Lincolnshire
COUNTY COUNCIL

discover libraries

This book should be returned on or before the last date shown below. NC1

To renew or order library books please telephone 01522 782010
or visit www.lincolnshire.gov.uk

You will requ
Ask

BRANDED

AND

LASSOED

BY
BJ DANIELS

MILLS & BOON

BRANDED

BY
BJ DANIELS

All the characters in this book have no existence outside the imagination of
the author, and have no relation whatsoever to anyone bearing the same name
or names. They are not even distantly inspired by any individual known or
unknown to the author, and all the incidents are pure invention.

First published in Great Britain 2012
by Mills & Boon, an imprint of Harlequin (UK) Limited,
Eton House, 18-24 Paradise Road, Richmond, Surrey TW9 1SR

© Barbara Heinlein 2011

ISBN: 978 0 263 89502 5

46-0212

Harlequin (UK) policy is to use papers that are natural, renewable and
recyclable products and made from wood grown in sustainable forests. The
logging and manufacturing processes conform to the legal environmental
regulations of the country of origin.

Printed and bound in Spain
by Blackprint CPI, Barcelona

USA TODAY bestselling author **BJ Daniel**s wrote her first book after a career as an award-winning newspaper journalist and author of thirty-seven published short stories. Since then she has won numerous awards, including a career achievement award for romantic suspense and many nominations and awards for best book. Daniels lives in Montana with her husband, Parker, and two springer spaniels, Spot and Jem. When she isn't writing, she snowboards, camps, boats and plays tennis. To contact her, write to BJ Daniels, PO Box 1173, Malta, MT 59538, USA or e-mail her at bjdaniels@mtintouch. net. Check out her website at www.bjdaniels.com.

I wanted to kick off this new series with a dedication to a good friend who has been in my thoughts.
This one is for Debra Webb, one of the strongest, most determined women I know and one heck of a writer.

Chapter One

Emma Chisholm heard the ruckus from clear back in the ranch kitchen. She wiped her hands on her apron as she walked toward the front of the sprawling house to peer out over the wide porch to the yard.

After a whirlwind courtship and marriage, she hadn't been prepared for her new home. Hoyt had warned her that his ranch was in the middle of Nowhere, Montana, but she hadn't been able to imagine anything this isolated or this huge.

She remembered thinking that day two weeks ago, when they'd driven north for three hours after picking up one of his ranch trucks at the airport in Billings, that she didn't really know what she was getting into—not with her new life. Or her new husband. After all, what did she really know about Hoyt Chisholm?

And what did he know about her? Very little since she had purposely skimmed over the past. It was a given that both being over fifty, they had things in their pasts they wanted to forget.

The thought that Hoyt might also have something in his past he wanted to hide had never occurred to her. That was an unsettling thought, she realized as she headed for the front of the rambling ranch house.

Even through the cloud of dust they were kicking up, she recognized the two young men brawling by the corral. Emma sighed, shaking her head as she watched two of her stepsons fighting. When Hoyt had told her that he had six sons, she'd been shocked. Funny how that hadn't come up when they met in Denver and found themselves flying to Vegas for an impromptu wedding.

She'd expected them to be boys, since that was what he called them. To her surprise, they were six grown men from twenty-six to thirty-three years old. But they definitely behaved like boys. Her six, big, strapping stepsons were typically involved in one squabble or another on a daily basis and she'd come to realize that Hoyt was usually the reason. The boys, all adopted, had apparently been raised without a woman in the house to give them any guidance and Hoyt dang sure wasn't providing any.

Emma saw her husband standing in the shade at the other end of the porch watching two of his sons rassle in the dirt.

"You just going to stand there, Hoyt Chisholm?" she asked as she stepped out on the porch.

He shot her that grin that had stolen her heart and clearly her senses, as well. How else could she explain marrying a man she barely knew to come to this ranch so far from civilization?

Hoyt took off his Stetson and scratched the back of his neck. She could tell that he wasn't going to do a darn thing about this. Just as she could see that he wanted her to accept the way things were on the Chisholm Cattle Company ranch. By now he must be realizing that wasn't going to happen.

Stepping off the porch, she walked around to the water faucet at the side of the house, snatched up the hose and turned the faucet on full force.

Hoyt, seeing what she was up to, quickly abandoned the porch as if he just remembered he had something to do in the barn.

Emma was tempted to turn the water on him, but she knew it wouldn't do any good. He'd just laugh and hightail it out of range.

His two sons were still rolling around in the dirt as Emma dragged the hose over and sprayed them.

"What the hell?" Colton said as he leaped to his feet.

"Don't you be using that kind of language around me, Colton Chisholm," Emma snapped and sprayed him again.

Tanner was on his feet, same as his brother, both now soaked to the skin, the dust on their clothes turning to mud.

Emma shook her head as she looked at the two of them and their hangdog expressions. Both were handsome to a fault.

"This is all your doing, Hoyt Chisholm," she called after her husband. "You're the reason they're always squabbling, each of them trying to win favor with you." She'd seen *that* within the first twenty-four hours of moving into the main house even though the "boys" had their own houses on the huge ranch that was Chisholm Cattle Company.

Of course, Hoyt pretended not to hear, but she could tell by the way he ducked his head as he stepped into the barn that he'd heard just fine. His sons were brought up wild. And he thought that was a good thing?

She turned her attention back to the two young men standing before her. They had both retrieved their hats and stood looking sheepish and wet and worried about what she might do next.

"I'd best not catch you fighting like tomcats again," she said, scowling at the two of them. "Now get on out of here before I give you another good soaking."

They tipped their hats and took off in the direction their father had gone. But within a few feet she could hear them arguing again.

She shook her head. It was time for Hoyt's "boys" to grow up, and she knew exactly what each of them needed. A woman.

Not just any woman. It took a special woman to domesticate a Chisholm man, she reflected, thinking of Hoyt.

As she turned off the water and coiled up the hose again, she told herself the hardest part would be finding the right woman for each of them. Since marrying Hoyt, she'd been thinking about how to bring this family together. It was clear that her stepsons had been more than surprised when their father had brought home a wife—and less than pleased. But she was determined to change all that.

She'd have to be careful, though, Emma thought, as she turned back to the kitchen and the apple pies she was helping the cook make for supper. If Hoyt or her stepsons got wind of what she was up to, there would be hell to pay.

But she was willing to take that chance. She smiled, thinking of her husband. The key was gentling a man, not breaking him. Love could accomplish the most amazing things, she told herself, hoping that was true.

She set her mind to which of her stepsons would be first to have his life changed forever with her help—and possibly a cattle prod.

COLTON CHISHOLM WIPED BLOOD from his split lip as he limped to his pickup. He told himself he'd gotten the best of the fight, but as he slid behind the wheel, he felt the pain in his ribs and wasn't so sure about that.

As he started the engine and roared down the road away from the ranch, he thought about just striking out and leaving Whitehorse and the Chisholm Cattle Company behind. He had plenty of reason most days.

But when he glanced in his rearview mirror, he knew he could no more leave this land than he could quit fighting his brothers for it. He was as much a Chisholm as the rest of them and he wouldn't be pushed out.

Not that his father didn't have him thinking twice about it, though. Everyone in six counties was talking about how Hoyt Chisholm had gone to the cattleman's convention in Denver and brought home a wife. And not just any wife. Emma McDougal Chisholm—a fifty-something buxom redhead with green eyes and a temper.

"The damn fool," Colton said to himself. What made it worse was that his father was plainly head over heels in love with the woman. And Emma...well, she seemed set on changing things on the ranch. He shook his head. Emma McDougal Chisholm had no idea what she'd signed on for. If she did, she'd be hightailing it out of town before sundown.

As Colton neared the highway on the long dirt road out of the ranch, he saw the postman, Albert Raines, pull up to the huge mailbox marked *Chisholm*. Albert waved to him and Colton slowed, pulling alongside as the postman got out and walked toward his pickup.

"Got a bunch of mail as usual," the tall, skinny postman said. "I was told to see that you got this personally, though." He handed Colton an envelope from the Postal Service.

At first he thought the postman was joking with him. "This about some new stamp designs?"

"Nope," Albert said with all seriousness. "It's a letter addressed to you that got lost. I brought it special."

"Thanks." He tossed it on the seat. He'd gotten other mail that had been caught in some machine and mangled and had ended up in an envelope just like the one Albert had handed him. No doubt it was a bill of some sort, since Colton rarely received anything else.

"Aren't you going to open it?" Albert sounded disappointed. "I heard it's been lost for fourteen years."

Colton chuckled. "I'm sure it will keep if it's been lost that long." He waved goodbye as he left and headed down the road to his house. He'd taken over one of the houses when his father had purchased a neighboring ranch a few years back. The house needed work, but Colton had needed space.

While the Chisholm ranch house was huge and rambling, it wasn't big enough for him and his brothers. All of them had moved out when they'd heard about their father's marriage, but they all still returned to the main ranch house for meals. Emma had seen to that.

After cleaning up, Colton headed into Whitehorse, anxious to get his errands done and get back for dinner. Emma had announced that she and the cook were baking apple pies. The way his brothers put away food, the pies wouldn't last long. Emma demanded that they all sit down to dinner each evening at the huge log dining room table at the ranch.

Crossing Emma had proved to be a bad thing, he thought, smiling at the memory of her turning the hose on him and Tanner. Emma wasn't very tall, but she was feisty as a badger—and just as dangerous when she was riled up. He figured that was one reason his father had fallen for her—and the reason this marriage didn't stand a chance in hell.

It wasn't until later, after picking up supplies, stopping to see if his saddle was fixed yet and having a cup of coffee while he waited at the local café, that Colton climbed back in his pickup and saw the envelope.

He thought about just tossing it. What was the point in looking at a bill that had gotten lost in the mail years ago? Hell, fourteen years ago he'd been eighteen, too young to have bills and who would have sent him a letter?

Curious now, he tore open the envelope and dumped out the contents.

A once-white small envelope tumbled out on his pickup seat. The moment he saw her handwriting, his heart stuttered in his chest and he found himself heaving for breath, the effort almost doubling over from the pain of his banged-up ribs. He stared at the handwriting, the return address and finally the postmark. The letter had been mailed fourteen years ago in May—right before Jessica left Whitehorse without even saying goodbye and he'd never seen her again.

He felt the heartbreak as if it had been only yesterday as he carefully eased open the back flap and took out the handwritten letter inside.

Colton,

I'm sorry we fought. But I can't stay here at the house any longer. It's only getting worse. I'm running away. I hope you'll come with me. I'll be waiting for you at our special place Friday night at midnight. If you love me, you'll meet me there and we'll go together. I have a surprise for you and can't wait to tell you.

Love,

Jessica

Colton felt as if his heart had been ripped out of his chest all over again. He let out a howl of pain as he reread the words. Jessica hadn't just taken off without a word. She'd sent this letter. Only he hadn't gotten it.

They'd had a fight the day before she left school, left Whitehorse, left him. He had been beside himself. He'd even braved going over to her house, knowing the reaction he'd get from her father.

Sid Granger had answered the door, his wife, Milli, behind him. "What the hell are you doing here? Haven't you done enough, you son of a—" His wife had grabbed his arm, trying to hold him back, but she was no match for her husband.

Sid had grabbed a baseball bat and chased him out to his pickup. "Jessica's gone and if I ever see your face around here again, I'll kill you."

In the days following, Colton had called the house, begging Sid to tell him where Jessica had gone. But the phone calls had ended with angry words and the slamming down of the receiver. They blamed *him* for Jessica leaving? He couldn't understand why. She'd loved him.

It was whatever was going on at home that had made her run away.

A few weeks later, he'd seen Mrs. Granger coming out of the Whitehorse Post Office.

"Please. Tell me where she's gone," Colton had pleaded.

"Go away." Millie Granger had glanced around as if she was afraid Sid would find out she'd talked to him. "Jessica's gone. She isn't coming back. And even if she was, she wouldn't want anything to do with you."

Colton hadn't believed it at first. He'd been inconsolable for weeks.

"She obviously wasn't the right woman for you," his father finally said after watching him mope around. "Trust me, her leaving is the best thing that could have happened. You both were too damn young to be so serious."

As weeks had turned into months, Colton had been forced to accept that the first woman he'd ever loved no longer wanted anything to do with him.

Now he stared at the letter and understood what had happened, why she'd never tried to contact him. She'd reached out to him, gone to their secret spot that night, only to have him fail to show.

How long had he waited for him, thinking he would come for her? The thought of her alone there that night, waiting for him, broke his heart all over again. He couldn't bear that she'd gone away believing he hadn't loved her, that he wouldn't have been there for her. He had promised to take care of her, look out for her, and when she'd needed him, he hadn't been there.

I never got the letter.

He hadn't been to their special place for fourteen

years—not since their fight and her disappearance from his life. As he drove out of town toward the ranch, he remembered the times they'd met there in secret. He would spread a blanket out for them beneath a stand of huge old cottonwood trees alongside the creek.

Even after all these years, he could remember the sound of the breeze in the leaves overhead, the sweet scent of the wild grasses, the cool coming up off the creek, the heat of her body against his.

It was in the shade of those trees that he'd first told her he loved her. They'd both been seventeen the first time they'd made love under that tree. It had been the first for both of them. Jessica had cried afterward and told him he would always be the only one for her. He'd told her he'd never let anyone hurt her again.

Colton drove past the Granger place, glancing in the direction of the house, as he had done for the last fourteen years. The house was set back off the road, almost hidden in a stand of trees. He never passed it without thinking of Jessica.

As he drove by the barbed-wire fence that marked the end of the Granger property and the beginning of Chisholm land, he slowed. Seeing no other vehicles coming down the road from either direction, he pulled in, stopping short of the barbed-wire gate.

The gate into this part of the Chisholm ranch property was seldom if ever used. The barbed wire had cut deep into the wooden posts, a sure sign that no one had been back in years. Once opened, he drove through the gate, then got out and closed it behind him.

The way in could hardly be called a road. It was a dirt path through some rugged terrain. Grass grew up between the two ruts, scraping the underside of his pickup as he drove until he reached the creek and the path petered out.

Parking in a gully where his pickup couldn't be seen from either the road or the Granger property, he walked the rest of the way, following the creek—just as he'd done as a teenager on his way to meet Jessica.

That night Jessica would have sneaked out of her parents' house and taken the back way, along the creek and through the barbed-wire fence onto Chisholm property, following the creek to the secret meeting place.

It had been Jessica who'd found the spot one night after a fight with her father. She'd wandered down the creek bank for half a mile to an oxbow surrounded by tall trees. She'd crawled through the barbed-wire fence onto Chisholm land—and realized she'd found the perfect place for them to meet in secret, her father being none the wiser.

Colton slowed his steps as he saw the tops of the trees in the distance and remembered the anticipation he'd felt each time he was to meet her all those years ago.

When he saw their secret spot, he stopped short. Jessica Granger had been his first real girlfriend, although they'd been forced to keep it secret because of her father. Sid Granger didn't want his daughter having anything to do with those wild Chisholm boys and no matter what Colton did, he couldn't convince him otherwise.

The spot didn't look as if anyone had been here in the past fourteen years since the land was posted and no one else had reason to come here. As he walked to the trees, stopping in the cool shade, he realized that the last person to stand here had probably been Jessica. His heart lodged in his throat at the thought.

For a moment he swore he caught a whiff of her

perfume. The scent took him back. He could close his
eyes and feel her in his arms as they lay entwined in the
shade of these cottonwoods after making love.

I have a surprise for you and can't wait to tell you.
Whatever it had been, he would never know, he thought
as he looked around.

What the hell are you doing here? He pulled off his
Stetson and raked his fingers through his sandy-blond
hair. Did he think he was going to find Jessica waiting
for him here? He laughed at the absurdity of it.

Hell, he couldn't even be sure she ever came here
that night. Maybe she'd changed her mind, sorry she'd
written him the letter, and had taken off on her own.

With a start, he remembered that Sid Granger had
called the ranch that night.

"It's Granger," his father had said after answering
the phone in the middle of dinner all those years ago.
"He wants to know if you've seen his daughter." Colton
had given his father a miserable shake of his head. "He
hasn't seen her. They broke up."

He'd never seen Jessica again.

If only he'd gotten the letter, he thought angrily. He
would have run off and married her in a heartbeat.

Colton took one last look at the spot under the trees.
"I'm so sorry, Jessica," he whispered on the warm
spring breeze rustling the leaves on the branches over
his head.

A part of him ached for what could have been. They
would have run away together. He could have gotten a
job on a ranch. She could have gotten a job cooking for
the hired hands. Or maybe he would have made enough
that she didn't have to work, especially if they'd gotten
a place to live along with his job.

He sighed, realizing that they had both been kids back then. The chances of his getting hired on some ranch would have been slim. Not only that, Jessica didn't know how to cook and she would have gone crazy living on a ranch. She'd always yearned to kick the dust of Montana off her heels and live in some big city. She had this idea that she would be a model. Or even a movie star.

"I'm going to be famous someday," she used to say. "You'll look back and say, 'I knew her when she was a girl.'" It used to make him sad when she talked that way because he knew he would never leave Montana.

What would he have done if he'd gotten the letter?

He would have figured something out, he told himself. He'd have had to. With her family being the way they were, he was all she had. She depended on him.

As he started to turn away, his boot toe caught on something. At first he thought it was a small root from the new growth at the base of one of the cottonwoods.

But as he reached down to free his boot, he saw that it wasn't a root but a leather strap protruding from the dirt. It was attached to something buried under one of the exposed roots.

He pulled on the strap and a small leather shoulder bag came up out of the dirt. The leather was discolored, the design faded over the years, but he recognized it at once.

His heart pounded against his injured ribs. Jessica's purse.

Chapter Two

Emma had just put the pies in the oven when the phone rang. She stared at it a moment, not sure she wanted to answer it after the last time.

"You want me to get that?" the cook asked. Celeste was a thirty-something woman, robust, flush-faced and tireless. What she lacked in a sense of humor was made up by her work ethic. At least that's what Emma told herself.

"No, I have it." Emma wiped her hands on her apron and walked to the wall phone in the kitchen. She picked it up on the third ring, praying it wasn't a repeat of the two other calls she'd gotten since arriving here.

"Chisholm Cattle Company," she said into the phone.

A beat of silence, then, "Mrs. Hoyt Chisholm?" The voice was a woman's. She sounded elderly and according to the caller ID, a local number.

"Yes." Emma held her breath, hoping the woman was someone from the nearby town of Whitehorse who'd called to welcome her to the area and wish her well on her marriage.

"You need to get out of that house before you end

up dead, too. Your husband is cursed when it comes to wives."

"I'm sorry, but what are you talking about?" Emma asked.

"The Chisholm curse. You've been warned." As the woman slammed down the phone, Emma jerked the receiver away from her ear.

"Something wrong?" Celeste asked.

"Wrong number." She hung up hoping the cook didn't see the way her hand was shaking. Emma wasn't ready to confide in either Celeste or the housekeeper, Mae. She'd seen how shocked they'd been that Hoyt had re-married. While neither of them had said anything, she'd noticed that they stayed to themselves, rebuffing any attempts she made to gain their trust—let alone their friendship.

"How long have you worked for Mr. Chisholm?" Emma asked Celeste now. She hadn't want to ask too many questions, hoping to gain the employees' trust by being helpful and pleasant and find out more about each of the women—and more about Whitehorse and how Chisholm Cattle Company fit into the scheme of things—as time went on.

That, she'd come to realize, wasn't going to happen.

"Just over a year," Celeste said.

"And Mae?"

"About six months."

Emma felt her brow shoot up in surprise.

"Not a lot of people want to work out here," Celeste said.

"Why is that?" She knew the wages were good and

Hoyt was congenial and easy to work for, from what she'd seen.

The cook seemed to search her gaze, as if she wondered if Emma was joking. Or testing her. "It's a long drive."

She could tell there was more, but that the woman wasn't going to tell her for some reason. "Surely *someone* lasted longer."

Celeste shook her head. "Not that I know of."

Emma wondered if it had anything to do with the Chisholm Curse. She hated to admit that the phone calls had shaken her a little.

"Those women who have been calling you, they're just jealous," her friend Debra had said when she called Denver later that afternoon. Celeste had left for the day and it was Mae's day off. Emma had the house to herself until supper when Celeste would return to help her cook for her large new family.

"Hoyt Chisholm must have been the most eligible bachelor in all of Montana," her friend said. "Don't let some old biddies get to you. He picked *you*. He loves *you*."

Yes, Emma thought. And she loved Hoyt. "Still, it seems odd." The last elderly neighboring ranchwoman's call hadn't sounded malicious. She'd sounded scared for her.

COLTON WAS WAITING BY THE ROAD when he finally saw the Sheriff's Department patrol car approaching. His mind was reeling from the letter—and what he'd found under the cottonwood tree.

Inside Jessica's purse he'd discovered her wallet with

her driver's license, $200 in cash and a bus ticket out of Whitehorse.

One one-way bus ticket? She'd said she wanted them to run away together. While she didn't have a car of her own, she knew he had his own pickup. Did she have so little faith that he would show up that she'd gotten the ticket just in case? He felt confused. The ticket had been for the 4:00 a.m. bus that would have left just hours after they were to meet at their secret spot.

Why had she thought she'd be leaving Whitehorse alone?

But if her purse was buried under the tree root, then how could she have left town? And why would she bury her purse? It made no sense. It made his blood run cold because he knew she wouldn't have buried it—just as he couldn't see how she could have left without it.

A terrible dread had settled into his bones by the time the sheriff's deputy pulled up next to his pickup and a female deputy stepped out.

She wore jeans, cowboy boots and a tan uniform shirt with a Whitehorse County Sheriff's Department patch on the sleeve. Colton felt his heart drop like a stone off a cliff as he recognized her. He swore under his breath. Just when he thought things couldn't get any worse. *"Halley?"*

DEPUTY HALLEY ROBINSON had told herself after moving back to Whitehorse that sooner or later she was going to cross paths with Colton Chisholm. When she'd left Whitehorse after junior high school, hadn't she sworn that one day she would return and make Colton sorry?

But that had been a young girl's dream of revenge. Halley was no longer that young, impressionable girl.

Lucky for Colton, she thought, since here they both were again, and oh, how the tables had turned.

"Colton," she said, secretly enjoying the fact that he'd remembered her.

"*You're* the new deputy?"

She smiled in answer. When the call came in, she'd been the only one on duty in the area. The county was a large one, stretching from the Missouri River to the south and all the way to Canada on the north.

"So, why don't you tell me what the problem is," she said, all business again. "You told the dispatcher you'd found Jessica Granger's purse and you believe something might have happened to her?"

He nodded, looking as if he now regretted making that call to the sheriff's office. Reaching into the cab of his pickup, he lifted out a weathered leather purse and handed it to her.

"It's Jessica's. I found it at a spot we used to meet."

She raised her gaze to his. "A *secret* spot, the dispatcher said."

He chewed at the inside of his cheek for a moment. "That's right."

"And there was something about a lost letter?"

Colton rubbed the back of his neck. His hair was longer than she'd ever seen it, but back in junior high, his father had taken clippers to all six of the boys, giving them buzz cuts. That was probably why she hadn't remembered the color, a combination of ripe wheat and sunshine that brought out the gold flecks in his blue eyes.

She felt that old quiver inside as her gaze me his. Colton Chisholm had been adorable in grade school.

It shouldn't have surprised her that he'd grown into a drop-dead good-looking man.

He reached into his jean jacket pocket and brought out a worse-for-wear looking, age-yellowed envelope. He held it as if not wanting to relinquish the letter to her, then finally handed it over.

Halley noted the postmark and the return address before opening the envelope. She quickly read what Jessica had written on the single sheet inside. The writing was young, girlish. She remembered Jessica Granger only too well. Jessica had been one of those annoyingly silly, all-girl girls while Halley had been a daredevil, tree-climbing, ball-throwing, horse-riding tomboy.

The letter, she noted, had been mailed fourteen years ago—only a few years after Halley had left Whitehorse brokenhearted because of Colton Chisholm.

Her gaze slid up to his again. He looked damn uncomfortable. Guilt? "What was it she had to tell you?"

He shook his head. "I didn't get the letter until today."

"You're saying you didn't meet her that night?"

"No. How could I since I never got the *letter?*" He sounded both angry and upset and she could see that he was more than a little shaken by this. He turned to get a United States Postal Department manila envelope from the pickup cab. He thrust it at her. "You can check with Albert if you don't believe me."

Halley wasn't sure what she believed. She was having a hard time separating the boy he'd been from the man standing before her. As a boy, he'd been too cute for his own good. Now he had a rough, sexy look about him that was enhanced by what was clearly a strong, worked-hard, ranch body.

She was sure women found him irresistible and wondered how many hearts he'd broken. It made her think
of her own fragile, small one that had taken a beating
all those years ago because of him.

"Jessica didn't phone you when you didn't show up?
Didn't try to contact you?"

His golden gaze met hers and held it. "I never saw her
again. I was told that she left town, just like she said she
was going to do in the letter. I tried to find out where
she'd gone, but…" He wagged his head and looked down
at the toes of his Western boots. "Her family wouldn't
tell me anything. Her dad didn't like me."

Imagine that. "You have a fight?"

He looked away toward the foothills, his face filled
with a pain that could have been guilt. Or she supposed it
was possible he'd really cared about this girl. It amazed
her that the thought could still hurt.

"It was just a stupid disagreement," he said finally.

"Over…?"

"Nothing, just dumb high school stuff."

He was lying. Halley wondered what the fight had
been about and whom he was trying to protect. Jessica
Granger? Or himself? Jessica had said in the letter she
wanted to tell him something that night.

"Would you have gone away with her?"

He swung his gaze back to her as if surprised by the
question. "I was in love with her. I would have done
anything she asked."

Halley nodded, unable to hide her surprise by his
impassioned response—or her quick flash of jealousy.
There'd been a time she would have given anything to
have the boy Colton had been feel that way about *her*.

"Why do I get the feeling there is a whole lot more

to this?" Maybe she just wanted to believe it because this was Colton Chisholm she was dealing with.

He didn't answer. The look he gave her said he feared she was incapable of believing anything he told her. He could be right about that. Clearly, she wasn't the only one who remembered their history. Call it puppy love, kid stuff, whatever, those old hurts lasted a lifetime.

"Why a letter? Why didn't she just call you and ask you to meet her?"

Colton hung his head, studying his boot toes again. "I don't know. Maybe her father wouldn't let her call."

"Or maybe she thought you wouldn't take her call."

He shot her an angry look. "We had an argument. Her dad didn't want her seeing me. It was complicated. None of that has anything to do with anything."

Halley lifted a brow, unconvinced.

"Look, I don't care what you think about me, I just need to know what happened to her."

"What do you *think* happened to her?"

Colton shifted, anger making his broad shoulders appear even broader. He looked ready to take her on, just as he had when they were kids. Except that he appeared to have already been in a fight. He was favoring his ribs and there was discoloration around one of his eyes. This time it hadn't been some skinny, spunky tomboy in the school yard who'd given him the shiner, though, she suspected.

"Let's cut to the chase," he said, a muscle tightening in his jaw. "Jessica wouldn't have left without her purse that night."

"So you think she's still out there," Halley said and felt a chill snake up her spine. "I think you'd better show

me this secret place of yours and I'm going to have to
keep this letter—at least until we get this cleared up."

COLTON DIDN'T WANT TO come back to the spot on the
creek. It had been tough enough earlier. Now it was
pure hell. He felt sick to his stomach as Halley parked
the patrol SUV in the clearing and cut the engine. She'd
insisted that he ride with her. He could feel her watching
him, looking for…what? Proof that he was everything
she thought he was and worse?

Hell, he'd never felt more guilty in his life. He'd let
Jessica down. Hadn't been there for her when she'd
needed him the most. Because in his heart, he knew
what they were going to find here. In his heart, he knew
Jessica had never left their secret spot that night.

The sun pounded down with a heat that stole his
breath. The quiet was deafening as they climbed out of
the SUV and walked along the secluded path toward the
stand of cottonwoods. It was as if every living thing had
deserted the area. Even the water in the small creek fell
silent.

"This is where I found the purse," he said when
they finally reached the grove of trees. "I tripped on
the strap." He could feel her gaze on him before she
glanced around. He could imagine what she was thinking. He felt anger rise in him again, but swallowed it
back. "I didn't kill her."

Halley's brow quirked up. "You're that sure she's
dead?'

"Can we please stop playing games here? We both
know she's dead. She wouldn't have left without her
purse and she damn sure didn't bury it herself under

that tree root." His voice broke. "You have to find her so she can get a proper burial."

"Where would you suggest we look for a body?" the deputy asked, clearly baiting him.

"Do you have any idea how hard this is on me?" he asked through clenched teeth. He had taken a step toward her, but now stopped, suddenly aware that her hand was resting on the butt of her gun. Did she really think he'd killed Jessica?

The heat, the quiet, the sickness in the pit of his stomach made him slump down on the edge of the creek bank. He put his head in his hands and fought back all the emotions warring inside him. "Please, just find her."

HALLEY PULLED OUT HER CELL PHONE, all the while keeping an eye on Colton. He hadn't moved from the creek bank. She got the number for Sid and Mildred Granger's house. A woman picked up on the third ring.

"I'd like to speak with Jessica Granger," Halley said and saw Colton lift his head. He frowned, the look he gave her appeared to question whether she'd lost her mind.

There was a beat of silence, then, "She isn't here. She doesn't live here anymore."

"Can you tell me where I can reach her?"

Another beat of silence. "May I ask who's calling?"

"Is this Mrs. Granger?"

"Yes."

Halley heard the hesitation in the woman's voice. "I'm Sheriff's Deputy Halley Robinson. I know this is unusual, but can you tell me when you last heard from your daughter?"

"A week ago. We got a letter. Has something happened to her?" The woman sounded scared.

"No, I'm sorry to upset you. But I would like to stop by and ask you a few questions. Something of your daughter's has been found. I'd like to return it."

"Something of Jessica's?"

"I'll come by now if that's all right. Is your husband home as well?"

"Yes, but—"

"I'll see you shortly." She snapped the phone shut and looked at Colton. "I talked to Jessica's mother. She says she got a letter from Jessica just last week. I'm going over there now to—"

"I'm going with you," Colton said, shooting to his feet. "She's lying. Jessica couldn't have written her last week."

A shaft of ice ran up her spine, even though the heat at the edge of the cottonwoods was intense. Why was he was so adamant that Jessica was dead unless…he'd killed her? She suddenly felt the isolation of this secret place where he used to meet his girlfriend. It wouldn't be the first time she'd stood face-to-face with a killer. But it would be the first time it was a killer she'd once loved.

"Why would her mother lie?" Halley managed to ask.

"I don't know, but she's lying. If Jessica was alive…" His voice trailed off, anguish twisted his handsome features into a mask of pain. "I want to see the letter she supposedly sent last week. I knew Jessica better than anyone."

Was that so? She had no doubt that Colton had known Jessica intimately if this secret spot under the cottonwoods was any indication. But if he'd known her so well, then why didn't he know what Jessica couldn't wait to tell him that night?

One thing was clear. Colton was going to the Granger house. Better he go with her.

"Okay, you can come with me. But if you cause any trouble, you'll be leaving their house in handcuffs, understood?"

He nodded and she couldn't help but notice how pale he looked. She'd never seen Colton Chisholm this vulnerable. She'd thought it would give her some satisfaction. It didn't.

EMMA FOUND HER HUSBAND IN THE BARN. He hadn't gone to move cattle with all of his sons except for Colton, which wasn't like him. She worried that he wasn't feeling well. Or that something was bothering him. Probably her. Maybe he was regretting his impulsive rush to the altar.

She'd noticed that he'd been spending more time in the barn with his horses lately. Apparently, this is where he went when he was upset about something. She stopped just inside the door to watch him as he curried a palomino mare. Hoyt was in his late fifties, just a few years older than she was. He was a big, physically fit man with a thick head of blond hair that made the gray in it hardly noticeable. But what had stolen her heart like a thief was his penetrating blue eyes and self-deprecating charm.

She wondered about the other women who'd passed through his life and this curse her latest caller had mentioned. Had those women only known the Hoyt who laughed a lot and lived hard? Or had they stuck around long enough to know this Hoyt, the quiet, gentle rancher who Emma loved and worried about?

At breakfast she'd noticed that he was quieter than usual. Now she was sure something was eating at him and wondered how long it would take before he confided in her. Or if he would.

She was sure the other women who'd been in his life had been younger, slimmer and no doubt more beautiful than she was. She couldn't help but wonder what had made him fall in love with her.

But whatever those other women had been like, Emma didn't think Hoyt realized yet that he had a woman strong enough that he could lean on her.

He turned as if sensing her presence. His face lit up at the sight of her and sent her heart racing and her pulse drumming in her ears. It amazed her that this man had the ability to do that to her. She didn't doubt that Hoyt Chisholm would be able to fill her with this same desire when she was ninety.

"Coming out here will only get you in trouble," Hoyt said as he reached for her. He pulled her to him, nuzzled her neck, making her skin tingle. She felt his fingers slip under her Western shirt and skim across her bare midriff.

As he drew back, his gaze met hers, desire burning like a hot, blue flame.

"Have you ever made love in a hayloft?" he whispered as he leaned in to kiss her.

"Never," she whispered back when she was able to catch her breath. Clearly he had something else in mind other than talking about what was really bothering him. If he thought he could distract her... Well, he was right.

"But you've secretly wanted to, haven't you?" He was grinning at her and she knew she would have given him anything.

"How is it you always seem to know my secret desires, Hoyt Chisholm?"

Without another word he took her hand and led her through the barn to the foot of the hayloft ladder. "Ladies first."

She saw the dare in his gaze and had a feeling no other woman had been up this ladder with him. Emma kissed him and began to climb.

"WHAT THE HELL is *he* doing here?"

Halley studied the man standing framed in the Granger house doorway. She vaguely remembered Sid Granger. She'd seen him around town when she was a girl because he'd worked for the city and probably still did.

"I need to speak with you and your wife," Halley said flashing her badge. It had little effect on Sid, though. He stood glaring at Colton, looking as if he wanted to kill him. "Mr. Granger, I have something of your daughter Jessica's."

She held up the purse, finally getting his attention.

"That's not my daughter's."

"It has Jessica's driver's license in it. I believe it *is* her purse." Behind him a small woman appeared in a housedress and long apron, the quintessential homemaker. Millie Granger? When the woman's eyes lit on the purse, her expression changed instantly. Suddenly she looked worried.

"Why don't you ask your wife if it's Jessica's purse," Halley said.

"It's Jessica's," Millie said in a small voice. "Let them come in."

Sid seemed surprised, but stepped back.

Halley shot Colton a look and said under her breath, "What did you do to make him hate you so much?"

Colton shook his head. "The son of a bitch was crazy when it came to Jessica."

They followed the Grangers inside the house.

The interior of the house came as a surprise. Given the way Millie Granger was dressed, Halley had expected a lot of doilies, ruffled curtains and crocheted pillows. Instead, the feel was more masculine, including the huge stretched and dried rattlesnake skin that hung over the fireplace. She shivered. She'd never liked snakes, but she shouldn't have been that surprised that Sid Granger did.

Sid turned abruptly the moment they were inside. "I don't want him in my hou—"

"Colton found your daughter's purse," Halley said, raising her voice over his. "As I said, her driver's license is in it along with a bus ticket from fourteen years ago and $200 in cash."

Sid shook his head. "How is that possible?"

"That's what we'd like to know. Did your daughter mention losing her purse?" she asked the mother.

Millie was a petite woman who looked as if she might blow away in a strong wind. The word *mousy* came to mind and, Halley noticed, Millie Granger was also clearly nervous. She was wearing a faded print apron. She kneaded the hem of it in her fingers, worrying at a hole in the fabric as she looked at her husband, as if fearful of what he might do.

Halley was wondering the same thing. Sid Granger's jaw was set, his body practically trembling with anger.

"There must be some mistake," Millie said in a small voice, her gaze still on her husband.

"You say you heard from your daughter last week?" Halley asked. Neither answered. "Is there a problem?" Clearly, there was, since Millie seemed to be waiting for her husband to say something.

"It's a family matter," Sid said through clenched teeth. "We don't discuss family matters with—"

"She ran away fourteen years ago," Millie blurted out, finally dragging her gaze from her husband. Sid shot her a lethal look.

Halley already knew from the letter Colton had received that running away had been Jessica's plan. "Was there an argument?"

Sid Granger had his lips clamped shut. He was still glaring at his wife.

"We didn't hear from her for a while," Millie said timidly. "But then we got a letter from her."

"So you've been in contact with her?" Halley asked. Again the Grangers exchanged a look. "You've *talked* to her?"

"She writes every year on her birthday, but there is never a return address and she mails the letters from different places. She doesn't want us to know where she is." Millie's voice broke.

"It's not us she is trying to get away from," Sid bellowed. "It's *him!*" He thrust a finger at Colton. "We lost our daughter because of him!" He took a menacing step toward him. "I want this man out of my house. *Now.*"

"Let's all settle down," Halley said, giving Colton a warning look as she stepped between the two men.

"Jessica got away from him and I won't have him—"

"You're the reason she was leaving," Colton snapped. "She would have done anything to get out of this house and away from you."

"Maybe it would be better if *you* left," Halley said, turning to glare at Colton. He was only making the situation worse.

"I'm not going anywhere until I see the letter from Jessica."

Halley would have liked to haul him out of the house in handcuffs just as she'd warned him. "If we could all just calm down."

"Not until that bastard is out of my house!"

"Sid, let the deputy tell us why she's here," Millie Granger said loudly, then quickly lowered her voice. "Please." She kneaded again at the tear in her apron, her voice again as tiny as she was.

The tension in the room dropped a notch.

"Could we all sit down?" Halley asked.

Sid grudgingly took a chair, scowling the whole time at Colton, who sat down on one end of the couch, Halley on the other. She wondered what he'd done to Jessica that warranted this much hatred from the girl's father. Was Colton right and it was just a father's love of his only daughter? Or something more sinister on either of the two men's parts?

"We need to be sure that Jessica is all right," Halley said. "Finding her purse raises questions, as I'm sure you realize. Could I see the letters from your daughter?"

This time Millie didn't look to her husband for guidance. She rose and, avoiding his gaze, went to a bedroom off the living room. She returned a few moments later with a small bundle of letters tied with a red ribbon.

She handed them to the deputy. As Halley undid the ribbon, she noted that there were over a dozen letters.

Before she could react, Colton stood and leaned over to snatch the top envelope from the pile.

Sid Granger shot out of his chair. Halley quickly took the letter back. But not before Colton had let out a cry that sounded almost like a sob.

"That isn't Jessica's handwriting," he said, his voice breaking, as he snatched another envelope from her hand, opened it and pulled out the short letter. He looked devastated. "These letters aren't from Jessica."

Chapter Three

Colton felt as if he'd been kicked in the chest by a mule. All these years her parents had believed she was alive because of letters that weren't from her at all?

"How could you believe the letters were from Jessica?" he demanded.

Millie was crying and wringing her hands in the cloth of her apron. Her husband looked as if he was trying to restrain himself. Colton was glad he hadn't opted to come here without the deputy because he was having the same problem not going for Sid Granger's throat.

"A person's handwriting can change," Millie was saying through her tears.

"If she was alive, why wouldn't she *call?*" Colton demanded. "Why was Jessica so afraid to let her own family know where she was unless she hated you so much—"

"You punk!" Sid Granger sprang to his feet. "It was you she was trying to get away from."

"Why would Jessica send me a letter asking me to run away with her if I was the problem?" Colton demanded, not backing down as he, too, shot to his feet.

"Colton," the deputy warned as she stepped between

them again. "Mr. Granger, I need to know why you're so angry at Mr. Chisholm."

Colton narrowed his gaze at her. Clearly, she was looking for just one more reason to hang him, but he stepped back, raising his hands in surrender.

"What was it you thought Mr. Chisholm did to your daughter?" Halley asked again.

Sid Granger seemed to have trouble speaking. He swallowed several times, his Adam's apple bobbing up and down. Tears filled his eyes. He hastily brushed them away with his shirtsleeve. Anger reddened his face. He opened his mouth, but nothing came out.

"He got her pregnant," Millie said from the rocker where she'd been sitting crying.

Colton took the news like a blow. He lowered himself to the couch. Looking up, he saw the deputy's face. She'd obviously been anticipating something like this. Was this the news Jessica had wanted to tell him that night?

"He knocked her up and refused to marry her," Sid finally managed to get out.

"No!" Colton bellowed. "That's a lie. I didn't know. She never…" His voice broke with emotion as it sank in. "I didn't know," he said more to himself than to the people in the room. He could feel Halley's gaze on him. He doubted she believed him any more than Sid Granger did.

"As Mr. Chisholm said, your daughter wrote him a letter before the night she was to leave," the deputy was saying. "That letter was lost and only delivered today. In the letter, she said she wanted him to run away with her. Do you know if she met him that night?"

"Why don't you ask him?" Sid snapped. "He's sitting right there."

"I'm asking you. When was the last time you saw your daughter?"

Millie spoke up from where the rocker. "I saw her that afternoon. She said she needed to run an errand. I wouldn't let her take the car so she had her friend Twyla pick her up."

"Twyla?" Halley asked.

"Twyla Reynolds." Millie looked to Sid. He had sat back down again and now had one arm over his face. "Sid, when was the last time *you* saw Jessica?"

"That evening after she came home," he said, his words muffled. "She said she was going to bed. I just assumed…"

"You have to understand," Millie said. "The letters… We wanted to believe that she was alive. If I noticed something different about the way she wrote, I just thought it was because she'd changed over the years."

"Didn't you ever wonder what she'd done with the baby?" Colton asked, still angry because something had been wrong in this house or Jessica would never have been at their secret spot that night. She would never have needed to run away. She would still be alive today.

He could see that Deputy Halley Robinson was asking questions as if she still thought Jessica might be alive. She was the only person in this room, though, who believed that now.

"I'd hoped that she had the baby and was raising our grandchild…" Millie looked away.

"I'd like to have a handwriting expert look at the letters that were sent to you," Halley said. "If you get any more, please try not to handle them so we can dust them for prints."

Millie nodded distractedly. "We weren't due to get another one for almost a year. I would imagine they will stop coming now."

Only if the killer finds out that Jessica's disappearance is being investigated, Colton thought. But the way news spread in this county, if the killer was still around, he would know soon enough.

"Do you have anything Jessica wrote before she left that we could compare it to?" Halley was asking.

Millie pushed herself to her feet. "I'm sure there is something in her room. It's just as she left it."

Colton started to rise to follow the deputy and Millie upstairs to Jessica's room, but Sid Granger stopped him.

"You aren't going in her room," Sid said, blocking his way. "If you hadn't gotten her pregnant…"

"Why don't you wait outside," Halley suggested to Colton.

He could have put up a fight, but he didn't have any fight left in him and there was nothing more to accomplish in this house, even if he could stand another moment in it. All he could think about was Jessica. She had been pregnant with his baby. But they'd been so careful. Not that any of that mattered now.

She must have been planning to tell him about the baby that night. Hadn't she realized that he would have been excited about the prospect of being a father? He would never have deserted her. Never.

As he left the house, he tried to swallow the lump in his throat at the realization that if he was right and

Jessica had never left the spot under the trees that night, then his baby had died with her.

"I think I have everything I need for now," Halley said a few moments later as she and Millie came out through the screen door to the porch and started down the steps to where Colton was waiting.

As she headed for her patrol SUV parked in the yard, she shot him a look. He could tell that she'd found more of Jessica's handwriting and it matched the letter he'd received fourteen years too late—not the ones someone had been sending her parents in the interim.

"I'll let you know what we find out," the deputy promised Millie who'd followed them as far as the vehicle and stood looking even smaller and even more terrified.

Colton saw her glance back toward the house. Sid stood in the doorway. Millie Granger visibly shuddered at the sight of her husband. As Colton looked toward the man in the doorway, he thought of the man's temper, his obsession with Jessica, his hatred of Colton. What if Sid had followed his daughter that night and caught her at the secret spot on the creek?

"You all right?" the deputy asked as she started the SUV.

He could feel her gaze on him as he suppressed a chill at the thought of what Sid Granger might have been capable of when it came to his daughter—was still capable of doing when it came to his wife.

"You didn't know she was pregnant."

It wasn't a question but he answered anyway. "No."

"I assume the baby was yours?"

He looked over at her, anger hitting him again with

sudden heat. "Why would you even ask that? You saw the letter. She wanted me to run away with her."

Halley nodded, but said nothing until they were back at his pickup parked at the edge of the road where he'd left it earlier. As he started to get out of the patrol car, she said, "I'm going to need a sample of your handwriting."

EMMA WOULD HAVE SAID she was the luckiest woman in the world if anyone had asked her just three seconds ago.

Moments before she'd been lying on the soft warm blanket on the pile of hay beside her husband, his arm around her, trying to catch her breath after their lovemaking. She'd been wondering if other people their age still felt like this, and felt bad for them if they didn't.

But then Hoyt's cell phone had vibrated on the blanket beside him and he'd snatched it up, checked to see who was calling, then he'd seemed to hesitate as if wanting to take the call and yet—

"Go ahead," Emma had said, sitting up to stretch. She knew how he was about business. Running this ranch was what kept him young.

"I really need to take this." He rose stark naked and walked down to the end of the hayloft.

Any other time Emma wouldn't have paid any attention, but something in the way Hoyt was standing, his back to her, his shoulders slumped over slightly, his voice low...

Her heart suddenly took off at a gallop as she noticed something that hadn't fully registered before. This wasn't the first time he'd checked to see who was calling and said, "I need to take this," and hurried out of the room. Or taken the call out on the porch. Or rushed downstairs. Or, like now, moved to the other end of the hayloft. These calls weren't about ranch business.

Ice-cold fear moved through her. She couldn't hear what he was saying but she could read his body language. There was secrecy in the way he spoke into the phone.

Emma tried to fight the terror that clutched her heart like a fist. She told herself that she was being foolish. Hoyt loved her. Only her. She had no reason to question his love.

He snapped the phone shut, turned toward her and she saw his face and knew. Her husband looked guilty as hell.

Emma had never thought she'd be one of those women who didn't want to know the truth. But right now, she felt too vulnerable, lying naked on a horse blanket in a hayloft after making love to the man she loved.

Quickly she hid her own face so he couldn't see her fear as she reached for her clothes.

HALLEY CALLED SHERIFF MCCALL CRAWFORD, who was in Great Falls tied up on a federal case, to update her on the Granger case.

"Sheriff Winchester, I mean, Crawford," McCall said with a small laugh.

The sheriff wasn't the only one who was having trouble getting used to her married name. Most everyone in town still referred to her as Sheriff Winchester. When Halley filled the sheriff in, McCall told her to let the state crime investigators take the case from here on out—and to wait for their arrival.

When the team arrived by small plane that afternoon,

she drove them to the crime scene, which a deputy had cordoned off, and waited to make sure nothing was disturbed.

Earlier, she'd told Colton to go home, warning him not to leave town.

He'd actually pulled himself together enough to chuckle at that on the drive back to his pickup from the Granger house.

"You must think I'm an idiot. You probably already suspect I'm a murderer. But do you really think I'm going to make a run for it?"

"I don't know, are you?" He'd given her an impatient look and she'd had to ask, "So tell me about Jessica."

"What do you want to know?" He'd sounded despondent.

"What was she like?" Halley remembered Jessica Granger, the girl Colton had started chasing at the end of junior high. Shortly after that Halley had talked her father into moving away from Whitehorse. "You were in love with her, right? There must have been a reason."

He had looked out the side window for so long she'd thought he wasn't going to answer. "You're not going to understand because she wasn't like you."

She'd shot him a look, not sure how to take that, but taking it badly, just the same.

"Jessica wasn't strong. She needed me."

"*That* was the appeal?" Halley asked in surprise.

He had finally looked in her direction. "Jessica needed someone to take care of her, to protect her from her old man. But I failed her."

"She needed protection from her father?" Halley couldn't help thinking about how she herself had needed someone to protect her from Colton Chisholm. She'd had to learn to fight her own battles. No one had come to her rescue. The thought drove the arrow even deeper in her heart and made her all the more angry that Colton, when he'd finally fallen for a girl, had fallen for one who he said himself was nothing like her.

"You met Sid," was all he said before climbing out of the patrol car.

She'd watched him go, seeing the toll this was taking on him, telling herself that a murderer might act the same way, especially if he couldn't take the guilt anymore.

Now, as Halley watched the crime techs begin the search for a body, she told herself her suspicions about Colton had nothing to do with how she felt about him today or all those years ago when he'd broken her tender heart.

The breeze stirred the cottonwoods as the creek whispered past. It seemed too beautiful a spot for the crime techs to be looking for a young woman's remains, but there was little doubt in her mind now that Jessica Granger was dead, that she'd died here.

Whether or not they would find Jessica, though, was another story. Halley suspected it would have been a shallow grave somewhere along this creek bottom. Which meant animals could have dug up the grave and carried away the bones years ago.

"I MIGHT NEED A LAWYER."

Emma had been picking at her supper but looked up now as everyone else at the table turned toward Colton. Like her, he'd hardly touched his food and he'd passed on apple pie. That wasn't like him. Hoyt hadn't eaten much, either. There was almost a full piece of pie on his plate.

"A lawyer?" she repeated. Since Hoyt's call in the barn, she'd tried to keep busy and think about anything but her own horrible suspicions.

"Why would you need a lawyer?" Hoyt asked.

Colton rubbed a hand over his jaw. "To make a long story short, there's at least one law enforcement officer in the county who thinks I killed Jessica Granger."

Hoyt froze, fork in hand. "*What? I* thought she left town."

Emma noticed that her husband had gone very pale.

"Apparently, she planned on leaving but I don't think she made it. Neither does the deputy now scouring a spot not far from here for her remains," Colton said, pain in his voice.

"I don't understand why they would think someone killed her," Hoyt said and Emma found herself studying her husband. Of course he'd be upset about such an allegation against his son, but when he set down his fork, she saw that his hand was shaking.

A bad feeling lodged itself in her chest as Colton proceeded to tell them about a lost letter, finding Jessica's purse buried under a tree root and calling the Sheriff's Department.

"Halley Robinson?" his brother, Tanner, asked with a smirk. "Isn't that the girl that you used to—"

"She's the new deputy," Colton said, shooting his brother a warning look.

Emma waited for Hoyt to jump in. When he didn't, she felt as if her world had suddenly shifted on its axis and nothing was as it had been just hours before.

"Isn't it possible the girl isn't even dead? They haven't found anything yet, right?" she asked.

Colton shook his head. "She wouldn't have left without her purse."

"What does the sheriff have to say about this?" Hoyt asked.

"From what I've been able to find out, the *sheriff* is busy in federal court on another case. This one has been turned over to the state crime team, but a fourteen-year-old possible murder isn't going to be at the top of their list of investigations. Even if the sheriff was in town, I'm not sure it would keep Halley from trying to railroad me."

"Well, you're just going to have to change this Halley person's mind," Emma said and saw her husband give her a sympathetic smile at her naiveté.

"Emma's is one approach," Hoyt said. "We'll also get you the best lawyer money can buy, just in case you can't convince this woman that you're innocent. I take it the two of you have some kind of history?"

"You could say that," Tanner said.

His other brothers had been feeding their faces, but now joined in. "Wait a minute," Zane said. "That's not that little dark-haired skinny girl—"

"She isn't so little anymore," Dawson said, laughing. "I saw her but didn't realize she was *Halley Robinson*. She's gorgeous." He let out a whistle.

Emma could see that Colton was at the end of his rope as Logan and Marshall chimed in with similar remarks.

"Let's take our dishes into the kitchen and let your father and Colton talk about this alone," she suggested, then stood and gave them each a look that sent the bunch of them quickly to their feet.

Colton shot her a thankful glance as she marched them all to the kitchen and closed the door behind them.

"Okay," she said once they were out of hearing range. "Tell me about this Halley Robinson."

HALLEY FOUND HER FATHER out in the south forty. He looked up as she came riding in. His face crinkled into a smile at the sight of her and she knew she'd made the right decision coming back to Whitehorse, Montana, with him.

He'd missed ranching and she knew the only reason he'd left here was because she'd been so unhappy. They were the only family they had.

"Hey, didn't expect to see you so soon," Geoff Robinson said as he finished tightening the top strand of barbed wire, then pulled off his gloves and turned all his attention to his daughter. "Everything all right?"

"I tried to call you on your cell," she said, swinging down from her horse.

"Oh, hell," he said feeling in his pocket. He grinned. "Guess I forgot it on the kitchen table. Sorry."

"It's all right. I needed the ride anyway." She'd been worried about him when she couldn't reach him and hadn't even thought to check to see if he'd taken his cell phone. He hated the damn thing and said one of the reasons he'd wanted to come back to Whitehorse was so he didn't have to carry it.

Still it worried her, him being out here alone, even though she could see how happy he was working on this old place.

"Should be able to get some cattle soon," he said now, smiling at her. "Just a big enough herd to make a little profit and keep us fed." His smile fell. "Rough day?"

"Had to go out to the Chisholm place," she said.

"Chisholm, huh."

"Colton Chisholm called the Sheriff's Department because he found his former girlfriend's purse buried in a spot the two of them used to meet fourteen years ago. There's a crime tech team searching for her remains as we speak."

"Is that right?"

She shot him a warning look.

"Sorry," he said, holding up his hands. "I know that boy drove you crazy but you held your own and quite frankly, I think—"

"I know what you thought," she said, cutting him off. Her father had told her she had to learn to fight her own battles. And she had. She knew he believed it had made her stronger, being raised like a son instead of a daughter.

But then he'd also thought that Colton Chisholm was just trying to get her attention all those years ago. Well, he certainly had her attention now.

Chapter Four

"I don't understand," Emma said after listening to her stepsons tell her about Halley Robinson. "Why would this woman have it in for Colton if all he did was have a crush on her?"

"He acted stupid around her," Tanner said. "Did stupid things like chase her with a frog and put gross things down her neck and knock her down in the school yard."

Emma sighed. She feared Colton was no better with women now than he'd been back in grade school with Halley Robinson.

"The funny part was that she always fought back and usually Colton got the worst of it, although he didn't let her know it," Dawson said, laughing. "Blackened his eye one time and almost broke his arm another. I'm sure Colton is the reason the Robinson family moved away. He just wouldn't leave her alone. That was until one day when he had to rescue Jessica from some bully."

Emma sighed more deeply. This was looking worse all the time. "What else do you know about Halley Robinson?"

Her stepsons shrugged. "She used to be this cute

little dark-haired girl with big brown eyes and now she's beautiful," Dawson said.

"She was too mean to be cute. She really did have it in for Colton before her family left town," Marshall said. "If she's now a deputy and she thinks Colton murdered his old girlfriend, who knows what she'll do to see that he hangs for it."

"They don't hang killers in Montana anymore," Dawson said. "But they could send him to the chair."

"Your brother isn't going to any chair," Emma snapped and her stepsons scattered like geese out the back door and across the lawn. She watched them go, her heart in her throat as she wondered about Colton's relationship with Jessica Granger.

That was the problem with being dropped in the middle of these strangers' lives. She knew nothing about her stepsons. She didn't even know her husband, as it was turning out. Just the thought of Hoyt sent another arrow to pierce her already wounded heart.

Love conquered all, right? Or broke your heart, she reminded herself remembering the look on Colton's face. Jessica Granger, whoever she had been, had broken his.

Celeste came into the kitchen with the last of the dishes. Emma fell in beside her to help, even though the young woman assured her it wasn't necessary. It was her house now. She could do dishes if she dang well pleased.

GEOFF ROBINSON COULD SEE THAT Halley didn't want to hear what he had to say about Colton Chisholm so he just shut his mouth and studied his daughter. She was the spitting image of her mother, Mary Lou, rest her soul. A beauty with a fire that would take a special man to appreciate.

He thought of the boy who used to follow Halley home from school, a gangly, towheaded Chisholm kid he'd heard had grown into a good man, a hardworking rancher and a good-looking cowboy.

Halley had always thought Colton Chisholm was a royal pain in the neck, but Geoff had seen something in the boy that told him the kid was all right—if a little misguided.

"You can't believe how he torments me," she used to complain.

"It's because he likes you."

She'd been so flabbergasted that she hadn't even been able to speak for a few moments. "He put a frog down my neck. Does that sound like he likes me?"

"It's what boys at that age do if they like a girl."

"I blackened his eye," she said, looking proud of the fact.

"Halley!"

"I told him I would break his arm if he pulled something like that again."

He'd realized then that Mary Lou would have been horrified to see the way he'd raised their precious daughter. But it wasn't until later that Geoff realized what he'd done.

Suddenly, the Chisholm boy was no longer tailing after Halley on the dirt road. Geoff had seen how miserable his little girl became, but he hadn't completely understood it until he found her crying on the porch one night not long after that. He asked her what was wrong even though he suspected he knew.

"Colton," was all she'd say. Apparently Colton had

stopped putting frogs down her neck or wrestling with her in the dirt. When Geoff saw the Chisholm boy in town with a girl named Jessica Granger, he knew that was the real heartbreaker for his daughter.

That's when he decided to get her out of Whitehorse. They both needed a change and that city life might be just what his wife would have prescribed for the problem.

But a part of him knew that she'd never gotten over her first taste of love—no matter how heartbreaking it had been. Is that another reason he'd wanted to come back here? He wanted his daughter to move on. He'd hoped her seeing Colton Chisholm again would do the trick.

As he studied Halley now, he saw a young woman who was equally at home in the city and the wild country of Montana. He hoped Mary Lou would be proud—he certainly was. But she still hadn't gotten Colton Chisholm out of her system. He was beginning to fear that she never would.

"Are you handling the case?" he ventured to ask.

"With the help of the state crime investigators out of Missoula. Don't give me that look. I believe a man is innocent until proven guilty."

"Even Colton Chisholm?" he asked, raising an eyebrow.

She gave him that crooked smile of hers, the one he suspected had gotten to the young, overly exuberant Colton Chisholm all those years ago. "Time will tell, won't it?"

He nodded, not worried. Halley was the fairest-minded person he knew. But what if Colton Chisholm was guilty of murder?

Her cell phone rang and he saw her face as she checked the caller ID.

"It's the crime team. I have to take this." She took a breath before she said into the phone, "Deputy Robinson."

He watched his daughter nod, then turn away. "What did the coroner say? A teenage girl? Cause of death? Uh-huh. Any identification on her? Right. I'm sure we should be able to get DNA from her family. Thank you for letting me know. "

"They found that girl's body," he said as Halley snapped her phone shut.

There was a look of determination on her face, the same one he'd seen when she'd announced she was going into law enforcement.

"They found a teenage girl's remains in a grave not ten yards from where her purse had been buried," Halley said. "Seems Colton Chisholm was right. Jessica never left their secret spot that night. The question is— Who did?"

WHEN COLTON GOT THE CALL the next morning, he was on a narrow dirt road, driving down to check some fence he'd thought might be down because several cattle had gotten out. He'd been trying to keep busy, but it was impossible not to think about Jessica and wait for the call he knew was coming.

Checking the phone, he saw it was from the deputy and no doubt the one he'd been dreading. He slowed the pickup to a stop, his heart pounding, and flipped open the phone. "You found her."

"You don't sound surprised. Why is that?"

He started to hang up. He was in no shape right now

to argue with Halley about his guilt or innocence or anything else. While he'd been expecting this call, it had still hit him hard.

"Don't leave town."

"I told you, I'm not going anywhere." He snapped the phone shut, feeling the effect of the news like a second blow. The moment he'd found Jessica's purse, he'd known she hadn't left that spot that night without it. He'd known then that something bad had to have happened to her.

But what? It made no sense that someone would kill her—let alone kill her there. No one else knew about their secret spot. Unless someone had followed her that night. Someone like her father.

Fury forced aside the heart-wrenching pain. Someone had murdered Jessica and his baby. He couldn't depend on Deputy Robinson to catch the killer—not when she appeared set on nailing him for the crime. He knew she'd called in the state crime investigators, but this was a cold case—fourteen years cold. What was the chance that they would be able to find the killer?

He was going to have to find the culprit himself.

Colton got the pickup going again, his mind racing. Who knew Jessica was going to their secret place that night? Earlier one of the Grangers had mentioned that Jessica had called her friend who had a car the day she disappeared.

Twyla Reynolds. She'd been Jessica's friend since the first grade, the two as different as night and day. As he recalled, Twyla had married some guy who worked on the gas rigs up by the Canadian border.

It took Colton several seconds to remember the man's last name. Brandon. Troy Brandon. He drove into town and stopped by the sheriff's department first to pick up the copy Halley had made him of Jessica's letter and to borrow a phone book. Back in the pickup, he tried the number. Twyla's line rang four times. He was about to hang up when she answered.

"Hello." He could hear little kids yelling in the background. *"Hello?"*

Colton hung up and headed for the address he'd found in the phone book.

EMMA HAD ALWAYS APPRECIATED IRONY. It hadn't escaped her that while she'd been busy plotting to help her stepsons find the perfect mates, her own love life might be on the skids. Earlier she'd wanted to confront Hoyt and demand to know what that conversation had been about.

But she hadn't. She told herself she couldn't bear the truth—not after just making love with Hoyt in the hayloft.

This morning, she felt foolish for not clearing up the matter right away. She trusted her husband. Of course nothing was going on. Still, she couldn't shake the nagging feeling at the back of her mind and the memory of the way her husband had turned his back on her all those times to take a call.

She thought of the strange phone calls she'd gotten. The parties on the other end of the line had been local women. Was it possible he was getting some calls like those, too? She should tell him about the calls she'd gotten. So what was stopping her?

She'd held her tongue because she knew it would hurt him deeply to hear that the community would say such things to his new wife. But Emma had to bring all of this to light and ease her mind. She hated that she felt a little wobbly, not as if someone had knocked the legs out from under her, as she had last night. But still not herself.

Something was going on with her husband, that much was clear, and it had something to do with a woman. She hadn't heard him come to bed last night, so it must have been very late, and he was gone early this morning after leaving a note that said he would be mending a fence up north and wouldn't be returning until supper time.

DEPUTY HALLEY ROBINSON HEARD the despair in Colton's voice when she'd called with the news. Did she really believe that he'd killed that girl? Or was it that she didn't want to believe it?

The law enforcement officer in her was determined to do everything she normally would in a case like this. Halley reminded herself that this wasn't her case, but that wasn't going to stop her. She had to know the truth.

One thing that was bothering her was that lost letter from Jessica. It seemed like too much of a coincidence for it to turn up now—after fourteen long years.

Colton hadn't had to come forward with the purse or the letter for that matter. Those actions did appear to be those of an innocent man.

But if he was guilty of the murder, then maybe it had been eating him up all these years and when he'd gotten the letter, he'd broken.

Except the part that seemed broken was his heart. He had looked devastated yesterday.

But what nagged at her about the letter was that it

proved nothing. He still could have met Jessica fourteen years ago. He still could have killed her.

Halley swung by the Whitehorse Post Office. Whitehorse was one of those small Western towns that had sprung up next to the tracks when the railroad had come through more than a hundred years ago. The first Whitehorse, now known as Old Town Whitehorse, was about five miles to the south, near the Missouri River Breaks.

The newer Whitehorse was only about ten blocks square with more churches than bars, a small weekly newspaper, a hardware store, several gas stations and a grocery store. The town sat on Highway 2, what was known as the Hi-Line.

As Halley pulled into the post office parking lot, she noticed that there were always more pickups parked around Whitehorse than cars. Ranching and farming kept the town alive, but only barely. She wondered again at her father's determination to come back here—and, more to the point, why she'd decided to return here, as well. She told herself that she didn't like the idea of living hundreds of miles from her father.

She refused to admit that it had anything to do with Colton Chisholm, a possible murderer.

The postmistress was busy in the back sorting mail. Halley rang the bell on the counter and waited. A few seconds later, Nell Harper came out.

Halley explained that she was interested in a recent lost letter and asked about the things that had been bothering her. How was it that the envelope had a postmark on it, but he hadn't gotten it all those years ago?

The elderly postmistress shook her gray head. She seemed as perplexed as Halley.

"Where exactly was it found?"

"One of the patrons said she saw a corner of it sticking out from between the wall and the counter. When I saw the postmark, I couldn't believe it."

"How could the letter have been there for the past fourteen years?"

Nell shrugged. "I guess it somehow fell down between the counter and the wall and just now worked its way out. It's a mystery to all of us, that's for sure."

"I assume something like this doesn't happen often?"

"Good heavens, no. Mail gets lost occasionally, but finding a letter after that much time…"

Yes, that's what bothered Halley. First the letter, then the purse, then Jessica's remains. It just seemed too coincidental. It was almost as if the killer had choreographed the whole thing so they would find the girl. But was the plan to also cast suspicion onto someone else?

"Who found the letter? You said it was one of the customers."

Nell nodded. "To tell you the truth, I'm not sure who spotted it. Hazel Rimes pulled it out and handed to me. You might want to talk to her."

As she left the post office, Halley made the call but got an answering machine. She left her number, asking Hazel to call at her earliest convenience.

TWYLA REYNOLDS BRANDON ANSWERED the door in a pair of cutoff jeans and a food stained T-shirt and Colton realized he'd caught Jessica's former best friend either in the middle of breakfast or just finishing. It was hard to tell. Most of her dyed blond hair had escaped from the scrunchie-held ponytail. She had a dish towel in one hand and a baby bottle in the other. And there was quite a large amount of drying food on her T-shirt. He couldn't even guess what kind.

"Colton Chisholm?" She said it as if he was the last person she ever expected to find standing on her doorstep.

That alone pretty much summed up their relationship in high school. He'd never liked Twyla and most of it was because of the stories Jessica told him about her. According to Jessica, the girl had been wild and promiscuous and confided all of it in detail to Jessica, who in turn had shared the stories with him.

"You shouldn't be hanging around a girl like that," he'd told Jessica.

She'd gotten her back up and quickly defended her friend. "Twyla's had a hard life. You have no idea what her home life is like. Anyway, I don't see what is wrong with her just wanting to have some fun—you know, cut loose and enjoy life. I like her."

He'd let it drop but he'd never understood why they had stayed friends. It had bothered him more than he'd let on. He'd convinced himself that Twyla was probably lying about her exploits with boys and even some older men. The fact that she would never give Jessica names proved it. That and the fact that as far as Colton knew, Twyla had never even had a date in high school.

Now he realized it wasn't even the lies Twyla came up with that had bothered him. It was the fact that Jessica seemed to enjoy telling him all about her friend's alleged sexual exploits, even when he'd told her he didn't want to hear about it.

"I need to talk to you," Colton said now, all too aware that Twyla had known that he hadn't liked her. Was it possible Jessica had told her that he'd tried to get her to end the friendship? Now he feared that Jessica had confided in Twyla as freely as her friend had in her.

At the sound of something breaking deep in the house, Twyla looked behind her. Colton could hear swearing, yelling and crying. Along with the noise came the strong scent of burned oatmeal, which could explain some of the stains on Twyla's T-shirt.

She turned back to him, stepping out of the house and closing the front door behind her. "Why would you want to talk to *me?*"

He wished there was somewhere they could talk besides the porch. The windows were open to the house and he could hear what must be her husband arguing with the kids.

"It's about Jessica," he said.

"Jessica?"

He thought by now the entire county would have heard about the remains found north of town and was thankful that Twyla apparently hadn't.

He held out the letter. "Go ahead. Read it."

She looked at the page as if she wished he hadn't forced it on her. After a few moments, she took it and read it.

Colton watched her face, wondering how much she had known fourteen years ago.

Partway down the page, her gaze shot up to him, then returned to the letter.

What had surprised her? "You didn't know she was running away?" Maybe he'd been wrong about Jessica confiding in her friend.

She hesitated. "I guess it doesn't matter now. Sure, I knew she was running away but...not with *you.*"

Colton stared at her, thinking he must have heard her wrong. He let out a humorless chuckle. "Who else would she have run away with?"

Twyla shrugged. "One of the others."

"Others?"

The woman looked at him as if he was the stupidest man alive. "You really didn't know? Seriously? When Jessica told me that she told you everything—and pretended *I* was the one who did…all those things with those guys—I thought for sure you were just playing dumb. But you really never caught on?" She shook her head. "So all this time you thought it was me." She gave him a pitying look. "You really didn't know your girlfriend, did you?"

Yesterday he might have argued that. But not today.

EMMA STARED DOWN AT THE top drawer of her bureau.

"Is something wrong?" Hoyt asked as he came into the room, startling her. His note had said he wouldn't be home until supper time.

She'd been putting away clothes fresh from the dryer and now realized that for several minutes she'd been standing there frozen to the spot. "Have you been in my drawers?"

Her husband chuckled as he came up behind her and put his arms around her. "Not yet, but I do like the sound of that."

"I'm serious, Hoyt. Someone has made a mess of everything in here." Emma liked things nice and neat, and just yesterday these drawers had been that. Now they had been rummaged through, as if whoever had gotten in them had been looking for something.

He let go of her and came around to look in the drawer where she had been staring. "Who would go through your things?"

She glanced over at him, hearing something in his voice. Fear? One look at him and she could see that he was upset. "What's going on?" she asked.

He cleared his throat. "Nothing, it's just that in my haste, I spoiled the surprise. I was looking for your favorite nightgown to check out the label so I could see if the shop had anything else in that brand."

Emma felt terrible. "Oh, Hoyt." She hugged him, resting her cheek against his broad chest. When she pulled back, she saw something in his eyes that made her feel even worse. He looked angry. "I'm sorry I spoiled your surprise."

"No, I'm the one who's sorry." He closed the drawer and pulled her to him. "I should have been more careful."

He kissed her slowly. It had always been like this, from their first kiss, from the first time he had touched her she'd been lost.

"Hoyt, the laundry is never going to get put away at this rate," she pretended to protest as he pulled her over to the bed.

"In a few moments, laundry better be the last thing on your mind, Mrs. Chisholm."

And it was.

It wasn't until later, after Hoyt had gotten a call and had some ranch business to tend to, that Emma had found herself standing alone again at another one of her open drawers. Why would Hoyt have gone through all her bureau drawers if he had merely been looking for her nightgown? He would have found it in the second drawer with the rest of her pajamas.

Emma thought of that moment of anger she'd seen in his eyes just before he'd kissed her. She couldn't shake the feeling that someone else had been in her house—and her husband, even though he was angry with that person, was covering for him or her.

With trembling fingers, she looked in her jewelry box. Nothing was missing, but again, someone had moved her favorite earrings from where she kept them. Same in the closet where the hangers were all shoved back, as if someone had been looking for something on the floor or the shelves behind the clothes.

Hoyt? That seemed unlikely, even with his story about surprising her.

That's when she caught a whiff of an unfamiliar perfume. It dissipated almost at once, but she knew that she wouldn't forget the scent if she ever smelled it again.

Someone had been in the room. Had searched it even though that made no sense. What could someone have possibly been looking for?

For a moment, she studied the room. Nothing was missing, as far as she could tell. But for whatever reason, her husband had lied to her about it. She'd seen how upset he'd been when he'd looked into the jumbled drawer and it hadn't been because she'd spoiled his surprise. No, this was like the secret calls he had to take, the conversations he didn't want her hearing.

And why had he come home early this morning after saying he wouldn't be back until supper time? He hadn't said and she hadn't gotten a chance to ask, she thought as she stepped to the window to see him take off in his pickup.

Where was he going in such a hurry? Emma feared it was to see the woman who used the unfamiliar perfume. She hated to think what kind of hold the woman might have on her husband.

Chapter Five

"Why should I believe you?" Colton said, taking a step back, as if he could distance himself from all this.

Twyla shook her head. "You've always thought I was a liar. Why change your opinion now?" She grinned. "Jessica told me she loved telling you what she'd done, all the details. She used to laugh at how shocked you were. It was all the more fun for her because you didn't know she was talking about herself."

Colton leaned against the porch railing for support. Inside the house, the swearing, crying and arguing had reached a new level.

"I've got to go…" Twyla didn't move, though. He could tell she wasn't in a hurry to go back in. She was enjoying herself at his expense.

He thought of the stories Jessica had told him about Twyla's conquests. And all the time it had been Jessica? He thought he might be sick.

"Who was the father of her baby?" he asked, his mouth dry as dust, his voice sounding strange to his ears.

Twyla merely shrugged. "She said it was some guy who picked her up one night when she hitchhiked into town. He was just passing through. That's why she needed to hit the rest of you up for money. She wasn't planning on keeping the baby. She was splittin' town alone, she told me."

He thought of the single bus ticket in her purse. Why had Jessica written him that she wanted to run away with him? According to Twyla, to hit him up for money. Clearly, she planned to leave alone. He could see himself letting her go alone that night, sending her money until they could meet up. He realized now that she wouldn't have been waiting for him in some town up the road, though.

Twyla seemed to realize that the copy of Jessica's letter still in her fingers and handed it back. "She told me you were her last resort. If she couldn't get what she needed from the others…"

"I get the picture." He thought about the first time he and Jessica had made love, her tears and his guilt that he'd taken her virginity. "I wasn't the first, was I?"

Twyla shook her head. "Her first, she told me, was when she was fourteen. Some older guy who'd been helping out at the ranch that summer."

Fourteen? He closed his eyes for a moment, squeezing them shut.

"She must have told you who the others were," he said.

Twyla shook her head. "That was the one thing she never told me."

"Then there is a chance she could have been lying about all of it," he said, knowing he was clutching at straws.

"You should let it go. What's the point after all this time?"

"Even if she wouldn't tell you, there must have been someone you suspected," he pushed.

She studied him. "You want proof." She seemed disappointed in him, then angry. "Why don't you ask your buddy Lance?"

"Lance Ames?" He choked out the words. "Now I know you're lying."

Twyla smiled as she opened the door to go back inside.

"Lance wouldn't—"

"Jessica went after whatever she wanted, including Lance," she said, opening the door. She paused in the doorway. "Since Lance was your best friend, she thought it would be a kick. Even if he'd told you, you wouldn't have believed him. If it makes you feel better, she had to get him drunk and he couldn't stand the sight of her afterward, but she didn't care. She got what she wanted."

How could Twyla be talking about the sweet, innocent girl he'd thought he had to protect? "If any of this was true, someone would have told me. It's nearly impossible to keep secrets in a small town."

She laughed at that. "You mean the way Lance told *you?*"

He suddenly had a vague recollection of a time in high school when he and Lance had gotten into some argument. They hardly spoke for months. With a start he realized when that had been—when he'd been wrapped up in Jessica. They had gone back to being friends soon after she'd allegedly left town.

"Jessica liked older men because they weren't about to talk," Twyla was saying. She gave him another pitying look. "She told me that you thought *I* was a bad influence on *her.* We used to laugh our butts off about that."

Twyla was still laughing as she stepped back inside the house and slammed the door behind her.

EMMA DID HER BEST thinking at a small café on the edge of town called the Whitehorse Café. This morning she took her usual table at a booth in the corner so she could see the door and have a view of everything that was going on.

In small towns like Whitehorse, the local café was the place to catch up on all the latest goings-on. Today though, because of the hour, the café was nearly empty. Only a couple of men were at the counter having coffee and talking about the cost of feed versus what you can get for a cow on the hoof.

Emma tuned them out. She had other things on her mind. Between worrying about her husband and her stepson Colton—

The café door swung open on a gust of cool morning air and Emma looked up to see a young female deputy enter. Since, as far as she knew, Whitehorse County had only one female deputy, this must be Deputy Halley Robinson, the woman determined to send her stepson to prison—if not the electric chair. If Montana had an electric chair.

"Excuse me, deputy," Emma said as the young woman started toward the far end of the counter.

The deputy turned toward her table and Emma got a good look at Halley Robinson. Her first thought was that she was much too pretty to be in law enforcement, let alone anyone who would want to hurt Colton. That sexist thought surprised her.

"Please, won't you join me?" Emma said and motioned to the booth seat across the table from her. "I'm Emma and I hate sitting alone."

She saw the young woman hesitate.

"Late lunch or just coffee?" Emma motioned to the waitress who came right over.

Deputy Robinson reluctantly slid into the booth. "Just coffee."

"Please have something to eat. April, bring us a couple of plates and a piece of that homemade apple pie." Emma quickly turned to the deputy. "Unless you'd rather split the banana cream?"

Halley Robinson smiled. "April, why don't you bring me the banana cream and Mrs. Chisholm the apple pie."

"So you know who I am," Emma said, liking the humor she saw in the deputy's big brown eyes. She could see why Colton had been so enamored of this woman when she was a girl. She must have been adorable because she was a beauty now. And smart, too. "But please call me Emma. I have a feeling you and I are going to be great friends."

COLTON FOUND LANCE AMES in the corral at the Flying Double A Ranch. Lance had inherited the ranch from his father and now raised some cattle, but his real love was horses.

"Hey, Colt, you're just in time," he said as he led a filly around the corral. "Have you ever seen a more beautiful horse?"

"Come out of the corral."

Lance stopped, his smile quickly disappearing. "What's wrong?"

"Out of the corral."

Lance called to one of his hired hands to take the filly back to her stall before he climbed the corral railing to jump down next to his friend. "It isn't your old man, is it? I heard he got remarried?"

"Dad's fine." Colton looked into the face of his best friend and told himself Twyla had lied. "I need to ask you something."

Lance shoved back his hat. "Fire away."

"Were you ever with Jessica?"

Colton saw the change in his friend's expression. He let out a curse an instant before he drew back his fist. The blow caught Lance in the jaw and sent him staggering back.

"Hold on," Lance said, raising both hands in surrender.

"You were my friend."

"I'm your *best* friend," he said. "If you recall, I tried to warn you about her."

"Warn me?" Colton took a step toward him. Hell, yes, he remembered now. That's what they'd had the argument about. Lance had tried to bad-mouth Jessica, and Colton wasn't having any of it. He'd thought his friend was just jealous. "You did a hell of a lot more than just try to warn me, didn't you?"

Colton took a swing, but Lance dodged it and caught him with a fist to the temple that made him see stars.

"I don't want to fight you, but I damn sure will," his friend said. "She wasn't the girl you thought she was."

He swore. "I keep hearing that and maybe you weren't the friend I thought you were."

Lance shook his head. "I guess that's a two-way street if you're going to believe Jessica over me."

Colton felt all the pain and anger and frustration surge inside him. He charged, barreling into Lance and taking them both to the ground. They fought as they had as boys, until Lance caught him in the ribs and, seeing the pain in his friend's eyes, rolled away from him.

"You okay?" Lance asked as Colton managed to lift himself up into a sitting position.

He thought about his stepmother telling him he was too old to be rolling around in the dirt. She was right.

After a moment he caught his breath and the pain in his ribs ebbed a little. "Jessica's dead." He saw Lance's shocked expression. "Someone killed her fourteen years ago. She was pregnant, but according to her friend Twyla, it wasn't mine."

Lance shook his head, his gaze taking on a faraway look. "It wasn't my baby if that's what you're thinking. I don't know what you heard, but Jessica put something in my drink at that party at the bridge you missed the fall of our junior year. The party that got raided by the sheriff."

"I remember how drunk you were, and upset. I thought it was because your old man had to bail you out of jail and grounded you."

Lance shook his head. "I swear I didn't even know what was happening until after it was over."

"You should have told me."

"Yeah," his friend said. "I tried and you might remember how that went. I figured Jessica would tell you. You should have seen the triumphant look on her face. I knew she'd only done it to come between you and me. And it worked."

Colton didn't think he could feel any worse. He was

wrong. Lance had been his friend since grade school and he trusted him with his life. "I'm sorry."

"Me, too," Lance said as he rose and offered Colton a hand up off the ground. "This all must have come as a real shock."

"Yeah." Colton took his friend's hand and let him pull him to his feet. He bent to pick up his hat from the ground. He told Lance about the letter and his visit to Twyla. "It isn't bad enough to find out that someone apparently murdered her that night. Now I find out that Jessica wasn't the girl I thought she was. I actually thought I was protecting her."

Lance shook his head. "Jessica was one messed-up girl."

"Yeah, I'm starting to realize that, and I think it all goes back to her family, her father in particular."

"Are you sure she was even pregnant?" Lance asked.

"I don't know. Her family believes it." He thought about some of the things Twyla had told him. "Apparently she liked older men." He remembered that Jessica had told him about an older, married man Twyla was seeing and had hinted that it was someone they all knew.

"Someone killed her and, if she was pregnant, then I suspect it was because of the baby," Colton said as he dusted himself off. His ribs hurt like hell and he was afraid he'd chipped a tooth. He really had to stop this. "I'm going to find the bastard."

"Shouldn't you let the sheriff do that?"

"The sheriff's not in town and the case is being handled by the state crime team. Deputy Halley Robinson is involved up to her pretty little ears and I'm her number one suspect."

Lance let out a surprised sound. "Not that girl—"

"Yep."

"You really do have a hell of a time with women, don't you?"

HALLEY HAD TO HAND IT to Emma Chisholm. She didn't mention Colton or the murder case the entire time it had taken them to have their pie and coffee.

Instead, the attractive older woman had steered the conversation to everything from a good piecrust recipe to the surplus of wildflowers this year to what it takes to be a deputy.

Emma had listened as if truly interested in Halley's training. "Did you always want to be in law enforcement?"

She'd explained how she'd taken some criminal behavior classes in college and gotten hooked. Before that she hadn't had a clue.

Then Emma had gracefully steered the conversation back to pies. "I hope we get some good apples this year. Do you have apple trees?"

"My father does in his yard. He bought a small ranch south of town," Halley said, surprised that she was enjoying the woman's company. "I rent an old farmhouse just outside of town. I haven't even looked to see what's growing in the yard."

"Well, if you have crab apples, let me know. I've been wanting to make a batch of crab apple jelly. I'd be happy to share."

They'd parted company out by Halley's patrol car. It wasn't until she was driving away that she realized how much Emma Chisholm had gotten out of her about her personal life.

The woman was so darn likable and self-deprecating that Halley had opened up, something she usually didn't do.

Now, though, she wondered what Colton Chisholm's stepmother had really wanted. Halley realized that she should have been more circumspect. The problem was that none of the questions Emma had asked had felt as if she was prying. She seemed genuinely interested.

Halley shook her head. All morning she'd been thinking about Colton because it had become obvious quite quickly that he was looking into her investigation. The man just didn't take no for an answer. And neither did his stepmother.

She found herself following his trail, first to Twyla Reynolds Brandon, Jessica's former best friend, and then to Lance Ames.

Twyla told her a story about Jessica's exploits, one that Halley couldn't help but react to with skepticism. The girl was a liar. She'd certainly lied to Colton. Why wouldn't she lie about everything else?

"This wild sex life that your friend had—are you sure she didn't make the whole thing up?"

"Maybe. Or maybe that's what got her killed. The last time I saw her she told me she was going to try to get money out of all of them. She said they couldn't very well turn her down, not when she told them she was pregnant."

Halley studied the woman sitting in a ragged recliner, a baby in her arms and several other small, dirty children hanging off the side of the chair. The house was a total disaster and Twyla looked as if she was fifty instead of thirty.

Twyla had been envious of her friend—that much

was obvious. Was that why Halley was having trouble believing any of this story?

"Anyway, why would she lie?"

"To make herself more interesting?"

Twyla shook her head. "I think she used sex to control men. Or maybe it was all about defying her parents. Can you imagine what her father would have done if he'd found out?"

Halley could after spending just a short amount of time with Sid Granger. "I assume you told Colton about this when he stopped by?" Clearly, Twyla would have relished every word.

"He used to treat me like dirt."

"Wasn't that because Jessica told him you were the one sleeping around and he believed her?"

"I suppose," she said grudgingly.

"So your friend really didn't do right by you, telling such stories about you. Didn't some of the boys at school think they were true and try—"

"That wasn't Jessica's fault," Twyla snapped. "It was Colton's. He's the one who talked about me to the other boys."

Halley didn't believe that. "However it happened, it all goes back to Jessica and the lies she told about you."

Twyla said nothing, just looked scornfully down at the baby in her lap.

"It wasn't that big a deal," she said finally. "Jessica and I used to laugh about how we were fooling everyone, especially Colton."

"I'll bet you did." Halley couldn't help but think about how mean kids could be at that age.

It had been a relief to leave Twyla's house and the

sour smell of baby spit-up and bitterness to drive out to the Ames ranch. The land stretched out as far as the eye could see. Halley put down her window, letting the warm summer air rush in.

Unfortunately, it did nothing to alleviate the bad feeling that had been growing with each person she talked to about Jessica Granger.

She found Lance Ames out by the corral. He had a cut over his left eye and a bruise along his jaw.

"I see Colton has already been here," she said, followed by a silent curse. She remembered Lance from school. He'd always been nice to her although he was Colton's best friend even then. She wondered if they were still best friends. The cut over the eye said otherwise.

"I need to know what you told him," she said, taking out her notebook and pen.

"You should talk to *him*," Lance said. "It was personal."

"I can see that. Why'd he hit you?"

"If you think this is bad, you should see him." The joke fell flat.

"You slept with Jessica."

Lance shook his head. "I told you—"

"Do you think he killed Jessica?"

"No way."

Halley nodded. "So he didn't know before now that you slept with Jessica."

Lance groaned. "She seduced me at a party. Truthfully, I'm surprised that anything happened, as drunk as I was."

That explained the cut and bruise. "So you're telling me—"

"I don't believe I was telling you anything."

"Why are you covering for him?"

"I'm not. You're wrong about Colt. He's the best man I know. He didn't do anything to Jessica but try to help her. It's Jessica you need to be looking into. That girl was seriously messed up."

Halley saw the guilty look Lance tried to hide. "You knew what Jessica was like but you didn't tell Colton."

He sighed. "I tried. It almost ended our friendship."

"He loved her that much?"

"It wasn't love. Jessica used him. She made him think he was the only one who could save her."

"Save her from what?"

Lance shook his head.

"Come on, help me out. If you really believe Colton is innocent, then help me. Who was she sleeping with besides Colton?"

He looked off toward the Larb foothills for a moment. "I saw her come on to a guy, a mechanic in town who was old enough to be her father." He made a disgusted sound.

"She came between you and Colton. You must have hated her."

Lance laughed. "I stayed as far away from her as possible."

"Did she hit you up for money?"

"Even Jessica wasn't that stupid."

"Why are you worried about your friend if you're so sure Colton is innocent?"

"Because I know him. He's determined to find out who killed Jessica."

"Why would he do that now that he knows she lied and cheated on him?"

"Colt feels as if he failed her."

Halley took that in. "How's that?"

"She was having some kind of trouble at home.
Colton thinks her behavior was a cry for help and that
he should have done something to save her."

"He told you this?"

Lance laughed. "Yeah, right. Colton has always been
so forthcoming." He shook his head. "He didn't have
to tell me. He's my best friend. I've known him since
kindergarten."

"You didn't tell him about the mechanic." Lance
shook his head and she could see that he was worried
what his friend might have done with the information.
"What's the man's name?"

"Deke Hanson."

"Is he still around after fourteen years?"

"Never left. He works at the garage in town."

EMMA FOUND HOYT SITTING on the porch when she returned home. She climbed the steps to take a seat next to
him on one of the half dozen old oak chairs and rockers
that had been in his family apparently for centuries.

The first thing she noticed was how quiet it was and
asked, "Where are your sons?"

"Got them all out workin' except for Colton. Don't
know where he is."

Something in his tone made her look over at him
sharply. She'd promised herself that she wasn't going to
ask. Better not to know. But that wasn't her way. "What's
going on, Hoyt?"

He looked out across the land as if he never got
tired of staring at it. The country up here was lush and
green this time of year. In the distance, huge cottonwoods formed a green canopy over the Milk River,

both winding their way toward the Missouri. Emma had fallen in love with the area the moment she'd seen it. Just as she'd fallen for Hoyt Chisholm.

"I know something other than the obvious is bothering you," she said and braced herself for the worst. "You might as well spit it out."

He smiled then and her heart broke at the sadness she saw in his blue eyes. "I did somethin'." She wanted to take her question back. She couldn't bear what Hoyt was going to say. "Fourteen years ago Jessica Granger contacted me. She told me she was pregnant with Colton's baby, but that she would give it up for adoption if she had the money to start over."

"Oh, Hoyt." Emma felt such a wave of relief, tears welled in her eyes.

"I knew better than to pay her off," he was saying. "But I couldn't let this girl ruin my son's life and you know damn well she would have."

Emma nodded. On that they could agree.

"Ten thousand dollars."

She let out a low whistle. "In *cash?*"

"Of course in cash. When we never saw her again, I thought she'd done just what she'd said she was going to do. I can't tell you how many times I've thought about that baby..." His voice broke.

Emma stared at her husband, seeing how hard it had been for him to go behind his son's back, but even harder to give up his own grandchild that way. Hoyt loved kids. That's how he'd ended up with six adopted sons, and it was no secret that he couldn't wait until this ranch rang out with the sounds of little cowboy boots.

After the initial shock and relief that this was at least part of the reason Hoyt had been acting so strangely,

Emma felt the weight of what her husband was telling her. Her mind began to whirl with the possible consequences of his actions.

"Does anyone else know?" she asked, wondering if the calls he'd been getting involved blackmail.

"No."

Emma knew she should have been relieved. "Colton said there was only $200 in her purse when he found it."

Hoyt nodded. "Maybe her killer took the money."

Emma felt her heart lurch at his words. "Hoyt, tell me you didn't meet that girl the night she died."

Chapter Six

After her visit with Twyla Brandon and Lance Ames, Halley was getting damn tired of finding herself trailing behind Colton. He was interfering with her investigation and it was time she set him straight on a few things.

She'd tried to call Hazel Rimes again, the woman who had allegedly found the letter from Jessica to Colton between the wall and counter at the post office. Still no answer. She left another message.

Halley couldn't shake the feeling that the letter played some important part in all this. She was suspicious as to why it had turned up now after fourteen years. It just seemed too coincidental somehow. The same with Colton finding the purse.

The problem was that she couldn't understand why, if he had killed Jessica, he had come forward with it. At first she'd thought that he was racked with guilt. Guilt did strange things to people. But she'd seen his expression when he'd found out that Jessica had been pregnant. His shock, his devastation, his anger had all been real.

She couldn't even imagine what he was going through now—given what Twyla Brandon had told him about Jessica and his fistfight with his best friend, Lance Ames. By now he must know that, according to Twyla, he wasn't the father of the baby, but then Jessica could have lied about that as well.

Halley worried that Colton Chisholm was a loose cannon, jumping on his big white horse and riding off to avenge Jessica's murder—no matter what she'd done to him. According to Lance, Colton blamed himself for not saving the girl.

But what exactly had Jessica needed saving from besides herself?

Whatever Colton was going through, Halley couldn't have him playing hero. The fool didn't seem to realize that he was chasing someone who'd already killed once and had gotten away it. There was more than a good chance that the person would kill again to keep that secret.

When she spotted his pickup coming out of a side road, she turned on her siren and lights and went after him. She caught his angry expression in his rearview mirror as she pulled him over to the side of the road. Climbing out of the SUV, she walked up to the driver's side of his pickup. He whirred down his window and gave her a disdainful look.

"There is no way I was speeding, so what the hell are you—"

"Your license, registration and proof of insurance, please, Mr. Chisholm."

"You aren't serious."

"Sir…"

He groaned as he dug out his wallet and then rummaged around in the pickup's glove compartment before handing her the documents she'd asked for. She studied each for a long moment, giving him time to settle down before she handed them back.

"Mr. Chisholm—"

"Aren't we past that?" he interrupted. "We've known each other since grade school."

"You're interfering with my investigation, Mr. Chisholm, and if you continue—"

"What are you going to do? Arrest me? Hell, you've been wanting to do that ever since you got back into town. So let's get it over with, *Deputy Robinson*." He shoved open his door, forcing her back, as he got out.

She started to reach for her weapon, but he merely held out his wrists. "Put the cuffs on. Take me in. Charge me." His voice dropped to a dangerous seductive level. "Or help me find Jessica's killer."

She started to open her mouth to tell him that it was her job to find the killer, not his, but he cut her off before she could get the words out.

"The only way you're going to be able to stop me is to arrest me," he said, that warm brown gaze locking with hers. "So let's do it."

"I'M NOT GOING TO ARREST YOU."

"Oh, yeah?" Colton said, worked up now. He knew he was on dangerous ground, but he couldn't help himself. He'd been through too much in the last twenty-four hours. "You'd better arrest me," he said advancing on her.

"Easy, Colton," she said, raising a hand as she stumbled back until he had her trapped against the side of the patrol SUV. "You don't want to do anything you'll regret."

He laughed. "Is there really anything I could do that would make you any more convinced that I'm a killer?"

When she didn't answer instantly, he said, "That's what I thought."

"You're wrong."

He laughed. "Nice try. But too little too late and not very damn convincing." He pulled off his hat and raked his hand through his hair in frustration. "I know what this is really about. It's about me making a complete fool of myself back in grade school, isn't it?"

"This has nothing to do with a few frogs down the neck."

"Like hell," he said, stuffing his hat back on his blond head before he pressed his hands on the warm metal of the SUV on each side of her, trapping her against her patrol car. He knew he was about to step over a line that he couldn't uncross, but he didn't care.

He was so close to her that he could see into the depths of her dark brown eyes. "You have that same look you did in grade school when you were about to slug me. Hell, now though you can just shoot me."

"Colton," she said in warning but there was a hitch in her throat as his gaze shifted from her eyes to her full bow-shaped lips. Every lick of common sense in him begged him to stop, but he was too worked up and damn but this woman had always had this effect on him.

He dropped his mouth to hers. He felt her gasp and then he was tasting her, pressing her against the side of the patrol SUV, intensely aware of the soft curves of her body. He felt her respond to the kiss, swore he could hear the pounding of her heart in sync with his own. But as he drew back, he expected to find that old fire in her eyes that was pure anger.

Colton braced himself for a blow. Or worse the cold,

hard steel of her gun barrel pressed against his already sore ribs.

But what burned in her eyes wasn't anger.

He heard a vehicle coming up the road and stepped back. Halley moved away, her back to him as a ranch truck passed, kicking up a cloud of dust.

"I'm sorry," he said to her slim back after the dust had settled. He was still shaken by the kiss, but all his earlier anger was gone. Now all he felt was an aching desire to kiss her again.

"I'll bet you're sorry," she said, turning to him again. Her face was flushed and he wondered if she was half as rattled by that kiss as he was.

"I'm not sorry about *kissing* you," he said. "I'm sorry about the way I treated you when we were kids. But you were just so impossible."

"Impossible?"

"Yes, impossible. I liked you, but every time I got near you, all you wanted to do was slug me or wrestle me to the ground."

Halley was shaking her head. "Apparently, you don't recall that you were the one who started it with your frogs and your—"

"I was a kid," he snapped. "And then we weren't quite kids anymore and I didn't know how to change things between us from what they'd been and you sure didn't make it easy. I liked you. But, quite frankly, you were as intimidating as hell."

"But Jessica Granger *wasn't.*"

"No. She… I really don't want to talk about her with you."

Halley shifted on her feet, looked off for a moment,

then settled her gaze on him again. "You have to stop looking for her killer."

He shook his head. "So we're back to that?"

"Colton—"

"I know. Stay out of your way."

"No, that isn't what I was going to say." She seemed to hesitate. "Instead of running ahead of me, how about helping me?"

He stared at her. "Is this some kind of trick?"

"No trick. Maybe I'm just tired of fighting you."

He couldn't help but grin. "That I will never believe."

"Well, believe this. I don't want to see you get arrested or, worse, killed."

He felt a ridiculous jolt of pleasure at her words. "So you're worried about me?"

"Surely you realize that whoever killed Jessica thinks he got away with it. If you continue digging—"

Colton laughed as he stared at the deputy. "You just admitted that you don't think I killed her."

TWENTY MINUTES LATER, Halley was still mentally kicking herself as she stepped from the hot sun beating down on the pavement to the cool shade of the automotive garage. Her face still felt blistering hot, but not from the summer heat. Her run-in with Colton had knocked her for a loop. And that damn kiss…

She touched her tongue to her lips, then caught herself and swore under her breath. If only she could quit thinking about all the things he'd said. She'd *intimidated* Colton Chisholm? He'd *liked* her? She knew it was silly. Hey, it had been junior high, but it still gave her a small thrill at the thought, which she quickly quelled. She was acting like the tween she'd been, and while it made her heart beat a little faster, she still had a killer on the loose that she was now more desperate than ever to find.

All her instincts told her that Colton hadn't done it. She felt a chill, though, as she remembered how her instincts had failed her not that long ago. There'd been another suspect she'd trusted back on the West Coast. She shivered at the memory of how close she'd come to getting killed because she'd fallen under the spell of the suspect. Her throat tightened at the memory.

One kiss and suddenly she believes Colton is innocent? Apparently, she hadn't learned anything from that earlier brush with death.

The garage smelled of grease and clanked with the sound of metal tools. There were three vehicles, one up on a hoist, the others with their hoods up, but no sign of anyone.

"Deke Hanson?" she called into the cavernous space. She had to yell again over the sudden loud whirl of a high-powered drill as one of the mechanics loosened a bolt.

A head appeared as a man rolled partway out from under one of the vehicles in the second bay. His face was smudged with grease, his dark eyes small in a web of squint lines. She estimated his age at somewhere in his late forties. "Yeah?"

Halley watched his gaze focus on her as she approached. First the uniform, then her face, then her chest. She saw his expression turn from worry to amusement. Some men seemed to think there was no reason to be concerned about a woman deputy. Apparently Deke Hanson was one of them.

"Deke Hanson?" she asked.

"In the flesh."

"I'm Deputy Robinson. I'd like a word with you." She realized that all the noise had ceased and that the other two mechanics were waiting to see what was going on. "In private."

Deke sighed and shoved off the side of the car to propel himself all the way out from under it. He got awkwardly to his feet, something she could see bothered him.

"I'm a little stiff today," he said, leering at her. One of the other mechanics chuckled from under a neighboring vehicle. "Big baseball game yesterday. I'm the star hitter." Another chuckle.

"Why don't we speak in your office?" Halley said and waited for him to lead the way.

"So what's this about?" he demanded once she'd closed the office door. Without his buddies around to hear him, he'd dropped the cuteness.

"Jessica Granger." She saw his eyes narrow, his jaw tense.

He licked his lips. "Who?"

"Your girlfriend fourteen years ago."

Deke looked away as he let out a bark of a laugh. "Honey, I've had a lot of girlfriends in the last fourteen years."

"It's *Deputy* and I think if you give it a moment you'll be able to recall Jessica. High school junior. Big age difference. Statutory rape."

"I never touched her."

"Oh, so you do remember her."

He swore under his breath. "Believe me, you don't forget a girl like that. She's the one who came on to me. Girls like that you have to fight off with a stick."

"Apparently, you didn't have a big enough stick."

He raked a greasy hand through his already greasy hair. Halley wondered what Jessica had seen in this man fourteen years ago. He would have been old enough to be her father back then.

"I already told you," he said defiantly. "I never touched her. She was a kid. I'm not stupid."

That was debatable.

"So you're saying you didn't get her pregnant?"

"Pregnant?" He laughed and she saw him relax a little. "That definitely wasn't me. After my wife popped out three in less than four years, I fixed that little problem. It's been sixteen years. You don't believe me, check with my doctor."

She did believe him. "But vasectomies don't always work so that doesn't exactly clear you, does it?"

He shook his head as if she just didn't get it. "The girl came into the garage with her *father*."

"You aren't telling me that she flirted with you in front of him."

"That's exactly what I'm telling you. I think she was just trying to get a rise out of him."

"And did she?" Halley asked, disturbed by the picture she was getting.

"She sure as hell did. He couldn't get her out of here fast enough. He threatened to whip my ass if I ever came near her. The bitch lost me a client. He never came back in again."

"And you never saw her again?"

"You better believe it. That girl was trouble and her old man… He was one scary dude when he lost his temper."

Her cell phone rang. She took it outside, letting Deke

Hanson get back to work. Her warrant for Jessica Granger's medical records had come through. Finally, she would know whether or not Jessica had really been pregnant.

COLTON WASN'T SURE HOW he should feel about Halley admitting that she didn't think he was a killer. Relief, sure, but he was still insulted that she had even considered that he might have murdered Jessica in the first place.

He was also a bit taken aback that she'd said she needed his help. That, he thought, was probably just to get him to quit looking for the killer on his own.

Whatever her reason, it hadn't dissuaded him in the least. He owed Jessica this and the more he'd thought about Jessica and who might have killed her, the more it brought him back to why she was running away in the first place. Something was going on at that house, specifically with her and her father.

It wasn't unusual for a father to be protective of his daughter, but Sid Granger seemed to have taken it over the top. Was it possible his overprotectiveness, if that's all it had been, had pushed Jessica to do the things she had?

Colton was convinced that Millie Granger knew the truth about what was going on in that house and why Jessica was so desperate to get out of it.

He called, ready to hang up if Sid answered. To his relief, Millie picked up on the second ring. "It's me, Colton Chisholm. I need to talk to you about Jessica."

"Yes." From the odd way she said it, he could only assume that her husband was nearby.

"Can you get away to meet me?" he asked, figuring

that she might talk without Sid standing over her. "Say twenty minutes at…" Where? It had to be a place they could talk where it wouldn't appear they had planned the meeting if it got back to Sid. "The grocery store." He could hear her ready to say no. "Or I can come to your house—"

"No, that's quite all right."

Twenty-five minutes later she joined him at the back of the grocery store. She pushed a metal food cart and kept looking around as if she was afraid she'd been followed.

"You shouldn't have called," she whispered, after making sure no one was close by. This time of the afternoon, the small store was practically empty.

"You lived in that house with your daughter," Colton said. "You had to know what was going on with her."

As someone crossed the aisle at the other end, Millie took a box of crackers off the shelf and dropped it into her basket. "What are you saying?"

"I wasn't the only one your daughter had been with, was I?"

She looked away.

"You *knew* your daughter was promiscuous?"

"I can't talk to you about this." She started to step away, but he stopped her.

"You have to talk to me. You accused me of knocking up your daughter and then killing her because I didn't want to marry her. Was she even pregnant?"

"Yes. That isn't something she would lie about."

"Oh, really?" he snapped, keeping his voice down. "She lied about everything else. Who was she seeing besides me?"

She shook her head.

"Jessica told me about some older, married man," Colton said. "She swore it was Twyla who used to sneak out of the house and meet him at night when his wife was sleeping. He had more to lose than anyone if he thought he'd gotten an underage girl pregnant."

Millie tried to step past him, looking stricken. "Please, I can't bear to hear this."

"Why are you protecting this man? Your daughter is dead. I would think you'd want to expose him."

"Sid and I did the best we could." She started to turn away.

Colton grabbed her thin arm and was surprised at the strength he felt there. "You *both* knew?" He felt her tense and let go. "Oh, my God."

She suddenly looked panicked. "It isn't what you think. Her father loved her. Everything he did, he did it because…he had to." She spun around, banging her cart into a stack of cookies. Several packages toppled off to the floor, but Millie Granger didn't slow down as she rushed off, one of the wheels on her grocery cart squeaking loudly.

HALLEY HAD JUST ASSUMED that Dr. Brian "Buck" Carrey was one of a long line of doctors who'd come to Whitehorse on his way somewhere else. The doctors were usually young, stayed only a short while, then moved on to greener pastures.

But when she stepped into Dr. Carrey's small office, she was surprised. The older man behind the desk looked as if he'd be more at home on the range than behind a general practitioner's desk. He wore a cowboy hat over his long gray ponytail. His face was tanned and weathered with deep lines around his eyes.

He broke into a huge smile as he pushed back his hat and considered her. "When they told me I had a deputy waiting for me... I had no idea it was going to be a filly."

Halley wondered if she would ever get used to this. Most places didn't think twice about a woman being in law enforcement. But then Whitehorse, Montana, wasn't most places. She could well imagine what the townsfolk thought about having a woman as sheriff.

"Dr. Carrey, I have a warrant to see the files of Jessica Granger," she said, getting right to business. "The last time she was in would have probably been about fourteen years ago."

"Before my time and call me Buck," he said before turning to call, "Margaret?" An elderly nurse appeared in the doorway. "Going to need some old files." He swung his gaze back to Halley. "Jessica Granger, that right?"

She nodded.

"I'll have to go over to the storage space," Margaret said. She was plump, in her sixties with short gray hair and a pleasant face.

"I'll go with you," Halley said handing her the warrant.

The files were stacked by date in a large storage unit that smelled of dust and age. It didn't take Margaret long to find Jessica's file.

"Did you know Jessica Granger?" Halley asked.

"I remember her," she said as she handed over the file. "I was sorry to hear that she might have been murdered."

But not surprised. Just as Halley wasn't surprised

that word of the murder was out. News traveled at the speed of wildfire in a windstorm through Whitehorse.

"So you *knew* Jessica?" she prodded.

"I wouldn't say that," the nurse said quickly. "I knew *of* her." She clamped her lips shut as though she wished she hadn't said that.

Halley opened the file, thumbed to the back, past the usual childhood injuries and illnesses, to Jessica's last doctor visit. She glanced from the page up at the nurse in surprise. "She *wasn't* pregnant." Relief flooded her. It was bad enough that the girl had died, but at least there hadn't been a baby involved.

This would be a relief to Colton as well. She couldn't help the thought. She'd seen how hard he'd taken the news that not only his girlfriend, but possibly also his baby, had been murdered. Even though Twyla had sworn it wasn't his, Halley was sure that Colton would always wonder.

Something caught her eye. "What's this about a call to Social Services?"

"Counseling, I would imagine."

"What for?"

The nurse hesitated before she said, "Possible physical abuse."

"She had bruises on her arms and strap marks as if she'd been restrained and *whipped?*" Halley said, reading the doctor's notation on the chart.

"She told the doctor—"

"Yes, I see what she told the doctor," Halley said as she turned the page and saw the notation. "She said it was a sex game she played with her boyfriend and he got a little rough? Is there any truth to this?"

Margaret shrugged. "She had a tendency to…"

"Lie?" No kidding.

"Prefer fiction over reality, possibly. When she came in, she was convinced she was pregnant and very upset that she wasn't."

Halley felt sick. Something had been terribly wrong with this girl. "Did you believe her, that the injuries were from a sex game?"

Margaret again hesitated before she met her gaze. "I can only tell you that the doctor decided a call should be made to Social Services and that the family should be…interviewed."

So the doctor thought something was wrong at home, as well. Flipping back through the file, she found a note indicating that the doctor had called Jessica's father. The note said the father had been defensive. "Was Social Services ever called? I can't find any notation that they were."

"You'd have to check with them."

Back at the doctor's office as Halley waited for a copy to be made of Jessica's file, she thought about her visit to the Granger house yesterday. The vibes at the house had been more than a little tense. She thought about Millie nervously kneading at her faded apron and the hole in it where the fabric had torn. There was something definitely off in that house.

But she reminded herself that Jessica's parents had just found out that their daughter was probably dead. She couldn't imagine what that would do to the family dynamics, especially since Jessica had been their only child.

Then again, something had been wrong long before that, since Jessica had been running away.

At the Social Services Department, Halley was led

by the receptionist into a small, hot room at the back. The woman behind the desk introduced herself as Alice Brown. When Halley showed her the copy of Jessica Granger's referral sheet, she said she was familiar with the case.

So the doctor *had* called. "I need to know what you found out when you went to the Granger home."

"I never went. I was informed by the mother that Jessica had run away. I filed a report and that was the last of it."

"You never investigated it further?"

"Jessica was out of the house," she said defensively. "Whatever was going on there, without her testimony, there was nothing I could do," Alice said.

"What do you suspect was going on there?"

The woman shook her head. "If Jessica returns…"

"That isn't likely, since someone killed her the night she tried to run away."

All the color drained from the social worker's face. "Oh, no. You don't think the father…" She shuddered at the thought.

So did Halley.

As COLTON LEFT THE supermarket after his brief rendezvous with Jessica's mother, his head was spinning. He'd seen the panic in Millie Granger's eyes. She was clearly terrified of her husband and Colton was sure now that Jessica had been leaving to get away from her father.

He climbed into his pickup and sat for a moment, trying to decide what to do next. "What the hell had been going on in that house?" he said to himself as he recalled the bruises he'd seen on Jessica before they'd gotten into the argument that last night he saw her.

"Who did that to you?" he'd demanded. Jessica had insisted that they meet at their secret place after dark. He wouldn't even have seen her injuries if she hadn't flinched when he touched her. He'd turned on the flashlight he'd brought to make his way back to his pickup later and had been shocked.

It wasn't the first time he'd seen bruises on her, but she always had an explanation. This time there was no explaining away the marks.

"I asked you who did this to you?" he repeated.

She moved away from him, covering the welts on her legs as well as the bruises on her arms. "Leave me alone."

"I can't. I want to help you," he said, kneeling down next to her.

But she'd pushed him away. "I told you to leave me alone. You tell anyone about this and I'll swear that you did this to me."

For a moment, he'd been too shocked to speak. "You wouldn't do that."

"Oh, yeah? Try me and you'll be sorry you ever met me," she'd snapped.

"I'm already sorry." He had grabbed his jacket and the blanket and left.

Now he felt desolate. Why hadn't he told anyone? He might have saved her life.

His head whirling, he started out of town toward home. He was thinking about swinging by the Grangers' on the way and confronting Jessica's father when his cell phone rang. It was Halley Robinson.

"What now?" he snapped.

"Is that the way you always answer your phone?" she asked.

"Only when I see that it's you calling," he said, then regretted it. "Sorry, I'm just not up for more bad news."

"I don't think what I have to tell you is bad, but either way, I still need to talk to you," she said.

He sighed. "I need to talk to you, too. I just had an interesting conversation with Millie Granger." He heard the deputy make a disapproving sound. "Look, you need to hear about this." He knew he had to tell her about the bruises, but he was hesitant. Jessica had threatened to make him look guilty—and now he had no way to prove otherwise. Colton knew that Sid Granger would deny laying a hand on his daughter. At this point, even Sid might be more believable to the deputy.

"Where are you?" Halley asked. "I'd prefer not to discuss this on the phone."

"I'm on the way to the ranch…" He squinted at the cloud of dust he spotted ahead. Out of the dust came a pickup. His father's. He saw Hoyt slow ahead and wave through the open window for him to stop. He had a bad feeling that his father had been coming to find him. Something was up.

"Is there somewhere we can meet?" Halley asked. "Is everything all right?" she added when he didn't answer, distracted by his concern about what his father might want.

"Just great," he said as he watched his father get out of his pickup. Colton slowed, seeing something in his father's face that set his heart racing. "I can't talk right now."

"Jessica wasn't pregnant. I thought you'd want to know."

He stopped on the edge of the road. His father was

waiting for him, standing in the middle of the narrow dirt road, looking as if the weight of the world was on his shoulders.

Jessica wasn't pregnant. Maybe all of it had been a lie. Maybe...

"I didn't mean to blurt it out," Halley said. "I just wanted you to know. I thought it would—"

"I really can't talk right now." He snapped the phone shut and got out of his pickup.

As he stepped to the middle of the dirt road, his father looked up and Colton saw his expression. His blood turned to ice.

Chapter Seven

"Son," Hoyt said as Colton joined his father in the middle of the road.

"What's wrong?" Clearly this was about something that couldn't wait.

Hoyt pulled off his Stetson and raked a hand through his graying hair. When his father had first returned to the ranch with his new bride, there had been a lightness to his step. Emma seemed to have taken years off him. But right now, in the harsh sunlight, Hoyt looked all of his fifty-six years and then some.

"I need to tell you something."

"And you thought in the middle of the road would be a good place?"

His father sighed as he pulled his hat back onto his head. "There is no easy way to say this. Jessica called me fourteen years ago."

"Why would Jessica call *you*?"

Colton listened, his pulse rising with each word as his father told him. He'd seen the fear in Hoyt's eyes and had known this was bad—he'd just never expected this.

"You paid her off?" He swore, turning away from his father, afraid what he would do. He couldn't believe this. "What if Jessica was pregnant with my child?" He swung back around, fisting his hands as he scowled at his father.

"You were *seventeen,*" Hoyt said.

"I don't give a damn. You had no right."

"Go ahead, take a swing," his father said as Colton stepped forward. "Get it out of your system. Can't say I wouldn't feel the same way if my old man had done what I did."

Colton wanted to. But a man didn't hit his father. He stood, shaking with rage. He'd been angry with Hoyt Chisholm before, many times, but never as angry as he was now and it scared him. He'd lived long enough to know that what either of them might say or do right now could destroy their relationship. He loved his adoptive father and that love kept him from saying the angry things inside him.

Hoyt had adopted him and his fraternal twin brothers, Logan and Zane, after their mother had died in child-birth. He'd raised them and three other sons mostly by himself all these years. Colton could never forget how different his life would have been if it wasn't for the generosity and love that Hoyt had shown him. He often forgot that they didn't share the same blood because this man was their father and always had been.

"I met her the night she disappeared and gave her the money, just as she asked," Hoyt said.

Colton was shaking his head. "Don't tell me you met her at—"

"The spot where I understand her remains were found. I had no idea the two of you had been meeting back there. Don't look at me like that. I didn't touch a hair on her head." His father's obvious disgust for Jessica felt like another blow.

Everyone had seen through Jessica but him, the dumb kid in love. The dumb kid who thought he would protect her because, as young as he'd been, he'd instinctively known that Jessica needed protecting.

"I wanted to tell you before I told the deputy," Hoyt said.

"You're only going to make yourself a suspect." He knew his father couldn't have killed Jessica, but that didn't mean Halley would believe it. "Deputy Robinson already has it in for me. Now she can add my family."

"You don't have to tell me how stupid I was—especially given what happened to Jessica that night. I'm sorry, I didn't like her, can't pretend I did. I probably shouldn't have given her the money, but I knew you, Colton. You would have married her even if it wasn't your baby."

"She wasn't pregnant. She lied."

His father nodded, not looking surprised in the least. "Even if she had been pregnant, she didn't have any business raising a baby. I thought I was doing what was best for my grandchild—*and* my son."

"Don't ever make that mistake again," Colton said and stalked back to his pickup. Once behind the wheel, he saw his father walk slowly back to his own pickup, his head down.

Colton swore and slammed his fist down on the steering wheel. Then he started the engine and left in a cloud of gravel and dust.

HALLEY THOUGHT AT FIRST it was Colton calling her back. She knew she shouldn't have been surprised that he was still digging into Jessica's death, but he had to be careful talking to Millie Granger. If her husband found out—

Where had that thought come from? From her growing suspicions about Sid Granger.

Checking her phone, Halley saw that it was the sheriff's department dispatcher calling. She said she had a call from Hoyt Chisholm and patched it through. She was surprised that he hadn't called sooner. The rancher had a lot of clout in the state. She wondered if he would try to strong-arm her into searching for suspects other than his son. Or if he would try to charm her. She'd heard he did both well.

Deciding it was time to find out, she said, "I'm out your way. Why don't I stop by?"

"Actually, it might be easier if I came to you, since I'm not at the ranch house. I'm on my way into town."

She spotted his truck coming down the road toward her and looked for a place to pull over. She wasn't sure that meeting him in the middle of nowhere was the best idea, but it was too late to do anything else as she saw him slow down.

Pulling over into a wide spot beside the road, Halley braced herself for the confrontation she knew was coming. As Hoyt Chisholm pulled in, she got out of her patrol SUV. This face-off would be bad enough with him standing beside her SUV or even worse if he got into her patrol car. She preferred standing, although he would tower over her five-foot-five frame.

He cut the pickup engine and got out, walking toward her slowly. He looked like a beaten man. So this was the way he planned to play it?

"There's something I need to tell you," he said after introducing himself and shaking her hand. His grip had been strong and he'd met her gaze with a steely blue one.

"If this is about Colton and my investigation—"

"It's about Jessica. I met her that night and gave her $10,000, at her request, to leave my son alone."

Halley had *not* been expecting this. For a moment she was at a loss for words. "Where did you—"

"At the spot where I heard you found her remains."

She was taken aback by this information, especially by how freely it was given.

"She was alive when I left her there. I had the feeling that she was waiting for someone else," he said, then seemed to straighten to his full height as if a weight had been lifted off his shoulders.

"The money wasn't found on her."

Hoyt nodded. "Colton told me there was only $200 in her purse. I have no idea what happened to the money I gave her."

"You didn't change your mind when you saw her? Get angry? Decide there was another way to keep her from ruining your son's life?"

He smiled then and Halley thought that while Colton might not be Hoyt Chisholm's son by birth, he'd definitely acquired his adoptive father's charm. "Would I have come forward if I'd taken my $10,000 back that night?"

Once she was over her initial shock, she said, "You had more motive to want her dead than your son did. Is that why you're coming forward now, to try to shift suspicion away from him?"

"Isn't it possible I just had to tell the truth? I thought

that girl had taken the money and left town." Hoyt rubbed a big hand over the back of his neck. "No matter how I felt about her, my son cared about her. I want to see her killer caught because of that."

He sounded so darn sincere, she actually found herself believing him. "What time of night was it when you left her there?"

"About eleven-thirty."

"What was the money in?"

"A large paper bag. The bills were hundreds. Old ones I took out of my safe."

"You're in the habit of keeping $10,000 in old hundred-dollar bills in your safe?"

He smiled again. "I do like to have some cash on hand. That particular money, though, was from the sale of a bull. I'd been paid with the old hundreds and I just hadn't taken them to the bank."

Halley remembered years ago hearing about one of the Chisholm bulls that had gone for $30,000. Cattle were Hoyt Chisholm's business and he'd done well by it.

"I appreciate your coming to me with this information," she said. "I may need to ask you further questions in the future."

"You know where I live."

EMMA HAD MADE A QUICK trip into town after Hoyt left, telling herself that she had to make tonight's dinner extra special.

When she returned home, she hadn't been surprised to see that all the ranch pickups were gone and Celeste hadn't arrived yet to help with supper. Hoyt, she knew, had gone off to find Colton. The rest of his sons were working somewhere on the ranch.

She had no idea where any of them were—including her husband. The thought had never crossed her mind before that she should worry about where they were. She'd always known that they would all show up come supper time. If they were moving cows, sometimes they didn't make it back for lunch, but they never missed supper.

Emma had brought fresh-cut flowers and the other necessities for the special supper she had planned. Celeste would pick up anything else they needed.

But as she stepped into the house, she stopped cold. At first she wasn't sure what had made her freeze just inside the door. Emma had never felt afraid alone out here on the ranch in the two weeks she'd been here. Even though it was miles from the next ranch and even farther from town, she'd loved the peace and quiet, the solitude.

She thought that was what was wrong with the world these days. People couldn't find solitude in the big city. That wonderful complete lack of noise and other people. It was why so many people always had a cell phone to their ear—they couldn't even stand being alone with their thoughts.

Now as she stood just inside the door, she could hear birds singing, the sigh of the breeze in the tall cottonwoods next to the house, a hawk crying out in the distance—and the pounding of her heart.

It took a moment to realize what had spooked her. Then she caught another whiff of it. Perfume. It was the same scent she'd caught just a hint of after someone had searched her bedroom.

Emma felt her heart drop like a stone. Another woman had been in her house again and she had a terrible feeling that Hoyt Chisholm knew exactly who that woman was.

COLTON HAD THOUGHT ABOUT skipping supper to avoid seeing his father. He was still furious with him, but he knew he'd have to contend with Emma if he missed the meal.

A part of him also realized after he'd calmed down some that he was going to have to face his father—and Emma. He had no doubt that Hoyt had confessed first to Emma. If she'd been around fourteen years ago, Colton was sure Emma would never have let Hoyt do what he'd done.

The moment he saw her, Colton knew that she'd been worried about the confrontation between father and son. She looked relieved to see him.

"We have company coming for supper tonight," she announced as she nervously straightened the bouquet of flowers at each end of the long dining room table.

Since Emma had come into their lives, there were flowers in the house and they dressed for dinner. Nothing elaborate, like tuxes, just clean boots, jeans and Western shirts. Hair combed. Hats off. Everyone freshly showered. She even had Hoyt saying a prayer before they ate.

In just two short weeks, Emma had made some major changes at the Chisholm ranch. Colton had to hand it to her. She seemed to be good for their father.

He studied her now, though, with some concern. She was acting as if everything was fine, but he could see by the way she fussed over the flowers that she was nervous. Since he hadn't seen his father since their meeting in the middle of the road, he figured Hoyt had gone to Deputy Robinson to confess and that's what had his stepmother on edge.

With a silent curse, he realized that he hadn't called Halley back. He told himself he would after dinner. Right now he was too upset. In fact, his stepmother's words had only now registered.

"What company?" he asked, noting that there was only one extra plate set at the table. Was it just him? Or did this seem like a bad time to have dinner guests? But of course he didn't tell Emma that.

Emma hurried off to the kitchen as if she hadn't heard his question. Often they had cattle buyers join them for dinner. Emma always said, "The more the merrier." She was so different from other nonranch-raised women who hated living on a ranch so far from town, and especially hated all the cooking that went with ranches and their crews and visitors. A woman like Jessica.

Who, he told himself, was the last person he wanted to think about right now.

His father had just come in through the side door when the doorbell rang. Emma came flying out of the kitchen, her expression one of anticipation and nervousness. The nervous part wasn't like her and Colton found himself looking toward the living room where his father had gone to answer the door.

He heard the door open, then nothing but what seemed like an awfully long silence.

"Please come in," Emma said, rushing to the guest at the front door. "Supper is almost ready. We're delighted you could join us."

"Emma?" Colton heard his father say and, unable to stand it any longer, got up to see what was going on.

His brothers had just come in through the back and looked expectantly toward the front of the house as if they knew something he didn't.

Colton spotted a car he didn't recognize parked out front an instant before he saw Deputy Halley Robinson standing in the doorway. *She* was their dinner guest?

Halley wore a pale yellow sundress that accented her dark hair, brown eyes and tanned skin. Her long hair, normally pulled back and tied up when she was on duty, now hung around her bare shoulders in soft curls.

He stood staring in wonder at how amazing she looked and realized his brothers were doing the same thing. A sharp pang of jealousy jolted him. Where had that come from? Halley Robinson sure as hell wasn't his.

Emma proceeded to go around the room introducing each of her stepsons.

As she came to Colton, he said, "We've met," and wondered what the hell the deputy was doing here. Clearly, someone had invited her to supper.

"Halley and I ran into each other in town today," Emma said, apparently realizing an explanation was needed. "I invited her to join us for supper."

"That was thoughtful of you," Hoyt said, an edge to his voice. He, no doubt, was wondering what the hell his wife had been thinking inviting the deputy sheriff who wanted to see either his son or himself fry for murder. Or both.

"Why don't we all have a seat?" Emma said.

The entire evening Colton felt as if Halley was watching him. He couldn't shake the feeling that she'd come out here merely to confirm her worst suspicions about him and his father.

He hated most that the whole time he'd been too aware of her every movement. For all his focused attention on her, it could have been just the two of them in the room. He'd barely touched his food and felt awkward and self-conscious, as if on a first date.

Nor had he said more than a few words and only those because Emma had been determined to include him in the conversation. He'd been afraid to open his mouth for fear of what might come out. He kept thinking about kissing Halley.

At Emma's suggestion, after supper was finally over, he walked Halley to her car. Not that he hadn't already planned to see the deputy out. "What was *that* about?"

She looked surprised. "Supper?"

"You know damn well what I mean."

"Your mother and I ran into each other today in town. She invited me and I took her up on it."

"She's my stepmother and I don't want you around my family."

Halley raised a brow. "It was just supper."

"You came out here to investigate."

She laughed. "Oh, you mean that story your *stepmother* told about you jumping off the roof onto a horse like you'd seen on television when you were five? I'm just trying to figure out how to use that against you." Halley shook her head and a sadness came into her gaze. "I had a good time. Please thank your...Emma for me again."

They both turned at the sound of the screen door

banging open. Emma came rushing out with a foil-wrapped package and handed it to Halley.

"I thought you'd like the last piece of apple pie."

"No, I couldn't—"

"Take it to your father. You're doing me a favor. I can't have my stepsons fighting over it," she said with a wink.

"I was just asking Colton to please thank you again for inviting me," Halley said. "I really enjoyed it and the meal was amazing."

Emma glowed in the praise. "You must come again soon." With that she turned and hurried off.

"I'm sorry you think I had an ulterior motive for coming out here tonight," Halley said. "Your stepmother is very persuasive. If anyone had an ulterior motive though, it's Emma."

"What are you talking about?"

She shook her head as she opened the door to her car, climbed in and drove off.

Colton had to move back or she would have run over the toes of his boots. He watched her drive away, her last words echoing in his head, and realized he hadn't told her about his talk with Millie Granger.

EMMA SAW COLTON'S EXPRESSION as he came back into the house and couldn't hide her disappointment that the evening hadn't gone as well as she'd hoped.

She'd thought that once the deputy saw Colton with his family, she would realize there was no way this young man could be a killer. She'd invited Halley to supper before Hoyt had dropped his bombshell. But she hoped that the deputy also realized after a nice meal at the ranch, that neither Colton nor Hoyt had anything to do with that girl's death.

"I'm glad Halley had a nice time," she said, just because she needed to say something as Colton came toward her.

She thought for a moment that he might tie into her but instead, he glanced past her, snapped his mouth closed in an angry line and, turning on his heel, headed out the front door.

She sighed and turned to find her husband standing behind her with a similar look on his face. No wonder Colton had taken off the way he had. "Emma, what were you thinking?"

In retrospect, she had no idea. Her new family had all acted oddly at supper, all of her stepsons but Colton flirting with Halley, and her trying to cover for both Hoyt's and Colton's silence.

"She seems like a nice young woman," was the best defense she could come up with.

Hoyt shook his head, pushed past her and took off toward the barn.

Emma sighed again, then turned back toward the kitchen, needing to work off her disappointment as well as her fear. Both Colton and Hoyt were furious with her. Both were suspects in a murder case and Emma worried that was only the tip of the iceberg.

She knew she was just trying hard not to think about her own worries since smelling the perfume in her house a second time.

As she began cleaning up the dishes, she thought maybe the night hadn't been a total disaster. She recalled the times she'd seen Halley Robinson steal a glance toward Colton.

It wasn't the look of a lawman at a suspect. Unless she'd lost her mind, Halley liked her stepson. Maybe more than the woman wanted to admit.

Emma just hoped she hadn't made things worse. But then how could it be any worse with both a son and his father now suspects and her fearing her husband was lying to her about…well, possibly about everything.

"HOW WAS YOUR EVENING?" Geoff Robinson asked his daughter when she stopped by his house to give him the piece of apple pie.

"Interesting," she said as she kicked off her sandals and tucked her legs under her on the couch, as she'd done since she was a little girl. She hugged herself as she watched him eat the pie.

"This is delicious. Please thank Mrs. Chisholm."

Halley nodded but seemed lost in thought, a small smile curling her lips.

He would have loved to know what that was about. "Anything new on the case?" He was instantly sorry he'd asked because the smile vanished.

"No. Just more disturbing information. Jessica wasn't pregnant. She apparently lied to get money from the men she was sleeping with—and Colton's father. Worse, it appears she was being physically abused. Possibly sexually abused."

"By someone in her family?"

His daughter frowned. "Probably, although Jessica tried to implicate her boyfriend. I can't rule out Colton Chisholm, even though I really like his stepmother and the rest of his family."

Wisely, he merely nodded. A day ago Colton would have been at the top of her list as a suspect. Clearly, something had happened to change her mind about him. Her father wondered what as he saw her touch her fingers to her lips and that small secretive smile appear again.

Her cell phone rang and she quickly checked it. "I have to take this." She got up and walked outside barefoot to the patio. A breeze stirred the new green leaves of the cottonwoods. In the distance, the Little Rockies had turned a deep, dark purple against the fading light. This far north it didn't get dark this time of year until almost ten.

Geoff Robinson finished the pie and waited for his daughter, praying that returning to Whitehorse had been the right thing to do—and, in turn, talking Halley into coming back here as well.

He'd thought it would be safer for her than out on the West Coast where she'd been working as a deputy—and had nearly been killed. But as he watched her, he knew she'd gotten more information about the Jessica Granger case and it wasn't good news.

"That was one of the investigators from the state crime lab," she said when she returned.

"Something wrong?"

"I need to go back to the crime scene. The state investigators are wrapping it up there. Not much evidence is left after fourteen years." She sighed. "A cold case like this...there's just little chance it will be solved and the suspects, well, they'll live the rest of their lives with everyone in town believing they're guilty."

He knew she meant Colton Chisholm. "Honey, you can only do so much. Maybe when the sheriff gets back—"

"I'm not going to stop digging into the case," she said,

pocketing her phone and giving him a smile. "With Jessica's purse and her remains discovered, the killer has to be worried. With a little push, who knows what will happen?"

Geoff Robinson was suddenly hit with a terrible premonition that coming back to Whitehorse had been a mistake.

Chapter Eight

The crime scene was bathed in twilight when Halley passed under the yellow tape. The team was packing up to leave.

A van with more techs had driven up from Missoula to take back the remains and the crime team. The lead tech told her that they had scoured the area for evidence all day, but after fourteen years there didn't appear to be anything to find.

She thought about taking a look at the crime scene herself, but she was dog-tired. If there had been anything to find here at the scene, she knew the crime techs would have found it.

She thanked them and left. By the time she pulled into her driveway in front of the old farmhouse she'd rented on the edge of Whitehorse, all she could think about was going to bed. It had been a long day. Not to mention emotionally exhausting.

She smiled at the thought, since kissing Colton Chisholm shouldn't have been that exhausting. Nor should having supper with his family. But just being near him...

She shoved that thought away as she climbed out of her car. The house was too large for one person, but she was too old not to have her own place. She hated to think how she would be able to afford heating the big old rambling place come winter, but for now it felt like home. In truth, she'd liked it the first time she'd laid eyes on the house. It was just far enough out of town.

"It rents cheap," the realtor had told her.

Cheap was exactly what she needed.

"You'll want to look around for a place you can buy."

Halley didn't see that happening. When her father had moved back, bought a small ranch, and she'd seen an ad for an opening as deputy, it had seemed like a good idea. She knew he was worried about her after everything that had happened at her last job. She had to admit that she was still shaken by her near death at the hands of a killer—a killer she'd foolishly trusted.

But now she was involved in a murder investigation and one of the obvious suspects was the one person she wasn't sure she could be objective about.

Halley had so much on her mind that she didn't notice at first that someone had jimmied her front door.

With a curse, she stepped back onto the porch and walked as casually as she could to her patrol SUV. Popping the lock, she opened the door and reached inside for her shotgun. As she closed the door quietly, the shotgun in her hands, she glanced toward the old farmhouse, listening.

The only sound was the breeze in the lilac bushes. It rustled the leaves and sent the now sickeningly strong smell of lilac into the summer night breeze.

She retraced her steps, climbing the porch to the front door and then easing it open. There was no vehicle in the yard and her instincts told her that whoever had broken into her house was long gone, but she wasn't taking any chances.

Her first thought had been a burglar, but she'd quickly rejected that idea. Since arriving in Whitehorse, she'd had little time to do more than buy some used furniture. She didn't even own a television or sound system. The small radio in her kitchen wasn't worth stealing and she didn't own anything a decent burglar would consider good jewelry.

No, whoever had broken into her house wasn't there to rob her.

Halley moved through the house, her weapon drawn. Her mind raced. It made no sense that someone would break in, so she figured it must be kids and that meant vandalism.

But as she searched each room, she saw no sign that anyone had been here. Nothing seemed to be missing or messed up.

As she neared the bedroom door, she slowed. The door was closed. She was nearly positive she'd left it open. Stepping to it, she took hold of the knob with her left hand, her right hand gripping the gun, and eased the door open.

The closet door was open—as she remembered leaving it. She glanced at the old vanity pressed against the wall. Her jewelry box sat on top, also open.

She could see even from where she stood that no one had been in it. One look and they would have noticed that she had very little jewelry and nothing worth stealing.

Realizing that the room was empty, she put her shotgun down and stood for a moment trying to reassure herself. No one was in the house.

But someone had been. Why? What had they been looking for?

She stood in the room, tired and irritable and a little spooked. The house felt different now. As a deputy, she'd worked with victims of burglaries and break-ins. The victims always said they felt violated, but she'd never had to experience it herself before. Mostly, it made her angry as hell.

She leaned the shotgun against the wall by the door, too tired to go back downstairs, even though she realized that she hadn't locked the front door. Not that it would matter since whoever had jimmied it had broken the lock.

Exhaustion pulled at her, even though it was still early. She stepped to the bed, wanting to just fall in under the covers without even undressing. As she tugged down the comforter, she heard the sound. Unfortunately, it didn't register until she'd uncovered what someone had left her.

COLTON MENTALLY KICKED HIMSELF as he started down the road away from the main house toward his own place. He hated the way he'd left things with his father, with Emma, with Halley. He'd been a jackass at supper.

But when he got around Halley, he had a history of doing everything wrong.

Except for the kiss. That had felt right, dammit.

He slowed at the county road, considering which way to turn. To the left and home? Or to the right and Halley's house? He knew the old farmhouse she rented just out of town.

He doubted that apologizing would get him anywhere

with her. But he wanted to see her. He hadn't gotten the opportunity to tell her about his meeting with Millie Granger and his conviction that Sid Granger had lost his temper and killed his daughter when he'd caught her running away. He'd believed she'd gotten herself pregnant and had been furious about it.

Colton sat for a moment longer at the crossroads, finally giving up when he couldn't shake the feeling that he needed to tell Halley as soon as possible. He turned right, swinging the pickup onto the county road, and heading for her house. He didn't care what kind of reception he got. It wasn't as if he was expecting her to welcome him with open arms.

As he drove, his window down, the cool summer night air blowing in, he noticed the first few stars pop out in the expanse of sky that spanned the horizon. On many nights like this, he'd seen the Northern Lights and always felt awed by the light show nature put on this far north.

As he turned down the road to her place, he was glad to see that Halley's patrol SUV and car were parked in front. He pulled in and sat for a moment, half hoping she'd heard his pickup and would come out on the porch. Probably armed with a shotgun though, he realized.

When she didn't, he debated leaving. Maybe this hadn't been such a good idea after all. A scented breeze blew in his driver's-side window. He could smell the lilacs in her front yard, still fragrant for a little longer before they would be gone for another year.

He remembered the way Halley's hair had hung around her shoulders, the soft look in her brown eyes and what she'd said just before she'd driven off.

Holy hell. Had she meant that Emma was trying to set them up?

He was reaching for the key to start the pickup and get out of there when he heard the scream. It came from inside the house.

In a heartbeat he was out of the pickup and running toward the house.

EMMA LOOKED OVER, SURPRISED to see that Hoyt had forgotten his cell phone on the nightstand, as it vibrated. He'd been keeping it with him, even when he went to shower, but tonight he'd left the house and forgotten.

It vibrated again and she reached over and picked it up. It wasn't until it vibrated a third time that she opened it.

"Hello?"

The laugh was soft and seductive sounding. "You must be Emma."

"And you must be…?"

"Aggie Wells." A beat of silence. "I take it Hoyt hasn't told you about me."

Emma felt her heart drop, but she tried to keep the pain from her voice. "What exactly should he have told me about you?"

That laugh again. "Why don't we meet and I'll tell you everything. Hoyt has that cattleman's assocatiation meeting tonight. Shall I come out to the ranch or—"

"Why don't I meet you somewhere?" Emma suspected the woman had already been out to the ranch several times. The perfume. The rummaged chest of drawers. The feeling that someone had been in the house.

"You pick the place," Emma said.

"I don't know Whitehorse that much better than you do, but I think some place out of town would be better. Do you know the bar out at the Sleeping Buffalo? Since it's a weeknight and early, we'll have the place to ourselves."

"I'll meet you there in an hour."

"I'll be waiting. I'll be the woman—"

"Don't worry. I'll recognize you." Emma snapped the phone shut and put it back on the nightstand. Then she headed for her closet to decide what to wear to meet the other woman in her husband's life.

COLTON HIT THE DOOR AT A RUN. As he burst in, he heard a second scream. It sounded as if it came from upstairs. He took the stairs three at a time. At the landing he ran launched himself at the open doorway.

Halley stood, back against the wall, eyes wide, her face white with terror.

For an instant he was too surprised to take in what was happening. He'd never seen Halley scared before, let alone terrified.

Then he saw the snake. The rattler was coiled just feet from her.

He moved with a speed that even surprised him, grabbing the comforter off of the bed and dropping it over the snake.

The ominous sound of the rattling snake still filled the room as he quickly bundled it up in the comforter and carried it down the stairs and outside where he shook out the snake. It slithered off into the darkness and he turned and hurried back upstairs.

Halley was just where he'd left her.

As he stepped toward her, he saw that her face was still bloodless, her brown eyes wide.

"Come on," he said taking her hand.

She seemed to stir, but she was still trembling. "Where are we going?"

"Downstairs."

"The snake?"

"Long gone. I'll come back up and make sure there are no others in the room, then I'm going to make you something to help you sleep."

"Sleep?" she asked as if he'd lost his mind.

"Sleep. You're exhausted."

She shook her head as if the last thing she was going to get tonight was sleep.

"Don't worry. I'm staying tonight."

Her eyebrow shot up and he saw some of the old don't-take-any-guff Halley Robinson in her expression.

"I'll sleep on your couch or on the floor next to your bed, whichever makes you feel safe. I'm not leaving you alone until we can get some decent locks on these doors."

Some of the color came back into her cheeks. "I'm a deputy sheriff and I can—"

"I know. You can take care of yourself." He could see that she was embarrassed. "There is no crime in being afraid of snakes. Especially rattlers. Truth is, nothing scares me more than coming across one."

She cocked her head, clearly not believing him.

"Honest to goodness," he said and then led her down-stairs to the kitchen.

She sat in one of the kitchen chairs while he checked the fridge, found milk and then a pan and began to heat the milk on the stove.

"Warm milk?" she asked, sounding amused.

"My dad used to give it to me when I couldn't sleep."

HALLEY HEARD THE CATCH in his voice and realized that his father must have confessed to him about trying to pay off Jessica. She could imagine how Colton had taken that news. She remembered how close he was with his father. She'd seen Hoyt pick up the boys from school. What kind of man adopted six sons to give them a good home? Apparently, a very kind, loving, generous one.

She knew that Colton's mother had died giving birth to him and his two brothers. Like her, he'd never known his birth mother.

"Are you all right?" he asked, studying her with concern as he stirred the pan of milk heating on the burner. He'd caught her glancing around the kitchen floor as if she expected to see more snakes.

"I. Don't. Like. Snakes."

"I remember, but I had no idea you were that afraid of them. Halley, I'm so sorry. I was such a jerk as a kid."

He had the most beautiful eyes. Between his eyes and his grin, was it any wonder she'd fallen for Colton so many years ago?

"Can you ever forgive me for what I did to you when we were kids?" he asked.

She wasn't about to tell him that when he stopped tormenting her, that was when he'd broken her heart.

"Here, drink this," he said as he put a cup of warm milk in front of her. "I'll be right back."

She picked up the mug, cupping it in both hands. The heat felt good, reassuring, just as Colton's presence in her house did. She liked having him here. The house felt almost cozy. She began to relax as she heard him searching upstairs.

Careful, girl, she warned herself. But how was she to know that she was a sucker for a man who came riding in to save the woman in distress?

She just never thought she would be that woman.

THE BAR WAS DARK AND empty just as Aggie had said it would be, except for the forty-something female bartender who was busy cutting up limes—and the woman sitting at a table in the back.

Emma had expected Aggie Wells to be young, blond and brassy. As she walked toward her, she had to work to hide her surprise and confusion. The brunette appeared to be about Emma's age, somewhere in her early fifties, and definitely not blond or brassy.

"So you're Emma," Aggie said, studying her, a slight smile on her face. "You're nothing like I expected."

The bartender called to Emma, asking what she'd like.

"Give her a stiff drink, honey," Aggie called to her. "She's going to need it." Aggie turned her attention back to Emma. "The usual? A margarita, blended with salt."

"You are certainly well informed," Emma said.

"Bartenders know everything," Aggie said with a grin. "The one at the hotel in Denver where you and Hoyt met is especially talkative—if you know what to ask."

"I'm touched that you have taken such an interest in my life," Emma said, trying hard to hide her surprise and her irritation. But she had to admit, she was just as curious about Aggie Wells.

Aggie wore a white long-sleeved shirt, open at the neck, and blue jeans. Her long legs were stretched out on the booth seat, her back to the wall, confidence in every line of her slim body, intelligence shining in her pale blue eyes.

Emma had the strangest thought. She would have liked this woman had they met in some other circumstance.

Aggie gave the order to the bartender, getting herself another bottle of beer with a tequila chaser. As Emma slid into the opposite side of the booth, Aggie drew her legs off the booth seat and turned to face Emma.

"Before you get me drunk, why don't you tell me what this is all about," Emma said.

"Fair enough. What do you know about your husband's past?"

Next to nothing, but she hated to admit it.

"Never mind. I already know he swept you off your feet, quickie marriage in Vegas." She made a disappointed face as if Emma should have been smarter. Emma was beginning to think the woman was right.

"Why don't you fill me in, since you seem to know a lot about my husband, as well as me. By the way, why is that exactly?"

"I'm the private investigator who's going to prove your husband killed his last three wives."

Emma was too shocked to speak. She took a long swig of her margarita, licked the salt from her lips and told herself to breathe.

"I take it no one's mentioned the Chisholm Curse to you?"

Emma thought of the phone calls and lied. "No."

Aggie gave her an impatient look. "You don't know

that Hoyt Chisholm's first wife, Laura, drowned in Fort Peck Reservoir and her body was never found?"

Emma knew his first wife had died soon after the two of them had adopted three little boys whose mother had passed away during childbirth. The father of the babies was unknown.

"I didn't know she drowned."

"On a fishing trip with Hoyt, just the two of them out in the middle of Fort Peck—a huge lake with more shoreline than California."

Aggie sounded angry.

"What is your interest in this?"

"I want to get the insurance company's money back," the woman said.

"Insurance?"

"Hoyt insured Laura and himself for a cool million."

Emma choked on her drink. Hoyt had said he needed to get an insurance policy on her. He'd said it was because she was now one of the owners of Chisholm Cattle Company. She'd agreed.

After a few moments Emma finally found her voice. "Of course the insurance company is going to want to believe it was more than an accident—"

Aggie smiled. "First wife, a million. Second wife, a million. Third wife, a million. See a pattern there?"

Emma didn't know what to say, since she hadn't even known about the other two wives. "Did your insurance company insure all three wives?" she asked.

Aggie shook her head. "Only the first one."

"Then how do you know—"

"I know. He didn't ask you to sign a prenuptial agreement, did he?" Aggie asked with a sly smile.

She knew her expression gave her away.

"That's the way he works it. No prenup, but he takes out insurance on them. If they try to leave him…"

"You don't know they tried to leave him."

Aggie gave her a pitying look. "Wife number one had filed for divorce before the boat trip. Wife number two had told several of her friends that she was leaving him. Wife number three—"

"Not every woman is cut out for living so far from civilization. Maybe I should have found out more about my husband before I married him," Emma admitted. "But I know that he loved me. That was enough."

Aggie raised a brow. "What if I told you his second wife, Tasha, died under suspicious circumstances and his third wife, Krystal, disappeared?"

"I'd say Hoyt has had some very bad luck with wives," she managed to say.

Aggie laughed. "Are you always this annoyingly cheerful?"

"Most of the time."

The P.I. shook her head.

"Look, Hoyt started to tell me about this past but I hadn't wanted—or needed—to hear about it. At this age, we all have a past we might want to forget."

"What if he killed his other wives and you're next?"

AGGIE COULD SEE THAT HOYT Chisholm's new wife was having trouble breathing.

"I trust my husband." The words lacked conviction. "I know my husband."

Aggie laughed and drained her beer bottle and followed it with the shot of tequila and a slice of lime. She motioned to the bartender for another drink.

Emma declined. It was obvious that she was anxious to leave and get home and question her husband.

"That would be a mistake," Aggie said.

"I beg your pardon?"

"You can't wait to confront him." She shook her head. "Very bad idea. Don't you think the others did the same thing?"

"You told the second and third wives about your suspicions in the first wife's death?" Emma sounded shocked and outraged.

"They had a right to know who they were married to—and now they're dead."

"I thought you said his third wife was disappeared."

"Hoyt recently had her declared legally dead."

Aggie's drink arrived and she downed the tequila first this time, sucked for a moment on the lime before taking a long drink of her cold beer. It felt so good going down. Almost as good as it was going to feel nailing Hoyt Chisholm finally.

She realized that Emma was studying her intently. "Your insurance company doesn't mind your drinking on the job?"

Aggie merely smiled. "I like you. I'd hate to see something happen to you. Take my advice. Get as far away as you can from Hoyt Chisholm or you're going to end up as dead as the others."

"Have you actually *met* my husband?"

"I've seen him and we've talked a few times on the phone."

Emma smiled. "What are you doing for dinner tomorrow night?"

A few moments later, Aggie was still chuckling to herself as she watched Hoyt Chisholm's new wife leave the bar. Emma had more guts than the others, that was for sure.

She studied the woman's ramrod-straight back, the way she held her head high, the squared shoulders. A woman who couldn't be rattled.

If Aggie hadn't noticed the way Emma Chisholm held her purse, she might have bought the act.

Instead, she watched with strange fascination as wife number four hightailed it out of the bar. Emma Chisholm was running scared.

But not of her husband.

That was the part that fascinated Aggie.

With a jolt that made her shove away her drink and sit up a little taller, Aggie realized there was more to Emma McDougal Chisholm than she'd thought.

Unless Aggie was losing her touch, the new Mrs. Chisholm had something in her own past she was worried about keeping secret.

Chapter Nine

Halley woke to the wonderful smell of frying bacon and freshly brewed coffee. She quickly showered and dressed before heading downstairs. After making her warm milk, Colton had again checked the entire house to make sure there were no more lethal surprises awaiting her.

He'd tucked her into her bed, kissed her on the forehead and gone downstairs to sleep on her couch. She'd had a devil of a time getting to sleep though, knowing he was just one floor below. But exhaustion had won out and she'd drifted off and slept soundly.

Now as she stepped into the kitchen, she couldn't help but smile. He had on her apron, a frilly thing that had come with the house.

"Nice apron," she said as she leaned into the doorjamb to watch him.

"I went into town and got a few groceries," Colton said, smiling at her. "Your refrigerator was sadly bare."

"I smelled the bacon," she said, breathing in the aroma.

"I made cheese omelets to go with it."

She raised a brow in surprise. "So you cook."

He laughed. "I'm just full of surprises."

Wasn't he though.

"Have a seat. Coffee?"

She nodded as she pulled out a chair and sat down, watching him as he poured a mug of coffee and handed it to her. She took a sip and smiled through the steam. "Thank you."

"My pleasure." He filled two plates with bacon, cheese omelet, hash browns and toast. She saw that he'd picked up some huckleberry jam for the toast.

"You thought of everything," she said, impressed. "Thank you again for last night."

He studied her openly for a moment. "Looks like you got some rest."

She touched her wet hair, suddenly self-conscious. She hadn't taken the time to pull it up, so her long hair hung around her shoulders. Her cheeks felt flushed from the shower, from the nearness of this man, and since she didn't have to be at work for a few hours, she'd donned a pair of jeans and a T-shirt. She had taken the time to dab on a little lip gloss, but that was it.

"I looked in on you before I went into town to the store," he said.

Halley felt a small shiver at the thought of him watching her sleep.

"No bad dreams?" he asked.

She shook her head and dug into her breakfast. "This is delicious," she said between bites.

Colton looked pleased as he cleared the dishes, then refilled her coffee mug and took a seat across from her again.

"I didn't want to bring up the Grangers until we'd eaten," he said.

Halley knew they had to talk about the murder investigation and Jessica. But moments before she'd been enjoying the companionable warmth Colton had brought to her kitchen. For a while, she was just a woman, not a deputy, and he was just a man, not the former boyfriend of the deceased, let alone a suspect.

Colton filled her in on his talk with Millie Granger. "I'm telling you her father is involved. Millie practically admitted it."

Halley thought he might be right. But practically admitting it wasn't evidence.

"She admitted he was always overly protective of Jessica, that she was his little girl—"

"None of that is unusual for a father."

Colton swore. "Something was wrong in that house and you know it."

Halley couldn't argue with that. "What are you saying?"

He shook his head, clearly not wanting to say what they were both thinking. The mousy, beaten-down wife, the teenaged promiscuous daughter... As a law enforcement officer, Halley had seen it before.

Halley wished they could have avoided this subject— at least for a little while longer. There was something she needed to ask Colton, but she hated to do it here in her kitchen. She finished her coffee and rose from the table.

"So she wasn't pregnant."

"No." Halley heard relief in his voice. "Apparently, she thought she was and she was upset when she was told that she wasn't."

"So she lied about it and that's probably what got her killed."

Halley didn't miss the irony. If the reason she was killed was because of the baby she said she was carrying, Jessica's lies had finally caught up with her. Colton seemed convinced that that had been the case. Halley was reserving judgment until all the facts were in. Somewhere in all the lies was the truth, and she'd learned that things were often not as they seemed.

COLTON SAW HALLEY BRACE HERSELF before she said, "I need to know if you were…physical with Jessica, grabbed her a little too roughly, possibly hit her."

So she'd found out about Jessica's bruises. Of course she would suspect him, just as he'd known she would. That was why he hadn't told her.

"Are you asking if we had rough sex?" He let out a humorless laugh as he shoved back the chair and stood. "No. That clear enough for you? I don't expect you to believe me, but I asked Jessica about the bruises because I was concerned that someone was hurting her."

"And what did she say?"

"She got upset, told me to mind my own business. If you must know, it's what we argued about the last time I saw her." He swore. "I didn't tell anyone. I should have, but she'd made it clear that if I did, it was over between us."

He saw sympathy in Halley's gaze. That made him angrier with himself.

"She didn't give you any idea of who might have been hurting her?"

"That's what I'm trying to tell you. It was her old man. Whatever was going on, it was why Jessica was so desperate to get out of that house."

Halley nodded.

He'd expected her to put up an argument and was surprised when she didn't. "You found out something. That's why you aren't telling me how wrong I am."

Halley seemed to hesitate. "Social Services were asked to do a check at the house. It never happened because Jessica disappeared before the social worker got out there. But the doctor did talk to the father. Sid Granger was belligerent and denied touching her in any way."

"Of course he'd say that."

Halley set her mug down on the counter and turned to him, crossing her arms over her chest as she leaned back against the counter. "I'm familiar with the pattern of abuse."

"I doubt it's a coincidence that Jessica was murdered so soon after Social Services and the doctor called about possible physical abuse in the home."

"Looks that way, but we still need proof."

"Sid Granger is guilty as hell and Millie knows it."

"Well, she's either too afraid to talk or she loves her husband and is covering for him. I'm not sure which. Maybe both," Halley said. "I'll see if I can talk to her alone."

"Good luck with that. She had to sneak off to the grocery store to meet me. She was scared to death the entire time, kept looking around as if she expected Sid to appear at any moment."

"In the meantime, steer clear of that family."

EMMA WASN'T SURPRISED to wake the next morning and find her husband gone. Hoyt had come home late. She'd pretended to be asleep, not wanting to have a discussion when they'd both been drinking and were tired.

This morning, after talking to her stepson, Tanner, before he headed off with a load of hay for a neighbor, she'd dressed in jeans, boots and a Western shirt and saddled up and ridden north. She found Hoyt stringing barbed wire with Dawson and Marshall.

Hoyt glanced over as she rode up and did a double take. "You ride?"

She laughed at his shocked expression and thought she couldn't love this man more—even under the circumstances. "There is so much we don't know about each other, isn't there?" She reached into her jacket pocket and handed him his cell phone.

He glanced at it, then at her. His expression changed and he put down the wire stretcher in his hand. "Why don't you boys take it from here. I need to talk to my wife."

Hoyt walked over into the cool shade of the trees where he'd left his horse and, without a word, swung up into the saddle. They rode under a vast Montana morning sky, white clouds bobbing along in all that blue, a cool breeze stirring the silken green branches of the ponderosa pines.

Emma breathed it all in. She refused to believe the strong, handsome, caring and generous man riding beside her was anything but that. Aggie was wrong. Those local women who'd called her were wrong. A woman knew in her heart what a man was really like, didn't she?

They stopped on a high ridge, Hoyt dismounting to reach for her. His large hands cupped her waist as he lifted her from the saddle and lowered her slowly to her feet.

What if you're wrong?

The thought blindsided her. She had followed Hoyt with a trust that, if misguided, could get her killed. With a start she realized that they had ridden far from another living soul. Even if she were to scream, her stepsons wouldn't be able to hear her. At the edge of the high ridge was a precipice that dropped a good twenty feet to a pile of stones. The fall would kill a person.

"Who told you?" Hoyt asked as his gaze met hers.

Emma swallowed. She hated to admit that she'd answered his phone, that she hadn't trusted him. "Aggie."

He let out a curse and stepped away from her to the edge of the rock cliff. "See all of that?" he asked, not turning around. "I own that and it means nothing without you."

She looked out at the land that stretched to the horizon.

"I don't blame you if you want to leave me," he said finally, his voice breaking with emotion.

The sound tore at her heart. She stepped to him, placing a hand on his warm back. "I'm not going anywhere."

He turned then, frowning at her. "That could be the biggest mistake you ever make, Emma."

HALLEY HADN'T SPOKEN TO THE Grangers since her last visit when she'd had to tell them that some remains had been found near the spot where Jessica's purse had been discovered.

Sid had opened the door, making a point of not asking her in. She'd had to give him the news on his doorstep. He'd been stoic, closing the door after no more than a brief nod and a mumbled, "Thank you for letting us know."

He hadn't asked where the remains had been found. Or if they were absolutely sure that they were his daughter's. Halley hadn't thought it was a good time to ask for a DNA sample. But, still, it was odd that he wouldn't ask where the remains had been found, which led her to believe that he already knew about the secret spot where his daughter had met not only Colton Chisholm—but also at least one other man.

Now, as Halley knocked on the door again, not only did she need to ask for a DNA sample, but she also had to ask about possible abuse of their daughter.

"I can't talk to you," Millie Granger said when she opened the door.

"Mrs. Granger, we have to talk. We can do it here or down at the Sheriff's Department."

Millie had been starting to close the door, but she now stopped. She looked so small and scared, Halley's heart went out to her.

"I want to help you by finding your daughter's killer."

"You can't help me," she whispered and Halley realized that Sid Granger wasn't at work. In fact, he'd been at home the other times Halley had stopped by as well. He suddenly appeared behind his wife.

"I thought you'd be at work," Halley said, caught off guard.

"I'm sure you did," he replied, his mouth twisting into a malicious grin. "I retired so I could spend more time with my wife. Which has been a godsend, given what she's been through. What we've both been through."

Halley suspected that his retirement had less to do

with spending time with wife than it did with keeping an eye on her. Why did he feel the need? she wondered. Had he been this possessive of Jessica and, after she was gone, turned that obsession on his wife?

"What do you want now? Haven't you given us enough bad news?" he demanded.

"I need to talk to the two of you," she said, not seeing any other way to handle this at the moment.

"Have you found my daughter's killer?" he asked.

"Not yet."

Sid nodded as if he had expected nothing less, then turned and walked back inside the house.

"Please don't say anything to upset him," Millie whispered as she let Halley into the house.

In the living room, Halley was even more taken aback by the large rattlesnake-skin hide that hung over the fireplace. She thought of the snake in her bed last night. A bite from that kind of rattlesnake wouldn't have killed her, so whoever had left it there for her had been either trying to scare her—or warn her off.

Neither Granger offered her a chair, but she sat down on the couch anyway. It took the couple a few moments to settle into chairs opposite her.

Halley began with the need for a DNA sample.

"What's the point? You're sure it's our daughter, right?" Sid asked.

"We will need positive identification. I thought you would want that as well." He didn't respond, so she continued. "Tell me about your relationship with your daughter," Halley said, taking out her tape recorder. "If you don't mind I'm going to tape our conversation."

Sid eyed it warily. Millie balled her hands in her lap.

"Fine with me," Sid said.

"So did you get along well with your daughter?" Halley asked.

"Jessica was my baby, my sweet girl," he cried. "I loved that girl more than…" His voice broke, tears welling in his eyes.

"She was the only child we were ever going to have," Millie said in her small voice. "We adored her. Didn't we, Sid?"

He nodded. "I would have given her the world. I just can't understand… It was that boy. He ruined my girl. I should have killed him when she told me what he did to her."

"What did Jessica tell you?" Halley asked and saw Millie tense.

Sid worked his jaw, fighting strong emotions, rage among them. "He took my girl's virginity."

"She told you that?"

"Only because I was waiting up for her one night after she'd sneaked out of the house to meet the little bastard. She'd been crying and her dress…" His voice broke again. "It was soiled. There were bruises on her arms. I wanted to go after him right then and there, but Jessica begged me not to. She said…" He swallowed hard. "She said she had wanted him to…" Sid shook his head and clamped his lips together.

"We forbid her to see him again," Millie said. "We thought she'd broken it off…"

Halley looked from one to the other, her gaze finally settling on the father again. "Did you punish Jessica?"

"We grounded her," Millie said.

"You didn't get physical with her?"

"What are you asking?" Sid demanded.

"Jessica had bruises that her doctor noticed when she

went in for her checkup about the pregnancy. It appeared that someone had been rough with her."

"It was that boy. She told me he hurt her sometimes," Millie said.

Sid shot his wife a look of disbelief as if this was the first time he'd hear this.

"Colton swears he never harmed her," Halley said.

"*Colton?* You two pretty tight, are you?" Sid sneered at her. "He hurt my girl plenty. He took everything from her—even her life." He was on his feet now. "I think you'd better leave before I say or do something I'll regret. I never touched a hair on my little girl's head. I couldn't even bear it when Millie..." He was crying again.

"I tried to reason with Jessica," Millie said. "And her father did everything possible to get her to come to her senses. No one loved our girl more than Sid."

Halley picked up the tape recorder and shut it off. "Why don't you walk me to the door, Mrs. Granger," she said as rose to leave.

Millie slowly got to her feet, avoiding her husband's scowl.

"I need you to tell me the truth," Halley whispered once they were out on the porch. "Did your husband beat your daughter?"

She seemed to struggle for a moment, before she finally spoke. "It isn't what you think. Jessica had this wild streak. Sid knew it ran on my side of the family. My younger sister went bad. He just didn't want Jessica going down that same path. What he did was for her own good."

"Apparently letting your husband beat your daughter didn't help a lot," Halley said.

"You aren't one to judge. We did the best we could with our baby girl."

"What about the way he treats you? Is that for your own good as well?"

Millie lifted her chin, anger sparking in her eyes. "He's my husband."

"That doesn't give him the right to—"

Sid appeared on the other side of the screen door. "There a problem, deputy?"

"I just wanted to double-check where the two of you were the night Jessica ran away." Halley improvised.

"I believe we already told you that," Sid said, glancing from Halley to his wife, not buying her story.

"It was my quilting night," Millie said. "I drive down to Old Town Whitehorse to the Whitehorse Sewing Circle."

Sid said, "I was home. As I already told you. Jessica told me she was going to bed. I never knew she was missing until Millie came home and found her bed empty."

Halley turned to Millie. "Why did you happen to check her bed?"

"I went up as I always did to check on her. It's an old habit from when she was a baby."

Sid rubbed his forehead. "I didn't know she'd sneaked out to meet that Colton boy." His jaw tightened again with anger.

The secret meeting spot wasn't that far from the Granger's house. Jessica could have walked along the creek behind her house. Halley wondered how far of a walk it would be—and if there was a path. If Jessica snuck out a lot, there could be.

Jessica had planned to meet Colton at the spot on the

creek under the cottonwoods. She'd met Hoyt Chisholm there at 11:30 p.m. and according to him seemed to be waiting around, as if expecting someone else.

Colton wasn't supposed to be there until midnight.

Was it possible that she was meeting someone else first?

The question was—who?

And the bigger question: Did her father follow her that night?

Chapter Ten

Halley had barely gotten back to the Sheriff's Department to type up her report when Colton called.

"I've been thinking about this morning," he said.

She thought of her kitchen, the wonderful smell of coffee and bacon, and Colton in the apron making her breakfast, and smiled to herself.

"It's possible there might have been someone Jessica confided in—other than her friend Twyla," he said.

So that's what Colton had been thinking about. Not this morning in her kitchen. She thought about that moment when they'd both left the house this morning. Colton had hesitated. She'd seen something simmer in his gaze.

They'd been standing just inches apart. She'd been so sure he was going to kiss her again that she'd almost leaned in.

"See you later?" he'd said and stepped back, as if needing to put distance between them.

She'd nodded dumbly, wondering about this overly gentlemanly Colton Chisholm. He hadn't tried anything last night and then this morning… "Later," she'd managed to say as he'd walked to his pickup.

Now mentally shifting gears, she asked, "You have an idea who that might have been?"

"Possibly. I saw her once after school talking to our guidance counselor."

"The married, older man?"

"He was married and he was probably ten years older than us."

She knew Colton must have seen something between Jessica and the guidance counselor years ago that had made him suspicious.

"He is still at the school," Colton said. "There is something else I should tell you. If he is the older, married man Jessica told me about, then he might have taken photographs of the two of them together."

Halley could hear how angry he was and couldn't help being surprised Colton hadn't pulled his cowboy-on-a-big-white-horse routine and already confronted the man. She said as much to him.

"I thought about it," he said with a humorless laugh. "Believe me, I wanted to go over to his house and… But I realized I had to let you handle this investigation."

He was finally trusting her to find Jessica's killer. Her heart swelled at the compliment. "Thank you. For telling me about the guidance counselor and for not going over there yourself," she added.

"Let me know what happens?" he asked.

She was still touched by his faith in her. "What's this man's name?"

"Mark Jensen."

THE BREEZE SIGHED IN the ponderosa pines. Nearby the horses ambled off to eat the tall green grass growing along the ridgeline.

"Emma, I should never have married you."

She stared at her husband, all her fears coming home to roost in those few words from his lips. She stumbled back from the edge of the cliff, suddenly needing to sit down. Lowering herself onto a lichen-covered rock, she felt a little better.

Hoyt sat down next to her. "I should have told you everything from the very beginning, but I knew once I did…" His gaze softened as he looked at her. "Aggie Wells has been calling me. I was going to tell you. I just didn't know how."

Emma saw the man she'd fallen so desperately in love with. "I know you didn't have anything to do with your wives' deaths or disappearance."

He chuckled. "Oh, Emma, it is that faith in me and your love that made me throw caution to the wind and marry you."

"You definitely have had bad luck when it comes to wives," she said.

He smiled at her. "Until now."

"You should have trusted me."

"You have no idea how difficult it was for me to even ask you out—let alone marry you. It still scares the hell out of me."

"Tell me you don't believe in some stupid curse."

"What else could it be?" he said.

"Bad luck? Or perhaps you married the wrong women."

He laughed, but there was no humor in it. "My first wife, Laura, I met at a college back East. She said she always wanted to live on a ranch and have a dozen children. When we found out she couldn't have children of our own, I suggested adopting. She had seemed so happy to get the three boys…" His voice died off for a moment. "They were just babies. I swear I didn't know she was leaving me—not until I got the divorce papers two days after she drowned. The boat trip on Fort Peck Reservoir was her idea. She said she needed a break from the boys."

"How did she drown?"

"We got caught in a storm. Fort Peck can be dangerous when the wind comes up. The boat capsized. When I surfaced, I couldn't find her. I dived time and again…" He looked away.

Emma could see how that could make an insurance company nervous. "You had a life insurance policy on her that paid double indemnity."

Hoyt turned to meet her gaze. "And I asked to take an insurance policy out on you as well." He let out another harsh laugh. "I told you it's because of the business, but we won't go through with it if it makes you feel better."

She shook her head, although she suspected that there was more to the story about Laura that Hoyt didn't want to tell her. Had they fought? Is that what had capsized the boat? Or had it really been the storm?

"Tell me about your second wife."

"Tasha was from California. She was up here on a dinosaur dig and she had this idea that living on a ranch would be romantic. By then I had adopted three more sons who needed homes."

"You had six boys to raise," Emma said. "I can see where you would want another wife."

"Tasha said she couldn't have kids of her own and

had seemed delighted to suddenly have six sons." His expression grew sad. "She had gone for a horseback ride alone even though I'd asked her not to until she'd spent more time on a horse. I found her. She'd somehow gotten her boot caught in the stirrup. She'd been dragged to death."

"Hoyt, I'm so sorry."

"I wasn't going to remarry, but a young woman named Krystal had been working at the house, helping Tasha… The boys had taken a shine to her. She had a boyfriend in Wyoming who was trying to get her back… I just couldn't bear for the boys to lose another person they cared about."

"So you married her," Emma said. "And she disappeared. Are you sure she just didn't go back to her old boyfriend?"

Hoyt shrugged.

"And then Aggie came back into your life and after seven years you had Krystal declared dead."

He nodded. "I swore I wasn't getting married again." He hung his head looking embarrassed. "For years I raised the boys alone."

Emma decided this wasn't the time to remind him that they were no longer boys.

"Hoyt, oh, honey." She moved to kneel at his feet and wrap her arms around him. "That's so horrible. No wonder you were afraid to love again."

"Aggie Wells is convinced that I killed all three of them."

"I know. She just doesn't realize the kind of man you really are. But she will, I promise."

He drew back. "Emma, what have you done?"

BEFORE THEY HUNG UP, Colton asked if Halley had talked to Millie Granger.

"I just got back from her house. I tried to talk to her but Sid was there. She is definitely frightened of him."

Colton swore. "I still think Sid killed Jessica. I suppose it's possible that if Millie starts to believe that he killed their daughter to keep the truth from coming out about the physical abuse, then maybe she will come forward."

"Maybe," Halley said. "In the meantime, it would help if Jessica confided in someone about what was going on at home."

"I suppose she could have confided in the guidance counselor even if she was sleeping with him." Colton sounded skeptical.

"We don't even know for a fact that any of what Jessica told you was true," she pointed out. "So tell me about this counselor."

"Mark Jensen was in his late twenties, so he'd be forty or so by now, a good-looking guy that everyone liked."

"Especially Jessica?"

"Yeah. The one time I saw her with him, he was very attentive and Jessica…she was flirting with him." He let out a humorless, self-deprecating laugh. "Twyla asked me why I never saw it."

"Because you didn't want to," Halley said.

"Yeah."

"Love does strange things to people."

"I'm not so sure that was love," Colton said. "I felt she needed me. She…hell, who knows what she wanted from me."

Halley thought about the first time she'd fallen in love. At least it had felt like true love. She could still remember the pain of seeing Colton with Jessica and realizing that he wouldn't be tormenting her anymore. Amazing that it could still hurt even after all these years.

MARK JENSEN LOOKED UP EXPECTANTLY as Halley tapped on his open door. Something passed over his expression that could have been worry as he took in her uniform shirt and the gun at her hip. She had called his house and been told by his wife that Mark was at his office at the school even though it was a Saturday.

"Mr. Jensen?" she asked.

Mark nodded a little too eagerly. "Yes."

"Do you have a minute?"

He glanced at his desk as if hoping he could find something important there so he could say no. Apparently finding nothing, he said, "Of course." He motioned her into his small office where she sat on a plastic chair across from his desk.

Since it was Saturday, the high school had a hollow, empty feel about it. She had seen only one other person as she'd walked through the building, a janitor. He'd directed her to the counselor's office.

Mark Jensen *was* a good-looking man, just as Colton had said. She'd had a couple of high school teachers she'd had crushes on and could remember that little thrill she'd gotten when one of them had complimented her on a paper or given her a smile after she'd answered a question correctly.

"I'm Deputy Robinson."

Halley noticed that Mark Jensen didn't look at her. "So what can I do for you?"

"I'm here about Jessica Granger. You might have heard—"

"Yes, terrible. I'm shocked."

"You remember her then?"

"Of course."

Halley pulled out her tape recorder from her purse and turned it on. "If you don't mind, Mr. Jensen, I'm going to tape this. It's standard procedure."

He picked up a pen from the desk and started playing with it nervously. "Sure. Whatever."

"What was your relationship with Jessica Granger?"

He looked uncomfortable. "I was her guidance counselor."

"Did she confide in you?" Halley asked.

"About what?"

"About her boyfriend problems, school problems, problems at home." She saw that she'd hit on something. "She told you about her trouble with her father?"

"She mentioned that he was too rough on her."

"*Rough* on her?"

"You know, too strict."

"You knew it was more than that."

He hesitated a moment then nodded slowly. "One day after class I noticed a bruise on her arm and asked her about it. She told me her father beat her and begged me not to say anything to anyone because it would only make things worse for her and her mother." He looked rueful. "I should have reported it, but I really worried that she was right. Even if Social Services got her out of there, her mother would still be in the house. Jessica said her mother would never leave her father. You don't think…"

"We're looking at all suspects," Halley assured him.

"I met Sid Granger only once. The man had a scary temper," Mark said.

"Jessica confided in you about running away, didn't she?" Halley asked.

Mark looked hesitant. "Yes, she told me."

"You and Jessica must have been close for her to confide in you."

"No more than any other student," Mark said quickly. He was flustered now.

"Mr. Jensen, I have to ask you if you slept with Jessica."

The counselor leaned back in his chair, dropping the pen to the floor. For a moment, she could see that he had thought about reaching down to pick it up, but changed his mind. "I'm not sure what you've been told…" he said, his eyes darting back and forth. "But I can assure you—"

"Did you believe you were the father of her baby?"

The counselor shot to his feet. "I'm going to have to ask you to leave."

"Jessica said the older, married man she was sleeping with kept photos of the two of them," Halley said. "I need to take a look in your desk drawers, Mr. Jensen."

"Just a minute. I know my rights."

She pulled out her phone.

"Who are you calling?" the counselor asked, sounding even more upset.

"A judge, to issue me a warrant to search your office. In the meantime, I'm afraid I'm going to have to read you your rights and take you into custody. Anything you say…"

Mark Jensen looked defeated as he slowly dropped back into his desk chair. There were tears in his eyes as he said, "I knew that girl would destroy me. You have no idea what she was like."

"I know she was underage, a good ten years younger than you were," Halley said.

He let out a bark of a laugh. "She seduced *me*. I was a babe in the woods compared to her."

"So you thought it was your baby," Halley said. "Jessica made demands on you?"

"She wanted me to run away with her. Just quit my job, leave my family, take off. And you know the worst part? I was tempted."

"Is that why you killed her, Mr. Jensen?"

"I want a lawyer," he said. "I'm not saying another word until I see a lawyer."

"You might be interested to know that Jessica Granger wasn't pregnant," Halley said.

He swore. "That lying bitch. I gave her $500 to get an abortion."

"When was that?"

He shook his head.

"Was it the night she disappeared?" Halley asked.

"A week before," Mark said.

Halley wondered if some of that cash was the $200 found in her purse. "But you saw her the night she was running away, didn't you, Mr. Jensen?"

"I told you. I need to talk to a lawyer. *Now*."

Later, after a deputy delivered the warrant, Halley got the janitor to break into the locked bottom drawer of Mark Jensen's desk.

She already knew what she was going to find. Still, some of the photographs came as a shock.

COLTON KNEW HE SHOULD be relieved after Halley's call. It appeared that Jessica's murderer had been caught. Mark Jensen hadn't broken down and confessed, but he might if his alibi didn't check out—and Halley managed to find the $10,000 that had disappeared that night.

The whole thing still felt like a nightmare. Colton couldn't believe the things he'd learned about Jessica or the fact that she was dead. Murdered.

Mark Jensen was guilty as hell—if not of murder then of having sex with a student. What had made him keep the photographs after all this time? No doubt because Jessica had that kind of hold over the man. Jensen hadn't forgotten her, couldn't.

Sid Granger was guilty as well. Even if he didn't kill his daughter, he had physically abused her. He was the reason she was running away. It bothered Colton that Sid might get off scot-free when he was at least partially to blame for Jessica's death.

Colton knew that Jessica had brought a lot of this on herself. But what had made her the way she was? Had it been some wild streak in her that even Sid Granger couldn't beat out of her? Or had it been his overprotectiveness that had pushed her to rebel in such a way? Colton would never know.

Colton was waiting for Halley when she came out of the Sheriff's Department that afternoon. He admired the way she'd handled herself. She made a damn good deputy. She was tough and yet all woman. He wished things had been different years ago.

"Could we have dinner or something later?" he asked impulsively.

Halley quirked a brow at him.

"Yeah, Halley, I'm asking you out on a date. You do date, don't you?"

"Yes." She sounded defensive.

He grinned. "When was your last date?"

"When was *yours?*" she shot back. Then she added, "Okay, you got me there. But I still don't think that's such a good idea. This is an ongoing investigation and—"

"Seven? I'll pick you up. Wear something sexy." He climbed back into the pickup before she could argue. He'd just driven away when his cell phone rang. It was Emma.

"I wanted to make sure you were at supper tonight," she said.

"I have a date," he said.

"A *date?*"

"Don't sound so surprised."

"Mind if I ask who this date is with?"

"Halley." He heard the pleasure in the small sound she made. "Wasn't that what you were hoping?"

"I don't know what you're talking about. We'll miss you at supper." She hung up, amusement in her voice.

He snapped his phone shut, realizing that he hadn't asked why she wanted to make sure everyone was at supper. Another surprise guest?

Feeling lost, he drove toward his place outside of Whitehorse. It was a small house, a two-story, much like the one Halley was renting. Like her, he hadn't done much to make the house a home. Living there had always felt temporary, as if he was just waiting for his life to start. Is that how Halley felt as well?

He couldn't help but think about this morning. He'd come so close to kissing her. Last night he had lain awake for hours on the couch, unable to sleep knowing she was just one floor above him. He'd wanted to go to her, but he hadn't. He didn't want to ruin things with her this time, so he was forcing himself to take things slow. He smiled as he thought about their date tonight.

Somehow, he had to make it perfect.

HALLEY WAS FEELING GOOD except that she was running late for her date. She had Mark Jensen behind bars. She still hadn't been able to verify his alibi, but he'd been charged with numerous felonies and wasn't going anywhere.

Mostly she was excited about her date tonight with Colton. She was practically giddy and chastised herself for being so silly. It was just a date. With Colton Chisholm!

She grinned as she climbed out of her patrol SUV and carried the small bags of groceries she'd picked up at the store. She'd been embarrassed that she'd had so little in her refrigerator last night.

As she started toward the house, she noticed the dark clouds that had moved in. It surprised her—and gave her a strange chill of apprehension. Halley didn't believe in omens, but if she had, this ominous sky certainly would have worried her.

The air felt heavy. Black clouds covered the sun, dropping like a blanket over the landscape. Pockets of deep shadows hunkered around the house as the wind whipped the trees, sending leaves flying through the air.

"So you really are renting this dump."

Halley dropped the two bags of groceries at her feet as Sid Granger stepped from the shadows of the sagging porch. Too late she saw his vehicle parked in the cloudy darkness beside the old barn out back. She realized it was no accident that he'd parked back there. He'd wanted to surprise her. He'd been lying in wait for her.

Chapter Eleven

"Little jumpy, aren't you?" Sid Granger asked, amusement and something more sinister in his voice, as he stepped from the shadows beside Halley's house.

Her hand dropped to the weapon still strapped to her hip. Her heart rate leaped, first out of surprise, then as she got a good look at him. He barely resembled the man she'd seen at his house earlier. His hair was disheveled, his clothes dirty. She could smell the alcohol on him as he staggered into the pale yellow of the ranch yard light that automatically came on as the storm moved in. He had a can of beer in his hand, and it clearly hadn't been his first.

But it was the look in his eyes that made her unsnap the loop on her holster and settle her hand over the grip.

"Mr. Granger, what are you doing here?"

"There a law against it?" He drained the last swallow of beer, tilting the can up and almost falling over backward. Then he crushed the can in his large, pawlike hands and leveled his gaze at her. "Colton Chisholm needs to pay for what he did to my little girl. I want to know what you're going to do about it."

Halley wasn't about to come to Colton's defense. Not

here. Not with a man as drunk and angry as Sid Granger. He was looking for a fight, but he wasn't going to find it with her.

She eased her hand off the weapon at her side, bent down and, never letting him out of her sight, picked up the groceries she'd dropped. "It's late and I haven't had my dinner. I'm mean when I haven't eaten." She started to step past him.

He grabbed her arm, squeezing her flesh painfully as he jerked her toward him. She smelled sweat and beer and an uncontrolled anger that she suspected was always just below the surface.

"I asked you a question," he bellowed, tightening his hold. "I saw how it was between you and *Colton.* You think I don't know about women like you? I had a daughter just like you. An alley cat who'd sleep with any big tom that came around. I learned the hard way how to handle a woman like you."

"And how is that?" Halley asked. His fingers dug into her flesh, making her wince. So he had known about Jessica's promiscuity and he'd just said he'd known how to handle a woman like that.

Sid Granger's gaze narrowed to tiny slits, reminding her of the rattlesnake she'd found in her bed.

When he didn't answer her, she said, "Bully them? Beat them? Put rattlesnakes in their beds? Is that how you handled it, Mr. Granger?"

He released her so quickly, it caught her by surprise. She stumbled back.

One of the grocery bags slipped from her grasp and fell to the ground again.

"What the hell did you just say?" he demanded.

She could see the confusion and what could have

been shock on his face, yet she didn't believe it. "I saw the rattlesnake on your wall. I know you put one in my bed. Don't bother to deny it. Just as I know you beat your daughter, and your wife stood by and let you."

His shock was replaced by a sadness so deep that his features seemed to dissolve in the storm light. "My baby girl. My poor baby girl. It's something in their blood. It makes them the way they are. Not their fault." The first drops of rain came out of the dark clouds like bullets. They smacked the old farmhouse's roof, ricocheted off the patrol car and pelted the two of them and the bags of groceries, one on the ground, the other dangling from Halley's fingers.

Over the racket she heard the sound of a vehicle coming and swore. Her date was early and she was running even later, thanks to Sid Granger.

He seemed to stir, as if seeing her for the first time. Suddenly he clamped a hand over his mouth as if he was going to be sick and spun away, half loping, half stumbling to his vehicle parked by the barn.

She watched him go as the clouds seemed to burst open and huge raindrops pelted down on her. She stood wondering if she had the wrong man behind bars for Jessica's murder as she heard a pickup turn into her drive. Colton was early—and she was worse than just not ready for what she feared might be the most important date of her life.

AGGIE WELLS HAD BEEN to the Chisholm ranch house before—just as Emma had suspected. But as she parked in front of the big, rambling house, she was still impressed. It was two stories, sprawling across what appeared to be a half acre of lawn. A wide porch ran across the front. The chairs and rockers all looked well-worn with a history that she envied.

"You are too emotionally involved in these cases," her boss had told her when he'd tried to take her off the Chisholm case.

"He killed those women," she'd argued, making him shake his head. "I'm getting the insurance company's money back."

"No, Aggie, you're not. You've gone beyond investigating this man. It's become an obsession. You're out of control, breaking laws, doing God only knows what to prove you're right."

She didn't deny that she broke the insurance companies rules and even a few laws. But visiting the Chisholm house when everyone was gone wasn't exactly breaking and entering. They left their door unlocked. Anyone could have walked in—and did.

She'd looked through the whole place, getting a feel for what it would be like to live there with a man like Hoyt Chisholm—and trying to learn everything she could about his new wife, Emma.

Aggie had known Hoyt would marry again. It was his pattern. His first wife had been close to his age, but the second two had been younger. Aggie had expected number four to be young as well and had been surprised to find Emma closer to Hoyt's own age—hers as well.

A change in his pattern? And just when she thought she had him figured out. So what was it about Emma? Aggie was looking forward to seeing the two of them together so she could judge for herself why Hoyt Chisholm had dared marry again—and to a woman nothing like the others.

She studied the house, worried that she was missing something important about this change in pattern, then, giving up, she opened her car door and stepped out into the fading light.

Storm clouds crowded the horizon. Wind howled at the eaves of the house and sent dust devils spinning across the yard.

Aggie frowned as she thought about the woman she'd met at the bar. Emma was stronger, more determined and definitely feistier than the others. Aggie had liked her and, from what she'd gathered during her in-house investigation, Hoyt was wild about her. At least for the moment.

She'd especially taken her time in the master bedroom and had searched it thoroughly, intrigued by the woman even before she'd met Emma.

With a chill, she remembered that the bed hadn't been made yet, the covers thrown back, the sheets in a tangle. She had stood there imagining the two of them in that bed. It had made her sick to think of how it would all end.

As it began to rain, she hurried toward the house, thinking again of the argument she'd had with her boss.

"Aggie, I don't understand what's happened to you. You used to be one of my best investigators. Then you took the first Chisholm case and something happened to you. It's almost as if—like his wives—you've fallen under his spell. Almost as if you've fallen in love with Hoyt Chisholm."

She grimaced now at how ridiculous her boss's accusations had been. This was about simple justice.

No, she amended as Emma Chisholm stepped out

onto the porch to greet her. There was nothing simple about this. Emma Chisholm was going to die and she didn't even realize it yet.

THROUGH THE POURING RAIN, Colton saw Halley in front of her house picking up a bag of groceries from the ground, a strange expression on her face. In a flash of lightning, he saw a vehicle come careening around the side of the house, Sid Granger's stark face illuminated behind the wheel.

He jumped out of the truck, having put on his slicker before leaving his house when he saw the thunderstorm to the south, and ran toward Halley. "Did that bastard do something to you?"

She shook her head, her hair wet and clinging to her face. She looked like she might cry.

"If he hurt you—"

"I'm sorry. I'm not ready for our date. I was running late. I…"

He stared at her through the rain as thunder and lightning filled the sky around them. "That's why you're upset?"

She nodded and he laughed as he took the groceries from her and said, "Then I guess we'd better get you inside."

He was going to say "and get out of those wet clothes," but the words caught in his throat as she looked up at him with those big brown eyes. Desire shot through him. He was no longer aware of the drowning rain or the lightning or the thunder that boomed so close it made the hair on the back of his neck stand up.

"We really should go inside," he said, his voice sounding strange, even to him.

He carried her groceries into the house, Halley trailing him into the kitchen, both of them leaving puddles on the floor. He heard her on her cell phone and realized she was calling the Sheriff's Department to have Sid Granger picked up.

He put the groceries on the counter and turned as she hung up. "You said he didn't hurt you." He stepped to her, gently touching her upper arm where bruises were already beginning to darken the skin.

"He grabbed me, but I'm all right. I had to put in a call to have him picked up. He's drunk and in no condition to be driving. I don't want him killing someone on his way home."

"Or taking it out on his wife?"

She nodded.

Colton stood inches from her, afraid of what Sid had done. "Something happened that has you upset. Something more than not being ready for our date."

Halley shook her head. "I'm not sure what happened. Sid had been waiting for me. He didn't exactly threaten me… But he did scare me and that made me angry. I mentioned the snake he put in my bed and he kind of freaked."

"He must have been surprised that you knew it was him."

"Maybe." She shivered.

"You really need to get out of those wet clothes." He turned away as he said it this time. "I'll put your groceries away while you change for our date." He hesitated, considering the items he saw in the grocery bags. Two steaks, a small bag of potatoes, sour cream, butter, asparagus and a bottle of wine.

Had she been thinking they would stay here for

dinner? The idea sent a wave of desire through him. "Unless you want to…" When he turned back around, there was a small puddle on the kitchen floor where she'd been standing, but no Halley.

A moment later he heard the sound of the shower running upstairs.

As EMMA WATCHED AGGIE during dinner, she thought maybe the woman was beginning to see that Hoyt wasn't the dangerous man she thought he was.

"This beef is delicious," Aggie had said, looking from Emma to Hoyt. "Did you raise it?"

He'd actually smiled as he answered that he had. At first he had been tense, but he'd relaxed as the dinner had progressed. Even her stepsons were on their best behavior and she could tell that Aggie was enjoying herself.

Emma was beginning to think she might have a knack for bringing people together. After all, Colton had a date with Halley tonight.

She smiled to herself as she listened to Aggie visiting with Hoyt. He'd been so sure that this had been a terrible idea. Emma had a theory that often when enemies were forced to sit down together over a meal, they came to see the other person differently. It humanized their enemy and made it harder to hate them.

"Emma, you are an amazing cook," Aggie said, turning to smile over at her.

"Thank you, but I had help."

"Don't let her kid you," Hoyt spoke up, then lowered his voice to add, "she's the one who turns out the great food from that kitchen. She is a woman of many talents."

Emma basked in his praise—and the sensual look he gave her. When she glanced at Aggie again, she caught her frowning. The woman quickly changed her expression but was quieter through dessert.

When supper was over, Emma walked her to the porch.

A warm summer rain fell in a dark sheet at the edge of the porch steps. Emma loved the sound, but felt a chill as Aggie came to stand beside her.

"Thank you for a wonderful meal and a very interesting evening," Aggie said, glancing back at the house. "You really seem to have turned this household around." She quickly added, "Hoyt said you make his boys dress for dinner—no cow manure on their boots, hands washed and even a prayer before they're allowed to eat."

"Just common courtesy where I'm from."

"And where is that, Emma?" Aggie's eyes had narrowed, and she was openly studying her.

Emma laughed. "It's enough that you're intent on investigating my husband. Do you still believe he killed all three of his former wives?" she asked pointedly.

"I have to admit, seeing him in his natural habitat does make me wonder," Aggie admitted. "But his last three wives are dead. I would think you're the one who should be worrying about that."

"I believe his third wife is still missing," she pointed out for the second time. "Unless you know something I don't."

Aggie prepared to run through the rain to her car. "You really are something. If one of his wives can survive being married to him, it just might be you,

Emma. But I wouldn't count on it. At least you've been warned."

"I appreciate your concern, but I'm not going to let it keep me up at night," she said.

"Oh, did I mention there was a witness on the lake the day his first wife died?" Aggie asked.

Emma felt her heart drop.

"The fisherman was too far away to hear what was being said, but he saw them both standing up in the boat as if they were arguing right before the boat capsized and no one ever saw Laura Chisholm again. It's just something to think about as you're about to fall asleep."

With that the investigator ran to her car.

HALLEY TOOK A QUICK SHOWER to warm up. She was still shaken by Sid Granger's strange visit—and the reminder of who was waiting for her downstairs. As she stepped out, she heard thunder, then a crack of lightning so close she flinched. She quickly toweled dry, not wanting to keep Colton waiting.

She'd thought about offering to make them dinner here at the house and had bought everything she needed. Going out with him under the circumstances didn't seem like a wise thing to do—especially after Sid Granger's visit.

In front of her closet, she stared at the few dressy clothes she owned. Five days a week she wore a uniform. On the weekends, she wore jeans and a T-shirt. She'd never had a good reason to dress up other than for a friend's wedding. The few men she'd dated took her fishing or canoeing or to a movie or bowling.

Colton had told her to wear something sexy. Sure.

Halley dug through her closet and found one little red print sundress. It was simple and not what she would call sexy. But it would have to do.

She slipped it over her head. The lightweight silken fabric dropped over her, settling on her curves. In her vanity mirror, she saw that her cheeks were fired with heat from her shower.

"You all right up there?" Colton called from the foot of the stairs.

"I'll be right down!" She dabbed a little lip gloss on, noting that her eyes looked overly bright. Fighting to still her excitement as well as her anxiety, she straightened and ran a brush through her thick mane of burnished hair. It fell around her shoulders in a dark wave, contrasting with the red of the dress and her slightly tanned arms and legs.

Feeling like Cinderella going to the ball, she slipped into her only pair of dress sandals and went downstairs.

Colton was waiting for her in the living room. He'd been standing at the window, looking out at the downpour, but he turned the moment he heard her approach.

Even in the dim light from the storm, she saw his eyes light up at the sight of her. "Great dress," he said and let out a low whistle.

She had to bite her tongue not to say, "Oh, this old thing?" Instead she stood feeling self-conscious and shy.

"We're going to have to make a run for my pickup," he said as he stepped toward her. "I'm sorry I picked a lousy night for our date."

"It's not your fault a thunderstorm blew in." She

met his gaze and felt a jolt. If he kept looking at her like that—

"We should go. I don't want to be late for our dinner reservation," he said, but didn't move.

Her heart began to pound harder, and she knew even before he lowered his mouth toward hers that he was going to kiss her.

Her pulse kicked up a beat as his lips touched hers. The kiss beside the road the other day had been quick and impulsive. This kiss was a keeper, slow and sensual.

It stole her breath. She leaned into him as he deepened the kiss. It felt so wonderful being in his arms. The thunderstorm boomed around them, but Halley felt as if she was in a warm cocoon. Desire spiked through her as hot and bright as the lightning outside the window. Her pulse pounded like the rain on the roof, her heart booming as loudly as the thunder.

COLTON DREW BACK FROM the kiss feeling as if one of those bolts of lightning had just struck him. He shook his head. He'd never wanted a woman the way he wanted Halley Robinson at this moment, but he'd be damned. He was taking her on a *date*. He wasn't carrying her upstairs right now and making love to her...

"We need to go," he said, his voice sounding strained.

Halley nodded, looking uncomfortable. Was she as disappointed as he was? He'd seen desire in her dark eyes. The same desire he'd seen the first time he'd kissed her.

"I'll get my jacket," she said, sounding as breathless as he felt.

They were soaked to the skin by the time they reached his pickup. Both of them had seemed at a loss for words as he started the truck and headed up the road toward the county highway. He'd wanted this date to be perfect, dammit, and nothing was going as he'd planned it.

Rain fell hard and fast. Every low spot on the road had filled with water. The dirt underneath was now slick mud. He felt the tires spin out and shifted into four-wheel drive. Not that it helped much, since in this part of the country the mud was known as gumbo, making a lot of roads impassible—this might be one of them.

He had gone less than a quarter mile up the road when, after busting through a deep puddle, the back of the pickup fishtailed around. He tried to regain control but on the slick mud, there was no way. The truck slid into the ditch and, even though he tried, he knew it was stuck until the road dried out. He doubted that even a tow truck could get him out tonight.

Colton swore. Nothing about this date was going right. When he looked over at Halley, he saw tears in her eyes. "I'm sorry. I wanted this date to be perfect and…" He unsnapped his seat belt and slid over to take her in his arms. "I wanted to do everything right, take it slow, not mess up with you again."

She smiled through her tears. "I think it's perfect," she said as her gaze locked with his.

He laughed softly as he brushed a lock of wet hair off her cheek. "Then I wouldn't change a thing."

Chapter Twelve

The day dawned warm and dry and beautiful, the storm forgotten except for the fresh smell the rain had left over the land.

Halley woke to see Colton propped up on one elbow lying beside her in her bed, smiling down at her. They were both still clothed and under the comforter he'd thrown over them late last night.

"I want to take you out to dinner tonight," he said. "A real date."

She chuckled at that as he bent to kiss her. They had stayed in the warm cab of the pickup, kissing and talking until the rain had let up a little. Then they'd made a run for the house. By the time they'd reached the front porch, they were both soaked and muddy from slipping and sliding that had ultimately resulted in a spill that took them both down in the warm mud.

Halley smiled to herself, remembering her first date with Colton Chisholm. It hadn't been that much different from the old days, except that there hadn't been fighting when they ended up wrestling in the mud.

After a hot shower and a change of clothing, he'd cooked the food she'd brought home. They hadn't made love.

"Sorry," he'd said as he'd covered his eyes and handed her a towel after their shower. "I don't make love on the first date."

Colton had proved that it wasn't just breakfast he excelled in cooking. They'd eaten their steaks, baked potatoes and buttered asparagus at her kitchen table as the storm raged around them. They'd laughed and visited as if they'd known each other their whole lives. In a way, they had.

Then they'd gone back upstairs and laid down on the bed, talking and kissing until they'd fallen asleep, holding each other.

Halley glanced at the clock. "I have to get to work. If I can get out to the county road."

"You should be able to make it if you go off road through the grass. I'll get one of my brothers to come over with a tractor and pull out my pickup. I think it has dried enough for us to get it out. So do I get to take you out tonight on a real date?"

"I liked our date last night," she said, leaning in to kiss him again.

"Me, too."

She started to tell him that she still didn't think their being seen together was a good idea right now, but he stopped her.

"Are you worried that you don't have the killer behind bars?"

"No." Right now both Mark Jensen and Sid Granger were behind bars. Last night she'd gotten a call from one of the other deputies that they'd picked up Sid and charged him with driving under the influence. He would have to go before a judge before he could get out of jail.

"I have to get going." She slipped out of bed and headed for the shower. A moment later she heard him outside the bathroom door.

"I'll call you later," he said. "Halley? I had a really good time last night."

She smiled. "I did, too."

COLTON HEARD ABOUT LAST night's supper at the ranch from his stepbrothers.

"I kid you not, the woman is a private investigator for an insurance company and from what I gathered, she's *investigating* Dad," Marshall said.

"For what?" Colton asked, although he suspected that he knew. He and his brothers had been too young to hear any talk when Laura Chisholm had drowned. When Tasha died, there was talk. It wasn't until Krystal disappeared that Colton had heard the rumors about his father.

He'd ignored them and so had his brothers. There were always rumors circulating around Whitehorse— especially if your name was Chisholm.

"So Dad's had bad luck with wives," he said and looked to his brothers for agreement. They had gathered out by the corrals—out of earshot of the house and Emma and their father.

"Three dead wives is more than bad luck," Marshall said.

"We don't know that Krystal is dead," Zane spoke up.

"Dad had her legally declared dead," Tanner reminded them.

"That doesn't mean—"

Colton cut off Logan. "Dad had nothing to do with their deaths."

"We know that," Dawson agreed. "But that isn't what that investigator believes. I was watching her at dinner. She hardly took her eyes off Dad. She's trouble. I remember the last time she came around. I thought I saw her coming out of the house. I told Dad, but he said I had to be mistaken. I wasn't."

The brothers stood looking at each other.

"I'll see what I can find out about her," Colton said.

HALLEY HAD FORGOTTEN THAT she'd left a message for Hazel Rimes to call her. When her cell phone rang later that afternoon, it took her a moment to remember who Hazel Rimes even was.

"I'm sorry," the elderly woman apologized for not getting back to the deputy sooner. "I was over in Great Falls, visiting my daughter and that bunch of wild animals she calls her kids." Hazel laughed. "I love them all, but it sure is nice to be home. But that probably isn't why you called me, to hear about my grandkids."

"No." Not that it probably mattered anymore. "I was just curious about the letter you found at the post office, the one that had fallen between the wall and counter."

"The letter to Colton Chisholm? *I* didn't find it," Hazel said. "I was just the one who handed it to Nell. No, let me think. Oh, yes, I remember, it was Millie Granger. She's the one who spotted it. I'd have never seen it. Only a little corner of the envelope was sticking out. It's a wonder anyone noticed at all. I guess Millie did because she was standing right there by the counter."

Halley felt her heart beat a little faster. "But she asked you to get it and give it to Nell?"

"That's right. Nell had gone back to get a package for me."

"Was anyone else there in the lobby with you and Millie?"

"Not that I remember. Oh, I can't swear there wasn't. My memory isn't all that great. You could ask Millie. She's sharper than me," she added with a laugh. "I'd have never seen that letter and it would still be there another fourteen years."

"I'm just confused about why Millie would ask you to retrieve the letter if she was right there."

"She said, 'You get it. I just had my nails done.' I didn't mind. Was there a problem with the letter?"

"No, I was just curious. So you both looked at it before giving it to Nell?"

"We were just shocked when we saw the postmark, let alone who it was from," Hazel was saying. "Millie had to remind me that her daughter had dated Colton Chisholm. Frankly, I barely remembered Jessica. She always seemed like such a shy, retiring girl. Kinda skittish, you know?"

Something like that. "Well, thank you for calling me back, and welcome home."

"It's good to be here. That's a long drive from Great Falls. I did stop in Havre for a bite to eat…"

Halley was no longer listening. Her heart drummed in her chest. Millie Granger was the one who found the letter from her daughter? Given the way she and Sid felt about Colton, there is no way she would have let that letter be delivered, was there?

Unless the postmistress had come back in and Millie had felt she had no choice.

Hazel finally quit talking and Halley was able to hang up. That lost letter had bothered her from the start. She had to pull over to the side of the road, her hands were shaking so hard and her head was spinning.

When her cell phone rang again, she thought it was Hazel calling her back for some reason or other. It was Colton.

"I need to ask a favor," he said.

"Sure."

"Would you see what you can find out about a woman named Agatha Wells. She's an investigator for Royalty Life Insurance Company."

Halley wanted to ask why he needed the information, but he didn't give her a chance.

"What time should I pick you up for our date?"

She glanced at her watch. "Why don't you make it eight? I have something I need to do before I head home."

"Is everything all right?"

"It will be once I check on something," she told him.

COLTON COULDN'T SIT STILL. He was anxious to hear what Halley had found out about the insurance investigator and excited about their date tonight. He had time to kill before he picked her up.

He felt badly that he hadn't worked at the ranch in days. His brothers were moving cattle this afternoon to summer range. He was thinking about saddling up and trying to catch up with his brothers and the cattle when he decided to give the insurance company a call on his own.

He had hoped that Halley would call him right back, but when he'd spoken with her, he could tell that she was distracted. He wondered if it had something to do with Jessica's murder. Had the school counselor's alibi checked out? Or had Sid Granger done something more to make her suspicious?

Finally, unable to wait any longer, he put in a call to Royalty Life Insurance and got an answering machine. He glanced at his watch and realized that the main office was on the East Coast and had already closed for the day. He'd waited too long.

He was about to hang up when the automated answering machine gave him the option of listening to the company's list of agents. He waited as the voice droned on and on, finally getting to the end of the alphabet and the name Agatha Wells.

Except he didn't hear the name. He thought he must have missed it and asked to hear the list again. No Agatha Wells. No Wells at all.

He'd just hung up when his cell phone rang. He saw that it was Halley and answered quickly.

"I got some information on Agatha Wells," Halley told him without preamble. "She is no longer employed by Royalty Life Insurance Company. Based on how little information the company president was willing to give me, I'd guess she was fired."

"Fired? When?"

"Apparently some time ago. As far as I could find out, she isn't employed by anyone right now."

Colton swore under his breath. Then what the hell

was she doing investigating his father? Or was that what she'd been doing last night at dinner at the ranch?

"Want to tell me what this is about?" Halley asked.

"I will later at dinner. I need to go. See you at eight." He disconnected and swung by the ranch to talk to Emma, wondering if her inviting the woman to dinner was a case of keeping her friends close and her enemies even closer.

HALLEY PARKED IN FRONT of the Granger house, noting that Millie's car wasn't parked in the yard. The garage door was open—and empty. It appeared that Millie wasn't home.

Halley climbed out of the patrol SUV, unsure exactly what she was doing here. Since finding out that it was Millie Granger who'd discovered the allegedly "lost letter," Halley hadn't been able to get it off her mind.

The evening was cool, a skim of clouds hiding the last of the sun's rays to the west. She could smell the cottonwoods and see the cotton floating through the air like snowflakes.

Halley had hoped to find Millie at home. Sid was still in jail. It was the perfect opportunity to talk to the woman alone—and Halley had a lot of questions, beginning with the letter Jessica had written Colton.

It seemed odd that Millie wasn't around. Maybe she was trying to get Sid out of jail. Or maybe she was taking advantage of this freedom and doing something fun. The latter seemed improbable.

As she walked toward the open garage, she tried to imagine Millie doing something just for fun, let alone kicking up her heels.

Like the house, the garage was immaculate. Everything seemed to have a place along the sides and back of the garage. Someone had actually written on the wall where each item went. Rake. Clippers. Snow shovel.

Halley made the circle, coming to a stop at the only spaces along the wall that were empty. Suitcase #1. Suitcase #2. Two empty spots, one larger than the other, were dark, the area around them faded from the sun, which had bleached the color out of the wall. Apparently, the suitcases had been stored here a very long time without being used.

That niggling feeling pulled at her again as she walked around to the front of the house, mounted the stairs and knocked, even though she wasn't expecting anyone to answer. On impulse, Halley tried the knob. Locked.

Backtracking, she entered the garage again, then tried the door leading into the house. It opened. She hesitated. Without a warrant, she was breaking the law. Anything she found couldn't be used in a court of law.

But the two missing suitcases seemed like a sure sign that Millie Granger was about to take a trip. Her husband in jail, it seemed an odd time for a woman like Millie to be packing. Unless the two of them were planning to take off together.

Halley opened the door and slipped inside. The house felt cool and dark as she quickly moved through the laundry area to the living room. Her gaze went to the rattlesnake skin on the wall. She shivered and felt a premonition so strong, she almost turned around and left.

At the top of the stairs, the landing opened onto three doors. The first one she came to was closed. She tried the door, glanced in and was startled to see a figure silhouetted against the window.

Her pulse took off, heart pounding after it, before she was able to corral herself—and make sense of what she was seeing. A faceless dress form adjusted to Millie's size stood at the window draped in a half-finished housedress. It appeared that Millie made her own clothing. Like the garage, the room was inhumanly neat, everything in its place.

Halley closed the door and stepped down the hall past a bathroom to the last doorway into the master bedroom.

Like the décor downstairs, the room had a masculine feel to it. The quilt on the bed had been made from blocks of material featuring Montana animals: elk, moose, bear, deer and antelope.

On the bed were two large suitcases that she could see at a glance matched the outlines on the wall of the garage where they had been stored. Now both suitcases were open and filled haphazardly with clothing.

Halley glanced toward the open closet. Her heart began to beat harder again. The closet looked as if someone had been tearing the clothing from the hangers. What hangers hadn't fallen to the floor hung at odd angles. Only one side of the closet was in disarray. Sid's side was in perfect order, all his clothing still hanging there.

The way the clothing had been dumped in the suitcases, it looked as if Millie was running for her life.

EMMA WAS SHOCKED to hear that Aggie Wells hadn't worked for the insurance company in years and might have been fired.

"I don't understand," she told Colton when he'd broken the news.

"Neither do I. Do you have any idea where she's staying in town?"

Emma shook her head, still in shock. She thought about the self-assured woman. "I met her for a drink out at Sleeping Buffalo, but I got the impression she was staying somewhere else. Somewhere closer to the ranch." She saw Colton's expression. "In retrospect I'll admit it might not have been a good idea to meet with her. Just like inviting her to supper might have been foolhardy under the circumstances."

"You think?"

She ignored his sarcasm. Any other time she would have made him apologize. But he was right. Sometimes she acted impetuously and it blew up in her face. This was not one of those times, she hoped.

"She told me she worked for the insurance company." Emma tried to remember the exact conversation. "Or maybe she just led me to believe that, I'm not sure. I got the name of the insurance company from Hoyt, now that I think of it."

"She's trying to prove that my father killed his other wives, isn't she?" Colton said.

Emma hedged, but saw that he already had heard— probably from one of his brothers, which meant Hoyt must have told them at some point.

"I assured her your father wasn't that kind of man."

Colton laughed. "I'm sure your assurance carried a lot of weight."

"The woman is obviously misguided."

"Did she say anything else that might give you a clue as to where I could find her?"

Emma groaned, suddenly feeling more nervous than she had when Aggie Wells had told her what she was up to. "If she no longer works for the insurance company, then why would she still be after your father?"

"It's possible she could be freelancing, taking old cases in hopes of getting a percentage of any insurance company's money she retrieved for them. Kind of like a bounty hunter or a private investigator."

"Wait a minute. I just remembered something. There was a matchbook on the table. It had a name on it. I think it said Whitehorse West. Is that a motel?"

He nodded. "It's along Highway 2 and the Hi-Line on the edge of town."

"Wait a minute," she said as he started toward the door. "What are you going to do?"

"Find out what she's up to," he said over his shoulder.

"Colton," she called after him. "Be careful."

HALLEY WAS ON HER WAY downstairs, the cold and silence inside the Granger house beginning to get to her when her cell phone rang, making her jump.

She headed out of the house the same way she'd come in as she answered it.

"I thought you'd want to know." It was the deputy who had picked up Sid the night before for driving while intoxicated. "Sid Granger just made bail."

"Who bailed him out?"

"His attorney."

Not his wife. So where was Millie? She must have had to run an errand, get some money, clean out a safe deposit box, buy gas for the car. It seemed odd that she had stopped in the middle of her packing, though. Had

Sid called from the jail? Had he expected Millie to post bail? When she didn't, had she been forced to call his lawyer?

Halley didn't like that scenario. That meant Sid would be headed home, already angry with his wife. What would he do when he saw the suitcases? Or had Millie decided to just take off, forget her clothes and put some distance between her and Sid and Whitehorse?

"He still seems to be pretty worked up, but we can't hold him any longer. Just wanted to warn you to watch your back in case he comes looking for you again."

Halley snapped the phone shut, realizing that she needed to move fast. It could get ugly if Sid caught her coming out of his house. As she came out of the garage, she saw the path that led around the side of the house.

She hesitated, glancing at her patrol SUV parked in front of the house. Sid would be here soon—unless he decided to stop off at the bar for a drink or two. Millie might be back at any moment as well.

But there was something Halley wanted to check out. She took the path to the backyard, pretty sure there was another path back there that led to where Jessica Granger had died.

COLTON KNEW HE HAD just enough time to drive into town and see if Aggie Wells was still staying at the Whitehorse West Motel before he had to get ready for his date.

He feared that if he put this off, the woman would skip town. More than likely she had someone she still knew at the insurance company who would tip her off that a Whitehorse deputy had been asking questions about her.

Everything was already planned for his date. He'd made reservations again at Northern Lights, an upscale restaurant in downtown Whitehorse for his date with Halley. He'd asked for a private table in a corner and the best bottle of champagne they had.

"Would you also like one of our flourless chocolate cakes for dessert?" the owner, Laci Cavanaugh-Duvall, had asked him with a slight chuckle.

"Whatever you suggest."

"A special date?" she'd asked.

"I hope so."

Now as he drove toward town, he studied the horizon, glad to see nothing but blue sky. He was determined that he and Halley would have a normal date tonight.

As he reached Highway 2, he turned toward Whitehorse. He hadn't gone far when he saw the motel's neon sign ahead and shifted his thoughts to Aggie Wells.

His every instinct told him that his father had good reason to fear this woman. Even after being fired, she was still determined to prove that he'd murdered his wives? Colton couldn't wait to find out her story. The woman was either a wacko or...

He slowed and turned into the motel lot, parking in front of the building marked "Office." There was only one car and two pickups parked in front of the dozen rooms. Even though it was summer in Montana, this part of the state didn't get a lot of tourists. The single car didn't look like a rental, but he had no idea what Aggie Wells might be driving. For all he knew, she could own one of the pickups.

"I'm looking for Agatha Wells," he told the young female clerk behind the desk. "She is staying here in your motel, right?"

"She was. She checked out last night late."

Aggie had left after having supper at the ranch?

"Did she say if she would be back? Or possibly where she was going?"

The clerk shook her head.

"I really need to talk to her. Did she leave a phone number where she could be reached? Possibly when she registered for the room?"

"I'm sorry, I can't give out that information," the clerk said.

"Can you tell me what room she was in?"

The young woman looked surprised by the request. "Number three, but she's not there."

"Have you cleaned that room yet?" He knew it was a long shot. But he also knew that with so few guests and little help because of it, things moved slowly in Whitehorse.

"No," she said suspiciously.

"I want to rent the room—as is."

"I don't think…"

He put cash on the counter.

She looked from it to him, then shrugged.

Colton knew it was a long shot as he took the key and walked down to number three. Opening the door, he caught the stale scent of the woman's perfume. He stood for a moment just looking at the room.

The bed hadn't been made and there were several towels on the bathroom floor. He noticed a glass on the nightstand and, using a clean washcloth, wrapped it up to take to Halley for prints.

At this point, he couldn't even be sure that the woman Emma knew as Aggie Wells was who she said she was.

He stuffed the cloth-wrapped glass into his jacket

pocket and took a look around the bathroom, then the rest of the motel room.

Just when he thought there was nothing more to find, he saw what looked like a scrap of paper on the floor by the bed. Stepping over and kneeling down, he discovered it was a part of a photograph. There were other pieces in the trash can next to the bed.

Colton dumped them out and fitted the torn pieces together.

With a jolt, he saw that the photo had been taken on the Chisholm Cattle Company ranch. The picture was grainy as if it had been taken from some distance, possibly with a telephoto lens.

But it had definitely been shot at the ranch—and no doubt in secret, he thought with a curse. He recognized the corral and part of the barn—and the people in the picture. The photograph had been taken within the last two weeks.

How else could Aggie Wells have taken a clandestine snapshot of Hoyt Chisholm kissing his new wife next to the barn?

Chapter Thirteen

The cottonwoods were thicker back here by the creek. Halley worked her way through them. This time of year the grass was tall, obscuring any path that had once followed the creek to Chisholm ranch property—and a spot for lovers to meet in secret.

But she had no doubt that there'd been a trail fourteen years ago, a trail that Jessica Granger had taken the night she was murdered.

It took her a while to find her way through the tall green grass and new cottonwoods along the creek bank. The evening air had grown cool, especially along the water. Cotton from the trees floated around her, scenting the growing twilight with the smell of spring.

Halley stopped suddenly to listen. She'd thought she'd heard a rustling in the grass and brush behind her, but could now hear only the breeze stirring the leaves and the soft babble of the creek beside her.

She felt jumpy. The last of the day's sunlight flickered down through the leaves into the deep shade beneath the trees. Working her way north, she continued to push through the lush grass. She was forced to move away from the creek to circumvent a thick stand of cottonwoods, but she hadn't gone far when she found what had once been a path.

It wound through the trees in sight of the creek. Halley moved a little faster. Sid was out on bail. Millie might come back. Both would see her patrol SUV parked out front. The last thing Halley wanted to do was get Sid riled up.

The only sound was the swish of her jeaned legs pushing through the grass and an occasional cricket chirp or the cry of a hawk soaring overhead. She couldn't turn back now. She had to follow this path and prove to herself that Jessica could have come this way that night.

Where the creek turned, Halley felt confused about where she was for a moment. With the sun down, she couldn't tell if she was still going in the right direction. She found a shallow spot to wade across, soaking her boots. Is this where Jessica had crossed? What if the water had been deeper?

Halley moved faster, feeling time slipping through her fingers. It was dark in the trees now and she feared she was lost. When she came to a barbed-wire fence that marked Chisholm property, she realized that this might all have been a waste of time.

Surely Jessica didn't have to crawl through the barbed wire every time she met Colton out here. Maybe she had gotten a ride and taken the road in. Maybe Halley was dead wrong.

Now, forced to bushwhack her way through the thick grass and dense stand of small new trees growing up on this side of the creek, Halley knew that if she was right, there had to be another way in here.

She was ready to give up when she burst out of a stand of thick brush into a small opening she recognized and was grateful that at least she wasn't as lost as she'd thought.

The twilight cast an eerie, pale light over the spot where Jessica's remains had been found. Halley's heart began to pound. She'd been right. Fourteen years ago there had been a trail of sorts making this spot well within walking distance from Jessica's house.

That night Jessica had pretended to go to her room, but she must have snuck out and headed for this spot to meet, first, Hoyt Chisholm, and then wait for Colton? Or had there been someone else she'd been waiting for besides Colton? Someone she was meeting first?

COLTON DIDN'T HAVE MUCH TIME, but he had to make sure that Aggie Wells was long gone. It took another $50, but he managed to talk the motel clerk into giving him a copy of the registration form the woman had filled out.

"Do you remember what kind of car she was driving?" he asked, noting that the plates started with a three, which indicated it had come from Billings. Billings also had the closest airport to Whitehorse. He was betting the car was a rental.

"White or tan. I have no idea what kind. They all look the same to me, you know medium-sized, kind of ugly."

He did know. "Did you happen to see a rental sticker on it?"

She started to shake her head, but stopped abruptly. "I did," she said, showing the first sign of excitement. She rattled off the name on the sticker.

It took a few calls and as plausible a story as he could come up with, but he finally was told that Aggie Wells had planned to return her car today before four, but hadn't shown.

"Did she ask about a shuttle to the airport?"

"As a matter of fact, she did. I believe she said she had a six-thirty flight."

"She probably didn't mention to where."

"Actually, she did. Phoenix. I remember because I used to live there. I said, 'Bet it's changed a lot since I lived there five years ago.' And she said, 'I wouldn't know. I'm only visiting. There is no place I call home anymore.' I thought that was a little strange."

"Not if you know Aggie," Colton said and hung up.

Why Phoenix? And why didn't she make her flight? Was she still around Whitehorse?

Glancing at his watch, he headed for his house to get ready for his date. He couldn't wait to see Halley.

But as he drove down the main drag, he saw Sid Granger coming out of the liquor store and turned into an empty space next to the curb.

Sid didn't see him until Colton was almost on top of him. He looked up in surprise. Clearly, he had other things on his mind as he clutched the bottle-shaped brown paper bag in his hands and stepped to the driver's-side door of his older-model car.

The man looked awful as he squinted at Colton. "What do *you* want?" Sid snapped as he reached into his pocket for his car keys.

"I want to see you go to hell for what you did to Jessica."

"I'm already in hell." Sid fumbled with his keys, his hands visibly shaking.

"You're going to pay for what you've done—one way or the other."

The older man quit fighting to get his key into the lock and turned to look at Colton. He let out a humorless laugh. "I'm already paying in ways you can't even imagine. Everything I've ever loved has been taken away from me. *Everything*."

With that he jammed the key into the lock and opened his door, shoving Colton back as he slid behind the wheel. The engine roared and he drove off.

The last thing Colton saw was the hard lines of the man's grimacing face. He realized that Sid Granger was crying—and apparently about to get very drunk if the size of the liquor bottle was any indication.

LOSING LIGHT, HALLEY looked around for another way back to the house. She'd heard a car just moments before and feared that Sid could be home by now and had found the suitcases Millie was packing. Halley hated to think what he might do. She could only hope Millie had taken off without her clothing and hadn't come back. Either way, her patrol car was parked in front of their house. Maybe seeing the patrol car would make Sid think twice before he took his anger out on Millie.

As she looked around, she saw an opening between the trees and took it. The route turned out to be the right one. When she reached the creek, she found where someone had laid an old board across the rocks, forming a makeshift bridge.

Halley felt as if she was following in Jessica's footsteps as she crossed on the weathered gray board, then saw the remains of an old trail through the grass.

Hurrying along the trail through the tall grass, she thought she heard something coming through the grass in the distance, but when she stopped, she heard nothing. Halley hated the spooked feeling that settled inside her.

She reminded herself that the sound could have come from one of the many deer in the area. Or something even smaller. It didn't mean she wasn't alone out here. So why was her heart racing faster as she began to run, brushing at tree limbs and fighting the grass that grasped at her jean-clad legs.

At the barbed-wire fence property boundary, she stopped to catch her breath. It was getting darker here under the trees and the air had cooled considerably. Halley told herself that she was acting silly. But still she couldn't shake the bad feeling. All she wanted to do now was get back to the Granger house.

Bushes had grown up along the old rusted barbed-wire fence, but at one low spot, someone had laid a large log over the fence, forcing it down next to a boulder—and making it easy to step over.

It appeared that Jessica had used this path often. But had it been to meet Colton? Or someone else? How many others had there been? Halley felt a deep sadness at the thought—and all of it had happened not far from her own home. If Sid had caught her—

As Halley started to step over the fence, the hem of her jeans caught on a strand of barbed wire. She bent to free it and saw a small torn piece of cloth fluttering in the breeze inches away, where someone else had gotten their clothing caught in the barbs.

The cloth was faded, the pattern hardly visible anymore, but, with a jolt, Halley realized that the scrap of fabric had dark spots on it. Blood? Her pulse began to drum as she realized where she'd seen the tiny print fabric before.

With her blood pounding in her ears, she barely heard the whisper of a sound behind her. She got her hand to her weapon at her hip as she turned, but it was too late to avoid the blow. The butt of a gun caught her in the temple, dropping her to her knees. She saw the barrel pointed down at her, the metal catching the last of the light.

A fleeting thought whizzed past. She was going to be late for her date with Colton. Again. As darkness crowded her vision, she fell face-first into the tall grass at her attacker's feet.

Chapter Fourteen

Halley opened her eyes to a fierce headache and a blinding bright light. She blinked and tried to turn her head.

"Did you really think I was going to let you mess up everything?" a female voice said from the dark of the trees.

Halley lay in the grass, tree limbs forming black patterns against the twilight. She held her hand up to shield her eyes from the strong beam of light and thought she must be losing her mind. The voice had sounded like…

Millie Granger lowered the flashlight and stepped over to her. Halley would have thought the woman had come to save her except for the pistol in her right hand, the flashlight in the other. The light now made a pool next to where Halley lay on the ground.

"Millie?" She couldn't keep the surprise from her voice. As she sat up, she rubbed the bump on her head with one hand and reached for her weapon with the other. The gun was gone, her holster empty.

She looked up at Millie Granger again, everything coming back to her. The butt of a gun slamming into her skull, hearing someone behind her, finding the blood-splattered scrap of fabric caught on the barbed-wire fence near Colton and Jessica's secret spot.

She'd recognized the tiny print fabric from that first day she and Colton had stopped by the Grangers'. Millie had been wearing that old faded apron, clearly a favorite, even though it had a tear in the fabric that had left a hole. She'd been nervously toying with the hole.

"I tried to help you solve this," Millie Granger said. "I practically handed the killer over to you, but you just couldn't leave it alone, could you?"

Halley stared up at her, trying to make sense of everything. Her head ached and she felt ill. She wondered how much time she'd lost. When she glanced at her watch, she was surprised that it had only been a few minutes.

"*Sid,*" Millie said as if Halley was stupid. "He was obsessed with Jessica and determined that she wouldn't turn out like my sister. He tried to beat it out of Jessica, but when he found out she was pregnant and followed her to that awful spot where she met the men, he killed her in one of his rages. I would have come forward, but he told me he would kill me, too."

"I don't think so."

Millie laughed. "Yes, I guess it is too late to sell you on that theory, isn't it?"

Halley stared at Millie. She seemed so different, no longer pretending to be the poor, frightened, beaten-down wife who lived in terror of her husband's temper.

"So it was all a lie to make Sid look guilty," she said. "You knew I would think he'd done it. You've been leading me there all along. You purposely worked him up so he would come over to my house last night after he'd been drinking."

Her smile broadened. "Very good. I knew it the first time you came to my house. I thought to myself—that woman is too smart for her own good. Too bad, too. You could have saved yourself a lot of trouble if you'd stayed home tonight. Maybe went out with your boyfriend. But you had to come over here, didn't you? What exactly were you expecting to find?"

"Evidence that would make your husband look even more guilty. That's right. You blew it, Millie. The school counselor's alibi checked out. Sid Granger was my number one suspect."

COLTON KNEW HE WAS running a little early as he pulled down the road to Halley's farmhouse. He'd dressed in his best boots, his favorite Western shirt and his newest jeans.

When he'd stopped by the ranch to give his dad and Emma the update on Aggie Wells, they'd both raised an eyebrow.

"Another date with Halley?" Emma had asked.

He couldn't help himself—he'd grinned and changed the subject to Aggie Wells.

"She didn't turn in her rental car?" his dad asked, sounding worried.

"She must have gotten word that we were checking on her employment and just took off rather than catch her flight," Colton said. "Any idea on why she was headed for Phoenix?"

Hoyt shook his head.

"Dad, if there is anything you want to tell me…" Colton said after Emma had left the room.

Hoyt looked up at his son. His face softened. "I have tried to spare you and your brothers from all this."

"I know you had nothing to do with anyone's death or disappearance. Why, though, is Aggie Wells so convinced that you did?"

His father shook his head. "I have no idea, but I'm worried about Emma. I'm afraid something might happen to her if I don't get her away from this ranch."

Colton had wanted to question his father more, but Emma had come back into the room just then to announce that Celeste was about to serve supper. He heard his brothers coming in through the back door and, telling his father he would talk to him later, left.

Now all he wanted to do was put everything out of his mind except for Halley. But as he pulled into the yard, he realized that Halley's patrol SUV was nowhere to be seen. He glanced at his watch, surprised that she was running late again and disappointed as he cut his engine to wait.

Colton tried not to worry, yet he couldn't forget Sid Granger with a bottle of liquor and out of jail. He told himself that as long as Halley didn't cross paths with him, she would be fine.

"You really did think Sid killed her?" Millie asked.

Halley nodded. "I thought it was Sid, but then I remembered that apron you were wearing, the yellow one with the small print? I noticed that first day that it had a ragged hole in it, as if you'd caught it on something. You were kneading your fingers in and out of the hole."

Millie looked regretful. "I should have thrown the old thing away, but it was the last of my mother's and one of her favorites."

"What I don't understand is why you were wearing it that night."

"I had to leave the house quickly because Sid came home before I expected him that night. He just assumed my friend had already picked me up to take me to the Whitehorse Sewing Circle. I was forced to hide out here in the woods." She frowned. "I don't know how you came to the conclusion that I was wearing it that night, but you'll never get a DNA sample from that apron. I washed all the blood out of it years ago."

"Why did you kill her?" Halley asked, not about to tell her about the scrap of fabric caught on the barbed-wire fence. There was still the chance that this wouldn't end the way Millie was hoping it would. Even if the woman killed her, she wasn't strong enough to move her body. Maybe the crime lab would find the fabric and test the stain on it. Once they found Jessica's blood on it…

"You're wrong, and unfortunately it's going to cost you your life," Millie said and glanced at her watch in the glow of the flashlight. "Sid is out of jail. He is furious and probably already getting drunk. When he comes home, he's going to knock me around—just for effect. Then, after seeing your patrol car parked in front of our house, he's going to come looking for you. You have no idea how dangerous my husband can be when he's this upset."

"He knows the truth, doesn't he? That's why you changed your plan," Halley said, realizing it was true and she knew when it had all come together for him. "I actually witnessed the moment he figured it out. It was when I accused him of putting the rattlesnake in my bed."

Millie smiled. "I thought it was a nice touch. Sid was so proud of that horrible rattlesnake skin that he'd insisted on putting over the fireplace. He likes going out and catching them. I used his equipment and went to one of the spots he's always going on about."

Halley shook her head, even though it hurt to do so. "I don't understand why you would you try to frame your own husband."

"With him in prison for multiple murders, I can finally do whatever I want without having to see his pathetic face every day."

"You hate him that much?"

"He's weak. I could have broken that girl. I could have beaten her mother's slutty ways out of her, but Sid couldn't bear it and look how it all ended."

Halley frowned. "Jessica's mother?"

WHEN COLTON'S PHONE RANG, he thought it was Halley calling to say she was running late again.

The last person he'd expected to be calling was Sid Granger.

"Is the deputy with you?" he asked the moment Colton answered.

"What?"

"I called your house and got your cell phone number. The deputy's patrol car is in front of my house. I can't find her. Or Millie."

Colton felt his heart rate spike at Sid's words—and the fear he heard in them. "No, I'm waiting for Halley. Why are you asking me... Sid?" He realized that the man had hung up.

Snapping the phone shut, he reached for the key still in the ignition, cranked the pickup's engine to life and headed for Sid Granger's house, his fear growing with each mile.

Why would Halley's patrol car be parked in front of the Granger house? She must have gone over there to talk to Millie. Now they were both missing?

His heart pounded, fear making him break out in a cold sweat. Jessica had been afraid in that house. For all her bravado and all her exploits, she was just a girl. A girl hell-bent on running away from that house.

Colton thought of the fear he'd heard in Sid Granger's voice and remembered the broken man he'd seen coming out of the liquor store.

What the hell *had* been going on in that house fourteen years ago? And what had happened now? His every instinct told him he had to find Halley—and fast.

"JESSICA WASN'T OURS," Millie said with disgust. "She was my sister's bastard, but rather than have the whole county talking about our family any more than they already did, I let everyone believe the baby was mine. My sister was living in Billings. It was easy enough to stay down there during the last of her pregnancy, then bring the baby back as my own."

"What happened to your sister?" Halley asked, her heart in her throat.

"She did what was best for everyone. She took her own life. An overdose, the coroner said."

Halley felt sick.

"You killed them both."

"I tried to *save* them both," Millie snapped.

"You followed Jessica that night and killed her."

"I didn't have to follow her. I knew where she was going. Just as I knew she was no good. She had my sister's blood running through her veins. I saw it when she was little, the way she always had to have Sid's attention."

Halley didn't think she could be more sickened, but she was wrong. "So it was really about competing for Sid's attention."

Millie lifted a brow, her face taking on as deadly a look as the gun in her hand. "What do you know about it? I could see the devil in her the way she sashayed around, thinking she was a lot cuter than she was."

"She was just being a little girl. Is that when you started beating her?"

"Spare the rod, spoil the child."

"That what your mother taught you?" she asked, re-membering the treasured apron the woman had hung on to all these years.

Millie took a menacing step toward her. "Don't you say anything bad about my mother. She was a saint. She taught me to be a *good* girl."

Halley shuddered at the look in the woman's eyes. "You didn't have to kill Jessica. She was *running away.*"

"What makes you think I wasn't glad she was run-ning away? I wanted to be rid of that girl. After Social Services called, I knew I couldn't use my usual methods to try to keep her in line and Jessica knew it as well. She had already brought shame on me by telling everyone she was pregnant."

"Jessica *wasn't* pregnant."

"Not this time anyway. At least the lie worked in her favor, now didn't it?"

Halley thought of the $10,000 Hoyt Chisholm had

given Jessica that hadn't been found yet. "You knew about the money she was extorting."

Millie laughed. "It was my idea to hit up those men who had taken advantage of her for the money. I figured if the tramp was going to lie, why not make it worthwhile?"

Halley was at a loss for words. "If you wanted to get rid of her and she was running away that night, then why did you have to kill her?" The reason came in a flash. "The money. You wanted it for yourself so you could leave, too."

She didn't deny it.

"The letters you told your husband came from Jessica…"

"Have you ever quilted? It's a wonderful hobby. And with the internet you can talk to quilters all over the world. Isn't that amazing? And they are such nice people. They would do anything for you."

"You had quilters mail the letters for you."

"I needed Sid to believe she was still alive until I was ready for him to find out differently."

"The lost letter," Halley said. It had started all the events in motion. "How did you get the letter?"

"Jessica confessed that in a weak moment she'd mailed the letter to Colton just in case his father didn't come up with the $10,000. It would have only complicated things. I followed the mailman the next day. The Chisholm mailbox isn't within sight of the ranch house. It was easy to get the letter back. At first I was simply going to destroy it."

"But you thought of a better way to use it by implicating Colton."

Millie smiled again. "I knew how Sid would react

if he thought Colton had killed Jessica. The plan was perfect."

"You dug up Jessica's purse so he would find it."

The woman cocked her head as if listening. Halley realized that Millie hadn't been telling her all this to get it off her chest or the relieve her guilt. She'd been waiting for someone.

"You think you have it all figured out," Millie said distractedly. "There is just one piece of the puzzle that doesn't quite fit."

"What piece is that?" Halley asked, her heart again in her throat.

"I didn't kill Jessica. Here's your killer now."

Halley turned, sensing at the last moment that they were no longer alone.

Chapter Fifteen

Jessica's former best friend Twyla Brandon came out of the darkness, a baseball bat in her gloved hand. She stopped within swinging distance.

"I see you found Sid's bat," Millie said with a nod and smiled at the younger woman.

"Twyla?" Halley said in disbelief.

"She's the daughter I should have had," Millie said. "Jessica was a terrible friend to Twyla. She used her in the worst possible way. Fortunately, I was there for her. She'd always come to me when Jessica was bad and tell me everything. Didn't you, sweetie?"

Even with her head still aching, Halley finally saw what she'd missed before. She thought she couldn't be more horrified. "You betrayed Jessica to her mother, knowing what Millie would do to her?"

Twyla looked down at the baseball bat in her hands. "I merely told the truth." When she raised her gaze, Halley saw the hatred reflected in the light from the flashlight beam. "Jessica used me in her warped, evil game. She thought it was so funny pretending I was the one who was the tramp. Do you have any idea what her lies cost me?"

"You could have stopped her."

Twyla snorted. "No one could stop Jessica. I begged her to quit telling stories about me, but she just laughed."

"I thought you both laughed at Colton's expense," Halley said. "You could have told him the truth." But even as Halley said it, she knew Colton wouldn't have believed her. He saw what he wanted to see in Jessica—a girl in trouble he thought he could help.

"You don't know the way he always looked at me, as if I was dirt under his feet," Twyla said. "Other people heard the stories and they believed them. If it hadn't been for Millie, I don't know what I would have done."

Halley looked from Twyla to Millie and back. "She got you to kill Jessica?"

"It had to be done," Millie said. "Twyla needed to do it. I couldn't take that away from her. Jessica had to be stopped."

It turned Halley's stomach at how sick the relationship was between these two women. "Millie used you. She's still using you. You think Jessica did a number on you? Well, it was nothing compared to what this woman has done to you."

Millie laughed. "Save your breath. Twyla knows what's at stake here. She has a family and children now. She can't let you ruin her life, and you will if we let you go. No one can understand what this poor young woman has been through but me." She nodded to Twyla, who stepped closer and raised the bat.

As COLTON DROVE UP into the Grangers' yard, he caught what he realized was a flashlight beam moving through the trees along the creek. Sid was heading north along the creek through the darkness.

Colton grabbed the pistol he kept under the seat and a flashlight and leaped from his pickup. At the creek, he followed the faint light flickering through the trees from Sid's flashlight, opting not to use his own. He could hear Sid ahead of him, moving fast.

Colton didn't need to wonder where he was headed. He tucked the pistol into his jeans and followed, unnerved to realize that Sid Granger had to have known about the secret spot where his daughter used to sneak off to.

How long had he known? There was no way of knowing. Just as there was no way of knowing if Sid was leading him into a trap.

He gave little thought to that prospect. He had to find Halley. Every instinct told him she was in serious trouble, as he followed the man, moving swiftly through the tall green grass and dense cottonwoods.

Colton felt his anxiety growing. Why had Halley come to the Grangers'? Had she also found this old trail and taken it to the secret spot on the creek where Jessica had died?

He heard Sid slow ahead of him. Suddenly, the light ahead was snuffed out. He could no longer hear Sid moving through the grass and brush. He froze in mid-step and listened. Darkness settled in around him along with a deathly stillness. Beyond the faint sound of the creek and the breeze in the leaves of the towering cottonwoods, he heard voices.

Then Sid was moving again, sounding as if he was running, the flashlight beam bobbing erratically, then water splashed and he heard a gunshot fill the air, then the boom of a shotgun and a cry that sent a flock of birds scattering from a treetop overhead.

Colton snapped on his flashlight and raced toward the horrible sound.

LIKE THE LAST TERRIFYING moment Halley remembered, this one happened just as fast. Twyla raised the bat and swung. Halley rolled, throwing herself toward the young woman, and only caught part of the blow on her calf. She grabbed at Twyla's legs and brought her down, scrambling to gain control of the bat, all the while knowing that Millie still held a pistol on her and that any moment she would feel the heat of lead ripping through her body.

Halley felt the cramping pain in her calf where the bat connected as she grappled with Twyla. The young woman was stronger than she looked and when Halley heard the gunshot she winced, expecting to feel the fiery pain. But instead, she saw Sid and heard his cry of pain from where Millie had shot him. He was still standing at the edge of the barbed-wire fence. He raised the shotgun in his hands, pointed it at his wife. Halley saw then that his pain had nothing to do with his gunshot wound but with what he was about to do.

He fired the shotgun and Millie let out the most eerie, horrible cry Halley had ever heard. The flashlight fell to the ground, the beam pointing at an angle that threw light on the pistol still in her one hand, the other hand cupping her stomach, which flowed dark red.

Losing her focus for just an instant, Halley felt Twyla slip out of her grip and grab for the baseball bat lying in the deep grass. Halley tried to get to her feet, but the cramp in her calf slowed her down just long enough for Twyla to reach the bat, and she was up and swinging it.

Sid grabbed the bat, wrenching it from Twyla before she could complete her swing and throwing it into the brush out of sight. Using the shotgun like a crutch, he took a step toward Millie.

He never reached her. He collapsed to the ground just few feet shy of her, dropping the shotgun.

Halley dived for the shotgun, but Twyla got there first. In the light from Millie's fallen flashlight, Halley saw a gleam come into Twyla's eyes and realized that the woman wasn't seeing her—she was seeing Jessica, the friend who had tormented her in the most terrible way of all.

Colton came out of the darkness at a run, tackling Twyla and throwing her to the ground. Halley grabbed the shotgun and spun around.

Millie had dropped to her knees in the grass. She still had the gun in her hand, but her gaze was on the blood pouring out of her abdomen.

"Drop the gun!" Halley ordered, aiming the loaded shotgun at her.

Millie Granger slowly raised her head. She started to raise the pistol, but all the life seemed to drain out of her. She fell face forward into the grass. Behind her, Colton restrained Twyla Brandon who was crying hysterically and trying to get to Millie. Both Millie and Sid lay dead in the grass just yards from where Jessica had died.

Halley retrieved her weapon from Millie's jacket pocket, then turning to Twyla she took out her handcuffs and began to read the woman her rights.

It wasn't until later, the crime scene secured, the coroner come and gone, and Twyla safely behind bars, that Halley fell into Colton Chisholm's arms, but by then the sun was up and their second date was officially over.

Colton had sworn he was going to take it slow, but

he blurted it out because he couldn't go another instant without telling her.

"I love you."

She smiled, a slow, sexy smile. "About time you realized that."

He laughed and gently touched her face as he looked into her big brown eyes. "You are so beautiful, but you know what I love about you most?"

"My sense of humor?"

He shook his head. "Your strength. You're quite the woman, Halley Robinson."

She stepped to him. "I love you, too," she whispered, and kissed him. "I always have."

Epilogue

Emma stared out the window at the wide open spaces that had filled her with such calm when she'd come to the ranch just weeks before. But she'd been a newlywed, happy and content and pinching herself at her good luck.

Now the sprawling ranch and the endless prairie seemed to echo the isolation of the Chisholm Cattle Company ranch. It hadn't helped that Hoyt had sensed her unease and hung around the house, instead of riding off with his sons.

A quiet tenseness had settled over them, as if they were both waiting for the other shoe to drop, and Emma knew it had to stop—one way or the other—as she heard her husband join her at the window.

"You need to get back to running this ranch," she said without looking at him. "I'll be fine."

"Trying to run me off, are you?" he joked, then sobered. "Or are you afraid of being alone here with me?"

Emma turned then to look into her husband's handsome face. She touched his cheek, loving that weathered face. An honest face, her mother would have called it.

"I could never be afraid of you," she said softly. She would never believe he had anything to do with the death of two of his wives or the disappearance of the third, no matter what anyone said or thought.

Hoyt didn't look convinced, as he took her hand and brought it to his lips. "Maybe I'm afraid for you."

Emma shook her head, smiling up at him. "There is nothing to fear as long as we're together."

They hadn't heard anymore from Aggie Wells since they'd discovered she had been fired from the insurance company she worked for. Hoyt had talked to her boss. He'd apologized and suggested that Hoyt get a restraining order if Aggie contacted him again.

But Emma knew Hoyt wasn't going to do that. Like her, he was just hoping the woman was gone from their lives.

"Now get out of here," Emma said. "I need to plan a special supper for tonight. Colton is bringing Halley."

Hoyt shook his head in mild amusement. "You think it's serious?"

Emma nodded, unable to hide her pleasure. "Halley is perfect for him."

"So you say." He glanced over at her and she saw the suspicion in his gaze. "You didn't have anything to do with that, did you?"

"Me?" she asked innocently. "Oh, did I mention that I also invited that nice young woman who just returned from college at Montana State University. Graduated in animal husbandry. I think she went to school with Dawson. She'd come home to help her father run their ranch."

"Emma…"

HALLEY SAT ON HER HORSE, looking out over the prairie. "You're right, this view is amazing," she said. The breeze stirred her hair, which hung loose over her shoulders. She turned her face up to the warm sunlight and breathed in the fresh scent of pine and summer.

On the horse beside her, Colton was looking at her, rather than the view. She could feel the warmth of his gaze, hotter than the sun overhead. Halley smiled to herself, remembering their third date. It had seemed as if it was never going to happen, given the way their other dates had gone.

It had been so clear that Colton wanted to do this right with her. She loved that about him. No more frogs down the neck, but she definitely had his attention.

They'd gone to dinner at Northern Lights, the nicest restaurant in Whitehorse, had champagne and candlelight. It wasn't until they were on the way home that they both had started laughing at the same time.

"That was so not us," Halley got out between laughs.

"Could it have been more awkward?" Colton agreed. He'd stopped laughing and had slowed the pickup. "You and I—"

"We don't fit the mold. Pull over."

He shot her an amused look, then pulled over onto a dirt road, coming to stop on a small rise out of sight of the highway. He put down his window and shut off the engine. No full moon, only a sliver on the horizon and a few scattered stars glittering above them.

"I wanted everything to be perfect our first time," he said, putting his arm around her.

"It *is* perfect," she whispered and he kissed her.

It *had* been perfect. They'd made love in the cab of his pickup—just like high school kids—and when they came up for air, the sky was ablaze with the real Northern Lights.

They'd talked and laughed, lying in each other's arms, their feet sticking out the open window of the pickup. That's when Halley knew with certainty that this was the man for her.

"Colton?" She blinked and saw that Colten had gotten off his horse. He was standing next to hers, holding her reins and looking up at her with such love in his eyes that her heart took off at a gallop.

"Do you know why I brought you up here?"

Her heart raced a little faster. "You said it was to have the lunch that Emma packed. I love Emma's food, so you'd better not be fooling with me."

He grinned, his brown eyes golden in the sunlight. He had his Stetson pushed back. The man couldn't have been more handsome, nor could she have loved him more than she did at that moment.

COLTON HAD PROMISED HIMSELF he was going to take it slow, but there was nothing slow about the beat of his heart when he was around this woman. He'd been drawn to her ever since they were kids. Now they'd been brought back together and he wasn't going to let anything keep them apart, if he could help it.

"Halley?"

"Yes, Colton?"

He looked into her big brown eyes. His heart pounded like a war drum. "Marry me?"

Tears filled her eyes and for one heart-stopping moment, he thought she was going to say no. He watched her bite her lower lip as she fought to hold back the tears. "Oh, yes!"

He lifted her out of the saddle and into his arms. "I love you, Halley Robinson."

She brushed at her tears. "I love you, too," she said on a ragged breath, then looked down at what he held out to her.

It was corny and clichéd, right down to the small velvet box, but some traditions felt right.

Halley's fingers trembled as she opened the box. She let out a pleased sound, her face lighting up at the beautiful Montana agate engagement ring.

"Oh, Colton," was all she said as he slipped it on her finger. She threw herself into his arms. Emma's wonderful lunch forgotten until later that afternoon when they sat on the edge of the ridge watching the afternoon sun dip behind the Little Rockies.

Colton could imagine the excitement back at the house when he and Halley told his father and Emma the news tonight at supper. Hoyt had always said this was where Colton belonged, but he'd never felt it until this moment.

His future lay in this wild, expansive land and this woman. They would make a home here, their children would grow up on this ranch. He could see it all now. As he looked over at his beautiful bride-to-be, he knew this is the way it was always meant to be.

* * * * *

LASSOED

BY
BJ DANIELS

All the characters in this book have no existence outside the imagination of
the author, and have no relation whatsoever to anyone bearing the same name
or names. They are not even distantly inspired by any individual known or
unknown to the author, and all the incidents are pure invention.

First published in Great Britain 2012
by Mills & Boon, an imprint of Harlequin (UK) Limited,
Eton House, 18-24 Paradise Road, Richmond, Surrey TW9 1SR

© Barbara Heinlein 2011

ISBN: 978 0 263 89502 5

46-0212

Harlequin (UK) policy is to use papers that are natural, renewable and
recyclable products and made from wood grown in sustainable forests. The
logging and manufacturing processes conform to the legal environmental
regulations of the country of origin.

Printed and bound in Spain
by Blackprint CPI, Barcelona

The one thing no one told me was how many good
writer friends I would make on this journey.
This one is for Amanda Stevens, who is always there
when I need her. I should add, she is also the scariest
person I know and if you don't believe it, wait until
you read her new Graveyard series.

Chapter One

The lights came out of the darkness like an oasis in the desert. Billie Rae glanced at the gas gauge on the old pickup, then in her rearview mirror.

She hadn't seen a vehicle behind her for miles now, but she didn't slow down, didn't dare. The pickup engine roared loudly, the speedometer clocked at over a hundred, but it was the gas gauge that had her worried.

She was almost out of fuel. Which meant she was also out of luck.

At the speed she was traveling, the lights ahead were coming up fast. At first she thought it was a small town. She hadn't seen one for more than fifty miles. But as she sped toward the glittering lights, she realized it wasn't a town. It appeared to be a fairgrounds aglow with lights.

Suddenly fireworks shot up from the horizon, bursting in the huge ebony sky stretched over this vast Montana prairie. She stared in surprise, realizing with a start what day it was. July 2. Two days away from the Fourth. She let the pickup slow to eighty as the booming fireworks burst around her, momentarily blinding her. The engine coughed. She glanced at the gas gauge. The pickup was running on fumes.

In her headlights she caught sight of the sign to the Whitehorse fairgrounds and another sign that announced Rodeo July 2–4. As the pickup engine coughed again, Billie Rae knew she'd just run out of options as well as gas.

She turned onto the dirt road that had a handmade sign that read Rodeo Parking and let the pickup coast in past dozens of trucks and horse trailers parked in the field around the rodeo arena. Just as the engine died, she pulled the truck into a spot between two pickups and turned off the headlights.

The highway she'd just come down had been nothing but blackness in her rearview mirror. Now, though, she wasn't surprised to see a set of headlights in the far distance. She'd known she didn't have much of a head start. Just as she'd known nothing short of dying would keep him from coming after her.

Billie Rae sat for a moment fighting tears. Her chest ached from the sudden loss of hope. Without gas she wasn't going any farther—as if she really believed she could ever go far enough to get away from Duane. She slumped over the steering wheel.

She'd left the house with only the clothes on her back, and now it was just a matter of minutes before he found her. Duane was no fool. He'd know the pickup would be running low on gas by now and that she hadn't stopped to fill it up since she had no money. She'd had to leave her purse behind—not -

that there was any money in it, thanks to Duane. He had kept her a virtual prisoner since their wedding six months ago.

None of that mattered now, though. She should never have run. Duane was right. There was no getting away from him. He'd get a good laugh out of her thinking she could. Hadn't he said he would follow her to the ends of the earth?

But it was what else he'd said when she'd told him she wanted out of the marriage that made her now begin to tremble in the dark cab of the pickup.

He had grabbed her by the throat and thrown her down on the bed. "You ever leave me and I will hunt you down like a mad dog and hurt you in ways you can't even imagine."

Her heart began to pound now with both fear and outrage. Duane had been so sweet, so loving, so caring before the wedding. Her mother had just died and she'd needed someone strong to lean on. Duane had provided the broad shoulder. He'd helped her through a tough time.

And then she'd made the mistake of marrying him. It wasn't that he'd suddenly changed. It was that once he put that ring on her finger, he'd finally revealed who he really was—a bully, a bastard, a batterer.

Her hands were shaking as she let go of the steering wheel. Her fingers ached from gripping it so tightly. Was she just going to sit here and wait for him to find her? He'd done his best to beat her down, but there was still a little fight left in her. She'd left him, hadn't she? That proved she had more courage than she'd thought and certainly more than Duane had thought.

She wasn't going back. Nor was she going to let Duane kill her. She had been a young, foolish, enamored woman when she'd married him, but once she'd seen behind the mask to the monster, there was no going back after that. She wasn't one of those women who thought their husbands would change. Or that it was her fault when her husband took out his bad moods on her.

But there was no denying she was in trouble.

Opening the door, Billie Rae climbed out of the pickup, surprised how weak her knees felt. Between booms of fireworks she heard a vehicle slowing on the highway before the small community fairgrounds. She didn't dare look and what was the point? She knew who it was.

She quickly worked her way through the pickups and horse trailers, following the sound of the oohs and ahs of the audience in the stands as the fireworks continued to explode over her head. The fireworks were going off closer together. One huge boom rattled in her chest after another. Soon the crowd would be dispersing and leaving.

She felt all her bravado leave as well. Soon everyone would be gone. Maybe she could find a place to hide where Duane wouldn't… Who was she kidding? Duane was going to find her, and when he did…

Glancing back through the parked vehicles, she caught a glimpse of a large black car driving slowly into the lot. Duane. He'd find the old classic Chevy pickup that had been his father's pride and joy. He'd find her.

She raced behind the grandstand in blind panic, knowing what he would do when he found her. She shouldn't have tried to leave him. She should have waited until she had a plan. But when Duane had come home earlier and she'd seen the rage building in him, she'd known how the evening would end and she couldn't let him hurt her again.

Billie Rae ran, blinded by tears and terror. If she could reach the stands, maybe she could disappear into the crowd—at least temporarily. Eventually, though, the stands would clear out and all that would be left would be her—and Duane.

As she came around the end of the grandstand, she collided with a tall cowboy. She'd been running for her life, glancing back over her shoulder and not looking where she was going, so she was hit hard, with her breath knocked out of her and her feet out from under her. If he hadn't caught her, she would have fallen to the ground.

"Easy," the cowboy said, his big hands gripping her shoulders to steady her. Tears continued to spill and she couldn't quit trembling. She opened her mouth to speak but nothing came out as she looked up into the man's handsome face.

He was dressed in boots, jeans and a fancy Western shirt. A gray Stetson was tilted back on his dark head. But it was the kindness in his brown eyes that had her riveted as the fireworks' grand finale continued.

Huge booms reverberated through her as brilliant

colors showered the sky around the two of them in breathtaking beauty. For a few moments, it seemed they were the only two people in the world. As if this show was only for them alone. The cowboy smiled down at her and she felt a hitch in her chest.

The fireworks show ended in hushed dark silence, then the large lights of the fairgrounds blinked on and Billie Rae heard the crunch of gravel under a boot heel at the other end of the large grandstand.

As if coming out of a dream, she swung her gaze to where a dark figure was heading their way. Duane. She would recognize that arrogant gait anywhere.

She tried to pull away from the cowboy, needing to run, but he held on tight to her as the crowd suddenly swarmed around them.

TANNER CHISHOLM WOULD HAVE scoffed at even the idea of love at first sight—until a few moments ago. When the woman had come running out of the darkness behind the grandstand and into his arms in a shower of fireworks, noise and beautiful lights, he'd taken one look at her face and fallen.

Time froze with fireworks going off all around them. When she'd crashed into him he felt as if his whole life had been leading up to that moment. He'd known in an instant that it was no accident that this woman had run into his arms on this warm summer night.

He stared into her wide brown eyes, as her dark curly hair floated around her shoulders. He saw the terror etched in her tear-streaked face, felt her trembling and realized that come hell or high water, he'd do his damnedest to move heaven and earth for this woman.

It was crazy, wonderful and totally out of character. He wasn't the kind of man who fell in love in a split second. But any man would have seen that this woman was running for her life.

"What's wrong?" he asked as she fought to pull away from him and run. He saw her look behind him again. A man was headed in their direction, fighting the crowd to get to them in a way that left no doubt the man was furious—and coming after the woman in Tanner's arms.

"Come with me." Tanner took her hand and pulled her through the crowd. He knew these rodeo grounds like the back of his hand because he'd grown up here, played under these grandstands, ridden in junior rodeo and had later ridden bucking broncs out in the arena.

The woman resisted for only a moment before she let him lead her through the crowd and the darkness toward the shadowy fairground buildings beyond the rodeo arena. From the way she was still trembling, he suspected that the man chasing her meant to hurt her. Or at least she thought so. The fact that she was more afraid of the man than a complete stranger told him the woman was desperate.

As he drew her between two of the fair buildings, he spotted the man fighting his way through the rodeo crowd. Tanner caught the man's expression under one of the large lights. The heightened fury he saw on the man's face made him worry he might have made things worse for the woman by trying to protect her.

Too late now. Whatever had the man all riled up, he wasn't going to be taking it out on this woman. Not tonight, anyway.

Tanner led her between two more buildings, weaving his way through the maze of dark structures, until he reached one he knew would be unlocked. Pulling the door open, he drew her inside, closed the door and turned the lock.

"Who is that out there?" he whispered, still holding her hand in the blackness inside the building.

Silence, then a hoarsely whispered, "My husband."

Tanner mentally gave himself a swift kick. He really had stepped in it this time. Only a fool jumped into a domestic argument. "Why's he so angry?"

She started to answer but he felt her freeze as she heard the same sound he did. Someone was running in this direction on the wooden boardwalk in front of the buildings. He didn't have to tell her to be quiet. He knew she was holding her breath.

The footfalls came to a stop outside the building, the last along the row. Past it was a line of huge cottonwoods cloaked in darkness. With luck, the man would think that was where they had gone.

Tanner could hear the man's heavy breathing and cursing, then his angry voice as he muttered, "You may have gotten away this time, Billie Rae, but this isn't over. When I find you, I'm going to make you wish you were dead. That's if I don't kill you with my bare hands."

The man stood outside the door panting hard, then his footfalls ebbed away back the way he'd come. The woman he'd called Billie Rae let go of Tanner's hand, and he could hear her fumbling with the door lock.

"Not so fast," Tanner said, reaching around her to turn on the light. They were both blinded for a moment by the sudden light. "I think you'd better tell me what's going on, because you heard what he just said. That man plans to hurt you. If he hasn't already," Tanner added as he saw the fading bruise around her left eye.

WHAT BILLIE RAE HAD HEARD her husband say wasn't anything new. He'd threatened her plenty of times before, and the threats, she'd learned the hard way, weren't empty ones.

"I appreciate what you did for me, but I can't involve you in this," she said, finally finding her voice.

The cowboy let out a humorless laugh. "I'm already involved up to my hat. Do you have someplace you can go? Family? Friends?"

Billie Rae opened her mouth to lie. Duane had moved her away from what little family and friends she'd had right after the wedding. She'd lost contact over the past six months. Duane had made sure of that. Just as he had thrown a fit when she'd suggested going back to work.

"Your work is in this house, taking care of me. That's your work."

"You don't have anyone you can call, do you?" the cowboy said. "Don't worry. It's going to be all right. I know a place you can stay where you will be safe."

Billie Rae wanted desperately to take the cowboy up on his offer but realized she couldn't. It had been bad enough when Duane had been after her alone. Now he would be looking for the cowboy he'd seen her with. "No, you don't understand. Duane will come after *you* now. I'm so sorry. I should never have put you in this position."

"You didn't. I'm the one who dragged you in here," he said as he pulled out his cell phone.

She tried to protest to whatever he was about to do, but he shushed her.

"I need a ride," he said into the phone.

She heard laughter on the other end.

"I need you to bring me my pickup. That's right, it's parked right where we left it before the rodeo. No, I can't come get it myself, Marshall, or I wouldn't have called you. The keys are in it. I'm in the last fairground building. There will be two of us. Make it quick, okay?" He snapped off the phone and gave her a reassuring smile.

Billie Rae wondered if she'd just jumped from the skillet into the fire. But there was something about this man that made her feel safe. It wasn't just the kindness she saw in his brown eyes.

There was a softness to his voice and his movements that belied his size and the strength she could see in his broad shoulders, muscled arms and callused hands.

This was a man who did manual labor—not one who either sat behind a desk or rode around all day in a car.

"I'm Tanner Chisholm," he said and held out his hand.

"Billie Rae Johnson." She realized she'd given him her maiden name instead of her married one.

"My brother Marshall is coming to pick us up in my truck, then we'll go out to the ranch where my stepmother, Emma, will make you feel at home. She'll insist you have something to eat. She does that to everyone. Humor her; it is much easier in the long run." He smiled. "You'll like Emma. Everyone does."

"I couldn't possibly impose—"

"Trust me, it is impossible to impose at the Chisholm ranch. If anything, Emma and my father, Hoyt, will want to adopt you."

She felt tears well and quickly brushed them away. "Why are you being so nice to me? You don't know me."

"I know you're in trouble and I'm a sucker for a woman who needs my help," he joked. "Seriously, whatever is going on, you need someplace to stay tonight at least and to give your husband a chance to calm down."

As if Duane was going to calm down, she thought with a grimace. All of this would have him foaming at the mouth with fury.

"I assume you drove to the rodeo?"

"A pickup. It's out of gas. But—"

"My brother and I will see to it tomorrow. It will be safe here tonight."

Maybe the truck would be safe but the brothers wouldn't be if they came to fetch it tomorrow. Duane would be watching it and waiting.

She had to stop this now. She knew Duane, knew what he would do to this cowboy. "You have to let me go," she said as she reached for the doorknob again. "You don't know my husband. He'll come after you—"

"I think I *do* know your husband," Tanner said and gently touched her cheek under her left eye with his fingertips. She flinched, not because her bruised cheek still hurt, but because she'd forgotten about her healing black eye and now this kind cowboy knew her hidden shame.

At the sound of a truck pulling up outside the building, Tanner said, "That will be Marshall." He opened the door a crack and looked out as if checking to make sure the coast was clear. "I come from a large ranch family that sticks together. I have five brothers. Your husband isn't going to take on the six of us, trust me."

Before she could argue, he quickly ushered her out to a large ranch truck. She noticed the sign printed on the side: Chisholm Cattle Company. Tanner opened the truck door, then taking her waist in both of his large hands, lifted her in before sliding into the bench seat next to her.

"Marshall, meet Billie Rae. Billie Rae, my big brother Marshall."

The cowboy behind the wheel grinned. Like his brother, Marshall had dark hair and brown eyes reflecting his Native American ancestry. Both men were very handsome but there was also something kind and comforting in their faces.

"I'd appreciate it if you got this truck moving," Tanner said, glancing in his side mirror. He turned back to Billie Rae, plucked a cowboy hat from the gun rack behind her and dropped it onto her long, dark, curly hair.

Marshall laughed. "So you got yourself into some kind of trouble and apparently involved this pretty little lady in the midst of it, huh?" He shook his head, but he got the truck moving.

As they drove out the back way of the fairgrounds, Billie Rae stared through the windshield from under the brim of the hat, afraid she'd see Duane in the dispersing crowd. Or worse, Duane would see her—and the name of the ranch painted on the side of the truck.

Chapter Two

Duane Rasmussen leaned against his father's pickup, arms crossed over his chest, his heart pounding with both anger and anticipation.

The fairgrounds were still clearing out. His head hurt from searching the crowd and waiting to see Billie Rae's contrite face.

She would come crawling back, apologizing and saying how sorry she was. She'd be a lot sorrier when he got through with her. The thought kicked up his pulse to a nice familiar throb he could feel in his thick neck.

As his daddy used to say, "A man who can't control his woman is no man at all."

He used to think his old man was a mean SOB. But Duane hadn't understood what his father had to contend with when it came to living with a woman. Sometimes just opening the door and seeing Billie Rae with that look on her face…

Duane couldn't describe it any other way than as a deer-in-the-headlights look. It made him want to wipe it off her face. He hated it when she acted as if she had to fear him.

He had told her repeatedly that he loved her and that the only reason he had to get tough with her sometimes was because she made him mad. Or when she acted like she was walking around on eggshells, treating him as if she thought he might go off at any moment and slap her.

Didn't he realize how that would make him even angrier with her?

Duane shook his head now. He'd never be able to understand his wife.

Like this little trick she'd just pulled, taking off on him. What the hell was she thinking? She'd been so sweet and compliant when they were dating. She'd liked it when he took care of her, told her what was best for her, didn't bother her with making any of the decisions.

He couldn't understand what had changed her. It was a mystery to him especially since he'd given the woman everything—she didn't even have to work outside the home.

He'd squashed all talk of her looking for a job after they'd moved. No wife of his was working. Every man knew that working outside the home ruined a woman. They got all kinds of strange ideas into their heads. Let a woman be too independent and you were just asking for trouble.

With a curse, he saw that the parking area was almost empty. Only a few stragglers wandered out from the direction of the rodeo grandstands. The rodeo cowboys had loaded up their stock and taken off. The parking lot in the field next to the fairgrounds was empty.

A sliver of worry burrowed under his skin. Where was Billie Rae? Still hiding in those trees to the west of the fairgrounds? The night air was cooling quickly. She wasn't dressed for spending the night in the woods, not this far north in Montana.

That was another thing that puzzled him, the way she'd taken off. She hadn't planned this as far as he could tell. He'd found her purse and her house key. She hadn't even taken a decent jacket, and it appeared she'd left with nothing more than the clothes on her back. How stupid was that?

He settled in to wait. When she got cold and hungry she'd come back to the pickup. She'd know he would be waiting for her, so she'd come with her tail between her legs. He smiled at the thought. Of course Billie Rae would come back. Where else could she go?

EMMA CHISHOLM TOOK ONE LOOK at the woman her stepson had brought home from the rodeo and recognized herself—thirty years ago. It gave her a start to have a reminder show up at her front door after all these years.

All of it was too familiar, the terror in the young woman's eyes, the fading bruises, the insecurity and indecision in her movements and the panic and pain etched in her face.

The worst part, Emma knew, was the memory of the tearful promises that would be forgotten in an instant the next time. But it was those tender moments that gave every battered woman hope that this time, her lover really would never do it again. They called it the honeymoon period. It came right before the next beating—and that beating was always worse than the one before.

It made her heart ache just to look at the woman. A part of Emma wanted to distance herself, deny that she had been this young woman, but if there was one thing she'd learned, it was that all things circled back at you for a reason.

"This is Billie Rae Johnson," Tanner said. "Her car broke down at the rodeo. I told her we had plenty of room and that we'd get her fixed up in the morning."

Emma smiled and held out her hand to the young woman. "I'm Emma. We are delighted to have you stay with us as long as you'd like." Her gaze shifted to Tanner.

He'd never been one to exaggerate or lie, but she didn't believe his story for a moment. Billie Rae was on the run. Emma knew the look, remembered it only too well. Her heart went out to Billie Rae.

"I don't want to be an imposition." Billie Rae was a beauty, but Emma knew that her stepson had seen beyond that. Tanner was like his father, who brought home those in need. Was that one reason Hoyt had fallen in love with her? Because he'd seen the need in Emma herself?

"I promise you it is no imposition," Emma said. "I love having guests, especially female ones. I'm so outnumbered around here."

"Thank you," Billie Rae said. She looked exhausted. No doubt she'd been running on adrenaline and fear for hours and was about to crash.

"Why don't I show you up to one of our many guest rooms?" Emma said quickly. "Since all six of the boys have their own places now, we have more empty bedrooms than you can shake a stick at. Then I'll get you a snack. It always helps me sleep."

Billie Rae glanced at Tanner, who smiled and nodded, then she followed Emma without a word.

"You have this whole wing to yourself," Emma said when they reached one of the rooms that was always made up for guests. "So please, make yourself at home and if there is anything you need, don't hesitate to ask."

"I won't be here more than tonight."

Emma smiled. "Get some rest. Sometimes it takes more than a night. You are welcome to stay as long as you need. You're safe here."

Billie Rae nodded, tears coming to her eyes. "You're very kind."

"No, I've been where you are right now." Admitting it was easier than she'd thought it would be.

For a moment, the young woman looked as if she was going to deny it or pretend she didn't know what Emma was talking about.

"I was with a man who kicked the hell out of me on a regular basis," Emma said, surprised how easily too the anger came back. "Oh sure, he was always sorry. It was for my own good. He loved me. It took me a while to realize it wasn't for my own good, just as it wasn't my fault and that nothing I did or could do would change him. He didn't love me. He didn't know what love was."

Tears spilled over Billie Rae's cheeks. "I'm just so embarrassed."

Emma took her hand and they sat down on the edge of the bed. "Embarrassed? Oh, sweetie, you have done nothing to be embarrassed about."

"I married the wrong man. He…fooled me."

She nodded. "But you got smart and left him."

"He told me he'll kill me and I don't doubt it," Billie Rae said, brushing angrily at her tears.

Emma shook her head. "He isn't going to find you here. Tomorrow you can decide what to do next."

"You don't know Duane. I'm afraid he'll find out that you all helped me and do something terrible to you."

"Honey, that's why there's a shotgun in this house. Trust Tanner. He's a good man." She studied the young woman for a moment. "I don't know if you believe in fate or not, but I can tell you this. Tanner finding you and bringing you here was no accident."

As DUANE SAT IN THE empty fairgrounds in the dark, he knew where he'd made his mistake. If he'd gotten Billie Rae pregnant right away, none of this would be happening. But instead he'd listened to his wife, who'd wanted to wait until they were "settled in as a couple," as she called it.

With a surge of angry resentment, he realized she just wanted to make sure the marriage was to her liking. That *he* was to her liking.

Duane swore under his breath. Wait until he got his hands on her. He'd show her. She would never pull a stunt like this again. He'd kill her if she did. That was if he didn't end up killing her this time. He flushed, embarrassed to be put in this position, as the scent of fried food still drifted on the breeze coming through the open window of his Lincoln.

The last of the lights of the rodeo vehicles had dimmed away to darkness in the distance, all headed west. From the faint glow on the horizon, Duane figured the closest Montana town had to be up the highway. He was hungry and tired and even his anger couldn't keep him going much longer.

Duane looked around. It was just his car now and his father's pickup.

Where the hell was Billie Rae?

He waited until the night air cooled to a chill before he put up his car window, started the engine and drove down to park by the pickup. Billie Rae would be coming back soon and he didn't want to miss her.

A thought struck him like a blow. Unless she'd left with someone.

That cowboy he'd seen her with?

He couldn't get his mind around that. But then he'd thought he'd made it clear to Billie Rae what would happen to her if she ever tried to leave him—or to anyone who helped her. She'd made a friend who thought she could come between them. That friend was no longer anywhere around, now, was she?

Duane had thought Billie Rae had learned her lesson that time. But apparently that hadn't stopped her from "befriending" someone else who thought they could interfere in his marriage to her.

None of this was like Billie Rae, he thought as the hours wore on, and he felt an uncertainty that rattled him. For the first time, he wasn't sure he knew his wife as well as he thought he did.

AFTER HER TALK WITH Emma Chisholm, Billie Rae showered, slipped into the cotton nightgown left for her on the huge bed and slid between the sheets that smelled like fresh air.

Emma had also left her a glass of milk and a plate of sliced homemade banana bread. Billie Rae had eaten all of it. She hadn't realized how hungry she was or that she hadn't eaten since breakfast that morning.

For the first time in a long time, she felt as if she could breathe as she got up to brush her teeth with the new toothbrush Emma had set out for her. The cool night air blew in through the open window next to her bed as she crawled back under the covers. The breeze billowed the sheer white curtains. She could see the outline of mountains in the distance, smell sage and hay beyond the fresh clean scent of the line-dried linens on the bed.

But it was the sweet scent of freedom that she gulped in as if she was a drowning woman finally coming up for air. She was still half-afraid to believe it, but lying here in this house, she was filled with a sense of peace like none she had felt since she'd married Duane.

Don't rest too easy. I'm still out here looking for you. And when I find you—

She took another deep breath, chasing away the sound of Duane's voice. Like Scarlett O'Hara, she wouldn't think about tomorrow. For tonight, she was alive and safe, and that was more than she had hoped for.

At a tap at her door, she said, "Come in," thinking it would be Emma.

"I just wanted to check on you and make sure you have everything you need," Tanner said, peeking around the door.

"I'm fine." More than fine. "Thank you."

"I'll see you in the morning, then," he said. "I'll be just down the hall."

She couldn't help her surprise. Emma said that all the Chisholm sons had their own places now. "I thought—"

"I decided to stay here tonight." He shrugged, looking a little embarrassed. "In case you…"

"Needed anything," she finished for him, smiling.

"Good night, then," he said and closed the door.

Billie Rae lay in the bed still smiling, remembering what Emma had said. Trust Tanner. She did. She closed her eyes, dead tired, aching for sleep, but quickly opened them as Duane's image appeared as if waiting to taunt her in a nightmare.

Trust Tanner? Do you really think that cowboy or his whole damned family can save you?

She touched her diamond engagement ring in the darkness, the thick band of white gold next to it a reminder of who she was. Mrs. Duane Rasmussen, as if she could forget it.

Were you listening to that preacher? Till death do us part, Billie Rae. And that, sweetheart, is the way it is going to be, come hell or high water. You understand me, or am I going to have to refresh your memory?

As she spun the band in a circle, she thought about what Emma had said about fate. Did she believe in fate? Tanner had saved her tonight, he'd brought her to this house, to his stepmother, Emma, who had known instinctively what Billie Rae was going through.

Maybe fate had brought her together with this family tonight, but Billie Rae knew she had to run again come morning.

Slowly she took off the rings to set them on the

bedside table. The diamond winked at her in the light of the star-filled night coming in through the sheer, billowing curtains.

You really think it's that easy to be rid of me?

She got up, stood in the middle of the room, unsure what to do with the rings. Her first impulse was to throw them away, but common sense won out. The rings were worth money and she was going to need some if she hoped to stay free of Duane. She put them in the pocket of her slacks.

As she climbed back into the bed and pulled the covers up, she felt stronger than she had since she married Duane. It had been fate that she'd met Tanner Chisholm and that he'd brought her to this house. She'd been ready to give up and go back to Duane, believing she had no choice.

But now she felt as if she could do this. She *would* do this. She had let Duane Rasmussen bully her for too long.

This time when she closed her eyes she pictured Tanner Chisholm's face. But she didn't kid herself that Duane wouldn't be nearby waiting to ruin her sleep.

TANNER WOKE TO SCREAMING. He bolted upright in bed, confused for a moment where he was. As everything came back in a rush, he swung his legs over the side of the bed, pulled on his jeans and ran barefoot down the hall.

His conscious mind told him it was impossible that

Billie Rae's husband had found her here. That there was no way the man could be in the house. Worse, that he could have found the bedroom where she slept and—

He shoved open the door. Faint light shone through the sheer curtains at the large window next to her bed. A shaft of light from the hallway shot across the floor, making a path into the room. Tanner felt his heart break at the sounds coming from the bed. He rushed to Billie Rae.

She came out of the dream swinging her arms wildly. He didn't have to guess who she was trying to fight off.

"It's me, Billie Rae. Tanner. Tanner Chisholm."

Her eyes were wild with panic. She blinked at the sound of his voice and slowly focused on his face in the dim light before bursting into tears.

"You had a bad dream, but you're all right," he said as he sat down on the bed and pulled her into his arms. As he stroked her hair, he whispered, "It's all right. You're safe. You're all right."

She clung to him, sobbing, her breathing ragged. He could feel her damp cotton nightgown against his bare chest. She was shivering uncontrollably from the cold, from whatever horror still clung to her from the nightmare.

He held her close, continuing to stroke her hair and whisper words of comfort while all the time he wanted to kill the man who'd hurt this woman.

"Your nightgown is damp with sweat," he said

after her breathing became more normal. Shadows played on the walls, the breeze whipped the sheer curtains and outside the window, a branch scraped against the house.

As he started to pull away, she cried, "Please, don't leave me."

"I'll be right back. I'm just going to get you something warm and dry to sleep in." He hurried to his room, rummaged through a drawer where he'd left some of his old clothing. He found a large soft-worn T-shirt and hurried back to Billie Rae's room.

She was sitting up in the bed, clutching the covers to her chest. He sat down on the edge of the bed next to her again. "Here, take off the nightgown and put this on." He turned his back. He heard her behind him struggling to get out of the damp nightgown and knew she was still trembling from her nightmare.

What had her husband done to her to make her so frightened? He recalled what he'd heard the man say outside the door at the fairgrounds. But he'd thought them merely angry words. It wasn't until he'd seen the bruised area around Billie Rae's eye that he'd realized why she was so afraid of her husband.

Now he heard her pull on the T-shirt and lay back against the headboard.

He turned to look at her, jolted again by that strong emotion he'd felt under the lights of the exploding fireworks. Her face was lovely in the faint starlight. He couldn't imagine her ever looking more beautiful or desirable. Or vulnerable.

"Do you think you'll be able to sleep now?" he asked, starting to get to his feet, knowing what could happen if he stayed.

Her hand shot out and grabbed his wrist. He slowly sat back down.

There was a pleading in her brown eyes, along with flecks of gold.

"You want me to stay?"

She swallowed and he could see the battle going on inside her reflected in those big eyes. As he looked down, he saw that she'd taken off her wedding rings. There was a wide white mark where they had been.

He raised his gaze to her eyes again. "Slide over. I'll hold you until you fall asleep."

He saw relief, gratitude and something he didn't dare think about too long in those eyes.

She slid over and he lay down next to her. She moved closer as if desperately needing to know he was still there. He put his arms around her and drew her to him. She fit against him perfectly. He nestled his head against the pillow of her dark, luxurious hair and breathed in her scent. She smelled of soap and summer. He closed his eyes, feeling the steady beat of his heart in sync with hers.

"Thank you," she whispered. "I'm sorry that I—"

"Shh," he whispered. "I'll be here as long as you need me."

BILLIE RAE WOKE IN THE wee hours of the morning from a wonderful dream. She lay very still, keeping

her eyes closed as she tried to get back into the dream.
But it stayed just out of reach, slipping further away,
and she finally opened her eyes.

She thought she was at home, so when the horrible dread she always woke with settled over her, she
closed her eyes again, pleading silently for the dream
and the man in it who had made her feel so loved.
Like in the dream, the arms around her didn't hold
her as tightly as Duane's did. Tanner held her gently,
not as if he feared she would get away, but more like
he wanted to keep her safe.

With a start, she came fully awake. She *had* gotten
away from Duane.

Tanner shifted in his sleep and for a moment she
feared he would let her go. She had never met anyone
like him. She hadn't dated all that much before she
met Duane. In college, she'd had to get good grades to
keep her scholarships and still help her mother, who
had by then been diagnosed with cancer, so she'd had
no time for a social life.

She'd never been held this tenderly, never felt this
safe and secure, never felt…the emotions she was
experiencing at this moment—not even the first time
she'd gone to bed with Duane. He'd been disappointed
she wasn't a virgin and that had spoiled their lovemaking for both of them. After that, he was always
much rougher as if he was punishing her for losing
her virginity to the boy she'd dated all through high
school and thought she was in love with.

Scott had been a nice boy, but just that—a boy.

After high school, they'd gone to different colleges. They'd stayed in touch for a while, but had grown apart. Billie Rae had been thankful for that since she'd known by then that Scott wasn't the person she wanted to spend the rest of her life with.

She'd met Duane right after her mother died. Looking back, she saw that he had taken advantage of the vulnerable state she'd been in. She'd needed someone to lean on and Duane had made sure he was there, taking over her life, running it.

The problem was that when she no longer needed him in that way or wanted him to run her life, it was too late. By then, she'd needed and wanted something different from him. But Duane wasn't a giving, loving man. Nor was he going to let her go. He'd whisked her off to Vegas for a quickie marriage, selling it as romantic.

Hadn't she known that night, standing in a gaudy wedding chapel on the strip in front of a justice of the peace and his wife, that she was making a mistake? She remembered feeling as if she might faint. Duane had told her she just needed food and that he would feed her right after the ceremony.

Instead, they'd flown straight home as the sun came up and he'd sprung the news on her. They were moving to North Dakota.

Tanner shifted again in his sleep. Billie Rae held her breath, afraid he would awaken and leave her. A part of the dream returned, startling her because there was no doubt that the man in it had been Tanner Chisholm.

She sensed him coming awake and turned in his arms to face him. It was still dark out. In the faint starlight, she could see his bare chest, a light sprinkling of dark hair that formed a V disappear into the waistband of his jeans.

She met his gaze and felt a bubble form in her chest. Her heart began to beat faster.

He started to pull away, but she cupped his jaw and he froze. "Billie Rae—"

Her thumb moved to his lips and she shook her head, her gaze holding his. She hadn't felt desire in a long time. It felt raw and powerful and urgent. Under normal circumstances she would have never acted upon it with a man she hardly knew.

She brushed a lock of dark hair back from Tanner's wonderful face, feeling as if she knew him soul-deep. Her fingers tingled at the touch. By the time the sun set tomorrow there was a good chance Duane would have caught up with her and, if not killed her, definitely hurt her.

There were some things she couldn't live with. Duane was one of them. The other was not acting on what she was feeling at this moment, knowing it might be her last day alive.

Slowly, she leaned toward Tanner and brushed a kiss over his lips. Her pulse thundered in her ears as he gently drew her to him. His kiss was light as the summer breeze coming through the window. His hands came up to cup her face in his warm, callused palms.

Desire burned through her veins like a runaway train on a downhill track. As the kiss deepened, his fingers burrowed into her wild mane of hair. She shoved back the covers, needing to feel the warmth of his body against her, desperate for his human touch after months of flinching whenever Duane reached for her.

Tanner drew her to him, rolling over on his back and pulling her on top of him. "Are you sure about this?" he whispered.

She kissed him, sat up and then grabbing the hem of the large T-shirt, she pulled it up over her head and tossed it away. She heard Tanner moan, and then his hands were cupping her breasts, his thumbs gently teasing her nipples, which were already hard as marbles.

He drew her down again, kissing her softly. She rolled off him and wriggled out of her panties, desperately needing to feel his warm flesh against hers. She heard him slip out of his jeans and then he was pulling her into his arms. He brushed a tendril of hair back from her cheek.

Their eyes locked as he slowly and sweetly began to make love to her.

Chapter Three

Duane woke in his car, cramped and out of sorts. He couldn't believe he'd had to spend the entire night in a fairgrounds parking lot in the middle of nowhere.

As he climbed out, he looked into the front seat of his father's classic pickup, expecting to see Billie Rae curled up there. He'd been so sure she would return, probably with some cowboy with a can of gas for the pickup and some romantic ideas for her.

But he hadn't heard a sound all night and the pickup front seat was empty. No Billie Rae. With a curse, Duane realized he was going to have to call his boss and ask for some time off.

As for his wife, he didn't know what to do. First, he supposed, he would search for her himself. Someone had to have seen her. If that failed… Well, he might have to contact a couple of associates he'd met through his work. The nice thing about his job was that he met people who could and would do things for him that he'd rather not do himself. A little pressure here, a little pressure there, and people knew better than to say no to him.

He pulled out his cell phone, swearing under his breath as he punched in the number and asked for his boss. The last thing he'd do was admit the truth. He didn't want anyone to know what the bitch had done, how she'd made him look like a fool, let alone that he couldn't handle his own wife. He'd never live it down if his buddies found out about this. Other men lost respect for a man whose wife ran off on him.

No, he would take care of this himself and no one back home would be the wiser. That is, as long as he found Billie Rae fast. And one way or the other, he'd have to convince her never to pull something like this again. Either that or his lovely wife would end up dead, a terrible accident that would leave him a grieving widower—and free to find him a wife who knew her place.

He came up with a lame excuse, but his boss seemed to buy it. As he hung up, he told himself it was now time to deal with the mess Billie Rae had made. Walking around to the driver's side, Duane unlocked the pickup with his key and stared into it for a long moment, thinking about Billie Rae taking it. The truck had been his father's, purchased new almost fifty years before. His old man had loved this pickup and cared for it like a baby.

Hell, Duane had never even gotten to drive it until the old man died. His mother had been the one to give it to him—had his father known he was going to fall over dead with a heart attack he would have made other arrangements for his beloved classic pickup.

But Duane's mother hated the truck and resented the time and money and care the old man had put into it. She'd given it to Duane out of spite, knowing his father was now rolling over in his grave to think that his son had the truck. Which made Duane even angrier that Billie Rae had the impudence to take it. The woman must be crazy. No one drove this pickup but him.

As he slid behind the wheel, he saw that she'd left the key in the ignition and swore. Her lack of respect… He couldn't wait to get his hands on her.

He reached to turn the key and saw that it was the spare he kept locked up. She'd broken into his desk? He hadn't even been aware she knew where he kept the spare key.

Duane felt that strange chill creep over him again. Billie Rae had been watching him, paying more attention than he'd thought.

He turned the key. The engine refused to turn over. That's when he saw the gas gauge. She'd run out of gas. That's why she'd stopped here.

The tap on his side window startled him. For an instant, he'd expected to see Billie Rae standing there instead of some old guy in a plaid shirt and a baseball cap.

"Trouble getting her started?" the old man asked.

Duane realized the man must be the caretaker in charge of the fairgrounds. He hadn't heard him drive up. Duane climbed out, pocketing the truck key.

"The wife. She didn't check the gas gauge before she headed to the rodeo."

The old man laughed and shook his head. "I'm surprised you let her drive this. A 1962 Chevy Fleetside Shortbed with a Vortec 350, right?"

Duane nodded as he watched the caretaker run his hand over the hood. His old man had to be turning flips in his casket. He'd never let anyone touch his truck.

"You don't happen to have a few gallons of gas I could buy from you to get her into town, do you?" Duane asked.

"I haven't seen her around town," the man said frowning, still talking about the pickup. "You new to Whitehorse?"

So Whitehorse must be the closest town. "You could say that. If I had a hose, I could siphon some gas out of my car," Duane said impatiently.

"No need for that. I keep some extra gas for the lawnmower."

Duane followed the man back to a shed, waited while he unlocked the padlock on the door and went inside, returning with a small gas can that felt about half full.

"I'll bring this right back," he said, hoping the man wouldn't come with him. He hurried off, returning shortly, and handed the man the gas can and a twenty-dollar bill. "Thanks for your help." He had a thought. "Hey, is there any chance I could leave the pickup in one of your barns out here. My wife is tied up and I need to get back to her. I can't come back to get the truck for a while."

"No problem. You can just pull it in that one," the old man said pointing at the closest barn. "It will be plenty safe there until you can pick her up."

"Great," he started to turn away telling himself he had no choice since he couldn't drive two vehicles and who knew when he'd find Billie Rae. Nor did he want anyone else driving the truck.

"You're going to have to teach your wife to watch that gas gauge," the old man called after him with a chuckle.

He was going to have to teach his wife a lot of things when he found her.

"Good morning," Billie Rae said shyly from the kitchen doorway.

Tanner looked up. He'd been sitting at the kitchen table having a cup of coffee with Emma, who'd been chastising him.

He knew she was right. He'd fallen for a woman who was not just married—but in a very vulnerable state right now. He *should* have known better than to get more involved with her for not just his sake but hers as well.

When he met her gaze now, he was afraid he would see regret in her eyes. The morning light brought out the gold flecks in those eyes. With relief, he saw that they were free of regret. Their eyes locked and, after a moment, a slight flush came to her cheeks before she looked away.

They'd made love and fallen back to sleep in each other's arms. When he'd awakened this morning, she'd looked so beautiful and so serene lying there, he hadn't wanted to wake her.

He looked down into his coffee cup now, checking his expression as he felt Emma's watchful gaze on him. She'd already given him hell, telling him that she couldn't bear to see him get his heart broken and Billie Rae wasn't ready for another relationship.

"Sleep well?" Emma asked smiling as she handed Billie Rae a mug of coffee.

"Yes, thank you," Billie Rae said dropping her gaze and blushing as she took the mug and sat down in a chair across from Tanner.

Tanner smiled across the table at her. She looked a hundred percent better than she had last night at the rodeo. There was no longer that deer-in-the-head-lights look in her eyes. Her long dark hair was still damp from her shower. He caught a whiff of her now too-familiar scent. She smelled heavenly. He couldn't help but think about their lovemaking and wish he had awakened her this morning.

Emma refilled his coffee cup, giving him another of her knowing looks. This one held a warning he couldn't ignore. He knew making love with Billie Rae shouldn't have happened. Legally, she was a married woman. But to his way of thinking, Duane had broken the vows, destroying that fragile thing that made a marriage.

He knew Emma was worried about him getting too close to Billie Rae and getting his heart broken. But he wondered if it wasn't already too late. Damned if he would ever regret what had happened between them, no matter what today brought. He didn't kid himself. He knew that Duane was still out there looking for Billie Rae—and that she knew it as well. Whatever was going to transpire between them, it wasn't over yet.

Emma kept up a cheerful chatter as she and the cook, Celeste, served homemade pancakes with huckleberry syrup. Tanner watched Billie Rae put away a dozen of the silver-dollar-sized cakes, smiling to himself. A good appetite was a sure sign that she was bouncing back.

"She doesn't want to hear any of this," Tanner said after Emma told a particularly funny story she'd heard about him as a boy. Billie Rae was smiling, looking relaxed, looking as if she belonged in this kitchen.

"I wish you'd gotten a chance to meet my husband Hoyt," Emma was saying. "He could tell you some stories about his boys. But Hoyt's off digging fence post holes with Tanner's brothers."

Hoyt hadn't been home last night when Tanner and Marshall returned from the rodeo with Billie Rae. Tanner's father, according to Emma, had been at a ranchers' association meeting about some rustlers operating across the border in Wyoming.

It was odd, though, that Hoyt had already taken off so early this morning. Tanner hadn't even seen him before he left. His father had been putting in long hours recently, almost as if avoiding home.

He frowned at the thought and hoped everything was all right between his father and Emma. He and his brothers hadn't been happy when their father had sprung a new wife on them. But once they'd been around Emma for five minutes, they too had fallen in love with her.

Tanner was told she was nothing like Hoyt's other wives. He'd been too young to remember Laura, his father's first wife. She'd drowned in a boating accident. Tasha, his father's second wife, Tanner had heard was killed by a runaway horse.

A third wife, Krystal, had disappeared shortly after Hoyt had brought her to the ranch. Tanner vaguely remembered her. After all that tragedy, his father had gone years without a woman in his life.

Then, out of the blue, he'd come home with Emma. She was older, closer to Hoyt's age, more full-figured, redheaded and had a fiery temper that had earned her respect from all of the men in the family. She'd changed things around here, but in a good way. And Tanner had never seen his father happier. Until recently, when he seemed to be avoiding being home.

"What would you like to do first this morning?" he asked Billie Rae after breakfast.

"Is there a pawnshop or jewelry store in White-horse?"

Tanner shook his head. "But there are several in Havre. I'd be happy to drive you."

"No, I couldn't possibly ask you—"

"You didn't ask. I'm volunteering, unless you need to go back to the fairgrounds for your vehicle?"

"The pickup I was driving isn't mine."

"Then I guess we don't need to worry about it."

She nodded but he saw the dark cloud move over her eyes. She had a lot to worry about. They both did. She was worried about Duane, and Tanner was worried that this woman who had come crashing into his life would leave it just as suddenly.

"It's a nice drive to Havre," he said. "We'll have lunch and shop for whatever you need. I could use the day off, but don't tell my stepmother."

Emma swatted him as she passed.

Billie Rae nodded, tears in her eyes. "You have all been so kind. I really wish—"

"No regrets." Emma stopped next to her chair to lay a hand on her shoulder. "No tears, either, not on such a beautiful morning," she said. "You two best get goin'. Make sure Billie Rae gets whatever she needs in Havre." Emma pressed a wad of cash into Tanner's hand along with another silent warning look.

He was to make sure nothing happened to Billie Rae and that he didn't make things worse for her—as if he hadn't already.

"We'll be fine," he told his stepmother. He had a

shotgun in his pickup, and this morning he'd put a pistol under the seat. He wasn't taking any chances—he'd already done that last night.

SHERIFF MCCALL CRAWFORD looked up to find a young woman standing in front of her desk.

"There wasn't anyone out front," the teenager said, looking nervous. She was slightly built, though tall and regal in appearance. Her straight shoulder-length hair was white blond, her eyes a clear, disarming blue. She had a pretty face that belied how young she really was, since on closer inspection McCall realized she was no more than a girl, probably not even out of high school.

"Can I help you?" McCall asked the girl.

"*You're* the sheriff?" She glanced at the open door and the name stenciled on it. "I thought the sheriff's name was Winchester?"

"I recently got married." It had been more than a year and a half, but McCall was wondering why she'd bothered to change her name, since everyone in town still called her Sheriff Winchester. "Why don't you have a seat and tell me what seems to be the problem."

"It's my aunt, Aggie Wells," the girl said as she pulled up one of the orange plastic chairs across from McCall's desk and sat down. "She's missing."

"How long has she been missing?"

"Several weeks now."

Several weeks? "Why have you waited this long to

report her missing, Miss…? I'm sorry, I didn't catch your name."

"Cindy Ross. My aunt is gone a lot with her job. But this time she didn't call or come home."

"Where is home?"

"Phoenix, Arizona. That's where I live with my father."

"And your aunt?"

"She stays with us when she's in town. Like I said, she travels a lot but she calls me every few days from wherever she is and always calls on Sunday."

"So you haven't heard from her since…"

"The second week of May, that Sunday. She called to say she would be flying home that afternoon."

"Called from…?"

"Here. Whitehorse. She said she was driving to Billings, leaving her rental car and would be coming in on the last flight. I was to pick her up but she wasn't on the plane."

"And there has been no word?"

"No. My dad said something must have come up with her job." The girl looked down in her lap. "But when I called her office, they said she'd been fired a long time ago." She looked up, tears in her eyes. "I'm afraid something has happened to her."

"What does your father think?" The girl met her gaze, but didn't respond. "He doesn't know you're here, does he?"

"He says Aggie can take care of herself and that she'll turn up. But I have a bad feeling…"

McCall didn't like the sound of any of this. She picked up her pen. "Your aunt's name is Aggie Wells?"

"Agatha, but she's always gone by Aggie. She's an insurance investigator. That is, she was."

"What was she doing in Whitehorse?"

"She said she was trying to prove that some man murdered all three of his wives."

McCall's head shot up from taking notes.

The girl nodded knowingly. "I thought you might know about the cases. The man's name is Hoyt Chisholm. Aggie told me that he killed his first three wives and now he has married again. Her last appointment was with him and his new wife. She said they'd invited her out to their house for supper."

McCall was unable to hide her surprise. Everyone in town knew about the deaths of Hoyt's first two wives, and the disappearance of the third one.

The recent scuttlebutt throughout the county was about his new wife. McCall had heard that some residents were taking odds over at Whitehorse Café, betting how long this wife would be alive.

"My aunt told me that if anything happened to her, I was to make sure that Hoyt Chisholm didn't get away with another murder." The girl burst into tears. "I know he killed her."

BILLIE RAE FOUND HERSELF enjoying more than the ride to Havre. Tanner pointed out landmarks and told her stories. She knew he was trying to keep her entertained, to distract her from thinking about her life and Duane.

But the one thing she couldn't stop thinking about, sitting this close to Tanner, was last night. He had been so tender, so heartbreakingly sweet. She had cried after they'd made love.

"What is it?" Tanner had asked, sounding stricken.

How could she tell him that she felt she'd ruined her life by marrying Duane? That she'd lost her chance to be with someone like Tanner. Duane was going to kill her. Or at the very least, have her living in fear and on the run the rest of her life.

She could never be with Tanner again. As it was, she feared she had already put him and his family in danger.

"I forgot what happiness feels like," she had finally choked out. He'd held her and she'd spooned against him, relishing the warmth of his body and the way this man made her feel, dreading when the sun would come up and she would have to leave him.

"That's the town of Wagner down there," Tanner said now, pointing at the few buildings left. It appeared most of the towns along the Hi-Line were shrinking, some little more than a sign and a couple of old buildings.

"Butch Cassidy and the Sundance Kid held up a train not far from here," he said. "It was allegedly their last robbery before they headed to South America."

The day had dawned clear blue, sunny and warm. The land was a brilliant spring-green and, with the windows down, the air blowing in smelled of summer. It was the kind of day she remembered from when she was a girl and still had her illusions about life.

Billie Rae breathed in the sweet scents, catching a hint of Tanner's masculine one. When she was with him, she felt her strength coming back. Duane had done his best to beat it out of her. She was almost surprised that she could feel like her old self. But Tanner reminded her of who she'd been. Who she could be again—except for Duane who was determined to kill every ounce of independence in her.

She tried not to think about where he was or what he was doing. She knew he would be furious wherever he was. Just as she knew he would be frantically looking for her and wouldn't stop until he found her.

She shuddered at the thought.

"Warm enough?" Tanner asked, noticing.

"Someone just walked over my grave." She regretted the quick retort immediately. "You know what I mean."

"I do," he said and quickly pointed out an old Spanish mission on the road ahead. She was glad he didn't mention Duane, but neither of them had forgotten about him, she knew. She'd caught Tanner checking the rearview mirror occasionally—just as she had been doing in the side mirror.

Duane would not give up. She just had to make sure

he never found her—or learned that Tanner Chisholm had been the one who'd saved her last night.

Hopefully Duane would also never learn about this trip to Havre. She hated involving Tanner Chisholm in the mess she'd made of her life any more than she already had. But she needed to sell the rings. Hopefully she could get enough to buy an old car and enough gas to put a whole lot more distance between herself and Duane before she found a job.

"You're going to have to deal with him, you know," Tanner said as if realizing she hadn't been listening about the old mission they'd just passed.

Billie Rae nodded. "I'm sorry. I just can't help thinking about him."

"How long have you been married?"

"Six months. We met in Oklahoma, where I was teaching kindergarten. Right after we eloped, Duane sprung it on me that he'd gotten a job in Williston, North Dakota, and we had to move at once. I didn't even get to finish the school year."

"You had friends in Oklahoma?"

She nodded. "I lost track of them once we got to North Dakota. Duane made sure of that. It's hard to accept that I'm the classic case. The abused wife. But Duane wasn't like this when we were dating. He was…" She let her voice trail off. "That's not true. The signs were there. He was controlling but I wanted to believe it was because he cared and just wanted what was best for me, like he said." She laughed at that. "I was such a fool."

"We've all been fools," Tanner said. "Myself included. But you realized your mistake and got away from him."

If only it were that simple.

"You don't know my husb…Duane," she said. She couldn't bear to call him her husband anymore. She hadn't only left him, hadn't merely taken off her wedding rings. In her heart she was no longer Duane Rasmussen's wife, and last night with Tanner she'd felt like a free woman, even though she'd only been kidding herself.

Under the law, she was still Duane Rasmussen's wife. Only technically, she thought, because there was no love in her heart for him. When had she stopped loving him? She didn't know. Just as she didn't know when she'd begun to hate him.

"He's…dangerous," she said, thinking that was putting it mildly.

Tanner let out a dismissive sound. "Only to a woman who can't fight back."

She shook her head. "He carries a gun, he kills people." And when he caught her, she wouldn't be the first person he killed in a rage. "Duane's a cop."

Chapter Four

It hadn't taken long for Sheriff McCall Crawford to verify what Cindy Ross had told her. Agatha "Aggie" Wells hadn't used her plane ticket—nor had she returned her rental car—a white SUV. Aggie had also been fired from the insurance company seven years ago.

"Can I be honest with you, Sheriff?" Wells's supervisor asked.

"Please."

"Aggie was one of our best. She was relentless. But something happened with this Chisholm case. Once she found out another of his other wives had died and a third had disappeared, she became obsessed. I'm afraid that for her the case became almost…well, personal."

"Personal in what way?"

The supervisor cleared his throat. "I know this is going to sound crazy, but at one point I thought she had fallen in love with Hoyt Chisholm. See what I mean? Crazy, huh? It made no sense. If she really believed he'd killed his first two wives for the insurance money, and possibly the third wife who disappeared, then she wouldn't fall for the guy, right?"

McCall knew that crazier things had happened.

"Aggie just got so worked up when she talked about him, and even when she was pulled off the case, she continued to work on it in her spare time. Now, that's…scary."

Yes, McCall thought. And possibly dangerous.

"I take it she was never able to find any evidence that Mr. Chisholm had anything to do with the deaths or disappearance of his wives?" she asked.

"No evidence at all. Maybe that's what drove her so crazy. I finally had to let her go. May I ask why you're inquiring about her?"

"Apparently she hasn't given up on proving that Mr. Chisholm's guilty," McCall said. "She was in Whitehorse a couple of weeks ago and she met with the Chisholms."

"Chisholms?"

"Mr. Chisholm has remarried." McCall heard the heavy silence on the other end of the line and felt her concern growing.

"I have to tell you, I am very disturbed she is still apparently looking into this, and now with a new wife…"

"If you know something—"

"I probably shouldn't have said as much as I have," the supervisor said, clearly backpedaling. "Like I said, it was just a feeling. Aggie took her job very seriously. Quite frankly, I think she might…no, never mind."

"If there is something else you need to tell me, please do. It's important that I know everything. The reason I called you is because Aggie Wells has disappeared. She had called her niece to pick her up at the airport the day after she had dinner with the Chisholms, but never arrived. Nor has she used her plane ticket or returned her rental car."

"Let me guess. Aggie told her niece that if anything happened to her to contact law enforcement because Hoyt Chisholm would have killed her, right?"

"Yes, as a matter of fact."

"She insisted the same memo be put in her employee file here," the supervisor said. "We all thought she was just being paranoid, but what if Aggie was right? What if Hoyt Chisholm killed his three other wives and now plans to kill the fourth one as well?"

THE RINGS BROUGHT LESS MONEY than Billie Rae had hoped.

"The diamond is flawed," one jeweler told her.

She had argued that Duane had told her how much he paid.

"I'm sorry but there isn't any way your husband paid that kind of money for this," the last pawn broker said handing back the ring.

Tanner had driven her to all of the jewelry stores and pawnshops in town. He had waited in his pickup while she'd gone inside, as she'd asked him to. For that she was thankful because the experience had been humiliating. They'd all told her the same thing.

Duane had lied about what he'd spent on the rings. She realized he'd probably picked them up from a pawnshop to begin with or gotten them from one of the criminal types he loved to intimidate. Duane enjoyed the benefits that came with being a cop— those being throwing his weight around and flashing his badge to get what he wanted.

"What will you give me for the rings?" she asked the owner of the last place in town. When he told her, she had nodded, fighting tears of both discouragement and anger. Duane had lied to her from day one.

She knew that shouldn't have come as a surprise, the way their married life had turned out. But by the time she pocketed the small amount of cash she could get for the rings, she no longer had any illusions about the man she'd married.

"You all right?" Tanner asked as she slid into the truck seat next to him.

She gave him the best smile she could muster.

He laughed. "Stupid question. Let's get some lunch. There's a great Chinese food place here in the mall. You like Chinese?"

She knew she shouldn't spend any more time with him. While she couldn't imagine how Duane could have somehow followed them to Havre, she knew the longer she was around Tanner, the more she was putting him in danger.

"You have to eat," he said as if seeing her hesitation.

She nodded, hating the thought of the time that would come when she would have to tell him goodbye. "And then can we see if we can find me a used vehicle?" she asked as he started the truck and pulled out into the traffic.

He glanced over at her, but said nothing.

They ate at the Chinese buffet, finishing up with the fried donuts. Tanner was amusing during their lunch, telling stories about growing up on the ranch with five brothers.

Billie Rae looked around the restaurant. It had been so long since she'd felt normal. Sitting across from Tanner, she was able to eat without her stomach knotting up in fear that she would say the wrong thing and ruin it. With Duane she was seldom able to finish a meal without him getting upset and upsetting her in return.

"I saw you looking at that guy over there," Duane would say under his breath.

"What guy? Duane—"

"If you do it again, I'm going to go over there and punch him in the face, you understand?"

Tears welled in her eyes now at the memory of those horrible nights they would leave a restaurant, her in tears and Duane becoming more worked up by the minute. Billie Rae had known what was going to happen long before they got home, and she was never wrong.

Tanner reached across the table and put his hand over hers. "Billie Rae?"

She swallowed and wiped at her eyes with her free hand. "I'm sorry."

"He can't find you here. He has no idea where you are."

She nodded. Tanner didn't remove his hand. She didn't, either. She loved the feel of his large, callused hands. In his long fingers she felt a wonderful strength that seemed to flow into her. She thought of those hands exploring her naked body last night and remembered that feeling of both pleasure and sadness.

Billie Rae knew she would forever ache for his touch. As she looked across the table at this wonderful cowboy, her regret was that she would never see him again after today, let alone make love with him again. It was a regret she thought she couldn't bear to live with.

She realized Tanner was waiting for her to say more. He actually wanted to hear what she was feeling? "I was just thinking how nice this is, having lunch with you."

"I was thinking the same thing," he said and squeezed her hand gently before letting go.

She felt that well of happiness that she'd experienced last night after they made love. She was happy. The word almost seemed alien to her because she hadn't let herself admit how unhappy she'd been for so long.

Billie Rae had gone into marriage believing it really was until death do you part. She just hadn't known that those words had a totally different meaning for the man she married.

"I love hearing the stories about you growing up on the ranch," she said.

"Where did you grow up?"

She told him about being an only child, her father dying when he was young and her mother raising her in a small house in Oklahoma City.

"My life was very dull compared to yours," she said. "I wish I'd had brothers who tried to talk me into jumping off the barn roof."

"Sure you do," he said with a laugh.

"So you're all adopted?" She loved listening to him talk about his big family. Billie Rae had always dreamed of a large family as a girl. She wanted the noise, the activity, the feeling at night of all of them under the same roof.

"Yep, Dad likes kids. He adopted three when his first wife was alive. When three more kids needed a home, he was right there to take us. He would have taken more if he'd had better luck with wives." Tanner seemed to realize what he'd said. He stammered, "What I meant was—"

"It's all right."

"No, you need to understand. Two of his wives died. Another...disappeared. Emma, well, he married her recently after being alone for years. He's had a rough time of it. But I've never seen him happier."

"You're trying to tell me there is life after marriage?"

"Yep. And there is no shame in getting it wrong—and getting out."

She smiled across the table at him. He had no idea how impossible Duane would make that. There was only one way she feared she would be leaving Duane and that, as he told her many times, would be in a body bag.

"Emma is wonderful," she said, refusing to let Duane ruin this lunch. "I'm happy for your father. If he is anything like you…" Billie Rae ducked her head, embarrassed because she'd again thought of lying in his arms last night. But talking to Tanner was so easy. She could be honest with him without fear that what she said would set him off.

This closeness she felt with this man both warmed—and frightened her. It was too tempting to take him up on his offer to stay at the ranch and try to handle the Duane problem through legal channels.

But Billie Rae had already tried that. Tanner didn't know what Duane was capable of. She did.

After lunch, they stopped at one of the few used car lots in town and Billie Rae realized quickly that she wasn't going to get much of a vehicle and still have gas money to leave town.

"You can't run far enough, if that's what you're thinking," Tanner said as they walked around the last lot. "Sometimes you have to draw a line in the sand and fight. Come back to the ranch with me. I'll help you. You'll be safe. You shouldn't have to do this alone. I promise. I won't let anything happen to you."

He reached over and took her hand, squeezing it gently, and she was reminded of last night when he had pulled her through the rodeo crowd and kept Duane from catching up to them.

Tanner pulled her to a stop and turned her to face him. "There is something I have to tell you. Last night when I saw you," he said as if he too had been remembering when they'd met. "You're going to think I'm crazy, but it was love at first sight. It wasn't that I saw this beautiful woman and fell in love. I felt this strong connection as if you were some missing part of me, and when I saw you it was like this jolt…" He stopped and looked embarrassed.

She cupped his strong jaw with her free hand and smiled as she looked into his eyes. "I don't think you're crazy. I felt it too."

"Then come back with me—"

"I can't. If you knew Duane you would understand. I have to go. I have no choice." Her heart ached at the thought of never seeing him again. But if she wanted to protect him, she *had* to leave. Whatever had happened between them, she couldn't put Tanner and his family in jeopardy any more than she already had because of her bad decision to marry Duane and then make a wild run across the Hi-Line.

"At least think about it?"

She'd nodded, but she knew she couldn't change her mind—even as much as she wanted to.

At the cheapest car lot, Billie Rae bought a small beat-up old car that seemed to run fine and got good gas mileage. She paid cash but the owner of the lot still needed her to fill out paperwork—all traceable when you have a cop on your tail.

"I'm going to need some identification," he said as he pushed the papers across the desk toward her. "Your driver's license," he said when she gave him what he took for a blank look. "I need to make a copy of it."

"I lost my purse," she said.

"Then I can't sell you the car until I have—"

"Put the car in my name," Tanner said and placed a hand on Billie Rae's shoulder before she could stop him. "It's better that way," he said to her after the owner had gone to make copies of Tanner's driver's license. "Duane won't know, right?"

She nodded numbly, thinking this would make what she had to do all that more difficult. Tanner had saved her last night in more ways than she wanted to admit and now here he was saving a woman he didn't really know again.

Billie Rae said as much to him and he laughed.

"I feel as if I've always known you," he said, and she thought he might be right. Sometimes she caught him looking at her as if he could see into her soul.

They *had* connected last night at the rodeo. She'd

felt it and yet even now she denied the feelings for so many reasons. How could she trust her emotions right now? She couldn't. Not to mention she was on the run from her husband.

But Billie Rae knew the real reason she had to ignore what she was feeling was because it scared her. Tanner was the man she'd dreamed of marrying. She'd loved being on the ranch with his family. It only made her feel worse about marrying Duane. She'd ruined her life and now the best she felt she could expect was to keep her husband from killing her.

"I can't go back with you to the ranch," she told Tanner as they walked out to the car she'd bought. "I won't put your family in any more danger than I already have. I got myself into this. I'll get myself out."

"Billie Rae—"

She put a finger to his lips and felt a frisson of pleasure course through her from just touching those lips. She shook her head, afraid of what she might say. Or worse, do. If only she could just lose herself in him again. To be in his arms...

He leaned in and kissed her, and it took all of her strength not to throw her arms around his neck and let him take her back to the ranch, back to a life she had only dreamed possible, where she was safe and loved.

"I wish there was something I could say or do to keep you from doing this," he said as he drew back.

"But I wouldn't force you even if I could. If you ever need me, though…"

Billie Rae had to fight tears. "Thank you for everything."

He pulled her to him, hugging her quickly as he whispered, "Be safe, Billie Rae." He stepped back. "Chisholm ranch will always be here if you're ever passing through again."

She realized then that he'd known she wouldn't be going back to the ranch with him. As she drove away, she tried not to look back. When she did, though, she saw Tanner standing beside the ranch truck watching her.

The look on his face seemed to say he knew there was little chance he would see her again. At least not alive.

Chapter Five

Emma Chisholm looked up to see the sheriff's SUV pull into the yard. At first she thought it was her stepson Colton's fiancée, Deputy Halley Robinson, stopping by, but the woman who climbed out wasn't familiar.

Going to the front door, she pushed open the screen and stepped out onto the porch. She hadn't been locking the doors for almost a week now—not since she finally felt confident Aggie Wells wouldn't be coming back.

Emma had just started feeling safe again. She'd noticed that Hoyt, though, was keeping his distance as if he really believed there was a curse on him and that Emma was doomed to die as well.

She couldn't bear the thought that he might regret marrying her. They'd been so happy. She thought of Hoyt tempting her up into the hayloft of the barn and their lovemaking. They'd proven that age didn't matter when it came to love and desire. Emma ached for her husband and had been determined to be patient with him. Once he realized that Aggie Wells was gone and that there was no stupid curse…or worse, that she might think for a moment he had anything to do with his wives' deaths…

Now, though, Emma felt her heart drop as she saw that the woman was the local sheriff. She'd heard that Whitehorse had a woman sheriff, but she hadn't heard how young and beautiful she was.

"Good afternoon, Sheriff," she said brightly as the woman flashed her credentials.

"I'm Sheriff McCall Crawford. You must be Emma."

"I am." Emma took her hand, amused by the surprise she'd seen on the young woman's face. Apparently the sheriff had been expecting Hoyt's new wife to be a trophy wife—not a short, plump redhead.

"I'd like to talk to you. Is your husband home?"

"No." Emma felt the first inkling of real anxiety. "Is something wrong?"

"I just need to ask you a few questions. When do you expect Mr. Chisholm to return?"

"He's working on the other side of the ranch. I don't expect him until late tonight. You know summer, with all this daylight, the men work late."

Emma realized she was doing too much explaining, giving away just how nervous she was. "Won't you come in, Sheriff? As they say, coffee is always on at any decent rancher's house. Why don't you join me for a cup back in the kitchen?"

The sheriff followed her to the kitchen and took a seat at the table while Emma set about getting the coffee and dishing up some of her freshly baked oatmeal cake that was still warm.

"Mrs. Chisholm—"

"Please, call me Emma," she said as she placed a brimming mug of coffee and a plate of warm cake in front of the sheriff. "Cream, Sheriff?"

"No, thank you."

Emma sat down across the table from the sheriff and, lifting her mug of coffee, studied the woman through the steam as she tried to still her raging nerves. "Something tells me this isn't a social call."

"Actually, I'm looking for Aggie Wells."

She knew the sheriff was also looking for a reaction and hoped to give her one she wasn't expecting. "A delightful woman. We had her to supper a couple of weeks ago."

"I heard that."

"Oh? Aggie told you, then." So the woman hadn't left town as Emma had hoped. Then why hadn't they heard from her? Because Aggie had been waiting until she had enough evidence to involve the sheriff?

"No, actually, her niece mentioned it. Apparently Ms. Wells is missing."

Emma put down her mug very carefully. The feeling of finally being safe evaporated like sun-kissed dew on the morning grass. "I'm sorry to hear that."

"I was hoping you might have heard from her."

"No, but then I didn't expect to."

McCall raised a brow. "Your business was completed with Ms. Wells?"

Emma laughed and helped herself to the cake. "I wouldn't say we had business together. I'm sure you know that Aggie Wells used to work for an insurance company. Apparently once she started a case, she had a hard time quitting until she was completely satisfied."

"And was she finally satisfied?" the sheriff asked.

"I think she was." Emma took a bite of the cake, closed her eyes and let it melt in her mouth. "Mmm." She opened her eyes and chuckled. "Sorry, but I do love this cake when it is still warm."

"You baked it?" McCall asked, glancing around the kitchen. "You don't have help?"

"Oh, yes, but I can't stay out of the kitchen. I love to cook and bake. It's a flaw." She felt the sheriff studying her, no doubt wondering about her other flaws. "The cook won't come in until later. It's the housekeeper's day off."

"When was the last time you saw Aggie Wells?"

"The night she came here for supper," Emma said, her heart in her throat. The sheriff wouldn't be here unless something had happened to Aggie. She couldn't help but think about her first reaction to the woman. She'd thought they could have been friends under other circumstances.

"Did she say where she was going when she left your house?"

"No. But since we didn't hear from her again, we assumed she'd left town."

"Do you know where Ms. Wells was staying?"

"No. I met her for a drink, though, out at Sleeping Buffalo." Emma could see that the sheriff was taken aback by how forthcoming she was being.

"Did anyone see you there together?"

She studied the sheriff for a moment, wondering if she didn't believe her—or if she was just looking for someone who might know how to find Aggie Wells.

"Just the bartender. A female." She described the woman, and the sheriff nodded as if she knew her.

"Mind if I ask what you talked about?"

"She informed me of her suspicions concerning my husband."

McCall had been in the middle of sipping her coffee but quickly put it down. "You weren't aware of your husband's past before then?"

"No, actually. I hadn't cared. I knew he'd been married and that he'd lost several wives. I love my husband, Sheriff. I trust him and I know he couldn't kill anyone."

McCALL HAD JUST GOTTEN back to her office and was sitting at her desk when she looked up to find a large man standing in her doorway.

His expression quickly changed from a slight frown to a smile as she greeted him.

"Sheriff Crawford," he said, stepping forward to extend his hand. His handshake was a little too firm, his smile a little too bright.

McCall instantly didn't trust him.

"My name is Officer Duane Rasmussen." He flashed his badge.

"May I see that?" she asked as he started to put it away. She could tell he didn't like being questioned even for something like this as he slowly handed her his shield.

She studied it and handed it back. "What brings a police officer from Williston, North Dakota, to Whitehorse, Montana?"

"It's a delicate matter," the cop said as he closed the door, pulled out a chair and sat down without being invited to. He leaned toward her, the smile this time self-deprecating.

He was good looking in the way a lot of ex high school football players are. She took him for a college linebacker who'd managed to stay in good shape, probably through hours in a gym.

"I'm looking for someone," he said.

She waited, knowing that if this was a professional investigation he would have come through normal channels and she would already be aware of the suspect through a bulletin.

This cop was off the leash.

"This is embarrassing," he said and did his best to look bashful. "It's my wife. She's not well. I'm worried about her. She took off without even her purse."

"What makes you think she's in Whitehorse?"

"I found my pickup at the fairgrounds where she'd run out of gas."

McCall lifted a brow. "She didn't take her own car?"

Some of his smooth veneer fell away. "She doesn't have her own car. She doesn't like to drive."

Alarms were going off all over the place for McCall. She didn't like this guy, was suspicious of his entire story and could see that he knew it.

"I was just hoping that you might have heard something that would help me find her," he said, looking as if he wished he hadn't come by to talk to her.

"What is your wife's name?"

"Billie Rae Rasmussen. But she could be going by her maiden name, Johnson."

McCall nodded and took down the cop's name and his wife's. "I'm sorry. I haven't heard anything, but I will keep an eye out for your wife. I'm surprised, if you're that worried about her, that you haven't put out an APB on her."

"I was hoping that wouldn't be necessary since I don't want to upset her. I just want to get her help. We've been trying to have a baby. I'm afraid she went a little berserk after this last disappointment."

"I'll need a description of your wife."

He pulled her picture from his shirt pocket.

McCall looked at the studio shot of the woman standing next to the man sitting across from her. The woman was small and pretty with a wild mane of dark curly hair and warm brown eyes. The sheriff asked for a more detailed description, jotted it down and handed the photo back.

"You have a number I can reach you?" McCall asked.

He gave her his cell phone number. "My wife is in a very…fragile state. I hate the thought of her out there somewhere…"

McCall nodded, wondering about the pretty dark-haired young woman in the photograph he'd shown her. There'd been something in the woman's eyes.…

He rose to his feet. She could tell he hadn't got whatever he'd come here for and doubted it was information about his wife. "Thanks for your time, Sheriff." He said the last word with just enough emphasis to let her know what he thought of a woman sheriff.

She watched him leave, worried about his wife. McCall had come across his type before. But in this one, she sensed fury below the surface. This was a dangerous man, and she suspected the wife knew it and that's why she'd run.

After Officer Duane Rasmussen left her office,

McCall told her deputies to be on the lookout for Billie Rae Johnson Rasmussen.

Now she had two missing women—one of them the wife of a cop, the other an obsessed insurance investigator after a man she believed had committed three murders.

McCall was thinking about that when her phone rang. "Sheriff Crawford," she said distractedly.

"I just found that vehicle you put the alert out on, the white SUV rental the missing woman was driving," a local highway patrolman told her. "It's down in the trees beside the Milk River, about ten miles north of town on River Road."

The same road as the one that went to the Chisholm Cattle Company ranch.

"The driver's side door is standing open, the keys are still in the ignition and there's a purse, the contents spilled on the ground nearby," the officer was saying. "No sign of the occupant."

"I'll be right there," McCall said and headed for her patrol car.

BILLIE RAE FILLED UP the car with gas, bought a map of Montana and tried to anticipate what Duane would do once he realized she wasn't coming back to his dad's old pickup.

From Havre, she had few options. She couldn't head north to Canada. Even if Duane didn't have the border patrol looking for her, he could find out if she'd crossed. She could head southwest to Great Falls. Or she could keep going west across the Montana Hi-Line toward Glacier Park. Either way she chose would be two-lane blacktop for miles.

Nor could she catch a commercial flight even if she had the money until she reached a much larger city, which would be several hours away minimum.

She still wasn't sure what she was going to do until she reached the junction on the outskirts of Havre and found herself turning south toward Great Falls.

Billie Rae had to fight the feeling that no matter which way she went, Duane would find her and it would all end the same way. So why run at all? Why not just turn around and go back?

Just the thought of Tanner kept her going down the highway. For so long she'd devalued herself, thinking she deserved everything Duane was dishing out. But Tanner Chisholm had made her feel whole again.

She prayed that Duane would never learn that Tanner and his family had helped her. She'd actually considered leaving some kind of trail so Duane would follow her and leave them alone.

This made her laugh. Duane didn't need a trail of breadcrumbs to find her. He could get the help of any law enforcement department. That's if he couldn't find her himself.

When she glanced in the rearview mirror, her heart lodged in her throat. No need to leave a trail. Duane had already found her.

A large black car came racing up behind her. She couldn't see the driver's face behind the glare on the dark windshield, and the car was too close for her to see the license plate. But her thundering pulse told her it was Duane.

She turned back to her driving. With growing panic, she saw that she was partway off the highway and headed for the ditch. She swerved back into her lane and glanced back again.

The driver of the black car swerved around her, sitting on the horn as the car zoomed past. She caught only a glimpse of the irate woman behind the wheel.

Billie Rae tried to catch her breath. Her heart was pounding and she felt sick to her stomach. That *could* have been Duane.

But it hadn't been. She was still free. Still safe. But for how long?

As she drove through the wide-open country, finally picking up the Missouri River as it cut a deep path through the state, she knew she had to come up with a plan.

She'd go as far as she could on what little money she had, then she would find a job, get an apartment and work until she had enough money to move on.

The hardest part would be establishing a new identity. She needed a social security number to go with that new identity. Or a job where she was paid cash and no questions were asked.

But she was determined. Tanner Chisholm had shown her what her life could be like with a loving, caring man. She desperately wanted that. The thought made her ache because she knew there was only one Tanner Chisholm and she'd just left him.

As the miles whizzed past and no sign of Duane's large black car coming up fast behind her, she was almost starting to relax a little when the right back tire blew.

Chapter Six

Stopping by the local sheriff's office had been a mistake. Duane had expected some country sheriff who would sympathize with his dilemma. If he'd known Whitehorse had a female sheriff he wouldn't have bothered.

Bitches always stuck together.

He'd driven into Whitehorse, which was the closest town to the fairgrounds, so he assumed that was where Billie Rae had gone. One of the locals had to have given her a ride. It stuck in his craw that someone had helped her. Maybe a woman. He swore under his breath. More than likely, though, it had been a man—possibly that cowboy he'd seen with his wife at the rodeo.

Whitehorse had turned out to be one of those small Western towns that dotted the Hi-Line of Montana. The towns had sprung up when the railroad came through. Many of them, like Whitehorse, had a main drag of brick buildings facing the tracks. Apparently in Whitehorse, though, they'd recently had a fire, because there was a gaping hole between two of the buildings.

After talking to the sheriff, Duane knew he now had to find Billie Rae before the local law did. Billie Rae couldn't have gotten far—not without any money or wheels.

But someone had helped her. Where would she have spent the night? In a local church? Do-gooders often put up the poor, helpless sorts who arrived in town without a car or food or money.

He was counting on her still being in Whitehorse. Sure, someone would be nice enough to give her a ride that far, but no farther since the closest towns were Glasgow, an hour away to the east back toward Williston and North Dakota, and Havre, an hour-and-a-half away to the west. The only other option was Canada, about fifty miles to the north.

He couldn't see her heading back the way she'd come, toward North Dakota. If she'd left town, she would either go north toward Canada or west toward Glacier Park.

But he still thought she hadn't gotten that far yet. Even if she'd talked someone into giving her a ride, this was a small town. Somebody would have seen her. All he had to do was ask the right people.

TANNER HAD GOTTEN BACK from Havre too late. By the time he'd reached the fairgrounds, there was no sign of the old pickup Billie Rae said she'd escaped from her husband in—nor of the black Lincoln she'd said her husband had been driving.

"I should have gone out there first thing this morning," Tanner had told his brother Marshall when he'd called him after leaving the fairgrounds.

"That would have been a boneheaded thing to do," Marshall said. "Didn't you say this guy is a cop?"

Now back at the ranch, he found his family sitting around the dining room table eating an early supper. It was clear that Marshall had told them what Tanner had been up to.

"The man's abusing his wife," he said, angry at the reproach he saw not only in his father's gaze but in Emma's as well. "I saw her black eye and the bruise on her cheek, but more than that, I saw her fear. Last night she was running for her life."

"Then she should have gone to the sheriff," his father said.

Tanner shook his head. "It would be her cop husband's word against hers. Even if he was arrested, he would get out on bail and be even more dangerous than he is now." Billie Rae was afraid of law enforcement and he could understand why, given she was married to a cop. "I tried to get her to stay. I told her I would help her," he said voicing his frustration.

"This woman really got to you, didn't she?" Emma said.

"I can't explain it. I saw her last night and…" He realized what he was saying and shut up. Emma, he suspected, would understand, but not his brothers. Unless anyone had felt something like that....

"She wasn't ready for your help," Emma said. "There really is nothing you can do until she's ready."

"But Billie Rae wants out. Otherwise, why would she have run when he told her he would kill her if she did?"

Hoyt shook his head. "Most of the time, the woman goes back. Better the devil you know than the devil you don't. A smart man never gets in the middle of a domestic dispute, especially for a woman he doesn't really know."

"Tanner is no smart man," Marshall joked. "He's determined to save this woman—even from herself."

"You aren't going looking for this husband again, are you?" his father asked.

"I drove out to the fairgrounds when I got back from Havre, but he wasn't there," Tanner said.

"I told him it was a stupid thing to do," Marshall said and shrugged when Tanner sent him a withering look.

"She's afraid he's going to kill her," Tanner said. "He threatened to if she left him and she did. She needs help. Why can't you see that?"

"We do see it," Emma said. "But she didn't want yours or she would have stayed."

"She's afraid she put us all in jeopardy by letting me bring her here last night," Tanner said.

"Son, by now she could be headed back to her husband, for all you know," Hoyt said. "You can't save a woman who doesn't want to be saved. I ought to know."

Tanner knew his father was talking about his third wife, Krystal. He'd saved her from an abusive situation, only to have her disappear shortly after they were wed.

"Did Krystal go back to her abusive boyfriend?" Tanner asked, ignoring his brother's warning look not to.

"Yeah, she did and he was only her boyfriend. This woman you think you rescued is *married*. Let it go, son," his father said, laying a protective hand on his shoulder as he got up from the table. "We've got fence posts to set before it gets dark. Come on, work is the best medicine for what's ailing you. That, too, I know from experience."

"Your father only wants to help. He's worried about you," Emma said after the others had gone outside. "But Tanner, trust what you feel and pray. She's going to need it."

SHERIFF MCCALL CRAWFORD found the patrolman waiting for her at the spot along the Milk River where he'd discovered Aggie Wells's rental vehicle.

As she walked toward the stand of cottonwoods where the white SUV had been abandoned, there was no doubt in her mind that whoever had left it there had been trying to hide it. Law enforcement had been looking for Aggie's vehicle since the niece had reported her aunt missing.

She felt her heart beat a little faster as she neared the officer and saw his expression. "You found a body?"

He quickly shook his head. "But it appears we might be dealing with foul play. There is blood on the driver's seat." He handed her a flashlight so she could look into the tree-shaded vehicle.

She shone the beam into the rental, quickly taking in what appeared to be blood on the driver's seat; two open suitcases in the back, with clothes strewn around; a purse on the ground, the contents dumped as if someone had gone through her belongings. Or had hoped to make this look like a robbery.

"Have you checked the area yet?" she asked the patrolman.

"Just the immediate area."

McCall looked into the deep shadows under the cottonwoods. She could see the gleam of the river's dark surface through the low branches. The water looked murky. She felt a sudden chill as she remembered watching her father's pickup being pulled from an old stock pond where it had been buried in the mud for twenty-seven years.

At least whoever had hidden this car hadn't opted to sink it in the river where it might not have been found for years—or ever.

That thought gave her pause. Why hadn't the last

person to drive this car done exactly that? Because they'd wanted the car to be found?

She glanced around. Maybe the person had been in a hurry. Possibly someone had been waiting for them up on the road, so they hadn't taken the time to do more than try to hide the car.

Too many possibilities, McCall thought. "Let's call in some help and broaden our search, and if we don't find her we're going to have to drag the river for her body."

As she reached for her phone, the question was still the same one she'd been asking herself since the niece had walked into her office. Where was Aggie Wells?

DUANE DECIDED THAT HIS best approach when he questioned the good people of Whitehorse, Montana, wasn't to admit that Billie Rae was his uncontrollable wife on the lam. That might garner unwanted sympathy for Billie Rae from the kind of people who took in strays and just felt the need to do good all the time—like whoever had given her a ride last night after the rodeo, the someone who just didn't know any better.

So it made sense that his best approach was to make her a dangerous felon and to flash his badge and put enough pressure on this town that someone came up with some answers. He figured if he moved fast, the local female sheriff wouldn't get wind of it.

He began to hit the churches, which were notorious

for taking in stranded motorists and people passing through town. There were a half dozen in the small town, more churches than bars. When he struck out there he tried the motels, thinking the good Samaritan had put her up in one for the night.

Striking out again, Duane was tired and hungry and losing his patience. He considered repeating the story he'd told the local sheriff to some of his friends in law enforcement. If he put an all-points bulletin out on Billie Rae, everyone in the northwest would be looking for her. With luck, some good ol' boy would find her and—

With a start he realized that Sheriff McCall Crawford could have already done that. Someone could have already found his wife. But then, wouldn't the sheriff have called him? Probably not, he thought with a curse. Not until she talked to Billie Rae herself.

Duane realized it was time to put in a call to a couple of buddies he'd met who worked for the Montana state highway patrol department. They were good ol' boys. He gave them the same story he'd told the sheriff. It didn't matter if they believed it or not. They'd see that he got his wife back.

Then he found a small café on the edge of town and ordered a cheeseburger, fries and a chocolate milkshake for a late lunch, telling himself it would be his word against his wife's. After all, he was a cop. And Billie Rae was…just his wife.

As he ate, he listened to the locals talking. He'd found you could learn a lot about a community by listening to the old guys talk in the local café. There was always a table or two of them and Whitehorse was no different. The talk was about range, cattle, water, weather and finally the rodeo.

Duane finished his meal, pushed the plate away and rose to go over to the table. "Gentlemen, sorry to bother you, but I heard you mention the rodeo." He took out his badge, flashed it and quickly put it away. He didn't need any smart rancher telling him he had no jurisdiction here. "I'm looking for a dangerous felon whose pickup was found at the rodeo last night. I was hoping you might have seen her."

"Her?" one of the old-timers said with a snort. Another one of them laughed as Duane handed him the photo he'd removed from his pocket of Billie Rae.

"You say this woman is a dangerous felon?" the man asked, disbelieving.

"The sweeter they look, often the more dangerous they are," Duane said, thinking how true that was. This woman was going to be the death of him, he thought.

"What's she wanted for?" another man at the table asked as the photo was passed to him.

"She killed her three children, ages eleven months, two and four years," Duane said without batting an eye. "Drowned them in the bathtub. The four-year-old fought for his life."

The men at the table wagged their heads in shock

and horror, and quickly passed the photo back to him, wanting nothing to do with such a woman.

"I was hoping you might have seen her," Duane said solemnly. "As far as I can figure, she caught a ride with someone from the fairgrounds into town."

The waitress had come up beside him. She'd obviously been listening. He let her steal a look at Billie Rae's photo before he put it back in his shirt pocket.

"Rachel might have seen her," the waitress said and hollered at the cook to come out. "She was telling me about some woman she saw right as the fireworks were over."

Duane felt a surge of hope as a heavyset cook came out of the back. He showed her the snapshot of Billie Rae.

"I can't say for positive," Rachel said, handing the photo back. "But I think it might be her."

Duane had been a cop long enough to know that often people liked to be a part of the drama by saying they saw something they didn't.

"Where did you see her?" he asked.

"By the grandstands."

"There must have been a lot of people there last night," Duane said. "What was it about her that made her stand out in your memory?"

She seemed to think for a moment. "I guess the reason I noticed her was because she was going the wrong way. We were all trying to leave and she was heading back in as if she'd lost something, you know."

"She looked upset?" he said.

The cook nodded. "She was crying. I thought maybe she'd misplaced one of her kids or something, and I was about to ask her if I could help, when I saw she already had help."

Duane felt his stomach roil. "She was with some-one?"

"One of Hoyt Chisholm's sons."

Chapter Seven

Billie Rae gripped the steering wheel as the car rocked, the flat tire flopping loudly on the pavement as she tried to keep control of it. She finally got it pulled over to the side of the road and climbed out to see how much damage had been done.

There hadn't been a lot of traffic along the two-lane, but now several semis passed blowing up a cloud of dust and dirt. Covering her eyes, she waited until they passed before she opened the trunk.

A motor home blew past as she looked in the trunk for what she would need to change the tire. She'd changed a tire once, but it had been a long time ago. Since Duane didn't let her drive and had sold her car right after they got married—

It made her angry how she'd let him make all the decisions in her life since they got married. But she'd learned early on not to argue with him. It was just easier—and safer—to go along with whatever he wanted than to argue, which always led to a fight.

She heard another vehicle coming and braced herself as she pulled out the bag of tools and waited for a truck pulling a trailer to roar past. Tanner, bless his heart, had made sure she had tools and the spare had air and some tread on it.

As she reached for the spare, she heard the sound of a vehicle slowing, then pulling up behind her. She turned to see a man in uniform climb out of a Montana highway patrol car.

ONE OF HOYT CHISHOLM'S SONS? Turned out there were six of them and they were grown men anywhere from their late twenties to their early thirties, and all six had been adopted by some big rancher to the north of Whitehorse.

Duane had gotten the information from the group gathered in the café.

"So what's the story on the Chisholms?" Duane had asked.

The waitress, not surprisingly, had turned out to be the most talkative. She told him about Hoyt Chisholm's four wives, two dead, one missing and one a newlywed, then about the six adopted sons.

"So you think he killed the other three wives?" he'd asked, not really giving a damn. All he really cared about was finding one of the man's sons—the bastard who'd apparently taken his wife away from the fairgrounds last night.

"There's this insurance investigator who thinks he did. Now she's up and disappeared. I heard they found her car by the river." She lowered her voice.

"My good friend works as a dispatcher at the sheriff's department."

Great. "So all six of his sons live on this big, old ranch of his?" he asked, trying to keep the woman on the subject he *was* interested in.

"Nah, I think they've all moved out. He keeps buying up ranches and the sons move into the houses that come with them."

"This guy must have money."

"Insurance money from those three wives," the waitress said under her breath. "Everyone is wondering how long it will be before he kills the fourth wife."

"So which one of them was at the rodeo last night with the woman I'm after?" he asked the cook, whom he had talked into sitting down at a booth with him and the waitress since the place was dead right now.

"It didn't really register when I saw him with her," Rachel said. "I was mostly looking at her. But later…" she added quickly as she must have seen him getting upset. "As we were driving out, we passed the Chisholm Cattle Company ranch truck and I noticed there were three people in the cab." She looked a little uncomfortable and Duane tried not to show how frustrated he was getting.

"I was still wondering if the woman had found her child or if she was upset about something else," the cook said.

Duane nodded, wishing to hell she would get on with it, but knowing better than to push her again.

"I saw the woman was sitting in the middle and Marshall Chisholm was driving. There was another brother riding shotgun, but I didn't get a good look at him before my husband went flying around them." She realized she'd just told a cop that her husband had been speeding. "He slowed down after that, but Marshall had already turned off, so I didn't see them again."

"You wouldn't happen to know where Marshall Chisholm lives, do you?"

Duane tipped the cook and the waitress more than either deserved and left with directions to Marshall Chisholm's house. Apparently it was a good distance from any other ranch house and miles north of town.

The perfect place to hide a woman who didn't want to be found.

BILLIE RAE WAS SURPRISED Duane hadn't called the law on her sooner, she thought as she watched the highway patrolman get out of his car. He'd always told her not to bother calling the cops on him because they all stuck together.

She'd learned that the hard way the one time she'd tried to get help from the police. But how had he known what she was driving? The car was in Tanner's name. Unless…

Her heart began to pound harder. She felt faint at

the thought that Duane had found Tanner and what he had done to him to make Tanner talk.

The patrolman was a big man with an angular face. He wore mirrored shades and touched his nightstick as he walked up to her, his face stern.

She leaned against the back of the car, her legs suddenly weak as water.

"Looks like you could use a little help," the officer said and picked up the bag of tools from the ground where she'd laid them. "Why don't you get off the road and I'll take care of this. Won't take but a few minutes."

Billy Rae licked her dry lips, her mouth like cotton. "Thank you," she said, choking out the words.

She stepped off the road as he went to work on the tire. He was right, it didn't take him long. She'd watched him, telling herself this was all there was to him stopping. Duane hadn't put the word out on her. She had nothing to fear.

But as she watched the highway patrolman she was suddenly aware of how little traffic there was on the highway. She was alone out here in the middle of nowhere with a man in uniform—and she had learned not to trust a badge of any kind.

The highway patrolman put the blown tire in the trunk along with the tools and slammed the lid shut. "There, you should be fine now. I'd suggest, though, that you get that tire fixed or buy another one. Where are you headed?"

"Great Falls." It was the only town she could re-member on the map.

"Good, it's not far up the highway. I'll follow you to make sure you don't have any more trouble."

"That's not necessary, really." She was trying hard not to let him see how upset his suggestion made her. The last thing she wanted to do was make him suspicious.

"It's not a problem," he said. "I'm headed that way, anyway."

All she could do was nod and thank him again.

Climbing behind the wheel, it took her a few mo-ments to get the car started, her hands were shaking so badly. He hadn't asked for her driver's license. Because he knew who she was, knew she didn't have it with her?

Billie Rae drove across the high bench for what seemed forever, the highway patrolman a couple of car lengths behind her. Finally the highway dropped down to the river and into the city of Great Falls. She pulled into the first gas station she came to and put down her window to let in fresh air as she tried to breathe.

What happened now? Would the patrolman detain her until Duane got here? She didn't think the man would hurt her, because he'd had the perfect oppor-tunity out in the middle of nowhere if that's what he had planned.

When she looked, she saw the highway patrolman give her a friendly wave, turn around and leave.

Billie Rae couldn't believe it. Her relief was so intense, she had to fight tears. Was it possible Duane hadn't put the word out on her? He'd always told her he had friends all over the country and that there was nowhere she could hide from him.

"Can I help you?"

Startled, she jumped and turned to find a young gas station attendant standing next to her open car window. It took a moment before she could speak. "I blew a tire. I was hoping—"

"Pop your trunk and I'll take a look at your tire." A moment later, the young man came back to the window carrying the tire. "You picked up a nail. I can patch it. Shouldn't take long."

She heard a cell phone ring.

The attendant looked at her as it rang again. "I think that's yours," he said as he took the flat tire and headed for one of the bays in the garage. On the third ring, she realized the sound was coming from inside the glove box of her car.

As she opened it, she saw the cell phone lying inside. For just an instant she had the crazy, insane suspicion that Duane had put it there. Or the highway patrolman when she wasn't looking. But that was impossible. Only one person could have put it there, she realized as she snatched up the phone.

"Hello?"

"I see you found the phone," Tanner Chisholm said. "Look, I'm sorry. I was worried about you. You wouldn't take my other offers but I thought at least you'd have a phone if you needed it."

She was so touched that for a moment she couldn't speak. "Thank you."

"Where are you?"

"Great Falls. I had a flat, or I would have been a lot farther down the road."

He was quiet for a moment. "I wish you'd stayed. It's not too late to change your mind."

She wished she could. She remembered the views from the ranch, the feeling of peace and solitude and freedom. She remembered what it felt like to be in Tanner's strong arms, to sit at the table with some of his family and feel safe.

The attendant came back out with her tire and loaded it into the trunk.

"I should go," she said.

"I bought another cell phone. You have the number now since I called you. Be careful and, when you get to where you're going, give me a call if you want to."

"I will," she promised and snapped the phone shut. As she started to put it back in the glove box, she saw the money Tanner had left for her and felt tears burn her eyes.

EMMA HAD BEEN EXPECTING the sheriff since the moment she'd heard about Aggie Wells's white SUV being found abandoned down by the river. The news had traveled like wildfire on the Whitehorse grapevine, not that Emma was on it since she was apparently too new in town, but Hoyt's ranch housekeeper had heard the news.

The moment she'd seen Mae Sutter's face when she'd come to work late that afternoon, Emma had known there was fresh gossip about the Chisholms.

"Spill it," she'd said to Mae, who'd looked surprised. But Emma was tired of beating around the bush with the cook and housekeeper. She'd tried to get close to them for weeks and they'd held her off as if she had a communicable disease.

Mae was a tiny thing. Emma had thought that a good gust of wind would blow the woman away. But Mae had turned out to be a lot stronger and more solid than she looked. She was also a good worker.

"I don't know what you're—"

"Save your breath, Mae. What's happened? And don't give me that innocent look of yours," she said to the housekeeper.

Mae straightened to her full height, all of five feet with her sturdy work shoes on, and tried to look indignant, but Emma could tell she was dying to tell everyone she knew—even her boss—who was involved.

"That woman who had dinner here the other night—"

"Aggie Wells," Emma said, trying to keep the tremor out of her voice. "What about her?"

"The sheriff questioned me about her," Mae said.

No surprise there. Emma put her hands on her hips

and gave the housekeeper an impatient look, knowing there was a whole lot more to it than that.

"They found her car abandoned by the river," Mae blurted out. "There was blood on the driver's seat. They're dragging the river for her body."

Emma had always been proud of her ironclad composure, but she felt all the blood drain from her face and had to sit down.

Mae got her a glass of cold water. "Are you all right?"

She nodded, knowing that Mae must be champing at the bit to tell everyone in the county about her reaction. Emma didn't care right now. "I liked Aggie," she said, tears in her eyes as she grasped the housekeeper's hand. "I know it sounds crazy, but I really liked her. I hope nothing happened to her."

Mae didn't look convinced. Nor was Mae surprised any more than Emma was when a few minutes later the sheriff drove up in the yard.

"I'll take care of this," Emma said, pulling herself together as she went to open the screen door and step out on the porch.

"Good afternoon, Sheriff," she said as McCall climbed out of her patrol SUV. "I thought we'd sit out here and talk, if that's all right. Would you like coffee or lemonade?"

The sheriff shook her head. "I need to speak with your husband."

Emma hadn't mentioned to Hoyt the sheriff's earlier visit when he and his sons had surprised her and come home for lunch. She hadn't wanted to upset him. She told the sheriff what she'd told her before. Hoyt wasn't expected back until late.

"You've heard," the sheriff said as she studied Emma still standing at the top of the steps.

Emma nodded, not up to playing games. She was still shaking inside and felt light-headed. "Have you found her?"

"No, not yet. When you hear from your husband, would you tell him to contact me as soon as possible?"

"Of course." She didn't need to ask why. Of course Hoyt would be the number one suspect, with her falling in at a close second.

The sheriff seemed to hesitate. "Did either of you leave the house that night after supper with Agatha Wells?"

"No. We were here the rest of the night." But she knew that wouldn't clear them. Hoyt had gotten up early the next morning and left. Emma didn't know where he'd gone, had just assumed it had something to do with the ranch.

She, herself, had gone into town that morning and didn't have an alibi for her whereabouts as she had taken a ride south to the Little Rockies to clear her head. The truth was, she hadn't wanted to stay around the house. She'd been too antsy, afraid of what Aggie Wells would do next.

When Aggie had left, her last words had been a warning that Hoyt Chisholm was dangerous, that he'd killed all three of his former wives and that Emma would be next.

Emma had hoped that having Aggie out to dinner would change her mind about Hoyt. It had been a foolish idea. At dinner Aggie had seemed to enjoy Hoyt's company, but later she was more convinced that Emma was living with a killer.

"Are you sure you wouldn't like some coffee or lemonade?" Emma asked the sheriff, hating the fear she heard in her voice.

"Thank you, but I need to get going," the sheriff said, turning to leave. "Do you know where your husband is working today on the ranch?"

Emma didn't. Hoyt had said they were putting in a new fence, but she had no idea where. He hadn't confided in her much about the ranch and his work lately. She'd told herself he had a lot on his mind, just as she told herself he hadn't been avoiding her. The thought that she'd been lying to herself about a lot of things scared her more than she wanted to admit.

After all this had come out about the deaths of two of his wives and the disappearance of the third, he had begged her to leave him. She had refused. It was after that that Hoyt had made himself scarce, as if he feared just being around her might put her in mortal danger.

"I assume you already tried to reach him by cell phone," Emma said.

The sheriff nodded. "It went straight to voice mail.

I left him a message. It's important I speak with him as soon as possible."

"I'll tell him. And you'll let me know what you find out about Aggie?" Emma called from the porch.

The sheriff had reached her patrol SUV. She glanced back at her and nodded.

What was Emma thinking? If Aggie's body was found, she and Hoyt could expect to see the sheriff at their door—probably with an arrest warrant for at least one of them.

DUANE FOUND Marshall Chisholm's farmhouse without any trouble. It was off the county road, back in a quarter mile and sheltered by a large stand of old cottonwoods.

He drove up to the two-story house, noting there were no vehicles parked in front. The large old barn out back had a tractor and some rusted farm equipment around it but nothing inside. The perfect place to hide a vehicle.

He pulled his car into the back of the barn deep in the shadows, then taking the tire iron from the back, went to have a look in the house. While he didn't believe Marshall was home, he couldn't be sure Billie Rae wasn't hiding inside.

He was only a little surprised to find the back door unlocked. People in this part of Montana were awful trusting. Duane let himself in.

The kitchen linoleum was worn and dated just like the appliances and cabinets, but everything was clean.

Duane couldn't imagine living alone and wondered about a man who could. No wonder the man had jumped at the chance to pick up a woman like Billie Rae.

The living room was neat as well, even though the furniture was also dated. It would seem that the son, even an adopted son, of a rich rancher could afford better furniture.

He climbed the stairs to find two bedrooms, one empty, the other with an antique metal bed frame and antique dressers that had probably come with the house.

Duane moved to the bed, pulled back the quilt and smelled the sheets. Billie Rae hadn't slept here. In the bathroom, he also found no sign that Billie Rae had ever been there.

Maybe she hadn't spent the night here, but Marshall Chisholm still had to know where Billy Rae had gone last night after he'd given her a ride to Whitehorse.

Duane settled in to wait for Marshall Chisholm to come home.

"ANY NEWS?" MCCALL ASKED when she reached her husband. As a local game warden, Luke Crawford was often involved with any law enforcement in the county. Since he'd been in the area checking fishing licenses and had a boat, he was now involved in the search for Agatha Wells's body.

"Nothing so far. We're dragging the river."

"I just spoke with Emma Chisholm again. After she and her husband, Hoyt, had Aggie out to supper the night she disappeared, Emma says neither of them left the house after that."

"You believe her?"

The sheriff thought about the new Mrs. Chisholm. She liked her and wanted to believe her. "Not sure. She's scared, which makes me think her husband wasn't in the house all of that time."

"From what you told me," Luke said, "Hoyt Chisholm has the most to gain by this woman's death."

"I spoke with the insurance company that Agatha Wells worked for. She was fired. Her boss said she became obsessed with the Chisholm case, convinced that Hoyt killed all three of his wives, including the third one who disappeared. I found out that he only recently had her declared dead."

"And now he's remarried. Wouldn't that explain the fear you saw in Emma Chisholm? I know that would scare me if your last three husbands met with accidents or just plain disappeared."

McCall chuckled. "I scare you already."

"True." She heard the soft, seductive tone in his voice and felt a small shiver. Could she love this man anymore? Not likely.

"I just needed to hear your voice," she said truthfully.

"Always glad to oblige. See you later?"

"Absolutely." She disconnected, and following a

feeling she hadn't been able to shake all day, she put out an all-points bulletin on Billie Rae Johnson Rasmussen.

BY THE TIME BILLIE RAE got something to eat from a fast-food place, filled the car up with gas and looked at a map to decide which way to go next, it was getting dark.

The emotional roller coaster of the past forty-eight hours had taken its toll on her. She felt wrung out and knew she wasn't up to driving much farther. The next large town was hours down the road and she didn't trust staying in the smaller Montana towns, feeling it would be too easy for Duane to find her.

She could almost feel him breathing down her neck. He wouldn't give up. It wasn't in his nature—not when he would feel justified for whatever he did to her. He would be driven and nothing and no one could stop him.

At least Great Falls was large enough that she should be able to find a motel, pay cash and get some sleep with some assurance she would be safe. At least for tonight.

She thought about changing her appearance, bleaching her dark hair, cutting it, getting a pair of glasses at the dime store. Instead, she picked up a baseball cap at a convenience store and stuffed her long hair up under it.

When she found a motel downtown, though, she

ran into the same thing she had when she purchased the car. No identification.

"I'm sorry, we need a credit card or some kind of identification," the older male clerk behind the desk told her.

"My purse was stolen," Billie Rae said. "I'm just trying to get home."

"Where's home?"

"Spokane." She picked the name out of thin air.

The clerk studied her. She was still wearing the blouse and slacks she'd been wearing when she'd made the run for it. She must look a mess. Tomorrow she had to buy some more clothing. Thanks to Tanner, she could afford a few items.

Billie Rae also realized that her "disguise" had been a mistake and quickly took off her baseball cap. Her long curly dark hair spilled around her shoulders.

Duane had told her she looked too young, that she should try to look older; people thought he'd robbed the cradle worse than he had. As it was, he was seven years her senior—him nearly forty.

She knew it bothered him, turning forty, and that was part of the problem. While he had begun to gray around the temples, Billie Rae could still pass for her early twenties, although she tried to dress and act older to please Duane.

"Well, I suppose it will be all right this time," the clerk said now.

She started to fill out the registration card as he

watched her. She was so nervous she wrote down her first name without thinking, then unable to quickly think of a second name, wrote down Chisholm. After all, the car was registered to Tanner Chisholm.

"Billie Rae Chisholm," the man said reading the card. She'd done better on making up an address in Spokane, Washington, but didn't dare make up the zip code.

"You don't know your zip code?"

"I keep forgetting it. We just moved there."

He nodded and put the registration card away as if he didn't believe anything she said but no longer cared. He gave her the key and told her how to get to her room.

By the time she reached the motel room, she was trembling all over and furious with herself. If Duane started calling motels in Great Falls, he would have no trouble finding her since she'd already made the clerk suspicious.

She thought about just leaving, hitting the road, trying to drive to another town or even another motel in Great Falls. But it would be the same thing all over again. Exhaustion overtook her. She plopped down on the bed, telling herself she would only rest for a few minutes before leaving, and fell into the sleep of the dead.

DUANE SAW THE LIGHTS coming up the road. One vehicle. Good, Marshall Chisholm was alone. Unless he'd brought a girlfriend, but Duane was pretty sure that wasn't the case or he wouldn't have picked up Billy Rae last night.

He smiled when he saw the cowboy climb out of his truck alone. Duane loved being right.

Marshall Chisholm was good sized. Duane wasn't all that sure he could beat him in a fair fight, but then there was no chance of that.

He waited until Chisholm opened the door and stepped in before hitting him from behind, knocking him to his knees.

The idea was to disarm him—not to knock him out. While he'd love to beat the hell out of the man who'd interfered in his marriage, he needed to know where Billie Rae was first.

"What the hell?" the dazed cowboy said when Duane stepped in front of him.

"Where is Billie Rae?"

The cowboy was on his feet before Duane could get a good swing with the tire iron. The blow didn't even stun him. Marshall Chisholm grabbed the tire iron before Duane could hit him again.

Seeing how this was going down, Duane pulled the gun just so the cowboy knew who was boss here. "Where is my wife?"

Marshall Chisholm took a step back at the sight of the gun. He rubbed a hand over his jaw, and his eyes widened just enough that Duane knew they were finally on the same page.

"Now you *remember?*" he said with a laugh. "Where is she?"

"You're the cop," Marshall said as if trying to get up to speed. Or maybe he was just reminding himself that he'd just slugged an officer of the law.

"That's right," Duane said, brandishing the gun. "And you're the son of a bitch who picked up my wife last night at the rodeo." He took a threatening step toward Marshall. "Now put down the tire iron and tell me what you did with her and where she is now." He fired a shot next to the cowboy's head. Wood splintered, the boom echoing through the house. "I suggest you start talking."

Chapter Eight

Tanner woke to an unfamiliar sound. It took him a moment to realize it was his landline ringing. After he'd put his cell phone in Billie Rae's car, he'd picked up another cell phone and had his number changed, but no one but Billie Rae had the number.

He'd slept badly last night and now felt groggy as he glanced at the clock. It wasn't even daylight yet.

As he reached for the phone, he realized it might be Billie Rae calling. He knew he shouldn't have called her yesterday evening, but he'd needed to hear her voice, needed to know she was all right, needed to be sure she hadn't changed her mind and gone back to her abusive husband. He'd also wanted to make sure she found the phone—and the money—he'd left her.

"Hello?" He heard the hope in his voice that it was Billie Rae and that she'd changed her mind and was coming back. He should have known that no call this time of the morning was going to be good news.

"Son, it's Dad."

"What's wrong?" Tanner sat up, now fully awake.

Had Hoyt heard something about Billie Rae? Was that why he was calling?

"It's your brother Marshall. He's in the hospital."

"What happened?" All Tanner could think was a car accident.

"He's been beaten up pretty badly, but the doctor says he's going to be all right. He's asking to see you."

Beaten up? How could he have gotten into a *fight?* Last night Marshall said he was heading home after they finished work late, that he was tired and going home to his house.

"He asked to see all of the family?" Tanner asked in alarm. Maybe his father was wrong and Marshall was worse off than they thought.

"Just you."

Thirty minutes later, Tanner found his brother sitting on a gurney in the emergency room of the hospital, Hoyt and Emma standing nearby. Marshall's head was bandaged and he had a dark row of stitches along his jaw.

When he saw Tanner, he asked their father and stepmother to give them a moment alone.

"Come on, Emma," Hoyt said, shooting Tanner a look that spoke volumes. He was responsible for this?

With a curse he realized who had done this to his brother. "I'll kill the son of a bitch," Tanner swore again, seeing red. He'd gotten in the middle of Billie Rae's marriage to a cop, of all things, and now he had gotten his brother almost killed. How could this situation be any worse?

Marshall shook his head. "I'm fine. But we have to find Billie Rae before he does."

The anger fled in an instant at the sound of her name, leaving him clearheaded. "You told him where she'd gone," Tanner said, no judgment in his tone. His brother had taken a beating because of him.

"Not on your life. I sent him north to the Canadian border to buy us time," Marshall said, sliding off the gurney.

"Sir, the doctor hasn't released you," the nurse said, rushing toward them. "He wants to keep you overnight. You have a concussion."

"She's right," Tanner said, putting a hand on his brother's arm. "I can handle this."

Marshall met his gaze as though assessing if he thought his brother was too emotionally involved, then he slumped back against the gurney.

"I'm so sorry," Tanner said as he and the nurse helped Marshall back up onto the gurney.

"This isn't your fault. I know what would have happened to Billie Rae if we hadn't helped her last night and so do you, but he's a cop, little brother. You can't kill a cop, even a bad one, and if you tangle with him you'll get yourself killed."

"I can handle this."

His brother shook his head. "Even when he pulled the gun on me, I wanted to go for the bastard's throat. I'm afraid that's exactly what you would have done and he would have killed you. I'm telling you, Tanner, this dude is dangerous. Just make sure he doesn't find Billie Rae until you can get her some kind of protection from this psychopath."

SHERIFF MCCALL CRAWFORD got the call before breakfast. Luke had left early since he was overseeing the dragging of the river. She had wanted to go with him but got held up with a phone call.

She had just hung up when the phone rang again. It was her deputy.

"We just found a grave not far from where Aggie Wells's car was abandoned by the Milk River," he said. "It's not our missing vic, though," he added. "These remains have been here for a lot longer than a few weeks."

By the time McCall reached the scene, Coroner George Murphy was crouched beside an open hole in the side of the riverbank.

"Looks like whoever killed her dug into the side of the bank, shoved the tarp-wrapped body in, then let the soft dirt slide down and cover her." He motioned to the bones lying on what was left of an old canvas tarp.

"Her?" McCall asked.

"Definitely a woman. I'd say in her late twenties."

McCall glanced at the gaping hole in the side of the bank. "How was it again that you found the grave?" She remembered finding her father's. It had been like opening Pandora's box and she suspected this grave would be no different.

"Apparently another dirt slide unearthed it—or maybe one of the searchers inadvertently did," the coroner said. "This morning I happened to spot a bone and a piece of the tarp sticking out."

"That was handy, wasn't it?" she said, never comfortable with coincidence. "Or maybe someone wanted us to find it. Any chance of matching dental records?"

"She's had some dental done," George said slowly, then met her gaze. "I think you might get luckier with her medical records. She had an abnormal amount of broken bones for a woman her age."

"Are you suggesting some medical reason for that?" McCall asked.

"Maybe. More than likely this woman was seriously abused in her twenties, I would say."

"You can tell all that from her skeleton?"

"It's the type of breaks. Facial, wrists, arms, ribs…" George looked a little green around the gills. He always did when things got ugly. For a man who didn't like knowing about the evil things humans did to one another, it was amazing the EMT was still willing to act as the county coroner.

"How long would you estimate that the remains have been there?"

George sighed. "Hard to say, but given the amount of decomposition…I'd guess, and remember this is just a guess, twenty-five years. Maybe less, maybe more." He launched into a speech about all the factors that made a body deteriorate, a speech she'd heard many times before.

"Let's get her ID'd as quickly as possible," McCall said and glanced through the trees where she could see Aggie Wells's vehicle. The wrecker was coming today to take it to the sheriff department's storage unit as evidence.

They'd been searching for Aggie Wells's body and now another woman's had turned up? And still no sign of Aggie.

McCall didn't like what she was thinking and was surprised when the very person she was thinking about called.

"Sheriff Crawford here," she said into the phone. She listened as Hoyt Chisholm told her why she needed to come down to the hospital, then said, "I'll be right there."

Duane sat in his car down the street from the small town hospital. He knew Marshall would warn whoever had been in the pickup that night with Billie Rae after the rodeo. All he had to do was wait and see who showed up.

Duane wasn't surprised at all when a cowboy drove up shortly after the father and stepmother had arrived. He recognized him from the high school yearbooks he'd found at the library.

Tanner was a big cowboy like his brother, but as

Duane had always said, "The bigger they are, the harder they fall." And this one was going down.

He smiled to himself as he waited for a few minutes to see if anyone else would show up. When no one did, he climbed out of his car and walked down the deserted street to the pickup the brother had arrived in. It had Chisholm Cattle Company printed on the side, Duane noted as he slipped under it and secured the tracking device.

Another benefit of being a cop, he was able to get all the toys that went with the job, along with anything else he wanted from the sleazebags he came in contact with on the streets.

Slipping out from under the pickup, he moseyed back to his car and checked it on his cell phone. "Modern technology," he said in admiration, pleased with himself, as he looked at the small screen. Now wherever Tanner Chisholm went Duane was sure to follow, and he had no doubt that this cowboy was going to lead him straight to Billie Rae.

"It's just a matter of time now, Billie Rae," he said to himself, then swore as he spotted a sheriff's department vehicle coming up the street. He slid down in his seat, swearing profusely as the patrol car pulled into the hospital parking lot.

He'd told Marshall Chisholm not to call the law or he would come back and finish him. Apparently the hick hadn't taken his threat seriously. Duane rubbed his jaw where the cowboy had got in a good punch. First Marshall had lied to him about where Billie Rae had gone. Duane had believed that under the threat of death the cowboy had told him the truth. But one call to the border after he'd left Marshall and he'd verified that Billie Rae hadn't been anywhere near the crossing.

Duane told himself he should have known better than to believe that she'd head for Canada. Billie Rae was proving she wasn't as stupid as he'd once thought. Obviously she'd known how easily he could find out if she'd crossed into Canada, so she'd probably gone in another direction. What he needed to know, though, was *which* direction—and how she was getting wherever the hell she thought she was going.

These Chisholm cowboys had been playing him. They really had no idea what a mistake that was yet. But they would soon.

As he watched the woman sheriff being met at the door by the parents of Marshall Chisholm, Duane knew it was time to get out of town. Apparently that was what Billie Rae had already done.

Wherever she was, he was counting on Tanner Chisholm leading him right to her.

TANNER CALLED BILLIE RAE the moment he left his brother's hospital room. The cell phone rang four times. A shaft of icy fear made his stomach roil at the thought that she'd dumped the cell phone, afraid her husband would somehow be able to follow her because of it.

Billie Rae answered on the fifth ring.

"It's Tanner. Are you all right?"

"What's wrong?" She sounded as if she'd been asleep. He'd forgotten how early in the morning it was.

"Tell me where you are."

"No, I—"

"Duane beat up my brother Marshall. He's in the hospital."

"Oh, no." He heard what sounded like her crying softly. "Is he all right?"

"He'll live but he's worried about you. He sent me to find you and make sure you were safe until something can be done about your situation." Tanner could hear her moving around.

"If Duane found out your brother was with us that night at the rodeo, then…oh, Tanner, he'll come after you next. He won't stop with your brother. You're in terrible danger. The rest of your family might be as well."

"You just worry about yourself right now."

Billie Rae let out a choked laugh. "I'm the one who put your brother in the hospital, the one who has put you all in danger."

"Listen to me, Billie Rae. None of this is your fault."

"You're the one who said I needed to draw a line in the sand."

"That was before I saw what Duane did to my brother."

"He's capable of doing much worse. But you were

right the first time, I can't keep running. He will go after anyone who helps me."

"My brother has filed charges against him," Tanner said. "The only place he's going is jail."

"No, you don't understand. Even if the sheriff finds him and arrests him, he'll be out within hours and even more furious. Tell your brother not to press charges."

"Billie Rae, it's too late. If you come back to Whitehorse—"

"And what? Get a restraining order against Duane?" She let out a humorless laugh. "Do you really think that would do any good? Tanner, I know about battered women whose husbands threaten to kill them. The husbands find a way to get to them no matter what and do exactly what they said they would."

Tanner wanted to argue, but he'd seen too many examples of women in the news who'd been killed by their husbands or boyfriends—or lived in fear of them even with their abusers behind bars.

"Then I will get you enough money so that you can disappear and Duane will never be able to find you," he said even as he realized it would mean he would never see her again, either. The thought hurt. But all that mattered right now was keeping her safe.

"Tanner, do you really think there is that much money in the world?" she asked. "Even if I could accept your too generous offer, I can't live like that, always looking over my shoulder. This was the reason

I hadn't tried to leave Duane before. And now I've gotten your brother hurt—"

"He's going to be all right. He told Duane you were headed for the border in one of our old trucks."

She groaned. "Once he finds out that your brother lied to him—"

"He isn't going after my brother again. The sheriff is putting a deputy outside his room until he is released. There is an APB out on Duane. Everyone will be looking for him. I'm betting he will get out of Whitehorse and not come back. It's you I'm worried about. Come back to the ranch. I'll make sure he never hurts you again."

"Tanner…" she said with a sigh.

"I know. You don't even know me."

"That's the amazing part. I feel as if I have always known you. This closeness I feel…" Her voice broke off.

"I feel the same way. I can't explain what happened the moment I saw you, but I don't want to let you go."

"And I can't let him hurt you or your family simply because you helped me."

Tanner heard something in her voice that scared him. "You can't go back to him. You know it will be worse for you. That's if he doesn't end up killing you. You can't go back because of me. Please, I can't let that happen."

"I can't run, either. You were right. I have to take a stand."

"*No,* I was wrong. Billie Rae—"

"Make sure you and your family are safe."

"My father and brothers will see to that. Billie Rae, I'm leaving right now headed for Great Falls. Meet me halfway between Whitehorse and Great Falls. There's an Indian casino called Northern Winds just outside of Havre. I'll be waiting for you in the parking lot." He heard her open the motel room door; he could hear traffic outside. He knew he was losing her. "And if you're still determined to go back to him after we talk, then—"

"Thank you, Tanner. I wish we'd met under different circumstances."

"Billie Rae. Billie Rae?" The line had gone dead. He called back but it went straight to voice mail.

Swearing, he started his pickup. If she was headed back this way, then he would see her on the highway. He would do whatever he had to do to stop her. He couldn't let her go back to that madman because of him.

All he could hope was that after she hit the road on the way back that she would change her mind and meet him at the casino. He said a silent prayer that she would be waiting for him when he reached Northern Winds as he pulled away from the Whitehorse hospital and headed west.

Tanner hadn't gone far when he checked his rearview mirror. He couldn't take the chance that Duane was still in town, waiting for him to lead him to Billie Rae.

But there were no other vehicles behind him as he turned onto Highway 2 and headed west toward Great Falls. Wherever Duane Rasmussen was, he wasn't behind him. Breathing a sigh of relief, Tanner settled in for the long drive, thinking about Billie Rae and fate and how he was going to stop her.

BILLIE RAE COULDN'T BREATHE. Wasn't this what she'd feared? She choked back a sob and closed the motel room door behind her. She'd never felt such pain—not even when Duane had hit her. The woman she'd been—before Duane Rasmussen—never dreamed she would find herself in this position.

Her heart ached and she felt sick to her stomach. She'd only made it worse by making love with Tanner the night before. What if Duane found out? She told herself there was no way that would ever happen. But they hadn't used protection. Last night she'd told herself it wouldn't matter. Duane was going to find her and kill her before she'd even know if she was pregnant.

But what if she was? She touched her stomach. Just the thought of having Tanner's child sent a wave of excitement through her. Then instant regret that she had now possibly endangered yet another life. What was she going to do?

You should never have left me. This is on your head. You forced me to hurt someone else. You deserve everything you're going to get.

She slid behind the wheel of the car and sat, trying

to pull herself together. Since she'd realized the mistake she'd made marrying Duane, Billie Rae had been desperate to get out—but she hadn't known what to do. Duane had made it clear that leaving him was out of the question. The fact that he was a cop made it all the more impossible.

She'd felt trapped with no way out and no one to turn to. Early on in their marriage, she'd had a friend she'd met at the small market within walking distance of their home. The friend had noticed Billie Rae's bruises and had tried to help her.

Not long after that, the friend had suddenly moved away without a word.

Billie Rae had inquired about her through a mutual acquaintance at the market and found out that a policeman had come around the night before her friend had left. Duane. After that Billie Rae hadn't let anyone get close, knowing the price they would have to pay if Duane found out.

Now she had involved the Chisholm family and it had gotten Marshall injured. She didn't want to think about what Duane would do to Tanner if he knew how much he'd helped her. And yet Tanner hadn't backed down for a moment. He was still ready to help her— even knowing now what Duane was capable of.

She felt such a well of emotion at the thought. Tanner was the kind of man Duane would call a fool. Duane would scoff at anything that smacked of chivalry. No doubt because he could never measure up and he knew it. That was why he resented men like Tanner Chisholm so much.

Thinking of Tanner reminded her of his smile, the warmth in his brown eyes, that spark that had brought the old Billie Rae back to life when he touched her. Tanner had already saved her in ways he couldn't imagine. But she couldn't let him get in any deeper.

After a few minutes, she could breathe again. She picked up the map, remembering something she'd noticed on it yesterday. It was a dangerous plan. A desperate plan. But for the first time in months, she felt she was finally thinking clearly. She almost felt like her old self—the strong, independent woman Duane had done his best to destroy.

For so long she thought she deserved what she got because she was the one who'd married Duane. *You made your bed, now lie in it,* her mother used to say.

No more. Anger boiled up from deep inside her. No more. She *didn't* deserve this. Nor did the Chisholms who had helped her. Tanner had been right. It was time to draw a line in the sand and fight.

It was time she took her life back.

Or lose it.

But at least she wouldn't go down without a fight, and if she was lucky she'd take Duane with her. Taking a deep breath, she braced herself, opened her phone and tapped in his number. Her hand was barely shaking as the phone at the other end began to ring.

"Hello?" He hadn't recognized the cell number.

Tanner had blocked the ID on it. She could hear Duane's car stereo in the background and wondered where he was. He turned down the music and repeated, "Hello? Who is this?"

Just the sound of his voice brought it all back. Fear knifed through her, and for a moment her courage faltered. She drew on the memory of the woman she had been in Tanner's arms, the woman Tanner Chisholm had seen in her, the woman he was bound and determined to save even if it meant risking his own life.

"It's me," she said.

The soft chuckle that came over the line sent a chill through her. "I wondered when I'd be hearing from you." Duane's words were clipped. Anyone else might not have heard the fury behind them. But she heard it and, if she hadn't known before, she knew now that he would beat her to death this time if she gave him a chance.

Terror gripped her and she couldn't breathe, couldn't speak, couldn't think for a moment. Then she reminded herself that Duane had been systematically killing her for months. He'd tried to suffocate her in a loveless marriage, beat her down, make her question herself, especially her strengths, and he'd hurt her in more ways than she wanted to admit.

"So you're ready to come home." His tone made it clear he couldn't wait to get his hands on her.

And that was exactly what she was depending on.

Chapter Nine

As Emma and Hoyt left the hospital, she saw her husband stop to take a call on his cell phone. He turned his back to her and she felt her heart drop—just as it had weeks ago when she'd feared her husband was having an affair. Instead the woman who he had been talking to back then was Aggie Wells, the former insurance investigator determined to see Hoyt hang for murder.

Hoyt hadn't wanted her to know that Aggie was not only back in town—but also that she was more determined than ever to see him go to prison for murder.

"Who was that?" Emma asked now as he put his phone away and joined her. She was half afraid it was Aggie. And at the same time, almost hoping it was. No one wanted Aggie Wells to turn up alive more than her.

Hoyt hesitated, then sighed. She'd made him promise there would be no more secrets. She still felt guilty about that because she had things she'd never told her husband, things she wanted to hide as well.

"It was Tanner. He wanted to tell me he was going after Billie Rae."

"He's his father's son," she said, not at all surprised—even after what had happened to Marshall, or because of it, Tanner would be all the more determined to protect the woman.

"He's a fool," Hoyt said as he led the way to the ranch pickup. The doctor was keeping Marshall in the hospital for observation even though her stepson had only a minor concussion. She'd seen how upset her husband had been after their visit with Marshall in the hospital and knew he feared that another son would be injured—or dead—before this was over.

She noticed how Hoyt glanced around the hospital parking lot. He was looking for Billie Rae's husband—or at least anyone who might fit that bill since the only description they had of him was what Sheriff Crawford had given them.

"Tanner's worried the husband might come after us, isn't he?" Emma said as she climbed into the pickup next to Hoyt.

He shot her look. "The man sounds crazy. It is cause for concern since his wife involved us in her troubles."

"Hoyt," Emma snapped as he started the engine and headed toward the ranch. "How can you say such a thing? The poor woman was running for her life. The man is an animal. Can you imagine what he'll do to Billie Rae if he finds her?"

Hoyt swung his head around to look at her. "Can

you imagine what he'll do to Tanner if he finds him with his wife? And what will have been the point? Women like that go back to the men who abuse them."

"Women like *what?*" Emma demanded, shocked by his last statement. She too was worried about Tanner. But she was also worried about Billie Rae. And her husband had hit a nerve. He didn't know she used to be one of those women. But like Billie Rae, she hadn't stayed—nor had she gone back in the way he meant, anyway.

"You know what I mean," he said. "I'm worried about my boys and now Tanner is going after the woman."

"You raised your sons to help those in need. The only reason Billie Rae would go back to her husband is to protect your boys, who by the way, are men. Are you going to let that happen?"

"What would you like me to do?" Hoyt demanded.

"This attitude of yours is all because you're so certain that your third wife went back to her abusive boyfriend." He'd told her about Krystal, a woman he'd tried to help by foolishly marrying her.

"She *did* go back. I hired a private detective. Krystal went back because she missed the drama, especially the honeymoon period, after he's beaten her up, when he pleads for her forgiveness, treats her like she's rare crystal, buys her things, promises never to hurt her again until he does and the cycle starts all over again. She was hooked on it and life with me was just too damned dull for her."

All Emma heard was the part where Hoyt said he'd had proof that Krystal went back to her boyfriend. "You hired a private investigator who had proof and you didn't give that information to Aggie?"

He stared straight ahead, ignoring her as he drove.

"No, you didn't give Aggie the information because you wanted to save face, because of your damned male ego. You'd rather have people believe you're a murderer." She was furious with this man she'd come to love more than life.

"Aggie Wells already believed I killed at least one of my wives," Hoyt snapped. "What could another one hurt? Anyway, you wouldn't understand."

"Oh, I understand just fine, Hoyt Chisholm. If Aggie had known about any of this—"

"She would still believe I killed Krystal. Don't you get it? She would think I couldn't stand my wife leaving me and that I went after her and killed her. Maybe killed the boyfriend too because shortly after that, both of them disappeared and not even the private detective I hired could find them."

This news took the wind out of Emma's sails. Hoyt was right. He would still look guilty, maybe even guiltier than he had.

He glanced over at her. "I'm not as stupid as I look. After I calmed down, I told the P.I. to get proof that Krystal was alive to give to Aggie. I thought maybe

then she'd believe that I didn't have anything to do
with my first wife's drowning or Tasha's accident.
But by then, both Krystal and her abusive boyfriend
had vanished."

Emma fell silent as Hoyt turned onto the road to
the ranch. "I'm sorry. You could have told me."

"I just did. It proves nothing." He reached over and
took her hand, all the frustration leaving his voice.
"This crazy cop husband aside, I'm still worried as
hell about you. I'm so afraid something is going to
happen to you."

"I'm fine as long as I'm with you."

He squeezed her hand. "How did I get so lucky as
to find you? Maybe that's what scares me. I feel like
I'm tempting fate."

"Don't be silly. I'm hard enough to get along with
that maybe *I'm* your punishment."

He laughed softly, but didn't disagree.

"I saw the sheriff talking to you. What was that
about?"

"She wanted to know the last time I saw Aggie
Wells. If I knew where she'd been staying. If she
happened to mention where she was going or what
she was doing. The usual."

Emma realized he'd been questioned by the sheriff
on numerous occasions before. But those times it had
been about his wives. Her heart went out to him and
for a moment, she hated Aggie Wells for making him
have to relive this all over again.

"So you told her the last time you saw Aggie was that night at dinner?" Emma said.

He shot her a look. "Are you asking me when was the last time I saw her?"

"No, I—"

"I didn't kill her, if that's what you're asking."

"I know you didn't kill her. I just thought—"

"That I might have met her the next morning?" He shook his head. "I never saw her again after that night at dinner and I hope to hell I never see her again. Any more questions?"

Emma shook her head, wishing she'd kept her mouth shut, but that was so not like her. Had she really believed Hoyt would meet Aggie the next morning?

"I have no idea where she is or what happened to her."

Emma could hear the fear in her husband's voice. It matched her own. Since Aggie's car had been found with, according to the scuttlebutt around town, her purse and suitcase, and blood on the driver's seat, the sheriff's department had been searching for her body along the riverbank.

"The sheriff asked where she could find me and I told her we were headed back to the ranch," Hoyt was saying. "I intend to stay with you until this cop who beat up Marshall is caught."

That sounded just fine with Emma. She'd missed her husband. Ahead she could see the main house at Chisholm Cattle Company. All Emma wanted to do was get home, go upstairs with her husband and make love. She said as much to Hoyt.

He swore under his breath. She thought that was his reply to her suggestion. Instead he was staring at the house as he pulled into the yard.

Emma turned to see that the front door was standing open, no other vehicles around and since Marshall's brothers, other than Tanner, were now all at the hospital…

"Stay in the pickup," Hoyt ordered as he pulled down the shotgun from the rack behind the pickup seat. Grabbing a handful of shells, he carefully closed the truck door and hurried toward the house and the open doorway.

Emma, who had never been good at taking orders, especially from a man, was hot on his heels. As she hurried up the steps and crossed the porch, she heard Hoyt moving cautiously through the rooms.

She would have followed him farther into the house, but she stopped just inside the door pole axed, her heart pounding as she breathed in the familiar scent of Aggie Wells's perfume.

The insurance investigator was no longer missing. She'd been in this house again, which meant she was alive even though her car had been found abandoned and the sheriff suspected foul play.

But it was the second realization that panicked Emma. Aggie Wells was still determined to prove Hoyt Chisholm a murderer—even if it was her own "murder" he went to prison for.

"BILLIE RAE?" There was now a sharp edge to Duane's voice.

"I'm still here," she said into the phone. She told herself to just breathe. She could do this.

"Right, and where exactly is *here?*" he asked as if she was a disobedient child. It was the same tone he'd used with her since she'd said, "I do."

"I'm broke down near a town called Fort Benton."

He swore. "Of course you are and now you need my help." There was smug satisfaction in his voice. She knew he was smiling and that, she'd learned, was when he was his most dangerous.

"How long will it take you to reach me?" she asked, needing to know where he was and how much time she had to prepare.

"I'm leaving Whitehorse now." She heard him put down his car window. A moment later a siren came on. He'd put the portable cruiser cherry light on the roof. "Give me the directions."

She told him how to get to the dead-end river road she'd seen on the map.

"How could you be so stupid as to go down a dead-end road?" he demanded, but didn't wait for an answer. "Never mind. The two to three hours you're going to have to wait for me will give you time to think about what you've done and how you intend to make it up to me." He hung up.

Billie Rae snapped the cell closed with trembling fingers, then went back inside the motel room for the phone book. She found the first address she needed, then checked the Great Falls map at the front and started the car.

She shuddered at the thought of facing Duane and feared she wouldn't have the courage to carry through with her plan. But she knew that if she showed any sign of weakness, she was a dead woman.

What sustained her was the knowledge that if she didn't make her plan work, Duane wouldn't end it there. He would still go after Tanner. In his mind, Tanner would be to blame for all of this.

Pushing the thought away, she concentrated on what she had to do. Tanner would be waiting for her at Northern Winds casino. He should be safe there. Just thinking about him made her feel stronger as she drove to the first shop on her list.

SHERIFF MCCALL CRAWFORD was just leaving the hospital after putting out a warrant on Duane Rasmussen when her cell phone rang.

"We have a positive identification on the remains found buried out by the river," Coroner George Murphy said.

McCall braced herself because she had a bad feeling she already knew.

"The remains are those of Krystal Blake Chisholm," George said.

Hoyt Chisholm's third wife, the one who disappeared almost thirty years ago.

"Cause of death?" she asked.

"A blow to the back of the head, according to the crime lab doctor who did the autopsy. It's all in the report, but I know you can never wait for the report, so I called you."

McCall smiled. "You know me too well. Thanks." Krystal Chisholm's murder cast a whole new light on the deaths of Hoyt Chisholm's other two wives who had died under questionable circumstances—and now insurance investigator Aggie Wells's disappearance.

"We found something among the remains in the tarp I think you're going to want to see," George said.

"I'll be right there."

As she walked into the autopsy room a few minutes later, she pulled on latex gloves and stepped over to where the box of weather-rotted scraps of canvas tarp and the remains had been placed on a gurney.

George handed McCall a piece of silver jewelry.

"The victim's?" she asked, wondering why he'd wanted her to see this.

He shook his head. "My best guess? It's part of a men's bolo tie." A lot of western-dressed men in this part of the country wore a bolo tie. It was as dressed up as they ever got. The tie consisted of two thin cords that formed a loop with the ends dangling down from some sort of decorative clasp that held the tie together.

"How would it have ended up with the body?" she

asked just wanting his take on it. She already had her own theory.

"The killer has the woman down, she reaches up and grabs the bolo tie, the silver clasp slides off."

Her thought as well. "Wouldn't the silver be more tarnished, though, if it had been with the body for the past twenty-five to thirty years?"

"Silver reacts badly to just about everything, latex gloves, ammonia, chlorinated water, air pollution, perfumes, hair sprays, even some foods like onions and eggs, anything salty unless the silver is plated with a thin layer of metal protection, which older jewelry wasn't," George said and then seemed to notice her looking at him sideways. "My sister works for a jeweler."

"Sorry, as you were saying…"

"Humidity alone can cause silver to tarnish."

McCall nodded. "So who knows how tarnished it would be, is that what you're saying?"

"Something like that," George said. "What do you think of the design?"

While he was squeamish about the violence of murder and what it did to the human body, he seemed to be getting into the investigation part of his job a lot more than when he first started, she thought.

She'd been turning the piece of silver in her fingers. If you turned it one way it appeared to be three tiny silver horseshoes welded together.

If you turned it the other way, it looked like three small C's.

She held it up. "One of a kind, I'd say." She was waiting for George's opinion, which she knew he was dying to give her. "Probably someone had it specially made at a jewelry store. Could be tiny horseshoes or—"

"We both know that it is three C's and that those three C's are for Chisholm Cattle Company," George said, losing his patience with her.

She laughed. "Why do I get the feeling you have something to back up that statement?" George was all about facts.

"In fact I do," he said stepping over to the laptop computer on a nearby desk, "I thought I'd seen Hoyt Chisholm wearing this very piece of jewelry and I was right."

McCall stepped over to look at a photograph of the cattleman taken at Whitehorse Days twenty-seven years before. Hoyt was wearing the bolo tie with the silver clasp, and he was with a woman. The cutline under the photo identified the woman as Krystal Chisholm.

DUANE HAD FORGOTTEN ABOUT Tanner Chisholm after Billie Rae's call. He'd been so excited at the prospect of getting to his wife that Tanner Chisholm had been the last thing on his mind.

That was, until he heard the soft beep from the tracking device on the seat next to him.

"What the hell?" he said as he saw Tanner's location. "The son of a bitch is following *me?*"

He almost ran off the road he was so busy staring at his cell phone screen. How was this possible? The cowboy had left Whitehorse before him. He must have stopped for gas or something. How else could Duane explain it?

Unless he was right and the bastard was actually *following* him.

All he had been thinking about after Billie Rae's call was getting to her. It was so like her to call—after she'd gotten herself into a pickle. Just the sound of her voice had gotten his blood boiling.

He chewed at his cheek for a moment now, giving this change of events some thought. Did he really give a damn about this cowboy? Wasn't getting to Billie Rae and settling this all he should concern himself with?

As anxious as he was to reach Billie Rae—there was always the possibility that she would get some wild idea to take off again—especially if someone encouraged her. He realized he couldn't let the cowboy follow him to her.

Another thought breezed past. What if Billie Rae had also called her cowboy savior, covering all her bets?

Duane swore. He was going to have to take care of Tanner. He watched the highway ahead looking for the perfect place to wait in ambush.

Chapter Ten

All it took was a couple of calls to jewelers in Glasgow and Havre. McCall hit paydirt on her second try.

"Chisholm, sure, I know him well," the elderly sounding jeweler said.

She described the clasp for the bolo tie.

"Yep, I made that, but not for Hoyt. It was an anniversary present I made for his wife to give to him," the jeweler said.

"His wife?"

"What was her name? Just a minute. I can look it up. I keep records back to when I started this business." She heard him digging in a file. A moment later he came back on the line. "Just as I remembered. An anniversary present, the clasp for the bolo tie and a set of cufflinks. Three tiny silver C's for Chisholm Cattle Company. I made them for Krystal Chisholm, October 16, 1984."

Twenty-seven years ago. Just about the time that Hoyt had married Krystal, McCall thought.

She asked if the jeweler could fax her a copy of that order, thanked him and hung up.

Earlier at the hospital, Hoyt Chisholm had assured her he knew nothing about Aggie Wells's disappearance. He'd sworn he hadn't seen her since the night she'd come out to the ranch to have dinner.

But given what she knew now, she wondered how long it would be before they found her body as well.

McCall sat for a moment before she placed the call to the county attorney. It was time to bring in Hoyt Chisholm before another wife ended up dead.

"AGGIE WAS HERE," EMMA SAID when Hoyt returned to where his wife was still rooted just inside the door.

"There's no one in the house. The front door probably blew open," he said as if he didn't hear her. He started toward her to put his shotgun back into his pickup.

"Did you hear what I just said to you?" she demanded. "Aggie was in the house again."

He stopped in front of her and frowned. "Emma—"

"Didn't you smell her perfume when you entered the house?"

He looked at her, shook his head and swore under his breath. "Where are you going with this?"

Did he think she was making it up? Imagining it?

"I know what I'm talking about. Don't you see what she's doing? She's trying to frame you for murder."

"She's been doing that for years," he said as he tried to step past Emma.

"Hoyt, I'm telling you she set this whole thing up, her disappearance, her car being found, the blood on the seat, the whole thing to make it look as if you killed her."

He shook his head. "I really don't want to talk about this." He pushed past her and headed for his truck.

"Hoyt Chisholm, do not treat me like I am imagining things," she said following him as far as the porch. "I smelled her perfume. She's been in our house again while we were gone. It's as if she knew we were all going to be at the hospital and—"

"And what, Emma?" he demanded as he turned from hanging up his shotgun on the rack behind the seats. He slammed the pickup door before he turned back to her. "Emma, why would she be sneaking around our house? For what possible reason?"

"She did it before."

"Yes, no doubt to let me know she hadn't given up sending me to prison." He swore under his breath. "Aggie Wells is the last person I'm concerned with right now."

"I smelled her perfume. She was in this house again." But she was talking to his back for he had turned and was headed out to the barn where he always went when he was upset—or didn't want to hear what she had to say.

As she started after him, Emma saw the sheriff's patrol car coming up the road toward the house.

TANNER KNEW HE WAS DRIVING too fast. He'd made good time. Even after his stop at the bank to get more money for Billie Rae and gas in the pickup in Havre, he was going to beat Billie Rae to the casino parking lot.

The casino wasn't far ahead. Just the thought of seeing Billie Rae again had his heart pounding with anticipation. He thought about the first time he'd laid eyes on her at the rodeo grounds.

He still couldn't describe the effect she'd had on him. Love at first sight? How was it possible to fall in love with a complete stranger in a nanosecond? It was easier to believe they'd been together in a past life and had found each other again in this one.

Whatever it had been, it had happened. In that instant, Billie Rae's face had lit up in a burst of fireworks and he'd felt his heart skyrocket. The fireworks had showered down from Montana's big night sky, the air smelling of summer and rodeo concession stand food. Music had played against the boom of the rockets exploding over their heads and he'd lost his heart.

That moment was frozen in time forever for him. But as odd as it sounded, maybe it had been luck that brought them together. That is, if they could stop this maniac after her.

Ahead, Tanner saw a large black car parked at the edge of the road. His heart lodged in his throat. Had Duane somehow found out where Billie Rae was going to meet him?

The black car pulled out, turned in his direction and headed down the highway toward him. Past it Tanner could see the casino in the distance. His gaze shifted from the black car approaching him to the casino parking lot.

He didn't see Billie Rae's small red car. He hoped that meant she hadn't arrived yet—and not that Duane had already stopped her.

His gaze shifted quickly back to the black car as it increased speed on the other side of the highway coming in his direction. The car was big and black, possibly a Lincoln like the one Duane drove, just as Billie Rae had described it and it was gaining speed quickly.

Tanner tried to see the face behind the steering wheel as it neared, but the sun was glinting off the windshield. He felt himself tense. He gripped the wheel tighter, bracing himself because he feared the driver of the black car was planning to swerve into his lane.

At the sped the car was coming, it would probably kill both of them if Tanner couldn't avoid the crash, but then Duane Rasmussen was a psychopath, wasn't he?

The car was within yards of him, still on the other side of the road. And then it was roaring by in a blur, throwing up dust and gravel on the edge of the highway. Tanner caught a glimpse of an elderly man behind the wheel with a shock of white hair as the car sped past.

Tanner had to hit his brakes to make the casino turnoff. As he fishtailed into the parking lot, his blood was still hammering in his ears. He'd been so sure the driver of the black car was Duane on a suicide mission that was going to take them both out.

Now as he brought the pickup to a stop in the parking lot, he had to take a minute to catch his breath. He glanced around the lot. Billie Rae wasn't here yet. He hoped that meant she was still safe. Police officer Duane Rasmussen was probably still back in Whitehorse. Or maybe already in jail.

Tanner tried to reassure himself that everything was going to be all right. Billie Rae would be here soon. He would talk her out of going anywhere near her husband. Somehow it had to work out because he couldn't bear the thought that he might never see her again. Or worse, that Duane would find her.

DUANE SWORE AS HE STARED at the GPS screen. Tanner Chisholm had been right behind him, then he suddenly stopped when Duane had found the perfect place to finish the bastard for good?

He tapped the screen on his cell phone and looked down the highway in the direction Tanner had been heading until a few minutes ago. No sign of a Chisholm Cattle Company pickup headed this way. Instead it appeared the pickup had left the highway and was no longer moving. Why would he pull off?

Duane looked at his watch. Turn back and find him? Or wait? Or keep going and take care of Billie Rae and then worry about Tanner Chisholm?

He tapped the screen again, thinking something was wrong with the tracking device. Maybe it had fallen off the cowboy's rig. The tiny icon representing the Chisholm Cattle Company pickup still hadn't moved. The location appeared to not be that far back up the highway.

What if Billie Rae's call had been bogus? What if she was meeting the cowboy back down the road? Duane tried to remember if there'd been a place back up the highway where Tanner and Billie Rae might have planned to meet.

With a jolt he remember seeing a large building set off the highway. A Native American casino.

Duane slammed the car into gear and, with tires throwing gravel, flipped the Lincoln around and headed back down the highway. If he was wrong about Billie Rae being with Tanner right now, he'd have to make this fast, which annoyed him to no end. He'd wanted to make the cowboy suffer enough that he wouldn't be stupid like his brother and call the law on him.

On impulse, Duane called the cell phone number

Billie Rae had called him from this morning. It went straight to voice mail.

"What the hell?" he said tossing the phone on the passenger seat as he floored the Lincoln.

He was driving so fast he almost missed the turn into the casino. The Chisholm Cattle Company pickup was sitting in the lot away from the few other vehicles, the cab empty.

Duane hadn't taken Tanner Chisholm for a gambler, but then he'd gambled with his life when he'd helped Billie Rae, hadn't he?

Parking next to a large motorhome out of sight of the cowboy's pickup, he sat for a moment considering his options. He didn't have the patience to wait for Tanner to come out. He was too anxious to get to Billie Rae.

But then again, she might be inside the casino with the cowboy right now.

The problem was he would have to be careful once inside. If he made a scene, he could end up in a Native American jail cell. He got out of his car. He didn't think walking into the casino wearing his shoulder holster would be the smartest idea, either. While he didn't have jurisdiction in Montana, he really didn't on the reservation.

But he also wasn't going in the place unarmed. He took off the holster, tossed it on the seat and removing the Glock, tucked the gun into the waistband of his slacks. The tail of his shirt covered it well enough.

If this place was like most casinos, it would be fairly dark inside.

Duane locked his car and walked toward the front door, hoping he didn't find the cowboy and his wife together gambling when Billie Rae had convinced him he needed to save her at the end of some dead end road up the highway.

If that happened, Duane wasn't making any promises about what he would do. But as it happened, Duane didn't have to go inside the casino.

BILLIE RAE LOOKED AT the pile of supplies she'd put in the car trunk, glanced at her watch and slammed the lid. Fortunately she didn't have far to drive, she thought as she slid behind the wheel.

She repeated the mantra that had been echoing in her head since Tanner's call. *Desperate times called for desperate measures.* She wondered, though, if Duane rationalized his behavior with the same kind of catch phrases.

The cell phone rang on the seat where she'd laid it. She checked to see who was calling as she drove out of Great Falls. Tanner. She wanted to answer just to hear his voice and take some comfort in it. But there was nothing more to say. She let it go to voice mail. If he knew about her plan he would try to stop her.

She couldn't let that happen.

Billie Rae knew how dangerous her plan was. So much could go wrong she didn't want to think about it. But she felt she had no choice. She had to stop

Duane from hurting anyone else and if that meant sacrificing herself in the process, then so be it.

Ahead she saw the sign for the dead-end road she'd seen on the map. Turning off the main highway, she drove down the narrow dirt road until it dropped precariously toward the river gorge below.

Billie Rae hit the brakes and sat for a moment gripping the steering wheel. Where was the road she'd seen on the map? What if it had washed out?

Setting the emergency brake, she climbed out of the car and walked to the edge. The wind whipped her hair around her face. She brushed it back and looked down. Her stomach knotted at what she saw. Far below was the river, a green snake of rock and rushing water.

The road she'd seen on the map was little more than a rocky two-rut path that had been cut into the side of the mountain high above the river gorge. Getting to it would require her to drive off this steep edge to reach it.

She couldn't do it. She took a step back, glanced at her watch. Time was running out. Duane would be here in the next thirty minutes, maybe sooner.

That's when she saw it. The swinging foot bridge across the narrow gorge. It was at the end of the road just like it had shown on the map. Billie Rae stared at it for a long moment, surprised that it was just as she'd envisioned it—except even from here, she could see it swinging in the wind.

This was pure suicide, she thought as she looked

from the swinging footbridge high over the river gorge to the road that ended at the bridge. The map had failed to give her any idea of just how narrow or how rough the road was. Add to that the large sign that prohibited anyone from going past this point unless for authorized use only.

She'd always been so law-abiding she actually hesitated, then reminded herself given what she planned this was a pretty minor infraction.

Taking a deep breath, she eyed the road for a moment, then gathering her courage, she got back into the car, released the emergency brake and, riding her foot brake, let the car drop over the rim into the river gorge.

TANNER FELT AS IF HE'D suddenly been dropped in Las Vegas. From the carpet to the noise and flashing lights of the gambling machines, it took a moment to get his equilibrium once he'd stepped inside the casino.

The place was huge and nearly empty, which made the beeps and dings echo through the large room giving it an end-of-the-world feeling as he walked through.

He couldn't help searching for Billie Rae among the few patrons and employees even though he didn't think she could have been here yet unless like him, she'd driven too fast. He wasn't all that sure that she could get that kind of speed out of the car she'd purchased—not to mention the fact that her car hadn't been in the lot.

But to be safe, he found the rear exit and checked to see if there was a back lot. No Billie Rae.

He found the men's room on his way back through the casino. He kept telling himself that once he had a chance to talk some sense into Billie Rae, she would come back to the ranch with him.

Hell, maybe by now the sheriff had already picked up Duane. Even if she couldn't hold him long before the cop made bail, at least Duane wouldn't be stupid enough to get into any more trouble in Whitehorse.

As he walked back to his pickup to wait, Tanner hoped Billie Rae would be here soon. He couldn't wait to see her. He glanced down the highway in the direction of Great Falls looking for her small red car.

He was almost to his pickup when Duane Rasmussen came out from behind a van and jumped him.

EMMA COULDN'T LOOK AT HER husband for fear she would burst out crying. She had taken his hand the moment they'd all sat down at the kitchen table and now gripped it tightly, afraid of what would happen if she didn't hang on for dear life.

As she looked across the table at the sheriff, she told herself this wasn't happening. "Are you sure I can't get us some coffee? Maybe some of that cake…" Hoyt squeezed her hand making the rest of her words dissolve in her mouth.

"You're sure it's Krystal," Hoyt asked the sheriff. He hadn't seemed surprised when McCall had informed them that Krystal Blake Chisholm's remains had been found not far from the ranch.

Emma refused to read anything into that. Hoyt must have suspected his third wife was dead after she and her old boyfriend had both disappeared. But hadn't he said the old boyfriend lived down in Wyoming? So how did Krystal end up buried up here? And where was the boyfriend?

Emma's mind whirled with such thoughts as she tried to concentrate on what the sheriff was saying.

"We have matched both dental records and the DNA which you provided when she disappeared," McCall said.

"So it really is her?" he repeated as if in a fog. He seemed to have aged right before Emma's eyes.

"Where did you find her?" Emma asked.

The sheriff seemed to hesitate, but she had to know the news would be all over the grapevine, if it wasn't already. "Near where we found Aggie Wells's vehicle." She was looking at Hoyt, obviously hoping for a reaction.

Emma sat up straighter. She'd erroneously thought the remains had been found on the ranch. Why else would the sheriff be acting as if she was about to arrest Hoyt at any moment?

"Near where you found Aggie Wells's car?" she repeated.

Didn't anyone else see what was going on here?

"You haven't found Aggie's body, though, have you," Emma challenged. Hoyt squeezed her hand. She pulled it free. "And you're not going to find it because Aggie isn't dead."

"Emma—"

It was the sheriff who cut Hoyt off. "Where would you suggest we look?" she asked, her eyes narrowing as she turned her attention on Emma.

"Aggie staged her disappearance," Emma said and Hoyt groaned next to her. "She isn't dead. I know that because she was here earlier today."

"You saw her?" the sheriff asked.

"After we got back from the hospital, the front door was standing open—Hoyt began to search the house. I smelled her perfume the moment I stepped inside the house."

"Emma," Hoyt pleaded again.

"I smelled her perfume another time when she went through our things in our bedroom. Don't you see what is happening here?" Emma cried. "Aggie is trying to frame my husband. She is so determined to be right."

The sheriff looked uncomfortable.

"Emma, the sheriff isn't here about Aggie Wells," Hoyt said. "This is about Krystal."

Sheriff Crawford nodded solemnly and then Emma knew even before the woman reached into her pocket that there was more. They had found some kind of evidence at the scene.

"I need to ask you, Mr. Chisholm, if this is yours."

Sheriff Crawford pushed a small plastic bag across the table. Emma caught sight of something discolored inside it. She recognized it at once—and so did Hoyt.

"Where did you get that?" Emma demanded.

"It was found with Krystal Chisholm's remains."

"That's not possible. Hoyt has his upstairs in his—" Emma was on her feet. She hurried up the stairs and opened the top drawer of Hoyt's bureau and rummaged through the wooden box. She knew she'd seen the bolo tie with the three C's on it in the box. It had to be there.

She found matching cufflinks but no bolo tie. She stood, trying to catch her breath from her panic, her fear, the run up the stairs. She'd been so sure the bolo tie had been in there even though she hadn't seen Hoyt ever wear it.

Returning downstairs, she found the sheriff and her husband waiting for her. Hoyt had his head down, looking like a guilty man. She wanted to snap at him, tell him to knock it off. She knew he was innocent. She knew that the reason he was behaving this way was that he felt responsible because he'd married Krystal, because he thought Aggie Wells had won, as if he'd always feared it was just a matter of time before he was arrested.

Three dead wives. Who wouldn't think he did it?

The sheriff didn't have to ask if Emma had found the bolo tie, but Emma still shook her head, her gaze going to her husband as she slid into the chair next to him and took his hand again.

"Mr. Chisholm?" The sheriff was looking at Hoyt. "Is this yours?"

He nodded, then glanced at the tape recorder she had turned on when the questioning began and said, "Yes, it's mine."

"When was the last time you saw it?" she asked.

He glanced at Emma, then shook his head. "It was part of a bolo tie I haven't worn in years."

"So you weren't aware it was missing?"

"No."

The sheriff rose to her feet. "Hoyt Chisholm? You are under arrest for the murder of Krystal Blake Chisholm."

Emma listened as the sheriff stated her husband his rights. "He didn't kill her," she cried as the sheriff pulled out her handcuffs. Hoyt pushed himself up from the table as if carrying the weight of the world on his broad shoulders. "I'm telling you he couldn't kill *anyone*."

Her husband turned, gave her a sad smile. "It's going to be all right."

The sheriff gave her a sympathetic look as she led Hoyt out the door. "You might want to call a lawyer for your husband."

Emma could only nod as she watched the sheriff escort Hoyt out to the patrol car, put him in the rear seat and drive away. She knew she should rush to the phone and call his lawyer and his sons, but what she really needed to do was find Aggie Wells.

Or maybe, she thought with a sudden chill as she looked out across the wide open country that was Chisholm Cattle Company, maybe Aggie was planning on finding her.

Chapter Eleven

Billie Rae drove the car down the impossibly narrow road cut into the side of the mountain wondering if she'd lost her mind. She had to creep along, dodging the rocks that would take out the oil pan, while at the same time avoiding the solid rock face of the side of the mountain—and the sheer drop off into the river gorge.

Once she'd turned onto the road, she'd also realized she couldn't change her mind. She would have to go to the end of the road. No way could she back up. She was committed.

"You should be *committed*—to the nut house," she said to herself. More and more she was realizing this was a suicide mission. Desperate times called for— "Just drive."

She could hear the wind rushing down through the gorge. It whistled through the gap in her car window and whipped at what little vegetation grew between the boulders on the mountainside next to her. Ahead she could see the bridge and felt physically ill at the sight of it swaying wildly in the gale.

Billie Rae concentrated on the road and tried not to look—or think—too far ahead. There was literally no turning back now. Duane would be coming soon. She had to get ready. If he caught her now…

Ahead she saw where the road abruptly ended in a pile of rock and dirt. There was just enough room to park the car. She didn't try to turn it around. If her plan worked, she would worry about getting out of here then. It was such a long shot that she would be leaving here at all she wasn't about to take the time now to turn the car around.

Climbing out, she felt the full force of the wind as it roared through the canyon. For a moment she froze as she watched the footbridge swing back and forth high above the rocks and dark green water below. Could she do this? Or had she played right into Duane's hands and given him the perfect place to kill her? This would give him such an easy out. He could get away with her murder if things went wrong and never serve a day in jail for it.

But then, Billie Rae thought no matter where she met him, he would figure out a way to get away with what he planned to do to her anyway. He'd gotten away with murder before. All the odds had been stacked in his favor, they always were. But she promised herself that she would end it here. One way or another.

She glanced at her watch. She could feel time slipping through her fingers. She had to move. *Now!* If Duane caught her just standing here, everything he'd said about her would be true. And everyone knew what happened to cowards.

Billie Rae cautiously moved to the rear of the car, feeling as if she was hanging on the side of the mountain by the skin of her teeth. Opening the trunk, she pulled out the large jacket she'd purchased, then taking the knife, began to cut into the cloth.

This morning after Tanner's call she'd known she had to use her husband's Achilles heel if she hoped to still be alive by dark. She'd found out about Duane's weakness by accident—something Duane had never forgotten—or forgiven.

"Did you hear about your big, tough husband?" one of the other cops she'd only just met, had asked her after too many drinks. They had been at one of the few parties with his fellow boys in blue that Duane had allowed her to attend—and the last after that night.

"Shut up," Duane said under his breath, but either the cop didn't hear or ignored the warning.

"So here we are chasing a robbery suspect and he hightails it up a six-story fire escape," the cop continues. "Duane starts up after him, me behind him. Then all of a sudden Duane looks down and stops dead. I crash into him and say, 'What the hell?' The dumb bastard, it turns out, is scared of heights." The cop broke up in loud guffaws.

The cop hadn't been watching Duane, but Billie Rae had. His face had been flushed with anger, a vein throbbing in his neck, his hands fisted at his sides.

She'd known Duane would never forgive the cop for telling that story—especially in front of her.

Two months later the cop was found shot to death in an alley. No suspect was ever found, but Billie Rae knew who'd killed him—and why. She also knew that had she told the police, no one would have believed her.

Just as no one had believed her the one time she'd tried to report the abuse.

"I'm going to give you some good advice," her husband's captain had told her after she'd taken a taxi down to the police station on a day she knew Duane would be on assignment away from the department. "Go home. Stop fighting with your husband. Work a little harder to make him happy."

Now she glanced again at the bridge hanging suspended over the gorge. She was about to take on the fight of her life with her cop husband. And how it ended would all depend on how badly he wanted to get his hands on her.

TANNER CAME TO in the dark. He was immediately aware of the pain—and his surroundings. He was in the trunk of a fast-moving car. He could hear the whine of the tires on the highway and smell exhaust. His hands were bound in front of him and he felt cramped even in the roomy space of what he knew was the Lincoln's trunk.

He wiped something sticky and wet from his left eye and tried to sit up. His brother Marshall had been right. He had gone for Duane's throat, charging him after the ambush even though the cop had quickly pulled a gun from under his shirt.

Tanner had gotten in a few good punches, catching the cop off balance. Duane had thought the pistol he pointed at Tanner would deter him. It hadn't. Tanner hadn't thought Duane would shoot him in the casino parking lot but the furious cop had definitely *wanted* to pull the trigger.

Duane had gotten the final blow, though. Tanner hadn't seen the butt of the gun coming until it was too late. He tried to block the blow, but his head had taken the brunt of it.

That's all he remembered although he was sure Duane had kicked him a few times when he was down. His ribs hurt like hell and he felt as if he'd been used for a punching bag. From what he could tell, there was a cut over his left eye which was bleeding and his nose might be broken.

He had no idea how long he'd been out—or how far they had driven. All he remembered was Duane saying that Billie Rae was waiting for them up the road.

It was too dark to see if there was a latch, something that could get him out of the trunk when the time came. He felt around, trying not to move too much, but didn't find anything. He didn't want the cop to know he was awake. Not yet, anyway.

Tanner felt he had the best chance of survival by pretending to still be knocked out. The element of surprise might be his *only* chance, he thought, remembering the fury in the cop's face when he'd jumped him.

What confused Tanner was how Duane had known he would be at the casino. Billie Rae wouldn't have told him. Tanner swore as he realized how stupid he'd been. Duane was a cop. He probably put a tracking device on Tanner's pickup.

He tried to think of when Duane might have had access to the truck. When Tanner had gone to the hospital to see his brother? The bastard had probably been just waiting for him to lead him to Billie Rae.

BILLIE RAE PUT ON the harness she'd purchased at the climbing store. She attached the rope the way the clerk had shown her, her fingers hardly shaking.

Don't think about all the things that can go wrong.

Don't think about Duane. Or the bridge. Or... Tanner.

Instead, she concentrated on what she had to do as she put the large jacket on over the climbing harness, coiled the rope she'd attached to the harness and put it in one large pocket of the jacket. The gun she put in the other pocket along with the extra cartridges. Hesitating, she took the gun from her pocket, lifted it to chest high and aimed it toward the bridge.

The weight of the weapon in her hands made her feel stronger than she really was, braver, almost invincible. She wondered if that was how Duane felt when he was armed. He spent hours cleaning his gun, handling it, holding it, aiming it. She shuddered at how often he had aimed it at her heart and threatened to blow a hole in her the size of a half dollar.

"You should learn to shoot," Duane said one night after a few beers.

"I don't like guns."

He'd laughed at that. "Only fools don't like guns. A gun can save your life."

"Or take it," she'd said.

He'd smiled at that. "I wouldn't waste a bullet on you, sweetheart. I'd kill you with my bare hands if you ever gave me reason."

The next afternoon, he'd come home early. "Come on," he'd said.

"Where are we going?" It wasn't like him to come home early. She feared something had happened at work and that they would be moving again. She'd only recently learned by overhearing Duane on the phone that something he did in Oklahoma was why he'd applied to the force in Williston, North Dakota. He'd told her it was because the job paid more but she'd found out that too had been a lie.

She'd later learned that he'd assaulted one of the suspects who'd said something to him that set him off. Two other policemen had been forced to pull him off the suspect. Unfortunately for Duane, some witness had gotten a little of it on his cell phone camera.

His fellow cops had covered for him so Duane had managed to get off with little more than a slap on the wrist, but the department was watching him—something Duane couldn't handle.

"We're going to the shooting range," he had announced the day he'd come home early. "No wife of mine is going to be afraid of guns."

"I'm not afraid, I just don't—"

"You're going to learn to shoot—and shoot well." She'd heard the warning in his tone and knew there was no arguing with Duane once he'd made up his mind.

Now she quickly slipped the gun into her jacket pocket again. Learning to shoot had been the one thing Duane had taught her that was finally going to come in handy.

The wind blew her hair into her eyes. She tied it back but still some tendrils escaped. Then she doubled-checked to make sure she had everything, before she glanced at her watch again. Duane could be here any minute. Slamming the trunk, she turned to look again at the bridge.

It was made of wooden slats that were no more than four feet wide. They were bound together with what appeared to be rope. Two other ropes that stretched from bank to bank acted as handrails. Each of those was attached vertically to the bridge platform every four or five feet with more rope.

Two steel cables anchored in concrete on each side ran under the bridge to give it reinforced support. But the cables were slack enough to let the bridge move and, boy, was it moving.

From this angle, it swayed in the wind as hypnotically as a pendulum. Billie Rae couldn't imagine trying to walk out on it—or how she would get to the middle where she needed to be when Duane arrived. She just knew she had to take that first step—just as she'd taken the first step to be free of Duane.

This time, she let herself think of Tanner as she slipped down the steep rocky slope to the bridge entrance. She was terrified of what she was about to do. Thinking of Tanner Chisholm gave her strength. At the base of the footbridge, she had to climb up to get on it.

A chain had been stretched across the opening with another sign that warned that the bridge was for authorized personnel only. Violators would be prosecuted. Like so many signs she'd seen out west, this sign had been used for target practice. It was peppered with rusted gunshot holes.

The holes made it hard—but not impossible—to read the smaller print at the bottom of the sign: Danger: Do Not Cross In High Wind.

She watched the wind kick up dust from the other side of the mountain, a gust wildly rocking the bridge before it settled back into just swinging.

Gathering all her courage, Billie Rae ducked under the sign and crawled up onto the bridge.

JUST THE THOUGHT OF Aggie Wells pulling their strings as if they were puppets made Emma angry. She had to calm down before she went back into the house after the sheriff left with Hoyt. She called the lawyer first, then each of her stepsons.

"Dad didn't kill anyone," said Dawson, the eldest of the brothers and the one they all agreed was the most responsible of the six. "Don't worry. We can take care of the ranch until we get him out. Have you called his lawyer?"

"Yes, he's headed down to the sheriff's department to see about getting Hoyt out on bail," Emma told him—just as she had the others.

That wasn't the problem—getting Hoyt out on bail, she thought after she hung up. It was finding Aggie Wells and getting at the truth. No way did Emma believe it was a coincidence that Aggie's car ended up abandoned near where Krystal's body was found. Or that the bolo tie clasp had ended up at the site.

Unless Hoyt is guilty.

The thought flew at her out of the darkness of her thoughts.

"My husband is not a killer," she said to the empty kitchen. Her voice echoed back at her and, with a chill, she realized how alone she was. The cook, Celeste, had called and made a lame excuse for why she couldn't make it today. Housekeeper Mae had called shortly after with an equally weak excuse. They were bailing off Chisholm Cattle Company as if it were a sinking ship.

She couldn't really blame them. Nor could she bear to think of Hoyt locked up—let alone him going to prison for a murder, or murders he didn't commit. Aggie Wells had to be behind this.

And if that was the case…Emma let out a cry as a thought struck her. *Aggie killed Krystal. How else would she know where the woman was buried so she could implicate Hoyt by putting the silver bolo tie clasp at the scene?*

She started to reach for the phone to call the sheriff when she realized she had no proof. It was all conjecture. She couldn't prove the bolo tie had been in Hoyt's jewelry box and he didn't seem to remember if it had been there or not since he'd said he hadn't worn it in years.

"Hoyt didn't do it." She said it loud enough that if the house wanted to argue she was up for it. All she got was an echo and realized she was arguing with herself because she was scared.

She was convinced Aggie Wells was alive and behind this. But did she really believe the former insurance investigator had gone so far off the rails that she would murder Hoyt's third wife just to frame him? That did seem extreme.

But Aggie had already been investigating the deaths of Hoyt's first two wives. What if she'd become so frustrated for lack of proof that she'd decided to kill Krystal and make it look as if Hoyt had, just so she could frame him?

"And then wait almost thirty years before she made sure the woman's remains were found?" Emma demanded of the empty room.

She was glad she hadn't called the sheriff. Her theory sounded way too far-fetched.

Just the fact that she'd smelled the woman's perfume in the house twice hardly proved that Aggie Wells was alive. Which begged the question, why hadn't she turned up?

Emma poured herself a mug of coffee and cut a small piece of the oatmeal cake. After staring down at the small piece of a cake for a long moment, she cut herself a larger piece as a thought crossed her mind.

If she really believed in Hoyt's innocence—which she did—then she needed to figure out what Aggie had been doing in her house. She took a bite of the cake. She really did make the best oatmeal cake, she thought, as she swallowed and had a sip of coffee. She could feel her strength coming back as well as her senses.

The reason for Aggie coming to the house at least the first time came to her like a shot out of the dark.

Aggie took Hoyt's bolo tie to frame him.

Emma felt a chill as she realized that had to be it. All of their bureau drawers had been gone through including Emma's jewelry box. She hadn't thought to check Hoyt's because he'd glanced in and said he didn't think anything was missing.

The only clue had been that lingering scent the woman had left behind. Emma had recognized it when she'd met Aggie at the bar at Sleeping Buffalo. When she'd accused Aggie of snooping around their ranch house, Aggie hadn't denied it. She'd given Emma the impression that she had merely been curious—and concerned—about Emma, Hoyt's fourth wife, after what had apparently happened to the other three.

Sitting up straighter, Emma saw how foolish she had been not to see this before. Aggie was so determined to prove Hoyt had murdered his first wife that she had become obsessed with being right. It had apparently cost Aggie her job at the insurance company.

But if she had killed Krystal… Emma had a thought that felt so right it scared her. What if Aggie hadn't killed Krystal to frame Hoyt—but to get rid of the competition?

Hoyt was an incredibly handsome man—not to mention wealthy and respected, a great catch. If Aggie had fallen for him while investigating him…

It fit. She wished she could ask Hoyt how Aggie had acted after his third wife had disappeared. Of course Aggie would have investigated the disappearance. That meant she'd been in Whitehorse, probably had been out to the ranch to talk to Hoyt.

But Hoyt hadn't been interested. He'd sworn off women all those years until he'd met Emma—and Aggie Wells had come back into his life. How would a jealous woman react to Hoyt getting married again after all those years?

Badly, Emma thought. So badly, though, that she would make sure Krystal's body turned up and that her own didn't? So obsessed that she had faked her own disappearance and made it look as if she too had been murdered?

Emma hugged herself as she realized just how obsessed that was. If she was right, then Aggie Wells was a very dangerous person with a very jealous streak.

She glanced toward the window, uneasy at the direction her thoughts had taken. The day was bright and sunny, the sky a brilliant blue, not a cloud in sight. Still she felt a chill wrap itself around her neck like a noose. Where was Aggie right now? Was she hiding in the hills, watching the house with binoculars? That seemed unlikely.

If Aggie wasn't hiding in the hills watching the house with a pair of binoculars then how had she known earlier that there was no one around so she could come back into the house again?

Emma took the last bite of cake and almost choked as the answer came to her.

Aggie Wells had bugged the house!

THE MOMENT BILLIE RAE stepped onto the bridge, she made her first mistake. Still on her hands and knees after slipping under the chain across the bridge entrance, she'd looked down. The rushing movement of the dark green water over the rocks far below threw her off balance.

She closed her eyes, held on to the wooden slats

of the bridge beneath her and tried to regain not only her breath—but her courage.

After a few moments, she opened her eyes, this time focusing on the other side of the gorge as she got to her feet. This end of the bridge was attached to a concrete base set back into the side of the mountain so the bridge was fairly stable.

But the moment she took her first step, she felt the bridge move under her weight. She clutched the ropes that formed the handrail. They felt insubstantial. She didn't look through the gaping hole on each side between the rope or through the wooden slats of the bridge beneath her feet, but she was well aware of how easily it would be to fall between the bridge floor and the handrail rope uprights and drop the fifty feet to the river and rocks below.

She couldn't move for a moment. The wind blowing down the canyon buffeted her hair, sending tendrils into her eyes. She could hear the river and the wind and a semi shifting down on the highway off in the distance, but she couldn't take a step—just as she hadn't all those years ago.

She'd been eleven the first time she'd ever seen a bridge like this. A boy she'd liked had asked her to go on a picnic with his family. The bridge spanned across a creek only about fifteen feet above the water. Nor was the bridge very long.

The boy had scampered across it and turned to look back at her, daring her to cross. She hadn't liked the feel of it, the way the footbridge swayed with each step she took, or the way the boy was watching her intently.

She'd gotten halfway across when the boy had started making it rock violently. Instinctively, she'd dropped to her hands and knees and gripped the rough edges of the worn boards in her hands and couldn't move.

The boy had felt badly for scaring her, for making her cry. He'd stopped rocking the bridge and offered to help her up, but she'd wanted nothing to do with him or his help and ordered him to leave her alone.

His father had come and talked her off the bridge. She'd never forgotten being in the middle of that bridge on her hands and knees. She'd never felt so trapped and nakedly vulnerable—until she found herself married to an abusive cop who would rather see her dead than free her.

At the sound of a car engine, Billie Rae turned her head to look back toward the road down to the bridge. Duane's large black car came to a stop on the rim of the gorge.

She turned back to the bridge and with an urgency born of survival, she took a step, then another, desperately needing to reach the swaying middle before Duane came after her.

BUGGED? EMMA ALMOST LAUGHED at how ridiculous she sounded and yet she went straight to the computer and typed in: How to tell if a house is bugged?

To her amazement a list came up with not only

inexpensive listening devices that could be purchased by anyone, but video surveillance devices as well. She'd had no idea how small or how high-tech the devices had become.

Just the thought that Aggie Wells could have been not only listening to their every word—but also watching them all this time—gave her more than a chill. As she read what to do about the problem, she realized that if Aggie was watching, Emma didn't want her to know that she was on to her.

Under the pretense of cleaning, she began to search the house for what the article called "conspicuous" places bugs or small video cameras could be hidden: lamps, picture frames, books, under tables and chairs, inside pots and vases. She hoped the sound of the vacuum would mask what she was up to—even if Aggie was watching her.

The devices were made to look like something else or hide in a plant or the edge of a frame on the wall, she'd read. Aggie could be watching her clean right now on a remote device as ordinary as a computer screen or even a cell phone. So Emma knew she had to be very careful if she didn't want to give herself away.

She discovered the first bug quite by accident. She was vacuuming the rug next to the bed when she noticed tiny pieces of plaster. It wasn't the first time she'd seen them in the same spot. The last time she'd been too distracted to think much about it since the house was old and the plastered ceiling had small cracks where the house had shifted.

But now she froze and slowly looked up to the smoke alarm on the ceiling. Her heart began to pound. The smoke alarm was new. Why hadn't she noticed it before? It was small and round and nothing like the other smoke alarms in the house.

Emma knew she'd been staring at it for weeks since some nights she couldn't sleep and— With a shudder, she realized Aggie had been listening to everything Emma and Hoyt had said in this bedroom. In this bed.

Furious, she wanted to take the vacuum attachment and beat the device off the ceiling. She had to refrain from doing that, though, if she hoped to find Aggie. Somehow she had to use this in her favor.

Leaving the vacuum running, she dragged a chair over and climbed up on it to inspect the smoke alarm. It didn't appear to have video. That was a relief.

Taking the advice she'd picked up on the internet, she put on headphones, then using her radio dial, listened near the smoke alarm for uniform distortion. The bleeps and recurring patterns indicated the presence of a covert listening device—just as the directions had said.

She finished vacuuming up the flakes of plaster that installing the alarm had caused. Not just installing it, Emma thought. Aggie had come back to the house a second time and messed with the alarm. Had it not been working properly? She could only hope.

Moving through the rest of the house, this time Emma knew what to look for and quickly found three more new smoke alarms. She could understand now why none of the family had noticed them. The devices were small and unobtrusive. The one in the kitchen was hidden on the other side of the overhead light, same with the ones in the dining room and living room.

Emma put the vacuum away, went back into the kitchen and poured herself a cup of coffee before sitting down at the table to plot the best way to draw Aggie Wells out into the open.

She had a feeling it wouldn't be necessary if Aggie thought she was alone at the house. Emma remembered how Aggie had repeatedly warned her that she would be the next wife of Hoyt Chisholm's to die.

She curled her fingers around the warmth of the mug. If Aggie had just been waiting for the time when Emma would be all alone in his big rambling ranch house, this was the time. No Hoyt. No stepsons. No cook or housekeeper. Just Emma, the fourth wife of Hoyt Chisholm.

Chapter Twelve

Duane could not believe what he was seeing. He'd turned off where Billie Rae had told him to, driven down the narrow dirt road, but when he'd come to where the road disappeared over the edge into the gorge, he'd thrown on his brakes with a curse thinking she'd meant to kill him.

Now as he stood next to the car, listening to the wind whistling down the river canyon, he hoped to hell he *was* seeing things. Billie Rae didn't really expect him to drive down that road cut into the side of the mountain, did she?

"What the hell were you thinking, woman?" he yelled. The wind blew his words back at him.

That's when he spotted her. She was standing at the entrance to a foot bridge that hung high above the river gorge. Who *was* this woman? Not the woman he'd married. Billie Rae had never been daring. He scoffed at even the idea. If anything he would have said his wife was timid. He thought of the way she often cowered away from him, which only made him more angry with her at the time.

So what had happened to her?

He frowned as he took in the small red compact car she apparently had been driving. Where the hell had she gotten that? From that cowboy? Or some other man she'd told her hard-luck story to? He ground his teeth at the thought that she'd told people about him. What went on between them was private. She had no business sharing anything personal with another person.

He watched Billie Rae start across the bridge.

"What are you doing?" he yelled again. She didn't seem to hear him as she took another step, then another.

He looked from her to the road. No way was he driving his car any farther down this road. He reached back inside the Lincoln, pulled on his shoulder holster and, on impulse grabbed the small unregistered handgun he'd taken off a drug dealer in Oklahoma. He stuffed it into the waistband of his slacks, covered it with his shirt, and slammed the car door.

As he walked away, he hit the automatic lock on his keys, heard it beep once, then pocketed his keys.

Billie Rae had stopped on the bridge. She was clinging to the rope rails. What was she doing out there in the first place? The damned fool woman must have changed her mind knowing he was going to be furious with her and now she was trying to get away from him by crossing the river?

He glanced to the other side and saw only a narrow

trail that led to what appeared to be some kind of weather station box used by meteorologists. The trail ended abruptly. Billie Rae was only going to find herself at another dead end. The stupid damned woman.

Well, if she thought he was going out on that bridge after her, she was sadly mistaken. She could just figure out how to get back and when she did, he would be waiting for her.

The road was rocky and rough and the dress shoes he was wearing were all wrong for chasing his wife into a river gorge. Duane swore as he started down the road, telling himself he would make Billie Rae rue this day.

TANNER HAD FELT THE BIG CAR slow, then turn onto a bumpy road. Is this where the cop was meeting Billie Rae? Or was this where he was getting rid of the passenger in the trunk?

He'd listened. Earlier he'd heard stereo music and even at one point, Duane signing along. The man couldn't carry a tune.

Tanner had tried hard not to bounce around on the rough road. He was hoping that Duane, in his hurry to get to Billie Rae, had forgotten about him. At least he was driving slow now—no doubt to protect his car—not his passenger.

The Lincoln had finally come to a sudden stop, throwing Tanner hard against the trunk wall. He had lain dazed, blinking in the darkness as he heard Duane get out of the car.

He heard the wind and then the cop swear. Tanner thought he smelled the river. Or at least water. All his senses seemed more acute. He felt something against his hip and realized it was his cell phone. It had fallen out of his pocket. He hadn't even thought to check for it, just assuming Duane would have taken it.

Picking it up, he hit 911. When the operator came on, he whispered, "Someone is about to be murdered. I don't know where I am. I'm locked in the trunk of a black Lincoln with North Dakota plates, off the road, north of Great Falls. Hurry."

He disconnected as he heard Duane get back into the car and cut the engine. This must be where Billie Rae had told Duane to meet her. Was she outside the car? He listened but didn't hear her voice, but he'd heard Duane yelling earlier though he hadn't been able to make out what he'd been saying with the howling wind rocking the car.

Tanner felt an overwhelming need to call her, let her know the police were on their way, but he'd feared with the music and motor shut off, the cop would be able to hear him since he could hear the cop moving around in the front seat. The car shifted as Duane got out again, slamming the door.

Tanner held his breath, assuming Duane would be walking back to the trunk and that any moment the lid would swing open and— He heard a beep and the doors all lock. Then there was nothing but the sound of the wind outside the car.

Listening hard, Tanner tried now to gauge how much time had passed. He keyed in the number of his old cell phone and prayed Billie Rae would answer.

BILLIE RAE WASN'T SURE she could do this. She'd never been afraid of heights, but as she started across the swaying bridge, she felt motion sickness roil in her stomach.

She took another step, sliding her hand along the rope railing to where it connected with the lower part of the bridge, forcing herself to let go and reach for another section of rope. The bridge swayed beneath her like a writhing snake.

Don't look down.

She thought she'd heard Duane yelling something at her, but realized she may have only imagined his angry bellow.

Then she heard him. Duane was yelling at her, his voice closer. She couldn't look back. She wasn't even sure now if she could pull off her plan because it meant not only reaching the middle of the bridge, but also turning around.

She kept moving, one step, then another. The wind whipped her hair around her face, rocked the bridge and kicked up dust from the mountain on each side of the gorge. She didn't look back, couldn't. Just a little farther.

She stumbled on one of the boards that had bowed

in the weather and almost fell. Tightening her grip on the rope on each side of her, she froze as she tried to catch her breath. Her heart was pounding so hard it hurt.

As she started to take another step, her cell phone rang. She'd stuck the phone in the pocket of her slacks earlier and had forgotten about it. The phone rang again.

She stopped moving across the bridge, willing herself not to look down. Gripping the ropes on each side of the narrow footbridge, she turned her head just enough that she could see the road cut into the side of the mountain. Duane was half way down the road, coming on foot. She squinted at the bright sun, the wind in her hair and the bridge swaying under her feet.

She'd thought it would be Duane calling her. But he wasn't on his cell phone. That meant… Tanner was calling. A bubble rose in her chest. He would have reached the casino by now and be waiting for her. The phone rang again.

Billie Rae thought of him worrying about her. She knew it was foolish, what she was about to do. She needed to get to the middle of the bridge. Duane was coming. The man was crazy. Who knew what he would do?

But she also desperately needed to hear Tanner's voice right now. She was too aware that it was probably going to be the last time she heard it.

Letting go of one of the rope railings, she started

to reach into her pocket. The bridge rocked wildly in a gust of wind and she lost her balance. She grabbed for the rope railing again, her fingers closing on it. Her heart lodged in her throat so tightly she could hardly draw a breath.

The phone rang again and she let out a cry of frustration and pain. She steadied herself, praying that Tanner wouldn't hang up before she could get the phone out of her pocket. She dug it out, balancing her weight on the bridge and trying hard not to think about Duane coming up the road toward her.

"Hello?" She had to raise her voice over the wind.

"Billie Rae, where are you?"

She couldn't speak; his voice filled her with sudden warmth and made her ache for what could have been.

"I called the police. They'll be here soon."

She felt her pulse begin to race. *"Here?"*

"I'm in the trunk of Duane's car. Tell me if he's far enough away that I can try to bust out."

She looked back toward Duane's car. "No," she said into the phone. "You shouldn't be here. Please don't—" The bridge rocked in another gust of wind, throwing her off balance again. She dropped the phone. It hit at her feet, bounced once, then fell between the bridge slats.

She watched the cell phone drop to the deep green of the river and rocks far below as she grabbed wildly at the rope, missing it, then lurching for it again. Her fingers clamped over the line and she teetered between the two ropes, her pulse thundering in her ears as she fought to regain her balance again.

"What the hell are you doing?" Duane's angry bellow sounded as if he was right behind her. He must have run the last stretch and was now at the other end of the bridge.

She didn't dare look back for fear he would be racing along the bridge toward her. Concentrating on nothing but her next step, she slid her hands along the weathered ropes, letting go only to grab the next section.

"Billie Rae, you stupid bitch! Get back here now!" Out of the corner of her eyes, she caught glimpses of deep green through the gaps between the wooden slats of the bridge floor as she took a step—just enough to remind her what was at stake if she failed.

"If I have to come after you…"

She heard a creak, felt the rope railing on her right grow taut and knew without looking that Duane was on the bridge behind her.

TANNER FELT AN URGENCY like none he'd ever experienced before. Something in Billie Rae's voice. Where was she? Close by. He'd heard the sound of the wind and a creak of boards. But it was what he'd heard beneath her words that had him frantically shifting his body around so his feet were pointed at the back seat of the Lincoln.

He prayed that Duane was far enough from the car

that he wouldn't hear the noise and come back, but he couldn't wait any longer.

He kicked the back seat, putting as much force as he could into it given how cramped his surroundings were. He kicked harder. He felt the seat give a little.

Repositioning himself, he braced against the wall of the trunk and kicked and pushed as hard as he could. He felt the seat give a little more.

He stopped to listen, afraid he would hear the beep of Duane unlocking the car doors—or worse, the trunk lid.

Hearing nothing but the wind, Tanner kicked again and again. The seat finally gave. He lay in the trunk breathing hard, then gave the seat a final push. He could see light coming in through the rear tinted windows.

Just a little more....

As he stepped out onto the bridge, Duane watched the water far below and felt the muscles in his legs begin to spasm. It was all he could do to keep standing. He clung to the rope rail, feeling sick to his stomach.

He couldn't move, couldn't breathe. Acrophobia. That's what the doctor had called it.

"It's not unusual," the mandatory police department psychiatrist had told him after the fire escape incident. "A large percentage of the population has the same problem."

"Acrophobia? What the hell is that?"

"It's an extreme or irrational fear of heights."

"Are you saying I'm irrational?" he'd demanded.

"It means that sufferers of acrophobia experience panic attacks in high places and often become too agitated to get themselves down. Isn't that what happened to you, Officer?"

Duane raised his gaze to look down the swaying footbridge to where Billie Rae had stopped moving. Maybe she was coming back. At the thought, he felt a rush of relief, of gratitude, almost love. If she came back, he wouldn't be forced to go out any farther on this bridge.

Maybe he wouldn't kill her. He'd just make her wish she was dead.

"I'm glad to see you've come to your senses," he called to her. "If you'd made me come after you…"

You don't want me to have to come after you.

Duane was startled by the sound of his old man's voice echoing in his head.

So what's it going to be, sonny? You think you can get away from me? You want to try? Or are you going to take what's coming to you like a man?

He'd been six years old that day when he'd stood in the field, his father standing at the edge of the barn door with a thick leather strap dangling from one large hand.

You going to take your medicine like a man or am I going to have to come after you? I guess I don't have to tell you what's going to happen if I have to come after you, do I, Duane?

"Come on back now, Billie Rae," he called to her when she still hadn't moved. He could tell by the way she was balanced on the bridge, her head and shoulders slumped, that she'd scared herself. She didn't want to go any farther. She would come back now.

"You want me, Duane?" she called back over one shoulder. "Then you're going to have to come get me. I can't move."

He swore under his breath. Hell, he'd just leave her there. She'd either starve or lose her balance and fall. Either way would work for him.

But his need to teach her a lesson with his hands pulled at him, taunting him. "Damn it, Billie Rae."

Duane looked back over his shoulder. It wasn't that far back to solid ground. If he turned around now... He started to, but then he saw Billie Rae glance back at him and remembered the night that dumb cop had told her he was afraid of heights. It was bad enough that she'd left him, bad enough that she'd put him through all of this, but now she was almost daring him to come out on the bridge.

Unless you're too afraid, you coward.

He stared at her, realizing she didn't think he could do it. She was planning on him getting scared and... what? Falling?

"You've made a big mistake," he called to her as he took a step toward her, then another. "You think I won't come get you?" His laugh echoed on the wind. "Oh, I'll come get you, Billie Rae. But you are going to wish to hell and gone that you hadn't done this."

SQUIRMING AROUND, TANNER worked his torso through the opening he'd made by kicking the back seat free. Now he just needed something to cut the plastic handcuffs. He managed to get the rear door open and dropped to his feet outside the car.

With a shock, he took in his surroundings. Duane had parked the car only feet from the edge of a precipice. Tanner stared at the river gorge for a moment wondering where the cop had gone. Was he really meeting Billie Rae here?

His stomach knotted at the thought.

He quickly reached into the car and unlatched the trunk. In the back, he found what he was looking for. A pair of pliers. He worked the pliers between his wrists, snapped the handles shut and snipped the plastic. The cuffs fell away.

For a few seconds, he searched through the tools to see if there was anything he could use as a weapon. He chose the tire iron, saw that it had what looked like dried blood on it, and quietly closed the trunk.

As he neared the rim of the river gorge, he peered over, saw the deep gorge, then looked upriver to where the narrow road that had been cut in the side of the mountain ended at a footbridge.

His heart dropping, he saw Billie Rae had stopped part way across the footbridge—the cop close behind.

Tanner began to run, the wind and dust blowing in his face, fear gripping him. He didn't want to think of what was going to happen when Duane caught up with her on the bridge.

Tanner wouldn't be able to reach Duane before he got to Billie Rae. The treacherous road made running at any speed almost impossible. Duane was now slowly moving across the bridge going after Billie Rae.

He could hear Duane yelling. So far, the cop hadn't seen him. Tanner had a feeling that Duane had forgotten about him. The wind howled in his ears. He could smell the river and the dust that kicked up along the steep bank of the gorge.

Billie Rae had started to move again, but the cop seemed to be gaining on her. Tanner ran up behind the car she'd bought. The cop still hadn't seen him apparently. He noticed that Duane was wearing a shoulder holster but he hadn't reached for his gun. Instead, he was holding onto both ropes suspended across the river gorge as if his life depended on it as he continued across the bridge after Billie Rae.

Tanner ran from behind the car over to the entrance of the bridge. A gust of wind whirled up dust around him and rocked the bridge wildly.

Billie Rae had reached the middle of the bridge. Suddenly she seemed to lose her balance. He felt panic seize his chest as he saw her drop to her hands and knees on the footbridge.

Duane was yelling obscenities at her as he clutched at the rope railing, the bridge swinging crazily. The cop was staring down at the river and rocks far below him. He wasn't looking at Billie Rae.

But Tanner was.

He saw her reach into the pocket of the large jacket she wore and attach what looked like a length of climbing rope to the steel cable that held the suspended footbridge in place.

Then she got to her feet again and turned around so she was facing Duane who was still yards away, the rope hidden behind her leg.

Tanner watched her hand sink into the pocket of the jacket again. He let out a silent groan, then said under his breath, "What are you doing, Billie Rae?" as he crawled up and onto the bridge behind Duane.

BILLIE RAE LOOKED DOWN the stretch of bridge swaying in the wind, estimating how many feet lay between her and Duane. He had stopped and now stood as if petrified and unable to move.

Unfortunately he hadn't come far enough out onto the bridge. She needed him to come at least another ten feet toward her—and the middle of the bridge.

Even from here she could see that his face was flushed, the large vessel in his neck bulging with fury and no doubt fear. It was a wonder he didn't give himself a heart attack, she thought.

"Get your ass back here, Billie Rae," he yelled, but his bellow had lost a lot of its bravado.

He didn't want to come out on the bridge. He was scared.

She saw how easily her plan could fail if he suddenly turned tail and rushed back toward the safety of the mountainside.

Worse, she realized with a start, Tanner had gotten out of the trunk of the Lincoln. A moment before he'd been behind her car, but now he had mounted the bridge and was coming up behind Duane.

If Duane turned now, he would see Tanner. She could see that Duane had on his shoulder holster. That meant he'd brought his Glock. She didn't doubt for a moment that he would shoot Tanner in a heartbeat.

"Duane," she called trying to sound as pathetic as he thought she was. She had to get him to come toward her another ten feet—six at the minimum. "I can't move..." Her voice broke. "I'm...scared."

He glared at her as if he thought she was mocking him. He stood with his feet spread apart as he tried to keep his balance, his hands gripping the ropes.

"Please," she cried. "You're going to have to help me."

"If I have to come out there, only one of us will be coming back," Duane yelled.

"You don't mean that."

"The hell I don't. It ends here, Billie Rae. I can't have a wife like you, don't you get it?"

She got it. "And I can't have a husband like you," she said under her breath. "Then just leave me here," she called back. "Divorce me."

He smiled, then let out a laugh. "You'd like that, wouldn't you?" The laugh died on his lips as they twisted into a snarl. "Over *your* dead body."

Her heart pounded as Duane took another step toward her, then another.

Come on, Duane. Just keep coming.

He stumbled on probably the same board she had and almost fell. He grabbed hold of the ropes, clinging to them. His face was livid with fury and fear. She could see the white of his knuckles on the rope and knew he was thinking about wrapping those fingers around her throat.

"We can stop this right now," she called to him. "You realize I'm not going to be your wife any longer—one way or the other."

"You got that right."

"Duane, I'm not going to let you hurt me again."

He laughed. "Then I suggest you jump."

He took another step toward her.

Billie Rae didn't dare look past him to where Tanner was cautiously moving along the bridge as to not let Duane know he was back there. She knew that she couldn't change her mind now. She'd come this far and if she wanted this to end, she knew there was no other way out.

That night after the day she'd stopped by the police station to report the abuse, Duane had almost killed her. She should have known Duane's boss would tell him that she had come down to the police station. She'd realized then that there was no restraining order or locked door that could protect her from the man she'd married.

And that was how they had ended up on this bridge, she thought. It had all come down to this moment.

Duane took another step toward her. She gauged the distance and reached into her other pocket and carefully closed her hand around the grip of the gun.

"It will be extremely effective at from four to seven feet. Seven to ten feet is optimum," the sales clerk had told her.

Billie Rae knew she couldn't let Duane get too close. If he lunged for her—

"It doesn't have to be this way," she called to him. "There is no shame in divorce."

The word shame seemed to strike a nerve. Duane swore and took another step toward her and another. Billie Rae watched him, gauging the distance.

She could see that he was perspiring heavily. He was fighting looking down, gripping the ropes. Each step was costing him dearly.

"The hell you will shame me, you stupid bitch," he spat as he lurched toward her.

Billie Rae felt a tremor inside her. Duane was closing the distance between them quicker than she'd thought he would—or could.

Had she really believed he would let her go, agree to a divorce, stop this craziness?

He had left her no choice, she told herself as he

advanced. As if she'd ever had a choice from the day she'd married him.

Duane lumbered forward, grabbing the rope in his big fists, lurching on the wildly swinging footbridge. His anger had trumped his fear. He was too blind with rage to even realize he was suspended fifty feet over a rocky gorge on nothing more than a few boards beneath his feet.

Now. She had to act now or… Billie Rae told herself she could do this. Only a few more feet and if she didn't do something…

The warning signs had been there. She'd noticed even before they'd married that Duane always had to have his way. When she'd tried to assert herself, they'd argued. He had a temper and said hurtful things, but he was always sorry.

She found giving in to him was easier. She hated fighting with him. She overlooked his moodiness and believed if she tried harder to make him happy, everything would be fine. She loved him. And he loved her.

She shuddered as she saw the pattern their lives had taken, her walking around on eggshells, Duane getting furious over nothing at all. Her trying to pacify him. Him needing to be pacified more and more.

And finally Duane taking out all that anger inside him on her.

Billie Rae suddenly thought of the boy her husband had shot soon after they'd moved to Williston.

There'd been an investigation, which had put Duane
in one of his moods. She'd tried to stay out of his way,
but he'd finally come looking for her as if he'd needed
to work off some steam by picking a fight with her
and slapping her around.

But she remembered what he'd said about the
killing.

"The boy was asking for it, so it was self-defense."

"I thought he didn't have a weapon?" she'd foolishly pointed out.

He'd given her one of his dirty looks and raised his
fists. "See these? They're a weapon. So that makes
it self-defense. Even if my weapon that day was a lot
bigger and a hell of a lot more lethal."

Fifteen feet, twelve, ten.

Billie Rae thought of that boy as she pulled the gun
from her jacket pocket and said, "That's far enough,
Duane."

Chapter Thirteen

Duane froze in mid-step as he saw her pull a gun from the pocket of the oversized jacket she wore. He'd wondered where she'd gotten the jacket since she'd left home without one, didn't have her purse so shouldn't have had money to buy one and this one was too large for her. The cowboy. She must have gotten it from him.

"What do you think you're doing, Billie Rae?" His voice sounded amused even to him. Then he remembered the day he'd taught Billie Rae to shoot.

At first she'd been afraid of the gun, which really made him angry. Then she'd finally taken it and seemed to draw on some inner strength because when she'd fired the automatic pistol she hadn't stopped firing until she'd completely obliterated the bull's-eye of the target.

He'd been astounded. "Are you sure you haven't fired a gun before?" he'd demanded.

"I told you, I don't like guns."

Duane realized now that she hadn't answered

his question about whether or not she'd fired a gun before. Clearly she had.

"Billie Rae, I thought you didn't like guns," he called to her.

"I don't," she called back. "But you've really given me no choice, have you, Duane?"

"You can't shoot your own husband. Come on, put the gun away before you shoot yourself."

In the years he'd been a cop, he'd faced his share of fools with weapons. He'd learned the telltale nervous gestures that could signal if the hand holding the gun was going to pull the trigger.

He stared at his wife now as if looking at a stranger. Her expression was one of calm, cold and calculating. Her eyes were on him, the gun aimed at his chest, her feet spread as she balanced on the moving bridge.

"You can't be serious," he said, even though he knew she was. It went against everything he believed about his wife. Even after that humiliating experience at the gun range, if anyone had asked him if Billie Rae could fire a gun at a human being, he would have guffawed and said the woman didn't have the killer instinct. Now he wasn't so sure.

Could she shoot her own husband?

A few days ago he would have thought the question ridiculous.

Right now, though, he had a bad feeling not only could she, she would.

The only question was whether or not he could draw and shoot her before she got off a shot.

He squinted his eyes against the afternoon sun as he tried to see what kind of gun she held in her hands. "What the hell?" he said when he saw that it was a pistol-shaped taser.

As part of his law enforcement training, he'd been hit with a taser and he'd nailed more than a few suspects with one. He was well aware of what happened when fifty-thousand volts traveling in two small darts struck a body.

His gaze shot to the vertical rope supports every four to five feet along the footbridge and knew that if she pulled the trigger before he reached one, he was in for a long fall—and certain death in the river and rocks below.

Just as Billie Rae had obviously planned it, he realized with a start. The woman had brought him here to kill him.

"You better hope to hell you miss," Duane screamed and lunged forward.

BILLIE RAE WATCHED IN horror as Duane threw himself forward as if he planned to run down the bridge and take the taser from her.

She pulled the trigger. The fifty-thousand volts shot out in two darts that penetrated his shirt to prick his skin.

Her heart in her throat, she saw him instantly lose all muscle control and drop, just like the clerk who'd sold her the taser said would happen.

Duane landed hard on the bridge and would have

fallen over the side except for one of the vertical ropes between the footbridge base and the rope handrails.

She only had an instant to stuff the taser into her pocket again and grab the rope before the bridge swung crazily with his fallen weight. Beyond him, she saw Tanner do the same. He was still yards from Duane.

He had stopped and was looking at her as if he couldn't believe what she'd just done. She couldn't, either. Worse, her plan hadn't worked.

Billie Rae clung to the ropes as a gust of wind rocked the bridge and she realized what Duane had done. He'd seen that she had a taser, he'd known what it would do and he'd managed to get to a spot on the bridge so the rope uprights kept him from falling off and dropping to the river below.

A sob rose in her throat as she watched him lying there. A part of her couldn't believe she'd shot him— even with only a taser. Worse, that her plan had been for him to fall from the bridge.

She closed her eyes against the image of him lying bloody and broken in the rocks below. Even though she knew it was him or her in the end, she felt sick to her stomach. How had it come down to this?

With a jolt she realized that she had only a few minutes before he regained control of his body. He would be even more furious. There was no doubt now that he would kill her, that she had chosen the spot she would die today.

Her gaze went to Tanner. They would both die

here today. Another sob rose in her throat. She was about to get them both killed.

"Stay back!" she called to Tanner, but he either didn't hear or refused to heed her warning as he began moving toward the spot where Duane had fallen to the bridge slats. Tanner had something in his hand. Something that gleamed in the sunlight. A tire iron?

Duane began to move. Billie Rae saw him trying to get his Glock out of his shoulder holster. He fumbled the gun out, lost his grip. The gun skittered across the planes of the footbridge to drop over the edge. Duane made a guttural sound, then reached for the gun butt sticking out of the waistband of his slacks.

Billie Rae let go of the rope rail with one hand and dug in her pocket for the taser and another cartridge. The wind seemed stronger now. Her eyes burned from it and balancing on the moving bridge was becoming harder, especially as she hurriedly tried to reload the taser.

With shaking fingers she took out the spent cartridge and fumbled to get the new one loaded into the butt-end of the taser, while out of the corner of her eye she watched Duane rise up, the gun in his hand.

A gust of wind swung the bridge. She dropped the cartridge. Like the cell phone, it hit at her feet, bounced and disappeared over the side of the footbridge.

Billie Rae let out a cry of frustration and fear as Duane managed to get to his feet. He pointed the gun at her. They were now no more than eight feet apart. She could see the gleam in his eyes, feel the hatred and anger coming off him in waves.

"This isn't the way I wanted to end it," Duane said from between clenched teeth.

The wind was whistling through the footbridge. That, Billie Rae realized, was why Duane was unaware of Tanner moving stealthily along the bridge behind him. When she'd called, "Stay back," Duane had thought she was warning *him*.

She fumbled in her pocket for the last cartridge. Duane was watching her almost in amusement. He would never let her load the taser before he shot her and they both knew it.

He took a step forward. She could tell he didn't want to pull the trigger and end it so quickly. He wanted to hurt her. Worse, if he shot her, how would he explain it? But she knew when push came to shove, he would shoot her before he'd let her taser him again—and that could be as much justice as she could get.

"I gave you everything," he said, pain in his voice. "You were my wife. I treated you like a princess."

"A princess you slapped around when you had a bad day," she snapped unable to hold her tongue as she was forced to hang on to the rope with one hand and frantically try to load the taser with the other.

He stopped now only a few feet from her. "I used to watch my old man slap my mother around. I hated him for doing it. But I didn't realize that women push you to hurt them."

"We ask for it, right?"

"Make fun, but Billie Rae, if you had tried harder not to set me off—"

"Stop lying to yourself, Duane. You liked beating up a defenseless woman," she pushed. "It made you feel like you were somebody."

His face twisted in anger. He raised the gun so she was looking down the dark hole of the barrel. "I'm sorry it has to end like this. I really am."

Just pull the trigger. Let's get this over with because I can't live like this anymore. "Yeah, too bad you didn't get to slap me around some more, huh, Duane?"

The face she'd once found handsome twisted into the monster he was. "Goodbye, Billie Rae." He grabbed for her with his free hand, his intent in his eyes. She was going off the bridge. Alone.

TANNER HEARD WHAT DUANE SAID as he came up behind him. As he swung the tire iron, the cop must have felt the movement behind him or sensed his presence. He half turned, catching the blow on his shoulder.

The sound of the report from the handgun echoed in the narrow canyon, but all Tanner heard was Billie Rae cry out. Duane fell back against the rope rail and almost toppled over, but caught himself.

He'd managed to still hang on to the gun as he half

turned, knocking the tire iron out of Tanner's hand. It fell to the bridge and Tanner lost sight of it.

As Duane turned the gun on him, Tanner grabbed for it and they wrestled on the bridge, making it rock crazily. Tanner's gaze shot past Duane to the spot where he'd last seen Billie Rae.

She was gone.

THE CARTRIDGE LOCKED IN the taser just an instant before Duane grabbed for her. He got a handful of her jacket in his big fist before she could raise the weapon and fire.

She saw his expression and knew that he had sensed Tanner coming up behind him because he only had time to shove her through the ropes of the bridge railing before he was turning to fire again.

Billie Rae saw it all in those few heart-dropping moments. As she fell off the edge of the bridge through one of the spaces between the ropes, she stuffed the taser back into the jacket pocket and closed her eyes.

She could feel the fear contort her face as she fell—not at all sure she would stop before she hit the river fifty feet below. The drop was no more than a few yards, but when the climbing rope attached to her harness caught and she stopped falling, the impact was more jarring that she'd thought it would be. It knocked the air out of her.

She dangled from the bridge cable high above the gorge and fought to breathe. She didn't dare look down. Above her through the bridge slats, she could see Duane and Tanner wrestling for the gun. Still gasping for breath, she reached up and began to ratchet herself back up toward the bridge like the clerk at the climbing store had showed her.

He had made it look so easy on the store climbing wall. It took all her effort to rise the few feet to the level of the bridge, the effort more difficult because of the growing wind. But all she could think about was Tanner. She had desperately needed him the night of the rodeo. Now he desperately needed her.

Just before Duane had thrown her off the bridge, she'd heard the report of his gun. But she hadn't realized he'd shot her until she looked down and saw that the jacket was soaked with blood.

She realized she was losing a lot of blood because suddenly she felt light-headed. She clung to the climbing rope as the bridge above her blurred. Just a little farther. Tanner and Duane were still fighting for the gun. She felt as if she could pass out at any moment.

Pushing herself, she ratcheted herself up the last few inches. As she reached the edge of the footbridge, she pulled out the loaded taser and prayed for a clear shot.

AS THEY FOUGHT FOR THE GUN, Tanner knew he was fighting for his life. It was almost impossible to keep from losing his balance and falling from the bridge. Duane was strong and wild with an insane need to finish what he'd started. Tanner fought with a craziness of his own, believing that Duane had already killed Billie Rae.

He found himself thrown against the rope railing as they grappled for the gun, the bridge threatening to spill them both into the river far below. Duane kneed him in the groin and Tanner stumbled back, falling to the floor of the footbridge. He would have fallen through the opening had he not managed to grab hold of one of the vertical ropes and get one leg wrapped around the wooden slats on the opposite side.

He was breathing hard from the exertion and the near fall when he looked up to find Duane standing over him. Duane had the gun in one hand and was hanging onto the bridge rope rail with the other. He was breathing hard, sweating, but smiling as he pointed the weapon at Tanner's chest.

Tanner saw the tire iron caught between two of the wooden slats of the footbridge floor. Duane saw it too and slammed down his foot on it before Tanner could grab it.

"You should never have come between me and my wife," Duane said. "Let alone assault a police officer with a weapon," he added as he kicked the tire iron off the bridge. He seemed to watch its descent out of the corner of his eye and Tanner knew exactly what the cop had in mind for him once he shot him.

Like the tire iron, he would be making that fifty-foot fall to the rocks and river below them.

That's when behind Duane, Tanner caught a

glimpse of Billie Rae dangling from the bridge. Tanner had never been so happy to see Billie Rae. She was bleeding but he couldn't tell how badly she'd been hit.

With a start, he understood the climbing rope and why she'd attached the end of it to the steel cable. She had been expecting that very thing to happen.

The woman was crazy.

Of course she was. Her husband had driven her to this point where she felt she had nothing to lose.

Tanner thought of her in his arms, her face in the light from the fireworks, the look she'd given him yesterday just before she'd left. She'd known that she couldn't run far enough from the man she'd married. She'd known that one day she would have to end it because if she didn't Duane would kill her.

He couldn't imagine having that kind of monkey on his back.

Duane thrust the gun out in front of him as he took a more careful aim for Tanner's heart. "It was a shame that I had to kill you. But after what you did to Billie Rae. The jealous lover pushing Billie Rae off the bridge when she told you she would never leave her husband."

"Do you really think that will fly?" Tanner said.

"You forget, I'm a cop."

BILLIE RAE CLUNG TO the edge of the swaying bridge, the wind in her face, her vision blurring from the loss of blood. She felt light-headed and feared she might pass out at any moment.

The battle between the two men had driven them both away from her. Duane was a good fifteen feet away from her now—on the edge of the taser range.

But there was nothing she could do about that. She was feeling faint and her arms were trembling from the climb up the rope. She felt as if she was going into shock.

Billie Rae thought about calling down the bridge to Duane to get his attention, but she didn't dare chance it.

She raised the taser and tried to steady it. The last cartridge was loaded. If she missed him—

Duane was clinging to the rope with one hand, the gun in the other aimed at Tanner's chest. She could hear the hum of his voice but she couldn't make out his words. There was no doubt in her mind he intended to kill Tanner, who was lying on his back unable to do more than cling to the moving floor of the footbridge.

Everything began to fade from her vision. She felt herself getting weaker, the taser slumping a little in her hands as the bridge rocked and her eyes dimmed.

She said a silent prayer and pulled the trigger.

TANNER HAD SEEN BILLIE RAE holding the taser. He could see that she was struggling to aim it.

"Any last words?" Duane asked.

"Burn in hell," Tanner said. The darts caught Duane in the low back. He fell against the rope railing and for a moment Tanner thought his weight would snap it—or flip the bridge and both of them off it.

The floor twisted and Tanner was looking down at the water below him. The river was dark now that the sun was lower in the sky, but the rocks just beneath the surface still shone like sun-bleached bones as the water rushed over them.

Duane seemed to teeter on the rope, his body bent over it. Tanner grabbed the weapon Duane dropped and now held it on the man suspended on the rope.

He would later remember it all happening in an instant. Duane suspended there. And then in a blink, gone.

But right now it seemed to happen in slow motion. Duane's heavy body looped over the rope, making the bridge twist to the side, before gravity finally claimed the weight of his limp body. Tanner impulsively grabbed for him as Duane fell over the side of the bridge. But there was no saving him from the river—or from himself.

Then there was only the sound of the wind but he knew that like him, Billie Rae was listening for the moment when Duane landed in the river below them. He saw her hanging like a limp doll from the climbing rope, her gaze blurred with tears.

Tanner listened, but there was nothing to hear over the wind.

He didn't look down either as he made his way toward Billie Rae. She seemed to watch him through her tears. And then he was pulling her up and into his arms and holding her and telling her not to worry.

"Everything is going to be all right."

In the distance he could hear the sound of sirens headed this way as Billie Rae slumped in his arms.

Chapter Fourteen

"I can't believe Emma would do this," Tanner said as he looked around the kitchen table at his brothers. The six of them had gathered at the main house after Marshall had discovered Emma missing.

Dawson shoved the note across the table. "Believe it. It's right there in black and white."

"She took all her things," Marshall said. "Her closet is cleaned out. Everything is gone."

Tanner shook his head. "This is going to break Dad's heart."

"How is Billie Rae?" Dawson asked, changing the subject.

"The bullet wound missed any vital organs," Tanner said. "The doctor is releasing her today."

"The police cleared the two of you?" Dawson asked.

He remembered the hours of questioning, the days of worrying about Billie Rae, the awful time spent next to her hospital bed fearing she might not survive. "McCall said it shouldn't be too long before the investigation is concluded and Billie Rae and I are exonerated."

"What is Billie Rae going to do now?" Zane asked.

"Go back to North Dakota for the time being." Tanner had wanted to go with her but she'd insisted she needed to do this alone.

"I can't believe the judge denied bail and Dad has to stay in jail until his trial," Logan said.

"The judge thought he was a flight risk." Colton had been quiet until then. The fact that he was engaged to a sheriff's deputy didn't make him all that popular right now.

"As if Dad would ever leave the ranch," Logan said and looked to the others as if needing to be reassured.

"Dad didn't kill anyone," Dawson snapped, getting to his feet. "Enough sitting around here moping. Emma is gone. We have to finish the fence. I'll go into town for the load of barbed wire. The rest of you get ready to string fence for the next few days. This ranch isn't going to run itself and we have no idea of how long before Dad is cleared and back home."

"Any word on those rustlers that were hitting ranches down by the Wyoming border?" Zane asked.

Dawson shook his head. "I'll ask around while I'm in town. But I can tell you right now, they won't be getting any of our cattle."

"I'm going by the hospital to see Billie Rae and then I'll catch up with you out in the north forty,"

Tanner said and watched his brothers file out of the house.

He stood for a moment, listening to the silence. It hadn't been this quiet since Emma had come into their lives. He missed her, missed the rich aroma of whatever she had baking in the big kitchen. She'd made the house warmer, made their lives warmer as well.

Tanner still couldn't believe she would turn tail and run at the first sign of trouble. It just didn't seem like her, he thought as he picked up the note off the kitchen table and reread it.

I'm sorry but I can't do this,
Emma

No matter what the others said, Tanner knew his father was going to be heartbroken. Emma had been the love of his life.

CINDY ROSS FIDGETED in the seat across from the sheriff. "I got your message?" She made it sound like a question. She smelled of soap and her hair was still wet from her early morning shower.

McCall could see the fear in the girl's eyes and wished she had better news. "We haven't found your aunt. As you know we found her rental car." She didn't mention the blood they found on the seat. McCall was still waiting for forensics to tell her whether or not it was Agatha Wells's blood. The lab was testing the blood stain against hair follicles found in a hairbrush in the suitcase.

Cindy's eyes widened in alarm. "You aren't going to stop looking for her, are you?"

The team dragging the river had discontinued their search for Aggie Wells. "Law enforcement will continue to keep an eye out for your aunt."

"That's it? That's all you're going to do?" the girl asked, sounding close to tears.

"Until we get another lead—"

"What about that body you found out there?" Cindy asked.

McCall wasn't surprised the girl had heard about the remains found near her aunt's abandoned car. "That is tied in with another case."

"I know you arrested Hoyt Chisholm for the murder of the woman's remains you found. It was one of his wives that he murdered. He's going to prison, isn't he?"

"The remains were identified as one of his wives, but until his case goes to trial—"

"You know he killed my aunt."

She didn't know that. But like everyone else in town, she suspected he might have. "Have you been in contact with your father?" McCall asked the girl, seeing how upset she was.

"He hasn't heard from her." From the way she ducked her head, McCall guessed the father wasn't happy about his daughter's coming to Whitehorse in search of her aunt, let alone her staying so long.

"You might consider going home," the sheriff said. She knew Cindy had been staying at a local motel, waiting for news of her aunt. "When we have any news of your aunt..." If they ever did, but she didn't say that.

Cindy had slumped in her chair, all the fight gone out of her.

"Do you have money to get home?" McCall asked.

"I have enough to catch the bus back," she said. "I just feel like I should stay here, though, in case—"

"Your aunt will expect you to be in Arizona, right? That will be the obvious place she would try to contact you."

The girl lifted her head, hope shining in her eyes. "You still think she might be alive?"

"We have no evidence otherwise at this point." McCall didn't want the girl to be so far away from her father when there was news about her aunt. After this much time and what they'd discovered on the seat of Aggie Wells's abandoned rental car, McCall wasn't expecting the news to be good.

BILLIE RAE WAS DRESSED and standing at the window when she heard Tanner come into the hospital room. She knew the sound of his boots on the hospital's tiled floor after all his visits over the days she'd been healing.

She had a lot more healing to do—and not just from the gunshot wound.

As she stared out at the beautiful Montana summer day, she heard him come up behind her. She ached to feel his arms around her, the touch of his lips against her skin, the whisper of his voice next to her ear.

She turned before he reached her, knowing how easily he could destroy her resolve. "I was just thinking about you," she said honestly.

"That's a good start," he said, his Stetson in his sun-tanned callused hands. He'd been working at the ranch when he wasn't coming to the hospital to see her. He looked stronger, his shoulders seeming broader. There had always been strength and integrity in this man. She'd seen it that first night at the rodeo.

But now there was something different about him. A calm assuredness—and she knew it had something to do with how he felt about her.

He could survive without her, though. She wasn't so sure she could without him.

"I'll come back," she said, her voice breaking as she looked into his handsome face and fought the urge to reach out and feel the smooth line of his freshly shaven jaw beneath her fingers.

"I'm planning on that," he said.

She met his warm brown gaze, saw how hard it was for him to let her go. But he'd helped free her of a man who had tried to hold on to her at all costs. Tanner would let her go—even if it broke his heart—and that was what she loved so much about him.

All the hours he'd spent visiting her while she was

in the hospital, he'd talked about everything but the two of them and the future. He'd known she wasn't ready for that.

"I should get going. I'm taking the train back to Williston."

"Do you need a ride to the station?" He sounded so hopeful, she almost weakened. But she couldn't bear another goodbye, especially one in a train station. This was hard enough as it was.

"I have a ride, but thank you."

At a sound behind him, Tanner turned to see his brother Marshall standing in the doorway. When he turned back to Billie Rae, he was smiling. "You couldn't have picked a better person to take you to the train." Then he stepped to her and gently brushed aside a lock of her hair to press a kiss to her forehead before stepping back. "You'd better get going. See you soon. Drive careful, Marshall."

Epilogue

When Tanner saw Billie Rae coming across the field, he thought he must be seeing things.

He'd imagined her coming back to the Chisholm Ranch so many times, this time didn't seem real.

He stood watching her, the sun beating down on him. He'd warned himself that it might be months before she'd come back. There was also the possibility that she wouldn't. She might want to forget everything about what had happened on the bridge that day—and him with it.

Sheriff McCall Crawford had stopped by to tell him that the investigation of Duane Rasmussen's death had been completed. Both he and Billie Rae had been cleared of any wrongdoing. Duane's body had been released, his remains cremated and sent to Billie Rae in Williston.

So many times Tanner had wanted to turn his pickup down Highway 2 toward North Dakota. He'd wake up in the middle of the night knowing that Billie Rae had cried herself to sleep. He couldn't bear thinking of her alone back in Williston and being forced to come to terms with Duane's death and the ashes of her marriage.

But he'd done what she'd asked and he'd waited, counting the days, then the weeks, watching and waiting for her, planning what he would say when he saw her again. He'd hoped she would call, but she hadn't.

In all that time, there had been no word from Emma, either. Tanner still thought it odd. They all missed her and had moved back into the main house to hold down the fort until the day their father was set free.

It had been a waiting game. The only thing that had saved him was work. They had put in miles of new fence posts and were still stringing barbed wire along with all the other chores of running such a large ranch.

Now as Billie Rae walked the rest of the way across the pasture to where he was leading an appaloosa mare back toward the corral, words failed him.

Billie Rae looked so beautiful. Her face seemed to glow in the morning sunlight. Her brown eyes shone with tears as she stopped a few feet from him, looking almost shy. Then she smiled and he realized he didn't need any words.

Tanner let out a whoop, dropped the horse's reins and ran to her. He picked her up by her waist and swung her around in a circle before slowly lowering her down to the ground.

He looked into the depths of her gold-flecked brown eyes and saw love shining out. "Welcome home, Billie Rae."

She smiled through her tears and it could have been the Fourth of July all over again. Tanner swore he felt fireworks exploding around them as he pulled her into his arms and kissed her.

BILLIE RAE KNEW the moment she saw his face that this was where she belonged—in Tanner Chisholm's arms. And then he kissed her and she couldn't believe how far she'd come from that night in July when she'd been running for her life and Tanner had caught her.

Fate? Maybe. Love at first sight? Definitely. She remembered looking up into the cowboy's face and feeling safe for the first time in months.

In the weeks since what had happened on the bridge, she'd struggled with her heart. If it had had its way, she would never have left Whitehorse or Tanner. But her head said she needed time. She had to go back to Williston and take care of the mess she'd made of her life by marrying Duane.

Billie Rae had also wanted time to be sure that what she felt was real. Now as she drew back from the kiss to cradle his face in her hands and look into his eyes, she couldn't imagine anything more real.

"There is something I need to tell you," she said.

He laughed and shook his head. "I love you too, Billie Rae Johnson."

She smiled. "That too." She brushed a lock of his hair back from his forehead and turned serious. Just last week she'd gotten the tests back. "How do you feel about being a father?"

His brown eyes lit up and he let out another whoop as he picked her up again and spun her in a circle.

"Put that woman down!" Marshall called as he came out the back door of the main house.

"Billie Rae and I are havin' a baby!" Tanner called back.

"Isn't that putting the cart before the horse?" Marshall asked, grinning as Tanner led Billie Rae over to him.

"She might be a little gun-shy of marriage," Tanner said, eyeing her. "But I was about to ask her." He got down on one knee. He'd been carrying the ring around in his pocket for weeks like a good luck charm. "Marry me and make me the happiest man in Montana."

Billie Rae let her heart answer.

* * * * *

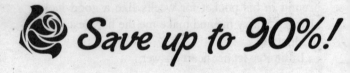